DEAD ZERO

A BOB LEE SWAGGER NOVEL

STEPHEN HUNTER

Simon & Schuster

NEW YORK   LONDON   TORONTO   SYDNEY

Simon & Schuster
1230 Avenue of the Americas
New York, NY 10020

First Simon & Schuster hardcover edition December 2010

SIMON & SCHUSTER and colophon are registered trademarks of Simon & Schuster, Inc.

For information about special discounts for bulk purchases, please contact
Simon & Schuster Special Sales at 1-866-506-1949 or *business@simonandschuster.com*.

The Simon & Schuster Speakers Bureau can bring authors to your live event.
For more information or to book an event contact the Simon & Schuster Speakers Bureau at
1-866-248-3049 or visit our website at *www.simonspeakers.com*.

Manufactured in the United States of America

1   3   5   7   9   10   8   6   4   2

Library of Congress Cataloging-in-Publication Data

Hunter, Stephen.
Dead zero : a novel / by Stephen Hunter.
p. cm.
1. Swagger, Bob Lee (Fictitious character)—Fiction. 2. Snipers—Fiction.
3. Marines—Fiction. 4. Afghan War, 2001—Fiction. I. Title
PS3558.U494D43 2010
813'.6—dc22
2010046773

ISBN: 978-1-4391-3865-6
ISBN: 978-1-4391-4993-5 (ebook)

For
Nick Ziolkowski
1982–2004
KIA, Iraq
"The Sniper from Boys Latin"

If there is any glory in war,
let it rest on a young man such as this.

"Surely, God has cursed the disbelievers
And has prepared for them a Flaming Fire
Where they will abide forever."

—KORAN 72:23

1. Pull pin. Hold unit upright.
2. Aim at base of fire. Stand back.
3. Press trigger. Sweep side to side.

—COMMON FIRE EXTINGUISHER
INSTRUCTIONS

PART ONE

WHISKEY 2-2

WHISKEY 2-2

ZABUL PROVINCE
SOUTHEASTERN AFGHANISTAN
0934 HOURS

Consciousness came and went; the pain was constant. It was the day after the ambush. The flesh wound in Cruz's right thigh still oozed blood and the entire right side of his body wore a purple-yellow smear of bruise. It hurt so bad he could hardly negotiate the raw landscape that strobed in and out of focus all around him in the harsh sunlight. But Ray Cruz, a gunnery sergeant in the United States Marine Corps, was one of those rare men with a personality of hard metal—unmalleable, impenetrable, unstoppable. Back at battalion, he was called the Cruise Missile. Once fired, he kept moving until he hit the target. Since 2nd Reconnaissance Battalion was a Special Forces–rated unit, it got all the cool jobs, and he was the go-to guy on patrol security, Agency snatch-and-grabs and various countersniper and IED problems. He ran Sniper Platoon. He was always there, in the shadows on the ridge line or the village roof—sometimes spotted up, sometimes not, with his SR-25, a beast of a .308 semiauto with a yard of optics up top—paying out survival for his people at long range in packages that weighed 175 grains apiece. He never missed, he never counted or cared about the kills.

Yet now, no one would confuse him for what he was. He was dressed in the loose-fitting, easy-flowing tribal garments of the Pashtun, the people of the mountains. He looked like Lawrence of Afghanistan. His brown face was crusty with beard and filth, his lips cracked. He wore sandals and a burnoose, obscuring his visage, and not one item of government-issue clothing. He was also among goats.

There were fourteen of them left. It is fine to love animals until you try to herd goats. The goats weren't into team spirit. They free-ranged, somewhat raggedly, depending on need or whim, and Cruz

was able to keep them moving roughly forward by constant screaming and beating with his staff. And when he swatted at them with
the staff, the weight went to his damaged leg and a new blade of
pain thrust up into his guts. They shat everywhere, without apparent effort or awareness. They attracted flies in clouds. They smelled
of shit and blood and dust and piss. They babbled constantly, not so
much a classic *bah-bah-bah* but more of a whiney singsong bleating,
like kids on a long bus ride. He hated them. He wanted to kill them
with the rifle under his robes, eat them, and go home. But he had a
goddamned job to do and he could not make himself quit on that
job. It wasn't will or habit, it certainly wasn't out of any notion of
the heroic or Semper Fi or memories of Iwo and Chosin and Belleau
Wood. It was just that his mind wasn't organized in such a way as to
consider alternatives.

The rifle shifted uncomfortably under his swirl of robes. It
was a little lighter than the SR-25, a Russian-designed, Chinese-
manufactured thing called a Dragunov SVD, with a skeletal wooden
stock and a longish barrel, looking a little like an AK-47 stretched in
a medieval torture machine. A battlefield pickup from some long-
forgotten firefight that its owner came out of second-place winner,
its strap bit into his shoulder and its rough surfaces gouged him as
it slipped this way or that. It was awkward, a heavy piece of crudely
machined parts, mostly metal, with knobs, bolts, buttons, ledges, and
all sorts of things sticking out of it. It represented the Russian school
of ergonomics that was "Fuck you, end user." A Chinese 4× sight had
been clamped on top with a strange range finder—it looked like a cartoon of a ski-jump slope—as part of the reticle information that only
someone from an East-bloc culture could dream up. He hated it. Yet
he was lucky to have it. And one magazine of ten 7.62 × 54 sniper-
grade Chinese cartridges.

It was all he had left. He'd started with a spotter, an ample supply
of food and water, and no bullet having blown six ounces of flesh off
his leg. The trek the long way around to Qalat would only be three
days in. After the shot, maybe a day of escape and evasion. Then his

spotter would put in the call, and a Night Stalker would helo them out and they'd be back at FOB Winchester in time for beer and steak. And the Beheader, as Ibrahim Zarzi, warlord of the southeastern Pashtun tribes, opium merchant, prince, spy, charmer, betrayer, Taliban sympathizer, and Al-Qaeda liaison was known, would be sucking poppy from the root end first.

But it didn't happen that way. Reality seldom follows mission-op outlines.

"Why send men, Major?" Ray had asked the battalion intelligence officer, the S-2, in the S-2 bunker, to an audience of the CO, the exec, and the Sniper Platoon lieutenant. "Can't our Agency friends send a missile? Isn't that what they do? Have some zen master pinball kid sitting in a trailer in Vegas flying a joystick take him out with a Hellfire?"

"Ray, I shouldn't tell you this," Colonel Laidlaw said, "but it's your ass on the line, so you have a right to know. The Administration has tightened up on the missile hits. Too much collateral. The UN squawking. This guy's complex is in heavy urban. You go all Hellfire on his ass, yes, you probably send him to his God. But you send two hundred other rug weavers along with him and you've got the *New York Times* violin section in full blast. These folks don't like that."

"Okay, sir. I can take him. I'm just worried about the E and E from Qalat. I want to get my guy out and also my own ass. Can we have Warthogs standing by to cowboy up the place if it gets tight? We won't have enough firepower to shoot our way out of anything."

"I can get you Apaches ASAP. Our Apaches. I don't want to lay on Air Force Warthogs because I've got to go through too many chains of command and too many people have to sign off on it. It's not all that secure."

The marines liked the Air Force guys because they thought the A-10 gun tubs were so well armored the pilots had the confidence to get down to marine level before they started blowing shit up and killing people. They thought their own pilots lacked the killer instinct— and the armor—for nose-in-the-dirt flying. They hung far off, launched Hellfires, then went home and slept between clean sheets after martinis in the officers' club. Some even had girlfriends, it was rumored.

So: no Hogs, maybe Apaches. That was it and it never occurred to Ray to come up with a turndown. If he didn't do it, somebody else would, and whoever that somebody was, he wouldn't be as good as Ray.

It had to be done. The Beheader—the nickname came because it was rumored he was the mastermind behind a kidnapped journalist who'd suffered that fate when he'd gone off on his own in Qalat to get the Taliban side of the story—was an eternal problem for marines in the southeastern operating area. When IEDs went off as command vehicles passed in resupply convoys, it was because the Beheader's spies had infiltrated and knew how to ID the one Humvee out of twenty-five that carried brass. When patrols were ambushed, and major ops had to be launched to get them out of the trouble they'd gotten into, and the shooters had mysteriously vanished into noth-ingness, it was suspected they had simply ducked into the off-limits Zarzi compound. When a sniper dinged a CIA operations officer, when a mortar shell or an RPG detonated with far too much accu-racy to be a random shot, when an Afghan liaison officer was found with his throat cut, all the signs pointed to the Beheader, who was in all other respects a wonderful man; a charmer; a handsome, well-educated fellow (Oxford, University of Iowa) with impeccable table manners who, when he allowed Americans, including high-ranking marine officers, into his home, boldly violated Islamic taboo by des-ignating a liquor room, where a superb bartender made any drink you could imagine served under a little paper umbrella.

"I want this guy dead'r 'n shit," said the colonel. "I had to fight command and the Agency to get a kill authorized. Ray, I'd love to push the button and watch the computer kids whack him, but it's not going to happen. You've got to walk in, drop him with a rifle shot, and walk out."

"Got it," said Ray.

The shooting site had to be the roof of the Many Pleasures Hotel, across the street from the Beheader's compound. Once a week, the man was predictable. At twilight on Tuesday—it was always Tuesday—he left the compound by armored Humvee and went into the Houri district, where he visited a nice young prostitute named Mindi, with eyes like almonds, hair the color of night, and ways and means beyond the imagination. And why didn't he just move her in? Well, concubine politics. He had three wives and twenty-one kids, and already wives number one and three hated each other; his second concubine was plotting against his first concubine; all the women were lobbying incessantly for a trip to Beverly Hills; and what little domestic tranquility that could be had would be shattered by adding Mindi to the mix. Thus it was felt that not only her sexual skills but the fact that she was deaf and dumb gave the Great Man a peace and serenity unavailable in his own hectic home.

In any event, Tuesday at twilight, he predictably strode from his house to the vehicle, a distance of some ten yards. It was then and only then that he was vulnerable to a shot. Shooting suppressed from a little over 200 yards out, with just enough angle to clear the wall but still access the target, Ray could easily put a Chinese sniper bullet into the Beheader in his five-second window of opportunity. Chaos would ensue, and the militiamen in the bodyguard squad would have no idea where the shot had come from and would certainly begin firing wildly, driving people to cover. Ray and his spotter would fall back from the Many Pleasures Hotel, rappelling off the roof and making their way into the crowded Houri district, just a few blocks away, where they would go to ground. They'd just be two more faceless, bearded Izzies in a city full to bursting with them. The next night, they'd exfiltrate the city, make it to a certain hill about five miles to the south, and wait for the Night Stalker to come pick them up.

"It sounds easy," said S-2. "It won't be."

On the first day, he and Skelton had passed a couple of Taliban patrols on the high track but attracted no interest from those wary fighters, whose gimlet eyes were used to piercing the distance for the sand-and-spinach digital camo of marine war fighters. The Tallys saw goatherders all the time, and if these two were a little more raggedy ass than most they saw, it didn't register. They moved at goat pace, without urgency, without apparent direction, letting the wiry little animals eat, shit, and fuck as their goat brains saw fit, but generally moseying in the direction of the big market at Qalat where their thirty-five treasures could be sold for slaughter.

As part of their security procedure, Whiskey 2-2 avoided villages, slept without campfires, ate rice balls and unleavened sheaves of dry bread, and wiped their hands on their pants and shat without toilet paper.

"It's just like the Sigma Chi house," said Lance Corporal Skelton as they came to the top of a rise and found a tricky path down the other side.

"Except you don't jack off as much," said Ray.

"I don't know about you, Ray, but I don't need to jack off much. I had a real nice time with that blond goat last night. She's a princess."

"Next time, keep it down. May be bad guys in the vicinity."

"She sure does moan, doesn't she? Boy, do I know how to please a gal or what?"

The two men laughed. Lance Corporal Skelton didn't have a Chinese sniper rifle under his robes and vests, but he did have ten pounds of HF-90M Ultralight radio, an M4 with ACOG, ten magazines, and a case containing a Schmidt & Bender 35× spotting scope. All that shit: he moved like an old lady.

They were in high plains country, trending north. The Paki mountains rose ahead, over the unseen border, mantled in snow and sometimes fog, more tribal territory where Americans couldn't go for fear of execution upon apprehension. The land they negotiated was rocky and hardscrabble, clotted with waxy, tough, gray vegetation. Rocks lay everywhere, and each hill revealed a new landscape of secret inclines and defilades, and it was all brown-gray, coated with dust or grit. They were right on the border between the rising plains and the actual foothills, and out here it was desolate. Except of course they knew they were being watched and always assumed some Taliban was gazing their way through the scope of a Dragunov or a nice pair of Russian binoculars. So no American-jock crap as young athletic fellows are wont to do, no air jump shots or long, deep fantasy passes; no scooping up the hot grounder and firing to first. No middle fingers, no mock-comic "Fuck yous," no hyperattention to hygiene, no acknowledgment that such things as germs existed or that Allah was less than supreme. Prayer mats, five times a day on the knees to Mecca; you never knew who was watching.

And, of course, somewhere up above lurked either a satellite or more likely a Predator drone configured for recon and riding the breezes back and forth behind a tiny turbocharged engine, so they were probably on monitors in living color in every intelligence agency in the free world. It was like being on Jay Leno, except for the Afghanistan part. So another sniper discipline was: don't look up. Don't look at the sky, as if to acknowledge that somebody was up there to watch over them.

2ND RECON BATTALION HQ

I didn't think it would take all this time," said the colonel.

"Sir," said his exec, "that's rough land. That's really rough land. And the goats. They seem to be having trouble with the goats. Maybe the goats were a mistake."

"S-Two, are they on schedule?"

"More or less," said the intelligence officer. "That goat market has been there for three thousand years and I don't think it's going anywhere anytime soon."

The colonel rolled his eyes to his exec. What was it with intelligence people? They always had a little bit of the I-wouldn't-be-in-intelligence-if-I-weren't-intelligent deal going on. This one, even worse, was an Annapolis grad and convinced he was on a straight run to become the next commandant.

"It's not the market, S-Two. It's the Tuesday shot. If they miss that, they have to hang out there in goat city undercover for another full week. They'll make a mistake and get nabbed and the Beheader will get to practice his specialty."

"Yes, sir," said S-2, "I only meant—"

"I know, S-Two. I'm just ragging on you because if I don't pick on somebody I'll have an anxiety attack."

Colonel Laidlaw stood in the S-2 bunker behind the base's many miles of concertina wire and sandbags. He had three patrols out, and word was brewing that the whole battalion was up for a major assault sometime in the next month and he had too many men down with malaria, too many in psych wards, and too many on leave. Battalion strength was about 60 percent, and recon battalions were smaller than rifle battalions to begin with. Nothing worked, one of his officers was showing disturbing signs of depression and replacing him would be a political nightmare, the intel that came through the Agency was always late and bad, and now he had two of his best guys way, way out on a limb. In other words, things were just about normal for combat operations.

He lit up what felt like cigarette number 315. It tasted just as shitty as cigs 233 through 314. He looked at what was before him on the monitor screen. It was Whiskey 2-2, from an altitude of about 2,000 feet, except that altitude was a magnification. Actually the bird was close to 22 miles up in the sky, rotating in a slow low-earth orbit, under the control of the geniuses at Langley, and it had cameras with lenses capable of resolutions nearly unbelievable only a few years before. They could probably tell if the Beheader had his eggs over easy or poached, if they wanted.

What Laidlaw and his staff saw from 0-degree angle on high and through the drifting smoke and the hum of tiny jihadi insects that buzzed and bit and were otherwise invisible, was the dark ripple, which was the crest of a ridge, running diagonally across the screen. On it a tiny, almost antlike movement that signified ambulatory life was held under the white, glowing cruciform of a center-lens indicator. A whole lot of meaningless numbers—Laidlaw wasn't good on tech stuff—ran across the border, the top, and the bottom of the image, and it took some getting used to. A compass orienter floated about the screen, establishing direction. With practice, you adjusted to the stylizations of the system, the 0-degree foreshortening, the brown-to-black-to-gray color scheme, the scuts of dust that blew this way and that, all the interfering digital reads and indicators, and learned to determine the difference between the two marines and the longer, squirmier forms of the goats, spilling this way and that.

"How much longer?" asked the colonel, meaning how long before the satellite continued its way around the earth and Whiskey 2-2 passed from view for another twenty-four.

"Only about ten minutes, sir," S-2 said. "Then they go bye-bye."

They knew that these semiabstract forms against the opacity of the large monitor were Whiskey 2-2 and not some group of actual goatherders by virtue of the cruciform that kept the camera nailed. It signified the presence of a GPS chip and a miniaturized transmitter in the grip of Cruz's SVD. The satellites told the chip where it was and the transmitter told the world what the satellite told the chip. This simplified the problematic issue of target acquisition and identification and meant that when the satellite was in range, it could eyeball the guys the whole way. But Whiskey 2-2 didn't know this and both S-2 and Colonel Laidlaw felt a little uneasy about it. It was, in effect, spying on their own men without permission, as if an issue of trust was involved. The colonel justified it by telling himself it was necessary in the case of an emergency evac, if Lance Corporal Skelton, hurt or killed, couldn't get to his radio and sing out coordinates. They could call in Air Force Warthogs and ventilate the area with frags and 30-millimeter while guiding in marine aviation for the extract if Whiskey found itself in a firefight.

"Who's that?" someone said.

"Hmm," said S-2.

"Where, what, info please," said Colonel Laidlaw.

"Sir, ahead of them on the same axis, on the hilltop a little back, I'm guessing maybe a half mile out to the west, that is, to the right."

To spare the colonel the agony of translating the directions into an actual location on the gray wilderness of the monitor, S-2 ran up to the screen and touched what the exec had seen first. No goats, that's for sure. No, it was a group of guys, slightly whiter against the dull sage of landform, only they were lengthier than goats and not moving, which meant they were in the prone. If they were facing in the right direction, they were on line to intercept 2-2's line of route.

"Taliban?"

"Probably."

"Is that a problem?"

"Shouldn't be. They ran into Taliban patrols twice yesterday and once earlier today. To the Tals, they just look like goatherders."

"Yeah, but those guys were on their feet, standing, eyeballing, moving in their own direction. These guys are setting up. This could be an intercept."

The marine officers continued to watch the monitor as the drama played out in real time before them. Laidlaw lit another cigarette. S-2 didn't say anything snarky. Exec didn't suck up. Sniper Platoon leader, twenty-two, refused to speak. It just happened.

The group ahead of 2-2 seemed to squirm, then settle. Damn, why hadn't the staff seen them come in; maybe their direction of origin would have been an indicator.

"How much time?" asked Colonel Laidlaw.

"Two minutes."

"Sir, I can reach Whiskey on the HF-90M. Give 'em a heads-up." That was exec.

"Sir, all due respect, but if you do that, Skelton has to hunker down, peel off his caftan, unstrap the radio, and talk into the phone," said S-2. "All those are tells. If these guys are bad or there are some other bad actors, say in caves, we're not picking up on, that gives Two-Two away for sure. The mission goes down. They get whacked for sure, or end up in a running gunfight."

"Shit," said the colonel.

"I don't like the orientation. Those guys are prone, they're setting up to shoot. Could the Agency have a team in there?" said Exec.

"I got negative from liaison on that not an hour ago," said S-2. "This is the only area op."

"Let it play out," said the colonel, "goddamnit."

They watched. The two small forces drew inexorably together, the raggedy fleet of goats spilling across the landscape on the ancient track in the hills, and the six possible ambushers set up orthodox Camp Lejeune–style for a shoot, legs neatly splayed, maybe one up on his knees working binocs, the others bending into scopes.

"I don't like this one fucking bit," said the colonel. "Where's our goddamned Hellfire when we need it. I'd like to punch those bastards out, whoever they are."

"They're probably birdwatchers from the National Geographic channel," said S-2. "Or maybe missionaries from the World Orphan Relief League. Or—"

But the question was answered. Two-two had reached its point of maximum closure with the unknown force on the hilltop and lay exposed to them.

From twenty-two miles up, the satellite watched with God's indifference as it picked up the spurting warp-speed blurs of muzzle flashes from the prone team, signifying high-rate-of-fire weapons.

"Ambush," said the colonel.

I t was raining goats. They flew through the air amid blasts of earth debris, some whole and bleating, some sundered and spraying blood, some atomized. The weather had become 100 percent chance of goat—red mist, gobbets of blasted flesh, unraveling intestines, the unself-conscious screams of animals suddenly sentient to the prospect of their own extinction.

Then Skelton launched. He pinwheeled fifteen feet through the air, his face a study in wonder, spinning, legs and arms extended, defying gravity as he sailed.

Ray lurched in that moment, saving his own life, for surely the gunner was shooting right to left, semiauto, had missed twice, hitting goat, the huge .50-caliber detonations unleashing waves of energy that flipped other goats airward and splattered them, then scoring a hard one that took Skelton solid, and then pivoted the huge weapon on the bipod another half a millimeter to plant one in Ray. But aiming for center mass, he was behind Ray on the action curve, and time in flight from half a mile out didn't help and the express train hit Ray on the outer surface of the right thigh. It hit no bones, broke nothing full of coursing fluids, and delivered nothing but energy.

Ray flew. He left the earth behind. He'd seen—and hit—enough guys with a .50 to know what the phenomenon looked like. Usually the delivered energy is so high—in the 5,000-foot-pound range—that a frail sack of blood and struts like a human being will flip through the air, sometimes as far as 30 feet, limbs askew, and land in a pile of wreckage. So it was with Ray, and he seemed to be in midair for a long while, and had a full measure of time to miss his mother and father, who had given him exactly what he wanted and needed, love and support and belief, and as well to miss the Marine Corps, which took over when his parents were called away, and which had given him so many opportunities to do that at which he excelled, and then he hit the ground in a stir of dust and stones and sprigs of leaf and twig. He spat out a missile of phlegm and grit, thanked God he hadn't landed on his back where such an impact would have driven the alien SVD into his flesh, possibly breaking some ribs and bruising his spine.

The surviving goats bleated pitifully, racing this way and that in utter panic, not even stopping to shit.

"Oh, God, Ray," he heard Skelton scream, "I am hit so bad, oh, Ray, he killed me."

"Stay there," he yelled back, "I'll get to you."

"No, Ray, get the fuck outta Dodge. Fuck, he blew a hole clear through my guts and I can't move, Ray, go, go, go."

Another burst of .50s lit up the ridge line, delivering more theater of destruction. Goats flew, dust detonated from the earth, angry chips of stone and metal sang through the air. Ray was just a bit out of the beaten zone, as he'd been deposited by the whimsy of physics off the crest line, maybe a little below it, while poor Skelton was exposed for a second delivery.

Ray squirmed left, pushed himself down, and wished he could get a good visual on his pard. If the boy was dead, no point in hanging around. If he was wounded . . . well, that was a different story, as he had his rifle and if he played it cool and those motherfuckers came to examine their kill, he could take a bunch of them down before they closed. Ray low-crawled a few feet back up, slipped behind the carcass of a dead animal and peered over the top. Neither part of Skelton appeared to be alive.

Cocksuckers, he thought, and swore there'd come a time when he put the dead zero on these operators and watch them sag to stillness under the request of his .308 hollow points.

But that would be in some distant future. For now, escape was the only sane possibility, and he slipped backward, well below the line of the crest, took a brief look around, and decided to head toward an arroyo a few hundred yards away that itself led to more complex geo-logical structures. He knew if he hastened, he'd leave signs and these Pashtun mountain fighters were wicked on tracking. So he made an effort to run on an indirect route to his goal, also moving from stone to stone, from low bush to low bush for at least the first hundred or so yards, figuring that by the time they got there, they'd have to stop, hunt for tracks, and it would take them hours to discover his true line, maybe not by dark, which would in turn buy him a night's worth of time to put distance between himself and them.

But where would he go? He could peel around and head back to the FOB. Then what had Skelton died for? Meaningless death seemed so cruel to Ray. If you get whacked to do something, to take an objective, to get somebody out of a jam, that was one thing. If your death is random, just an abstract function of the physics of being at a certain place when a certain piece of lead flew through it, what have you got? You've got nothing.

He considered as he dashed his odd, springy, half-legged way down the crest, then doubled back to the arroyo. He had his rifle, he had a magazine loaded with 7.62 × 54 Chinese match, his leg hurt like fucking hell but didn't seem to have suffered any structural damage, and he could get through something as negligible as pain. He had a head start on these clowns if indeed they were hunting him, and they may have been just a mob of jihadis who'd recently recovered a .50 Barrett from a wrecked Humvee and decided to amuse their savage selves by blasting some goatherders and weren't much interested in elaborate games of pursuit.

He considered, he decided. Mission up. Finish the goddamned thing. Qalat by Monday night, then kill the motherfucker called the Beheader, then go home and cry for Billy Skelton.

2ND RECON BATTALION HQ

The suspense was murder. S-2's IT set up the satellite feed with the usual contempt that ITs have for the technically illiterate, though he knew, as did the whole battalion, that Ray and Skelton had been bounced. He couldn't keep the speed and sureness with which his fingers flew to keys out of the equation though, that special IT thing that the officers regarded as mysterious and unknowable. That was just him.

There had been no radio contact the long night through. Either Skelton's HF-90M was junked by a slug or had fallen into a ditch or, as Marine Corps radios have a tendency to do, awarded itself an R & R in the middle of a combat operation, who knew? Commo people had been trying to reach 2-2 on the right freak, and on emergency freaks, Air Force freaks, even Afghan army freaks all night long. Not a goddamned peep.

The image came up, the gray-green-black-brown surreal reality, Zabul from space as brought to you via station W-CIA in lovely downtown Langley, Virginia, and beamed half a world away to a roomful of tired marine officers smoking too much, worrying too much, and angry too much.

The cruciform was untethered, as it always was. It seemed to move in a search pattern but it was really the television lens, aloft in the ether twenty-two miles over the Hindu Kush, that was moving. It was searching for the frequency of the GPS chip and transmitter embedded in the grip of Ray's rifle.

It drifted, this way and that, seeming to float without a care in the world as before it the panorama of the ragged landforms of Zabul fled, mostly dust broken by rocks and ridges, except the part where the rocks and ridges were broken by dust.

"Goddamn," said Colonel Laidlaw, halfway through Marlboro number 673. "Make it work faster, Lance Corporal."

The lance corporal didn't answer, not out of rudeness but because he knew the colonel's style was to make comically infantile demands as a way of amusing everybody within earshot.

And then—

"Lock-on! Lock-on!" said the lance corporal.

Indeed, as a glowing message in the bottom quadrant of the screen made clear, the frequency hunting doohickey in outer space had located Whiskey 2-2's signal and clenched it between its electronic jaws. The terrain that lay before it looked like—well, it looked like any other terrain in Zabul.

"Is it him?" Exec wondered. "It could be some Taliban mother-fucker with a shiny new rifle."

"Where is it, S-Two?" the colonel demanded humorlessly. "I need a location."

"Yes, sir," said S-2, reading the satellite coordinates and trying to relate them to the geodesic survey map he had pinned to a table. He calculated quickly. "I make him to be about seven miles east of the location of the ambush, still moving on a line to Qalat, still aiming to come in from the west."

"Jesus Christ," said Exec. "He's got goats."

It was true. Somehow, some way, the survivors of the goat massacre had managed to track Ray down amid the arroyos, switchbacks, and fissures of Zabul and had reassembled around him. Yes, that would have to be him, a slightly glowing figure at the center of the smaller but just as annoying platoon of goats, moving down a dusty trail.

"That is one tough Filipino," said S-2.

"I believe he's got some conquistador blood and maybe a little kamikaze DNA in him. Nothing stops the Cruise Missile," said Ray's section lieutenant.

"Look!" said S-2. "Is that what I think it is?"

He pointed.

Down at the bottom of the screen, slightly hidden behind a fusillade of rushing integers from a digital readout that no one in the room understood, not even the IT, six glowing figures picked their way across the landscape. They had arranged themselves in classic tactical diamond formation, with a point man and two flankers out a hundred yards in each direction. They moved, it was evident, with easy, practiced precision.

"They're hunting him," someone said.

"S-Two, give me a range."

S-2 did the calc and said, "They're within a mile. They've got a vector on him too. I don't think they're tracking. They're moving too fast to be tracking."

"How the fuck did they stay with him during the night?"

"I don't know, sir."

"Those fucking goats are slowing him down."

"But if he doesn't have the goats, then he attracts attention. He's got to stay with the goats, and he knows it."

"S-Two, get your Agency liaison on the horn and see if we can authorize a Hellfire into these guys."

"I'll try, sir, but they're very close to the vest with the Hellfires these days."

S-2 made the call; clearly it didn't go well. At the frustration point, the colonel took over.

"This is Colonel Laidlaw. Who am I speaking to, please?"

"Sir, it's McCoy."

The colonel saw McCoy: thirty-five, redheaded, from Alabama, the ops chief's right-hand boy, a former Delta commando.

"Look, McCoy, I've got a sniper way out on a limb and six bad boys moving in on him. You can see it on satellite feed yourself."

"We're watching it even now, Colonel. This is the Beheader mission, right?"

"That's it. Look, I want to put a Hellfire blast-and-frag from a drone into those guys before they get much closer or before they separate too far for one strike. You've got a Reaper floating somewhere in the area?"

"Sir, I have to advise negative on the request. Sorry about your kid, but our directive is only to strike ID'd targets and then only with Langley clearance. I just can't do it."

The colonel gave the guy a few minutes of choice Marine Corps invective, but McCoy wouldn't—couldn't—budge and the ops chief was out in some hamlet or other reaching the hearts and minds of the Afghan people by teaching dental hygiene or constitutional democracy or something.

"Okay," said the colonel to S-2, handing the phone back. "Keep trying. Go to 113 Wing at Ripley. Maybe we can send an Apache."

"I'll try, sir, but I don't think an Apache can get there in time, and I don't know that bringing a noisemaker like that into the area will sit well with command."

"Goddamnit," said the colonel and went back to watching as the pursuers closed in on the pursued.

Ray was awakened that morning by a tongue. Too bad it belonged to a goat and not a beautiful woman.

He'd run hard through the arroyos in the dark, falling several times and remembering not to curse when he hit the ground. No moon made the trip an ordeal. But he had to keep moving and knew that if he didn't, the leg would stiffen up on him and make the going even more torturous. He had to get as much out of himself as he could. But the arroyos weren't a subway line; none of them led directly to Qalat, so he was always following one until it veered in an inappropriate direction, then scrambling up its rough walls mostly by hoisting himself upward with his staff, reaching the crest, slithering over the crest, and sliding down into another one that more or less seemed to be heading where he wanted to go. He knew he wasn't making the best speed, but if he committed to the crests, his silhouette would be available to any hadji with stolen American night vision, or he might bump into a Taliban unit or opium smuggler or some Pashtun revengers, all of them richly festooned in AKs and RPGs. It wasn't the sort of neighborhood where you wanted to bump into folks.

Near dawn, he'd had it. He'd been running hard since the hit. His body could take more than most of the bodies in the world, but it had reached its limit. He found a relatively smooth area and nestled behind a rock; sleep overtook him quickly, a black blanket of dreamless escape.

The goat's tongue smelled of shit, like everything in the 'Stan. Ray bolted up, felt the pain in his black-blue-green leg jack through him and squelched a cry. The fucking goats had found him. What goat-brain skill enabled them to stay with him in the dark? Sure, they

could scamper over the landscape as if it were the surface of a bil-
liard table, but was it smell, his lingering presence in the wind, that
led them through the dark on a beeline to him? Another nuzzled up
and licked his face and showed something like dumb-beast love in its
moist and sentimental eyes. It bleated and shivered, shat of course,
and then nuzzled him for affection again.

"You skaggy bastard," he said, but still awarded the goat a neck rub
in payment for his loyalty.

Breakfast: rice balls, dates, and some warm water from the goat-
skin water bag strapped to him. Fed and hydrated, he shot an azimuth
with a much-abused Boy Scout brass compass originally manufactured in England in 1925, found a landmark for orientation, and
began the trek anew.

It was the day after the ambush. The pain was constant, but consciousness inconsistent. It seemed he passed out several times while
walking. The goats nestled against him or ran off on adventures and
he enacted what goat discipline he could. Around him, the land was
definitely not changing; it was still the endless sea of rough ridges,
small hills, scrub vegetation, dust everywhere. He had to move faster
because tomorrow would be Sunday and he had to make Qalat by
nightfall so he could infiltrate on Monday, recon, and set up the shot
for Tuesday afternoon; it was Tuesday afternoon or nothing, because
he couldn't last a week in the city—surely sooner or later someone
would notice that he spoke no Pashto or Dari or any of a thousand
other tells that would give him away. In fast, out fast—or no game
at all.

He reached a crest, scurried over it, the goats bleating and yapping
all around him, taking shit breaks or lunch breaks on the waxy vegetation. He got over the ridge, then slipped, put stress on the leg, felt
a specific pain rise out of the general pain and hit him hard, almost
enough to bring him down.

Water? No. He wouldn't have enough for tomorrow if he started
sipping every time he felt like it. But the leg hurt so goddamned bad.

Okay, he told himself, *take a little rest. You've got another two hours of daylight, you can punch through the night with greatly reduced efficiency, you can grab a couple of hours of snooze time until a goat alarm clock sings "I've Got You, Babe" in your ear.*

He awarded himself a little break.

He hunkered down, keeping his leg straight, squirmed until he'd found something near comfort as it might be defined in combat in Afghanistan, and set about paying off his oxygen debt. In a few minutes, he felt somewhat refreshed, no Semper Fi! or Gung Ho! bullshit, but some slight blurring of the generalized fatigue.

Time to go.

He thought also that it would be a good idea to take a fast recon of the area, just in case. He shimmied up to the crest of the ridge and in the low prone peered across the landscape he had just traversed. It looked a lot like the landscape he was just about to traverse. He saw the serrations of a hundred bayonets lined up, so the world was nothing but serrations—jagged rises and falls, edge beyond edge of them, endless, in that colorless color of the Afghan high desert, dun, dust, pale pink, mocha brown, whatever, even the plants were brown. High clouds piled up above, cumulus thunder bringers, the only clean, bright thing in the world, marble or alabaster. To the east, the mountains of Pakistan, much higher. He knew if he turned, he'd see the shadows of the Hindu Kush one hundred miles away. You could see the biggest mountains in the world from a long way out.

He was almost ready to pack it in when he saw them.

Oh fuck, he thought.

He slipped back, diddled with his caftan, performed the complicated negotiations necessary to free up the SVD strapped to his back, and came back to the ridgeline.

It took a while to relocate. The original indicator had been a jiggle of movement on a crest line way off, where movement shouldn't have been. Sliding the rifle to his shoulder, popping the lens caps, he settled into a steady prone as he cantilevered over the hump of the crest line, poking the rifle barrel through some vegetation for clearer vision. He found his spotweld, which yielded his perfect eye relief, and his fingers flew to the focus ring of the crude Chinese tube. He checked to make sure the sun had no angle to bounce off his lens in give-away reflection, played with the focus, twisting this way and that, wishing he had Marine Corps–issue 10× magnification instead of ChiCom 4×, cursed the elaborate reticle with its goofy ranging system that blocked out too many details, and reoriented on the suspect area, letting the substandard lens of the Chinese optics resolve into finite detail all that could be resolved.

Nothing.

I know I saw something.

He decided to give it a few seconds. *I would have seen them on a crest. Now they're behind the crest. They'll be on top of another crest and—*

He watched them come over, emerging headfirst, then disappearing as they scattered down the slope of the rill they'd just crossed. Khaki clad, bloused boots, burnooses obscuring their features, bearded men with necks wrapped in shemaghs in the green-black pattern so beloved by many. Bandoliers loaded with mags crisscrossed on their chests. Wait, one guy wore a baseball cap, khaki or sage, and he was the one with the heavy .50 Barrett, that monster rifle just at the limits of luggability, a twenty-five-pound ordeal as awkward as an iron cash register, and good for one thing only, nailing Johnny Pashtun at a long way out. The others were AK-ed up, standard for this part of the world, and one had a couple of RPGs over his back.

It was the guy in the ball cap who gave it away, even to the 4× of the Chinese scope. Yes, he was bearded, yes, he was nut brown from the cruel Afghan sun, yes, he moved with the wiry, wary grace of the Pathan warrior who'd haunted these climes for a thousand years, mixing it up with Alexander's spear chuckers, assorted Hindu invaders, and then troops from a Victoria, a Mikhail, a George W., and now a Barack. Yes to all that, and yes to one other thing as well: he was white.

We don't have much light left, Mick," said Tony Z.

"Hey, I don't want to hear that. What I want to hear is, Mick, let's push harder, goddamnit."

"Mick, let's push harder, goddamnit," said Crackers the Clown.

"Not funny, Crackers."

The team saw just hills, hills, hills before them in the fading light. At last report the guy was less than half a mile away, and they were closing. But the shot at a daylight takedown, much hoped for, was rapidly disappearing. Mick didn't want to do a night thing. Guys shooting, flashes, bad vision, only one set of night vision goggles between them, no long shots, no, you couldn't tell what might go wrong and very little ever went right at night.

On the other hand, if the guy saw them, he might set up and start picking them off from far out with his long gun. Then, assuming he wasn't the first to go, Mick might have a chance at taking him down with the motherfuckingseventonsofagonybullshit .50 Barrett he carried with him. You could do a guy at a mile with the thing, and Mick had done enough of it to know.

Which set him off again: Aghh! He had the sniper team cold-bore dead zeroed and yet he missed, maybe a little puff of breeze edged the first 750-grainer that way or this and only blew goats into the air; the second freight train missed too, goddamnit, and then he found the stroke and blew one guy thirty feet in the air, cranked to the other as he was disappearing and blew him aloft like a Frisbee sailing across a college lawn. Then he worked the beaten zone with the rest of the mag, blowing more goats to barbecue heaven and hitting the one visible body a second time so hard it landed in two pieces.

Then, when they got to the kill zone an hour later, after a slow, tactical approach, no fucking second body.

"You see blood?"

"A few spots down here, Mick. But clearly, not a big, huge gut wound; he won't be bleeding out."

"I saw him go bye-bye from midair," said Tony.

"Even a glancer from a motherfucker like this will send a guy off like a V-2. I hit a guy in Bagra once at just the right angle and it actually blew him out of the windshield of his car and about thirty feet down the road. Man, that was one surprised dude." It was a nice warm memory and Mick cherished it.

Thus the conclusion: one of the marines had gotten away.

"It's time to cut to the chase," said Crackers.

"Wait a minute," said Tony Z. "See, we're already *on* the chase. This *is* the chase. So how can you cut *to* the chase *from* the chase?"

"Fuck you," said Crackers.

"Knock it off," Mick said. "We got a pursuit on our hands. Guy has to have been hit, he can't move fast. He'll probably lay up in a cave. We have to track him and take him out."

"Mick, I didn't sign up for an adventure movie. I'm just here for the hit and the grins." That was crazy Crackers, like Mick, once a soldier, and young.

"We are getting top dollar to deliver two heads. We will deliver two heads. Crackers, with your forces background, you're the jock, why don't you run the man down for us."

"I left my track shoes at the motel," said Crackers.

Now, nearly a day later, at nightfall, they knew they had to be close.

But Tony Z said, "I'm thinking we ought to deviate, go around him, and let him come to us. He's been pushing hard and I saw him fly, so I know he's hurting beaucoup from a glancer. He'll have to hunker down. He's only a marine. He ain't Superman."

Mick wasn't ready to commit.

"Let's think about this a little while. I want this thing done up right."

One of the hadjis—he had three, Taliban boys whom on other

days Mick might have blown away without a thought, but his passport to safety in the tribal areas depended on this one—spoke his gibberish and Tony Z, who understood it, told Mick, "Mahoud says there's a path low around this set of hills, mostly flatland. We could probably get ahead of him that way."

So tempting. No more chase shit. No more waiting for Marine Hero to get the first shot off and go for him, he-man with Barrett. Mick was a soldier, as he'd been a football hero, because he was so big. He'd known from childhood that he had the strength to make people obey, and he didn't mind, rather enjoyed it, ultimately becoming addicted to hitting people to get their attention. Alas, it was a hard habit to break, which is why each of the various colorful entities that had paid him to do violence on their behalf had grown tired of his disciplinary problems, his thief's axiomatic greed, and the way he subverted every team he ever joined to his own ends. He was finally even cashiered out of Graywolf for shooting a surrendering hadji on CNN, a bad career move if ever there was one; now he had another client, less picky about certain moral distinctions.

He checked his big gizmo Suunto watch, that Finnish bubble of high tech that could almost predict the future it was so complex, and saw he had just a few minutes until he could get a position fix.

"We'll wait here till I call MacGyver. We'll see where he is."

The dark advanced shadows across the raw land, and a little night breeze kicked up dust or sand. One of the hadjis began to chew some suspicious weed or other, maybe for night vision, maybe for martyr's frenzy. Tony Z hung next to Mick, crouching, lovingly fingering his AK. Tony was a gun guy; he had a Wilson custom .45 in a shoulder holster and a Ruger .380 plastic pocket pistol with a laser sight floating around in his cargo pants pocket.

Mick, happy to be shed of the weight of the Barrett for a few minutes, slipped off his backpack, unlashed its flap, and withdrew a chunk of silicon technology called a Thuraya SG-2520 encrypted satellite phone. It was what held this whole mad little trip together. It looked like any other cell of the usual dimensions, 5.5 by 2.1 by 0.8 inches, but its distinguishing feature was a kind of plastic tube on top, which, when pulled, yielded a good five inches of stout antenna that enabled it to use the Thuraya constellation of forty-eight low earth–orbiting satellites if the GSM satellite coverage was not available. Other than that, it had the usual phone shit, a screen, a keyboard, all in gray Jetsons plastic. It was preconfigured to one number. He pushed call.

He waited, knowing he was about to send his voice into outer space, where it would bounce off various metal orbs full of circuits and chips and nanotechnologies, until it finally beamed down to a cell phone somewhere in America (he didn't know where) and a man humorously calling himself "MacGyver" would answer. The best thing was: the call was completely private.

"You're early," MacGyver said.

"We're close. The issue is: should we press on in the dark and overtake or try and get around him and set up an ambush on the other side? I need to know his position and if he's still moving."

"Which option do you prefer?"

"I don't like night action. Too much can go wrong. I'd prefer to set up and whack him tomorrow as he comes into town."

"Excellent. Of course you're wrong, so do exactly the opposite."

"Mr. Mac—"

"He's gone to earth for the night. I saw him on the big screen just a few minutes ago. I can give you his exact coordinates, to the meter. I can get you close enough to smell the goats. You'll find him conked out. Get up close, shoot him about a thousand times, and get the hadjis to get you out of there. That's what you're being paid way too much for."

Mick got out his pen and notebook and wrote down the exact mathematics of the sniper's location.

"Bogier, get this done. Are you hearing me?"

"Yes, sir," said Mick, hating the asshole, and then he closed down the transmit.

"Okay," he said, and drew his two white teamboys close to map it out, figure an approach, and plan the kill.

UNIDENTIFIED CONTRACTOR TEAM

At the base of the hill, the guys shed everything, stripping down, hadjis too, to pants and shirts. Even if it dropped to the thirties and froze them solid, Mick didn't want the heavy caftans or the schemeggahs slopping this way and that, roughing up the dust, scraping rocks, catching on thorns or sprigs. The guys could shiver; he just didn't want them to make noise.

The map was only so helpful. It identified the major landforms, even to the degree of suggesting approaches, but not the boulders and rock faces that gave those approaches practical meaning. Far better was his own recon through the AN/PV5-7 night vision goggles. As he took each man around to his starting point, he let them on the night vision set to get a good look-see of what lay before, how the rocks fell, how the arroyos trended, where the small trees for leverage were. He reminded them of the rules: no one was to rise above waist level until 0430; if they saw anybody walking upright, blast him. It would have to be the marine, awake, continuing his journey. Other rules: Do not fire at gun flashes, as the odds decreed you would be shooting your own teammate. And watch for goats. The guy wasn't dumb; he'd tether goats to himself, and run the risk of goat piss against the fragile restiveness of the beasts, who'd bleat and whimper at the approach of a predator. So you didn't startle a goat. If you moved low, quiet and easy, the goats would not be a problem. Afterward, they could butcher an animal and have a nice breakfast.

Since Mick, with the night vision, was almost certain to be the one to reach the hilltop first and would have the good vision to make the shot, he would signal them with a cowboy yeehaw when he'd scored. If for any reason that hadn't happened by 0500, then 0500 became go time. They were to continue to the top, slide in on the sleeping marine, and let him have it. There wasn't much else to say. It was pretty simple: infiltrate and execute. What could possibly go wrong?

Then he left each guy and slipped back as noiselessly as possible to his own starting point.

He checked his watch. It was now 0330 and the 0430 deadline was predicated on the assumption the distance was about 200 meters; it should take each man about an hour to edge, inch by silent inch, to the summit.

Mick began his crawl. He'd left the Barrett behind as there was no point in dragging it along; it was no close-quarters weapon. He had a Beretta 92 with a wicked Gemtech suppressor sticking from its snout like a can of frozen orange juice. At close range, it would finish up this asshole and get them the hell out of town in time for martini hour at the Kabul Hilton. He slithered, pulling his way along, enjoying the chilled air and the freedom from the ache of the big Barrett he'd been toting for three or four days. This was the cool part, the part he always loved, the special part of special ops work: the silent stalk. He enjoyed his own war craft, his ability to undulate silently, to ignore on will alone all the prods and pricks and pokes of the rough ground and thorny vegetation he crawled over. He moved more quickly than the others because through the night vision goggles, he could see what rocks lay ahead, where the breaks were, where the smaller brush collected, and so his progress was more assured.

He made it to the crest in less than half an hour. He found a larger rock and eased around it, hearing at the same time the gentle moaning of a goat or two. In the green world of the goggles the goats glowed incandescently, about 30 yards ahead. Three or four seemed tethered to what had to be the sniper, some kind of less-glowing form concealed in robes on the ground, heaving in and out with movement as the lungs took in air and then spent it, once in a while kicking.

Shoot him, Mick thought.

But it was a long shot for a pistol, particularly one wearing a suppressor that might change the point of impact off the sights, which were hard to see even in the ambient light's amplification. He had him. Wait it out. Be disciplined, wait it out, when 0500 gets here, we'll all hit him at once and pump his ass on the ground.

Mick sat back and waited, selecting memories to keep him toasty through the long hour. Hmm, the two Japanese girls in Tokyo that night? Or that CBS correspondent in Baghdad, the Brit? Man, she was hot and she'd done half the guys in Delta. Or what about the black gal in Dar es Salaam. Boy, that was a night, even if he'd caught a dose. Or . . .

In this fashion, he passed the time quickly, pausing now and then for a recon through the night vision to make sure the guy was still there, snoozing fitfully on the ground amid his screen of goats. Their bleats and baas came softly through the night but the goats were so intent on keeping warm that no man-scent alarmed them. They drifted and moseyed around the sleeping form and meanwhile Mick explored the brothel of his memory for suitable pornographic energy to keep himself distracted from the slow slippage of time on his Suunto or the numb chill spreading through his lower extremities. He timed it perfectly, jigging to release at roughly 0450, giving himself plenty of time to clean off and settle in.

A last check of the pistol. Shell in chamber, yes, hammer down, yes, safety off, yes, magazine seated, yes, suppressor can cranked tight against the threading, yes. He rose to knees, then to haunches, the gun in one hand, steadying himself on the rock with the other and enough of a sleeve hike to show the face of the watch as the Suunto digits dissolved steadily toward 0500 until they yielded that number exactly.

He took a breath, raised himself full, shouted, "Go!" in his loudest sergeant's voice, acquired the pistol in his support hand, and began moving ahead, examining the world through his goggles. He watched as incandescent goats fled at his approach, except for those tethered to the sleeper, and they bucked and busted against the ropes that secured them, sensing death on the come. The animals began a chorus of anguish, their voices involuntarily rising in pitch and urgency as those who could flee fled and those who couldn't tried to, desperately.

Mick got within twenty feet and fired, saw the drama of the operating pistol as it ejected a shell through its slide blowback, fired again against the much shorter cocked trigger pull, and then settled into a rhythm and fired three more times, and for just a second saw the impacts of his bullets as they puffed gas into the sealed fabric around the body and then it was obliterated.

The others were close enough, and on Mick's shots they fired, AKs blazing hot in the night, the extreme percussion of the small arms in the stillness of the air, the bullet strikes that stitched a beaten zone and ripped and tossed and pummeled the guy on the receiving end, who even as he was being speared multiple times by warheads moving at two thousand feet per second, began to issue copious amounts of blood-soak through his robe.

A goat fled by Mick, knocking his leg. Of the three tethered goats, two were hit by late-burst uncontrollables, and twisted angrily under the impact, knowing they had been killed; the survivor simply pulled desperately against his rope, finally broke it, and sped off.

"Cease fire, cease fire," Mick yelled.

The guns went quiet except for one Izzie joker who'd evidently just changed magazines and was determined to get his full money's worth out of the labor of the switch. His last thirty rounds served as the coup de grace, "Taps" and a fare-thee-well to the poor sonovabitch all shot to hamburger in his robes.

Then total silence except in the ringing inner ears of the shooters. Mick sniffed the delicious home-at-last smell of all the burned powder, felt a bit of wind whipping against the boys. One of the Taliban fighters kicked the two dead goats aside, and Mick bent to expose the corpse and was surprised to note that it wasn't a man but just another goat, its legs tied, its muzzle tied, itself very dead from all the wounds that had pretty much shredded its torso.

Suddenly a flurry of SureFire beams came onto the mess and the blood was as boldly bright as Mick's fuck-up.

"Shit," said Mick. "Shit, shit, shit."

"How the fuck—"

"What the—"

"The satellite said he was here," said Mick, uncomprehending. "He was here, the eye in the sky, it said he was here."

It was Tony Z whose SureFire found the gizmo. It lay under the dead goat, soaked in blood, clotted with dirt, but enough metal showed for Tony's beam to catch. He bent, plucked them out, a small cylinder of metal the size of one joint of a man's finger and a little, almost featureless plastic box.

"That's the GPS chip and transmitter," said Mick. "Fucker either knew or figured out how we were tracking him, and suckered us with it. Smart guy. Didn't just toss it and clear the area but set us up to waste the night while he moved on. Goddamn his ass."

It was then that the two Taliban guys started to chatter between themselves excitedly.

"What're they saying?" Mick asked Tony.

"'Where's Mahoud?' That's what they're saying. 'Where's Mahoud?'"

Where *was* Mahoud?

It only took half an hour to find him, by backtracking over the hill along the axis that had been assigned to Mahoud in the ascent. The peep of sun over horizon bringing rapid pink illumination to the vast sky was a big help as well.

He hadn't made it very far.

Tony leaned over the still figure, facedown on the dust of Afghanistan, and pulled his head up for examination. There wasn't much to see. His throat had been deeply and expertly cut from earlobe to earlobe. Not many of the anatomical structures remained unsundered, as if the cutter had truly enjoyed sending this one to Allah.

"I would say," said Tony, "we are dealing with a very angry individual."

QALAT

He sat in the shadows, drinking tea. Under his robes, the SVD with its unyielding structure and all its knobs, prongs, jutting edges, and lengthy barrel had to be wedged to the side, its sling loosened and the beast itself carefully adjusted so that it nestled against the length of his body, braced against the stiffness of his very bad leg. The leg itself, stressed beyond stress, now announced loudly that it had no further interest in completing the mission.

Ray sat far back in the crowded marketplace, at some kind of outdoor rude wooden cafe that looked rustic and slatternly, and he'd just finished some kind of meal, a mystery meat that had to be goat (except, wasn't meat supposed to be brown or red and not naval gunboat gray?), a thin gravy, lots of surprisingly good rice, and those patties of baked dough the Afghans ate, the ones that looked like Pop-Tarts but had no jam inside. But all in all, it could have been the best meal of his life, if for no other reason than that he was alive to enjoy it.

Tea: good, sweet, loaded with energy.

Rest: good, after the ordeal of the past few days.

Crowds: very good. People swirled everywhere in this city of thousands, most of them nut brown men in strange headgear or head- and face-obscuring turbans, dishdashas in blazing colors or patterns obscuring bodies, the necks draped in long scarves—graceful, scrawny, furtive, loud, animated, with faces that looked like the beaten hide of an African shield. Many were Pashtun tribals, openly carrying daggers or AKs that nobody was going to take from them; many were city folk, in suits with shirts but no ties. Many were women, some in tribal outfits, some in the Afghan version of the latest hot look from a New York they saw only on CNN satellite pickup, some young, some old. But so many of them. They traveled by every conveyance known to man, from bike to motorbike to motorcycle to tri-wheel covered motorcycles to pickups to full-blown lorries to the odd sedan, all of them competing for space with other life-forms, dogs, goats, even the occasional cow and some humped, hairy beasts that looked like *Star Wars* creatures. The place baked in the odors of combustion and methane and probably piss and keefe too, and a kind of blue haze of dust and exhaust hung low over everything.

Nobody seemed to have noticed Ray. It helped that he was dark, that his eyes were deep and brown to a degree that could have concealed an Islamist's serpentine way of thinking even if it only concealed a rigorous Catholic boyhood, and that he was thin, wiry, ropey, graceful, and with his thick dressing of robes, almost anonymous. The exoticism of his face could easily have been Mongolian, Chinese, Tartar, Uzbek, anything; it surprised nobody.

His plan: to sit here till twilight. In the falling darkness, he'd mosey the several blocks to the warlord Ibrahim Zarzi's compound and examine the Many Pleasures Hotel across the way. Getting into it shouldn't be too hard. The idea was to rent a room there tomorrow morning, sleep a bit, then carefully ease his way up to the roof. No door or lock could stop him, for he was as clever in the ways of penetration as he was clever in the ways of evasion.

He'd slide into shoot position just a few minutes before it went down. He wouldn't be at the building's edge, but as far back as possible while still retaining the angle. He'd thought this out; it wouldn't be the classic sniper's rested shot, off something like a bench. No, he'd be in character as the tribal wanderer until the very last, squatting on the roof. At the proper moment, he'd rise, lifting the rifle with him. If there was some structure upon which he could lean to stabilize himself, that would be excellent. If not, he'd take the kill shot offhand. It was only a little over 200 yards and he had superb offhand skills, something not many snipers build on but which had obsessed him one year at Camp Lejeune as a weakness in his game.

He could hit that shot one hundred out of one hundred, no problem. He might even have time for a follow-up, put another one into the already stricken man.

In the courtyard there'd be chaos, craziness, insane hubbub. It would take a few minutes for things to calm down, for someone to issue orders to Zarzi's well-armed militia, for the pathetic Afghan police or the hopelessly incompetent Dutch peacekeepers to be called. Ray would use that time to dump the rifle, and slip out of the hotel and off into the crowds.

Ray took another sip of tea.

It was as good a plan as could be imagined.

But it didn't deal with the problem.

The problem was: there was a mole somewhere who'd given him up to the contractors.

He was blown. He was hunted.

Now what does a nice Catholic boy do about that? He hadn't figured it out yet, but he knew one thing. He'd have to slit some more throats.

UNIDENTIFIED CONTRACTOR TEAM

The city shimmered before them in the afternoon sun. It almost looked like Oz or Mecca or the Baghdad of the many tales, white and dignified, sprawled across the plain under the mountains, except for the fact that it was utterly crappy. It had a skyline that consisted of a few decrepit buildings of the sort that were old fashioned in 1972 when they'd been built, and the rest low-rent ramshackle construction improvisations, none more than a couple of stories high, thrown together more or less on the fly, wherever. Mick and his pals wandered farther, heading downtown.

What lay farther along was, to the Western mind, somewhat baffling: a maze of dusty, crowded streets lit up by a riot of color and confusion, Arabic signs amid universal symbols like small Coke bottle signs, a brand of Japanese gasoline, pictures of kabobs, the ubiquitous BankAmericard and MasterCard symbols, Indian teas. Other identifiables amid the clutter consisted of but were not limited to carts, shops, tents selling mostly woven things gaudy with color, pots, guns guaranteed to fire at least fifty times before exploding, kabobs, rice balls, custard, more pots, whatever. The vehicles seemed from 1927, many of them with an odd number of wheels, many painted extravagantly. You could not move in the place without raising a shroud of dust, for less than 2 percent of the roads were paved.

Mick had ditched the ball cap—a long-billed SureFire giveaway for big-time customers in the trade—for his own turban, and by this time, he'd become expert in draping it so his features were obscured. The sunglasses and beard helped, but what helped most was that Qalat was still tribal, meaning really lawless, and there were enough

Westerners about of dubious pedigree that the addition of a few more didn't set off signals. He didn't have to pretend to be native, just psycho, not a stretch for him. Plus, he was escorted by two heavily armed Tals, whose glares and do-not-approach hand signals were enough to keep him safe from all but the most insane militia. And there was Mick's size, impressive, and his body language, which said fuck-not-or-die, and his own AK-47, the Barrett being stashed in the foothills, to be picked up if time and circumstance permitted. Then too he had Tony Z and Crackers the Clown, also festooned with AKs, robes, grenades, daggers, and dust, and those two serious pilgrims amplified the fuck-not-or-die message.

Mick's ears were still red. Such a reaming he'd gotten. Mr. Mac-Gyver had not been a happy camper, wherever he was, whomever he worked for. Mick winced at the conversation, held at 0730 that morning.

"Make me happy," the control had said in answering and when Mick merely swallowed, accepting that which was about to be bestowed, his voice box seemed disconnected from his brain. Mr. MacGyver had said, "You bastard. You moron. You idiot. You had his location, the cover of darkness, the advantage in numbers, firepower, ruthlessness, aggression, and experience, and yet he defeated you. Bogier, you were highly recommended but you are a total loss. Where is he?"

This was the part Mick dreaded.

"Qalat. I guess."

"You guess? You guess?"

Mick laid it out, the trick with the GPS transmitter, the throat-cutting of Mahoud, the night lost in slow approach and final assault, and the fact that if the marine was six or seven hours ahead of them, he was already there or damn near.

"Who knew he was that good? He was really good."

"So not only did you fail, but he also ditched the GPS, which means we won't be able to track him on any screen? Is that right?"

"I guess so."

"You've got it. That's you we're tracking, that's what you're say-ing."

"I guess so."

"You guess so. You guess so. You were paid to do a job and he has outfought you at every turn. Who is he, Superman?"

Mick wanted to say, Hey, asshole, you were the one who told me the GPS was him, so it was you he outfoxed, not me. What was I supposed to do, assault the position or set up perimeter security with six guys? Yet he also knew it was his refusal to close when he had the chance and instead wasted another hour and a half jerking off while his team positioned itself that had really cost them badly. No way they could catch up now.

"What do you want us to do?"

"Ever hear of a lovely Japanese thing called seppuku? Gut split-ting. Just open your guts with a very sharp blade and die quietly, all right?"

Mick waited as MacGyver's rage crested.

"All right," the control finally said, "you've left us with a very big problem. I will have to make some arrangements from this end. You go into Qalat and find a place near the compound. I may need you to move quickly if I can get done what I need to do. You call in at 0700 hours tomorrow your time, and we'll see where we are."

"Got it," said Mick. "Out and—"

But he was talking to dead air.

UN PEACEKEEPER HUMVEE

PLATOON C, 5TH ROYAL DUTCH MARINES
ROYAL DUTCH MARINE OUTPOST
QALAT
ZABUL PROVINCE
SOUTHEASTERN AFGHANISTAN
2300 HOURS

Ray popped the lock, slid in. These royal marines must be aching for a bad suicide bombing because their post security was so porous anyone could get in or out. It probably represented their absolute hatred of this job and this country. Imagine: you join the Royal Dutch Marines well aware that you're not going into combat anytime soon, and that you're basically signing up for a lifetime sinecure with cool guns; but you end up in an outpost in a slum city on the edge of the wildest area in Pakistan, surrounded by men who want to kill you. And your job, really, isn't to win any war, it's to represent some politician's alliance with an American ideal that has nothing to do with the Netherlands. Wouldn't you be depressed? And if you're depressed, you quickly turn fatalistic and lazy, and the next thing you know, you're getting by on luck alone. Maybe you'll get blown up, maybe you won't, now pass the hooch, please, and a little of that fine Afghan keefe that will help the time fly faster.

So while the Dutchmen explored their morose natures inside their sandbagged building, he'd slipped under the barbed wire and gotten into the Humvee, one of several parked outside. The guard posts weren't even manned by Dutchies, but by Afghan army troopers and they were at low readiness, so Ray had no trouble getting by.

He cracked the plastic dashboard, peeled the broken shielding off to reveal the ignition wiring, probed it with his knife blade, and in a bit it had stirred to life; he let it idle, peeped up to make sure no one in the guard post had noticed and that no drunken, high Dutchie was coming to check. He was momentarily secure.

He looked to the radio, saw that it was the standard mounted high-frequency AN/MRC-138, a higher-powered version of the PRC-104, the universal talk box of the war on terror. Ray knew it well, having been a radioman sometime in an ancient Marine Corps past, and turned it on, watching it pop and crackle to life as a small red light reached peak intensity, signifying full power, then went to the frequency knob, turned it slowly, and finally acquired 15.016 MHZ, the battalion operating freak. With no mountains in between, it ought to be a loud-and-clear chat.

He held the push-to-talk button down, and spoke into the phone.

"Whiskey-Six, this is Whiskey Two-Two. Do you receive, over."

"Whiskey Two-Two, this is Whiskey-Six, roger. Authentification, please."

"Olympic downhill," said Ray.

Commo tumbled out of protocol.

"Ray, Jesus—"

"Whiskey-Six, do you have Six Actual there, over."

"Negative, Two-Two, I'll get him, over."

"Whiskey-Six, negative, no time now. Be advised Two-Two is on-site and will execute tomorrow. I say again, Two-Two on-site, running hot, straight and dead zero, will execute as planned tomorrow and then exfiltrate by any means possible. Scrub the chopper pickup, Two-Two will hump it out the soft way. Do you read, over?"

"Copy that, Two-Two, will advise Six Actual 'On-site and will execute to—'"

"Whiskey Six, that is all. Two-Two out."

Ray cut off the power, hung the phone on its cradle.

He turned off the idling engine, eased out of the vehicle, low-crawled seventy-five feet to the sector of fencing farthest from the guard post, staying out of the lights, and took his cuts and punctures while slowly picking his way through the lower coils. That wasn't easy but far from impossible, for the barbed wire was meant to slow down, not stop, incursion. A little beyond the wire, he found shadow and rose and slipped away to the site where he'd cached his SVD. Tomorrow was shaping up to be a very interesting day.

2ND RECON BATTALION HQ

Jesus Christ," said Colonel Laidlaw, "and kiss my ass! He made it. The Cruise Missile made it."

S-2 asked, "He didn't say anything more? No details, no—"

"I had the idea he was stressed," said the corporal who'd been on radio watch. "He didn't want to talk at length. He just communicated the message—those are his exact words, sir—and signed off. I have no idea of the origin of the call. He had all call signs right, authentification code right, and I know Sergeant Cruz well and recognized his voice."

"That's fine, Nichols, you can go now," said the colonel, and the young NCO rose, left the bunker tent, and headed back to his duty station.

The colonel, in his nighttime sweats, the exec still in camos, and S-2, also still in camos, sat around the working table under the now-dead monitor on which they'd watched the fate of 2-2 play out. Cigarettes were consumed, and the colonel had the whiff—just the tiniest—of bourbon to him.

"Should we notify higher HQ, sir? The Agency liaison? At least helos at Ripley so we can put a bird airborne to get him out if he calls in again and needs emergency extract, no matter what he says tonight."

"Negative, negative," said the colonel. "I don't like the way they were jumped and that the shooters knew exactly who they were."

"Sir, it could have just been Taliban assholes. They'll shoot up anything and say it was God's will."

"These guys were not Taliban. They were too disciplined. They were all in prone, they were in a good tactical array, when they moved, they moved professionally, not like hadjis going to a book burning. And let's not forget: they hit the target. No, we'll keep this to ourselves. It's our party, we invented it, it's our man, our materiel, our mission. No, this is for us. Tomorrow I want a patrol in force to head out on the road to Qalat and I want a lot of other smaller patrol activity in that sector. I want Humvees all over the place, lots of corpsmen and sniper teams. Lots of marine presence and I want the troops on the alert in case Ray needs help fast or needs a place to go to with a pack of hadjis on his ass."

"Yes, sir," said the exec. "I'll draft the orders."

The colonel turned to S-2.

"Will we be able to eyeball him from above at that time tomorrow, or is the satellite somewhere helpful, like Hawaii or Omaha?"

"We only get real-time satfeed from 1400 through about 1530 tomorrow, sir."

"Ach," said the colonel. "That is not pleasing. S-Two, try to think of something that might please me. Think real hard. I know you can do it."

"Sir, I can request that the Agency task a recon Predator tomorrow and get us a real-time feed while this thing is going down."

"And what are our chances that these wonderful folks will cooperate with us?"

"I would say somewhere between zero and negative two thousand."

"That is not pleasing to me."

"Sir, I will take a Humvee, with your permission, and personally make the request."

"Tell them if they don't, I'll call in an artillery strike on their operations bunker."

"Sir, I don't think they've got a sense of humor. These people take themselves very seriously. But I do know a guy. In person, maybe I can get something set up. I know if we go routine channels through radio request, some Army dental hygiene unit will be in an ambush somewhere up-country and they'll get all the drone action."

"Then you do that, S-Two. You do that and get me my picture show."

"I'll do my best, sir."

"Good. Now everybody get some sleep. And pray for Ray if you're religious. And if you're not religious, pray for Ray. That's an order."

ROOF OF ABDUL THE BUTCHER'S

GUIZAR STREET
TANBOOR NEIGHBORHOOD
QALAT
ZABUL PROVINCE
SOUTHEASTERN AFGHANISTAN
0700 HOURS

Bogier felt a little less edgy. He'd fucked two houris in a house of ill repute in the district, and at least had his rod problems quieted for a bit. He'd taken two dexes and a Chinese red tiger and his mind was racy with energy. All his boys had gotten a little shut-eye, and the two Izzies seemed in good spirits, and not likely to cut his throat while he slept. Now he had to call in, see what was going to happen. Maybe they could all go home. That would be the best result.

He got out the Thuraya, activated it, pressed the button, and waited. In time Mr. MacGyver picked up.

"Did you have a good time at the whorehouse?" he asked.

"We all needed some R and R, Mr. MacGyver. Those satellites don't miss a trick, do they?"

"Not when you're carrying that GPS with you. Funny, I didn't think you were a doggie-style guy."

"Wow, that's some satellite."

"Joke. Bogier, even the great MacGyver has a sense of humor. So now you've gone to ground less than half a mile from the compound."

"That's right, sir. And I've eyeballed the Many Pleasures Hotel. It's the usual fucking joint. Not exactly a Holiday Inn. Ugh, negative stars in Frommer's."

"I don't need to know the details. Here's the play. Get one of your Izzies into the place tomorrow morning or afternoon. He's got to get to the roof somehow, and plant that GPS. We need a satellite lock-on to watch and see what goes down."

"Is that where the marine is shooting from?"

"Bogier, if I don't tell you something, it's because I don't want you to know it. So no questions, that's still the deal."

"Got it. Sorry. But it's the only site with enough elevation to get a shot into the compound."

"You're a genius, Bogier. No flies on you. Let's get back to tomorrow, shall we? After you plant that GPS, I want you to surveil. You set up all around. You cover each entrance. There can't be that many."

"No, sir."

"You make sure the marine has entered the building."

"Suppose he's there already?"

"We don't think he'll take the chance. That's our best thinking. He's suspicious now, but he doesn't know anything. So why put himself there with that big rifle and wait? It'll make more sense to him to slide in late, check into a room, and cut his exposure to the minimum. Plus he's got to buy some rope tomorrow, because he doesn't want to come off that roof by stairway or an elevator built in 1891. He'll want to get down fast, and rappelling is the only way, and it's clearly within his skill set."

"Yes, sir."

"You're looking for a man with a rifle under his robes. You think he's hit? So wouldn't he be moving tentatively?"

"Yes, sir, and if a .50 grazed him, he's purple from shoulder to ankle. He'll be moving *very* tentatively. Would it be easier to tell the police an assassination attempt—"

"No. Because they will surround the hotel crudely and he will go away. Then he will return to his HQ and make a formal report on everything that has happened and questions we don't want to be raised may well be raised. No, we want him in that hotel."

"And we take him on the roof?"

"No. You make certain he's in the hotel, then you call me with the definite, then, if I were you, I'd take cover."

MANY PLEASURES HOTEL

S oon came the call to evening prayers. Soon the sun set. Soon tea would be drunk, food would be eaten, life in all its manifold pleasures would be experienced by the rich and all its manifold pains by the poor. The city would go silent.

In that falling dusk, the man known as the Beheader would leave his large house and walk to his jet black armored Humvee for a fuck with a woman without a voice. He would not make it. A bullet the size of a pencil tip would enter his body at well over 2,300 feet per second from a cartridge of the equivalent of an American .30-06 and would blow out several of his blood-bearing organs, most notably his heart. He would be dead before he fractured his expensive Dallas cosmetic-dentistry whitened and straightened teeth on the cobblestones.

Or something like that.

Ray looked up and down the street. No sign of any police or militia presence. An orange personnel carrier, bearing the emblem of the Royal Dutch Marines, had ground down the street once at around two, but since then all was normal, as lorries, bikes, scooters, to say nothing of hundreds of merchants and citizens and donkeys, even the occasional fleet of goats, filled the busy street that housed the hotel, directly across from the gated compound of Ibrahim Zarzi, warlord, politician, and best-dressed man of 1934.

His leg pain was muted somewhat by a morning of rest in a flea-bag near the railway station, and a couple of kabobs for nourishment from a street-side vendor outside and half a bottle of aspirin from what passed as a "drugstore" in Afghanistan. He could have had keefe or bennies or dex or red who's-your-mamas? or rolling chocolate death or whatever, but stayed with the regular stuff. He'd also had about a gallon of the sugary tea.

Now, amid the hundreds, virtually indiscernible from them, he hobbled down the street, face down, his bad leg aching, the rifle suspended by the strap around his shoulder and threaded down his pants leg. It might print if he wore it across his back, or someone in a crowd might jostle against him and feel the presence of steel. It dangled, the butt of its stock directly in the armpit, the long skeleton of wooden stock extending its length ridiculously, the receiver group against his hip, the fore end and barrel down the side of his leg. He'd taped the magazine under the wooden fore grip, to keep the thickness of the thing, with its Chinese scope clamped up on top in some sort of steel frame, at a minimum. It meant that when he came to shoot, he'd have to take a second to rip the mag from its bonds of tape, quickly peel any filaments of tape away, slam it into the mag well, then pull and release the bolt as he rose and put himself in the offhand shooting position.

He didn't need to tell himself, but he always did anyway, a kind of mantra: breathe, relax, let sight settle, focus on crosshairs not target, press not pull, follow through, pin trigger. He'd done it a hundred thousand times.

He entered the hotel. It was ancient, somewhat Anglified in its shabby dignity and brass fixtures, and in pre-Soviet invasion days had been a haven for the hippies who came to rural Afghanistan to enjoy the local crops unmonitored by police agencies. The Reds had turned it into a troop barracks, and when the Taliban kicked them out it had languished, as under those stern boys not a lot of traveling had been done in the country. Since, er, "liberation," it had enjoyed substantially more prosperity, and now and then a particularly adventurous journalist or TV crew would stay there, in for an interview with the Beheader, who sometimes kept his appointments and sometimes didn't.

Ray slid up to a desk and was greeted by the suspicious eyes of a clerk and he abated that suspicion by sliding over a 250-rupee note and his beautifully forged Afghan identity card, which had him down as Farzan Babur.

No words were necessary, nor were signatures. The fellow took the note and returned thirty-five rupees in change, and pushed over a key, which wore a brass tag with the number 232 on it. Ray bowed humbly, took the key and the dough, and sloughed to the stairway.

"Got him," said Tony Z-for-Zemke, a forces washout who'd done nine years for Graywolf Security before being cashiered out on the same surrendering-pilgrim gig that had gotten Bogier fired. Since there were no radios, Tony Z had come running across the street, dodging bikes and donkeys. "Mick, I got him. Definite. A 'limp,' some kind of awkward thing under his robes if you looked. Clearly had a load on under all the Izzie shit he was wearing."

"See his face? White guy, marine?"

"Scruffy black beard, face held low, maybe a little browner than you'd expect. Maybe he's Asian or Mexican or some weird shit like that. You know, diversity's the thing these days. Not a native, his skin wasn't rough enough."

"Okay," said Mick, "get the other guys and fall back to that cafe. I'll make the call."

Mick slipped back, tried to find some privacy on the busy roadway, couldn't, slipped into a street that led nowhere except to stalls of Afghan wares—the kind of crap these people sold—felt good when one of his Izzies came up to offer screening, and got the phone out, unlimbered the antenna.

"Yes, yes?" MacGyver demanded.

"We got him."

"You're positive?"

"You didn't give us a pic. What I have is a non-Afghani in tribal garb and turban with apparently a bad leg heading into the hotel, just as predicted. He had some kind of shit under his robes, obviously the rifle. My guy couldn't get a close-up look-see, but all the indicators are there."

"A white man? American white?"

"Ahhh—" Mick's doubts came out.

"Well?"

"My guy said maybe he was a bit brown. Could have been Hispanic or maybe even Asian. He—"

"Bingo," said Mr. MacGyver. "Now get undercover."

2ND RECON BATTALION HQ

**FOB WINCHESTER
S-2 BUNKER
ZABUL PROVINCE
SOUTHEASTERN AFGHANISTAN
1904 HOURS**

Heeere's Johnny," said Exec.

"I am goddamned," said Colonel Laidlaw. "I am getting that sergeant a medal."

The cruciform locator on the screen centered on downtown Qalat, exactly at the site—authenticated breathlessly from maps by a triumphant S-2 who'd gotten Agency coop by calling in every favor he was owed, plus offering his firstborn if necessary to three separate officers—of the Many Pleasures Hotel across from the Beheader's complex, as seen from a discreetly cruising Predator drone a few thousand feet overhead. Ray's GPS was talking to its friends in the sky and by magical technical shit beyond the imagination of the colonel the chatter was being intercepted and used to pinpoint the GPS's location, and the camera in the Predator laid out everything perfectly, despite the readouts all over the screen, the other small screens from other feeds, the gray-green-black color scheme.

They could see the walled complex, the big main house, the garages out back; they could see the incandescent scuttle of ants that were men, the glow of cooking fires on the property, a silver ribbon where a stream ran through it. Outside the walls, a human glow-worm passed to and fro, this being the blur of pedestrian traffic. The white square roofs of the odd vehicles caught in this river of humanity showed clearly. It was the best movie Colonel Laidlaw had ever seen. He watched the hotel, slightly obscured under the cruciform of the locked-on locator, and saw the street scene from his memory, as on two occasions earlier on the tour he'd been a guest of the Beheader.

"Here comes the Humvee," said S-2.

Indeed from one of the smaller buildings in Zarzi's complex, the square roof of the armored vehicle scuttled forward, scooted between buildings, and came to rest in the driveway along one wall, perhaps thirty yards from the main building. The glowing signatures of underlings scurried this way and that. They seemed to form a security cordon right at the house itself, and it didn't take long for the door to open—so sharp was the long-range image that the narrow slice of the door, viewed from above, was clearly resolved—and a figure stepped out.

Laidlaw remembered him: he was a tall, stately man, handsome, always well dressed and exquisitely groomed, who favored Savile Row suits under beautiful lavender pashminas and an elegant if discreet fez of some kind of highly glossy material, possibly silk or velvet, neatly encompassing his silver-gray hair. His vanity was watches. Patek Philippe, Rolex, Fortis, Breitling, always something beautiful and complex. He had deep brown, extremely empathetic eyes.

"Get ready to die, motherfucker," said Exec.

All eyes switched to Ray's site on the roof, 230 yards out, revealed by the cruciform.

At that moment, so hot it burned their eyes, so fast it had to be a phenomenon of explosive energy, a smear of white ruptured and radiated outward, sending waves of electronic disturbance across the screen and in another second the image itself wobbled crazily, as if a giant wave had reached and smashed into the light unmanned aircraft, disturbing its equipoise and threatening its survival.

"S-Two, what the fuck was that?"

"Detonation," said S-2.

PART TWO

SEARCH MODE

CASCADE MEADOWS, IDAHO

J ulie came out of the office where she'd been checking the expenditures at the Missoula barn when she heard the racket, watched the horses jump and shiver in the corral. The helicopter settled slowly out of the blue western sky, and in its rude, invasive way kicked up dust and energy everywhere. It certainly was an impressive machine, a huge green hull with lots of portholes, a bubble canopy behind which sat two men in goggles looking very insectoid, landing gear, struts, insignia—USAF—under the great swirl of the blade at idle. It looked like it had emerged from CNN, on the television set.

A hatch opened and, as she expected, it was her husband's friend, a man named Nick Memphis, now a hotshot executive with the FBI. They'd been trying to reach Swagger for some time now, but he wouldn't talk to them. He was sick of them and, in a way, of the world, or at least the world they represented. He no longer read anything but big, fat World War II novels from the forties and fifties. Television annoyed him, he hated his cell phone and the e-mail process, and wasn't interested in iPods or iPads or whatever they were, BlackBerries, all those little electronic things. Hated 'em. Mostly all he did was work like a bastard around the place and take his daughter Miko to junior rodeo events, which she usually won or placed high in, proving to be, at twelve, a fearless competitor in the barrel race.

But after Nick, another figure emerged, familiar and yet not immediately recognizable. She searched her memory and then it came to her. Trim, pantsuited, waves of raven-black hair, a certain elegance, Asian: yes, it was a woman named Susan Okada, a mysterious figure who had appeared from out of the blue nine or so years ago with a gift that had lightened everybody's life and spirit—the child

Miko. She knew without having been told that Susan Okada worked for that mystery entity that went by the three initials C, I, and A, and knew that if Susan were here, it meant, without being stated, that an old favor was being called in. Perhaps Susan's presence established some principle of obligation, a call to duty, whatever. They needed him and there would be no turning them down this time.

"Hi, Julie," called Nick as he got to the house.

"Nice ride," she said.

She hugged him, kissed him, and did the same to Susan: you could not but love a woman who had somehow gotten you your second daughter, through some magic hocus-pocus making the bureaucracy and the waiting and the traveling and the interviewing all vanish.

"It's so good to see you," she said to Susan.

"I hear Miko's turned into a rodeo champ."

"She knows what she's doing on a horse. Of course we pushed the rodeo, thinking the horses would keep her away from boys, and we ended up with both horses *and* boys."

She drew them onto the porch and into the living room. It was a beautiful, big house, the house of a man of property and success. That was certainly Swagger. He'd become something a bit more than prosperous and now owned fourteen lay-up barns in six states, enjoyed referential relationships with the veterinary practice in those locales, the key to the whole thing, and really it was Julie, an organized and determined woman, who kept the wheels turning and the engine grinding forward into the black. The pension from the Marine Corps and the medical disability pay was only the frosting, ammunition money.

But then she turned to Nick.

"I know this is business. You didn't come by helicopter for small talk."

"Sorry for the melodramatics, but you can't get his attention any other way. He's not even opening e-mail or accepting registered letters, much less phone calls. We wouldn't be here if we didn't think we had a real situation."

"I'll go get him. And I'll pack. I'm guessing you'll be taking him with you."

"I'm afraid so, Julie. He knows the stuff and we need someone who knows the stuff. I know he's sick and tired of us. *I'm* sick and tired of us. But still . . . it's a real situation."

"And a tragic one," Susan Okada added.

Swagger, in jeans and a blue work shirt, sat across from them, his coffee untouched. He was sixty-four now and almost always in pain. The goddamned cut on his hip—exactly where all those years ago he'd taken the bullet that shattered the hip and almost killed him—had never really healed properly and gave him trouble every day. Yet the painkillers turned him groggy and he hated being groggy, so he just got through it. Riding horseback was a special agony, so he traveled most places these days by his three-wheeled all-terrain vehicle, beneath a straw Stetson, much weathered, and a pair of sunglasses too cool, he thought, for such a worthless loafer. His hair had never turned white but stayed a kind of pewter gray, wiry like his old man's, with a will of its own, and would only answer to butch wax; his cheeks had sunk for some reason and he thought he looked like a death's-head, but when he saw how many men his age had turned to blobs, he supposed he ought to be grateful. He still had the face of some kind of Comanche warrior from some forgotten age; he still carried himself with regulation Marine Corps grace and posture, as some systems imprint so deep they never go away.

"You're a hard man to reach," said Nick.

"I'm not good for much," he said. "That last one nearly killed me. I'm still tired from it. All I do is sleep or think of sleeping. Or dream of drinking. Can't have a drop in the house, or I'll suck it down. Been on the wagon thirty years and there ain't a day I don't miss it. Without all these damn women around, there's no way I'd stay sober."

"Don't listen to him," called Julie. "He's just playing the martyr to the choices he made himself. It's not attractive."

"Let me lay this out," Nick said. "Give it a listen, tell me if you don't think you can contribute. Miss Okada's agency got aboard when they heard what's going on. She wouldn't be here if this weren't a situation."

Swagger looked at Okada, who other than an opening hug had said nothing to him. All that seemed so long ago: the mad, twisted run through the Tokyo underworld, the deaths by blade, the oceans of blood, the loss of some good people so tragic and hurtful even all these years later, and his own survival, the terrible luck of it, when he fought a man with swords who was a hundred times better than he was and somehow survived it.

But there was this other thing. He had already lied: he said he dreamed of sleeping and drinking. But he also dreamed of Susan Okada. In ways that were too solid to be denied, he knew that she was The One. It just had to be, exactly as it never would be, their lives on different sets of railroad tracks heading in different directions, further separated by class, education, experience, levels of sophistication. So it could never, ever be and he'd never, ever act upon it, but at the same time, the unattainability, the taboo, the so-wrong-wrong-*wrong* of it made it delicious, a private, somehow comforting agony that he held close, telling no one. First thing he'd done, damn him, was to check her finger for a wedding ring and it was bare. That pleased him in ways he couldn't have predicted and it also frightened him.

"Hey, how come you're not getting any older?" he said to her. "I turned into the cranky old neighbor in the dark house by himself and you're still, what, on the cover of *Vogue* three times a year?"

"Four, but down from five," she said. "But you're right, I am eternally twenty-eight, even if certain inaccurate documents insist I'm thirty-eight. And you still look like Hector on a break from a hard day's night on the plains outside Troy."

"Them damned Greeks," he said. "You cut 'em all down, and the next day, they're back, just as pissed as before!"

"Okay, guy," said Nick. "I know you're old, old friends. But let me get to the pitch. Here it is. And it's why the Bureau and the Agency are working together, despite a long history of political animosity."

Nick leaned forward.

"About six months ago, in Afghanistan, the Second Reconnaissance Battalion of the Second Marine Division, Twenty-second Expeditionary Force, operating in Zabul province, asked for and received permission to deal with—kill—a warlord local intel suggested was secretly allied with Taliban and Al-Qaeda forces. The marines were losing people in ambushes, IEDs, sniper attacks, and the like. It all led to this guy."

"Do I need to know his name?"

"If you haven't been watching television, his name won't mean a thing to you, Bob," Susan said.

"So," resumed Nick, "a sniper team was sent. Led by a very able guy. Idea was to mingle with the locals, come in from the Pakistani-border side of town, hit the guy with a rifle shot, and beat it before the locals got organized. The rifle was a Dragunov, expendable, untraceable."

"Got it."

"A day out, the team got hit. We don't know what happened, but they were jumped by another sniper team and the spotter was killed, the commo equipment was totaled, the sergeant, we think, was hit."

"I'm guessing he didn't turn back."

"You got that right. Very impressive individual. Your type of guy. You, in a way, twenty years ago at the top of your game. Gunny Sergeant Ray Cruz, full name Reyes Fidencio Cruz, forty-two years old, father a retired lieutenant commander, U.S. Navy, of Portuguese ancestry named Tomas Cruz, mother a Philippine national, Urlinda Flores Marbella. He grew up essentially on the big naval station at Subic near Cebu City, where his dad became head of the golf club as a second career. The kid should have been a pro golfer. Instead he became a sniper."

"Good for him."

"Pretty outstanding guy. Everybody wanted him to go to Annapolis, but he went to UCLA instead. A shooter. NRA junior champion small bore, three years running. Went distinguished in high power in a single summer before he was twenty. Talent with the rifles. High IQ. Good grades. Just the best."

"Not your country-boy sniper type. Why isn't he running a software company somewhere?"

"Because his parents were killed in an auto accident and it really upset him. He joined the marines in ninety-one, won a batch of marksmanship awards, served with distinction in the first Gulf thing. He was offered commissions up the wazoo but wanted to stay a sniper. He thought it was a growth industry, I suppose."

"He was right."

"Was he ever. This is his fifth deployment after two in Iraq, two previous in Afghanistan. Hit twice, fast recovery. Incredible record all the way through. Now this is a guy who could have quit at any time, gone to work for big dollars at some security multinational. He could have taken a commission, retired a colonel, gone to work for GE or somebody. He could have started his own tactical school, run SWAT people and wannabes through for a thousand bucks a head a day and lived in the big house. He could have joined the Bureau, Secret Service, the Agency, State Department security, any outfit with initials instead of a name. Fool for duty. Stays operational, stays in the suck. Seems to love the suck. Goes out on this mission and gets whacked and keeps on going, full-tilt boogie."

"What happened?" Bob asked, loving the sniper already—*where are we going to find more people like him?*—and fearing the answer.

"Somehow, again, we're not sure how, he survived the first hit, he worked some fancy clever game on his pursuers and evaded them, and he made it to the target, but they were on his tail."

"How do you know all this?"

"He was carrying a GPS and transmitter and the satellite could track. At the battalion's S-Two bunker they were getting a real-time feed from a recon drone the whole time. It was Monday Night Football. They have his signal at the shooting site at the time of the hit."

"He made the hit?"

"There was no hit. There was a mysterious explosion. Thirty-one people died."

"That was on TV too," said Susan.

"Another night I must have missed," said Bob.

"The hotel—he was on the roof—was cratered. Nobody knows how or why. Missile? Doubtful, as we had no Reapers in the area—"

"The drones are our program," said Susan. "We had no missile activity at that time. I've gone over the records very carefully. Ugh, I went there, a princess like me, and talked to the on-the-ground people."

"Maybe your outfit even has secrets from you."

"This isn't *The Bourne Conspiracy,* Swagger," she said.

"What's that?"

"Never mind."

"Gas-main explosion. IED," continued Nick. "Ammo cache, bomb factory, nobody knows, and our forensics people weren't invited in to go through the wreckage. The Dutch made an investigation, but I've seen it, it was poorly done, and they were clearly uncomfortable outside their protected compound. It's wild and woolly out there. Maybe the blast was legit, we don't know. Things explode in tribal Afghanistan all the time."

"And this Ray, he was blown up."

"That would seem to be the case."

"What a waste. Remind me again what we get out of this thing?"

"No politics. Only cop stuff. And here's where it gets interesting," said Nick. "The blast seems to have seriously shaken the target, a fellow named Ibrahim Zarzi, also known as the Beheader. He left the city—Qalat—and moved to Kabul. He's hereditary aristocracy, well educated, cosmopolitan, he's got money, lots of it, don't ask why or where it comes from. Anyhow, about this time, conditions in Zabul province improve, no more ambushes, no more bombings, and Second Recon makes it home with no more battle deaths. Everybody gets a promotion."

"And this guy Zarzi," said Susan, "he suddenly becomes an aggressively pro-American player in Kabul. He makes overtures to State, they ask us to look into it, and we vet him up one side and down the other. Supposedly, he's now clean, he's broken all his old associations, walked away from the sources of his fortune."

"Drugs?"

"He was dirty. Now he's clean. We had him at a safe house in Kabul for a week, at his insistence, and polygraphed him, drugged him, interviewed him in English and in Pashto, Agency, FBI, DEA, State, everyone, did the full nine yards' dance on him, and he comes up clean. Very attractive guy, he may be emerging as a candidate for president in the upcoming elections. We view that possibility as very encouraging and are working discreetly to make it happen."

"You can't trust 'em," said Bob.

"People do change. It happens. We worked this bird hard and we believe he's genuine. I don't know how he could fake something like that and get it through all the vetting we laid on him. So our new policy is: you *can* trust them. The future depends on it."

"Maybe you're seeing what you want to see."

"Fear of that remote possibility shouldn't preclude our making full use of this development," she replied. "The trust has to start somewhere or your daughter Miko will be serving in Kabul."

Bob grunted, signifying that he didn't quite buy it. But then he moved on.

"So what does all this have to do with me?"

"As part of State's initiative to upgrade Zarzi's profile before the fall elections, he's coming to DC in a couple of weeks. You might call it a sort of further test, see how he stands up to that kind of DC pressure. Lots of things have been laid on. Debriefings both at State and at the Agency, news conferences, speeches before the foreign policy Council, a big national talking heads broadcast, and finally a medal ceremony at the White House, where all the biggies will be in attendance. He'll announce his candidacy for the presidency, and a big Mad Avenue firm will take over the election. He's our man in Kabul."

"And?"

"And Ray Cruz isn't dead. He's alive. He's back. He's all snipered up. And Ray Cruz has said he will finish his job. He will hit his target and complete Whiskey Two-Two's mission. He'll take Zarzi down."

"How do you know all this?"

"He told us."

Pablo trundled discreetly around the pool with a wireless telephone on his tray. He wore a tropical shirt, white shorts, and sunglasses. He was a good find. He'd also connected Mick with several high-end hookers, a very nice supply of blow, and every third drink off the hotel's books. Behind him, the glass, turquoise, and alabaster crescent of the building itself formed a bulwark against the offshore Atlantic breezes, so that even the palms were still. The sun sparkled off the pool's glossy blue waters. Many young women in bikinis the size of thumbprints were lounging about and most of them would sneak a peek at Mick once in a while. No surprise, since he had the hard body of an NFL linebacker—muscles without fat, all of them nicely bunched and protuberant—and the tattoos were all professional and elegant and military, not jailhouse shit with crude images of Jesus bleeding out on the cross or some chick named Esmeralda woven into hearts and violets. Mick took another sip of his Knob Creek on the rocks as Pablo reached him and presented the phone.

"Señor?"

"Can you throw it in the pool?" Mick asked.

"It would not be a good idea."

"Agh," said Mick. Who knew he was here? No one. That meant someone with the connex.

"Hello?" Mick said.

"Bogier. Enjoying the view?"

MacGyver. He thought he was done with that asshole. It played out as per, and indeed the agreed-upon large sum had been wired to Mick's account. Mick had also decided it was time to quit Kabul, in case someone caught on to something and marines came looking for him. So he awarded himself liberty. Maybe it would stop the ringing in his ears.

"I was until I heard from you."

"Don't be testy."

"I'm on vacation. I'm whipped."

"Vacation's over. A detail has come loose."

"And that would be?"

"The guy you were paid to handle? Well, chum, you didn't handle him. He's back."

"Hey," said Mick, "you guys cratered that hotel. He was there, I put him there for you, and you pushed the button and ka-boom, no more hotel. By the way, thanks for almost killing me too. However you did it, that sucker blew like a nuke. Man, that was a payload."

Mick remembered. How could he forget? He was a little off the street with his screen of Izzies in the alleyway. He disconnected the phone, turned, and signaled the war party to fall back. Then a screaming came across the sky, and the det went. Jesus fucking Christ. He had been around explosions his entire professional life. He'd set them, he'd planned them, he'd been inside a couple, he'd been close enough to a couple to catch a ride through the air for twenty-five feet, he had a thousand pepper marks on his otherwise glorious body from supersonic debris. But nothing like this. Explosions have personalities and they express ideas, they are not all the same. This one carried the message of serious mega destruction. It wasn't a warning or an exclamation point, it wasn't witty, ironic, amusing, or earnest. It was the end of the world in a very small package and it literally evaporated the hotel in a single nanosecond with a percussion that seemed to drive the oxygen from the surface of the earth and in the next nanosecond deposited a rain of dust, wreckage, human and animal parts, chunks of iron and masonry, windowsills, curtain rods, shards of glass on everything for miles around. It knocked him down. What the fuck. That was a goddamned blast and a half.

"It was thermobaric. We warned you to take cover. Did you need an engraved invitation?"

"The timing was a little off. It came in ahead of sked and capped thirty-one pilgrims and almost buried yours truly under a pile of heads and arms."

"Cry me a river why don't you. That's the suck, your chosen workplace. You're in this particular operation, you'll work it through to the end. Got it? We don't have time to do a recruitment drive. We pick you and you don't have the latitude here to say no, mister."

Unsaid: whoever MacGyver was, his power in finding and reaching Mick here or in the Cat's Eye cafe in Kabul where all the coyotes hung meant again: he had the connex. A phone call from him could bring major heat beaucoup fast on Mick's ass.

"Not on the same bill," said Mick. "That one's over. This one's starting up. Same fee structure. I don't work cheap."

"Corporate, aren't we? 'Fee structure,' very Graywolf. Yes, of course, lots of money for you."

"Okay," said Mick, "come to think of it, I would like to fry this little bastard for good."

"I'm sure he feels the same way about you. Can you reassemble your team?"

"Tony's with me, Crackers went home to his wife and kids in Fayetteville. I can get him back, no problem. What's the play?"

"This time, not only are you hunting this character, but so are the FBI and the CIA and just about everybody else. So you've got some competition. But to make it harder, they just want to stop the guy. You have to kill him, Mr. Mission Impossible."

"That's what I do."

"Little evidence of that yet, friend, though I understand you're hell on goats. He's trying to finish the mission you stopped him from completing. He wants to put a bullet in Ibrahim Zarzi, the Afghan politician, who arrives in Washington for a high-profile visit in two weeks. This time, you stop him, permanently. He is under no circumstances to whack Zarzi or fall into police hands and go all Chatty Cathy on us."

"Leads, you have leads?"

"The Bureau-Agency team handling this has gone to an old guy named Swagger, a former marine sniper with a lot of experience in these games. He's you with brains, talent, imagination, stamina, and guts. I've seen the file."

"The Nailer. A classic oldie. I've heard of the guy."

"I'll bet you have. He makes Ray Cruz look like a kindergartener. Swagger has the best chance of nailing Cruz, so you'll be given all sorts of little gadgets to make tracking Swagger something within your Neanderthalic reach."

"If I get 'em together, I have the okay to dust 'em both? I don't like the idea of pulling down on a knight of the round table, but there may not be another way."

"Bogier, don't go soft on me and start humming 'Halls of Montezuma.' Collateral's part of the business. This one is about getting the job done by any means possible. Don't fuck this up."

"Get over it. I didn't fuck up the last one. I delivered. Your thermobaric nuke didn't quite do the job."

"Bogier, this is unbelievably crucial. At your level you can't possibly understand what's at stake. But trust me: you must come through on this. No pussy, no blow, no uppers or downers, no new tattoos, no three hours in the gym every day. You get it done."

"I have it."

"We don't like to use coyotes. But we have no choice. Show us we haven't misjudged."

"Roger, wilco."

"And one more thing: no witnesses."

CASCADE MEADOWS, IDAHO

He told you?" Bob asked.

Nick reached into his briefcase and pulled out a file, reached into the file and pulled out a decrumpled piece of yellow paper now preserved in cellophane. It was a Marine Corps incoming radio communication form. Nick handed it over.

Bob saw the operator's name, the unit designation "2-2 Recon" and the date, sometime last week, and the time, 0455. He read the message:

"'Whiskey Six, this is Whiskey Two-Two. Authentification Olympic downhill. I say again, Olympic downhill." There was an asterisk scribbled in pencil next to the transmission, and at the bottom, after the footnote style, next to the parallel asterisk the operator had written, "No record of 'Olympic downhill' as verifier."

Unrecorded was the radio operator's response, which must have been something like, "Codes and verifier invalid, who are you, Two-Two, over, what is your situation, why are you in communication with this unit?"

Ray just bulled ahead, and the young man had written down:

"Whiskey Two-Two is on-site and will proceed with operation as planned. Target will be destroyed sometime next two to four weeks. Hunting is good, morale is high. Semper Fi. Out."

"The kid thought it was some kind of joke, but it went into the log and the next day, the CO's looking at the log. He used to be the exec and he remembered Two-Two. He got on the phone to division and on to marine headquarters at Henderson and then to us."

"So the thinking is," Bob said, "Cruz survived the blast and didn't limp back to his FOB but instead went AWOL big time as a way of going rogue. Somehow, he got out of Afghanistan and found a way back. Now he's pissed at what he has decided is some kind of betrayal that killed his spotter and thirty-one Afghans. Maybe he's a little nuts. So he's going to whack this politician anyway, just out of spite."

"Something like that."

"Come on. That doesn't make any sense at all. Especially now that the Afghan is on our side, publicly and loudly. So Ray is now betraying his country and his service. It's like he's working for *them*. He couldn't have been captured and turned?"

"Seems unlikely, but there are cases like it."

"That's not Ray," said Swagger, who now believed he knew Ray or at least could feel the way his mind operated. "No, he's got some other, deeper game in play. He's got another objective, and we're not smart enough to see it yet."

"Maybe we shouldn't worry about motive at this point," said Susan. "Maybe we should just deal with what we have and figure out how to stop it."

"So my part in this is to be your sniper consultant," Swagger said, looking as if each of his sixty-four years had cost him a thousand dollars' worth of grief.

"You're with us every step of the way. We want you to eyeball the possible shooting sites and tell us where he'd shoot from, what he'd see that we wouldn't. We want you to analyze his ingress and escape routes, his fallbacks, his hides, all the things that even our best experts might miss. We want you to be him when we game out possibilities or permutations. We need your intuitive access to his heart and mind over the next few weeks."

"So you can kill him."

"If it comes to that," said Susan, whose specialty, now as then, was delivering the hard truth. "Nobody wants it, but there are other issues at stake. We have to stop him, Bob. Do you have any idea how humiliating it would be to this country internationally if an Afghan politician under our sponsorship was publicly assassinated by a marine sniper?"

Nick outlined the deal. Bob would actually carry an FBI badge and be legally entitled to represent himself as an "FBI investigator," though not an "agent" or a "special agent." The consultancy fee would be substantial, not that it was about money. Under certain circumstances, with written authorization, he would be permitted to carry a firearm and make arrests. He would be granted all authority and respect within the federal system and the military in accordance with his police powers. He would report directly to Nick and Susan. He would have an unlimited travel budget.

"My heart is with the sniper," he said. "You have to know that going in. I want to get him out of this fix, get it straightened out. I don't want to kill him."

"We know that. We need that. We're buying that."

"Then my first move is to Camp Lejeune. I want to talk to his CO, his peers, and get a sense of him."

"We'll make the phone calls," said Nick. "Oh, and raise your right hand."

Bob complied, mumbled the appropriate yeses, and, cranky and old and ever so tired, realized he was back to taking the king's gold, which meant he might have to do the king's killing.

U.S.-MEXICO BORDER
27 MILES WEST OF NOGALES, ARIZONA
0356 HOURS
THE NEXT MORNING

The van was dirty and spotted and squalid, a '92 Ford Econoline with Arizona plates. It smelled of unwashed bodies, long nights, junk food, and urine. But its suspension was sound and its engine tuned. It looked like any van from a coyote outfit, and it looked like it had made many journeys to and from el Norte.

Now it prowled dusty trails, switchbacks, and arroyos in the dark of night, but slowly. Dust rose. No moon guided them. The landscape was raw and ugly, mostly tall, spiny vegetation that could kill you. Bilal drove, trying to stay on the donkey track before him without headlamps, and his Mexican contact Rodriguez, a veteran of many crossings to and from, sat next to him, squinting to read the map and compare it with his memory.

Behind them, crouched in the darkness of the cargo area this side of a black curtain, were two elderly gentlemen named Dr. Faisal and Professor Khalid. Both were educated men, unused to roughness in transit. One was a university lecturer, the other an engineer of some renown. They had never met before this little adventure, but they immediately recognized in the other a kindred spirit. They could not stop talking excitedly about politics, literature, spirituality, poetry, science, history, and the law, and it seemed each knew everything about these topics there was to know and like men everywhere, of every creed and kind, upon discovering such a commonality of spirit, each wanted to totally destroy the other. The arguments! They were driving Bilal, an earthier sort, crazy with this kind of endless aggression.

"Old buzzards," he said, "shut up. We need to concentrate." It turned out that of the several languages spoken by the passengers in the vehicle, the only one all four shared, if imperfectly, was English.

"The young," said Dr. Faisal. "So rude these days."

"He is such a pig. Bilal, you are a pig, you have no manners, no respect," said Professor Khalid.

"These two," said Bilal. "They know everything about nothing and nothing about anything."

"At a certain age," said Rodriguez, "they all go off a little like that. It should be right around here."

"You should know I do not like this 'should be,'" said the testy Bilal. He was a rangy man around thirty-five, all sinew, extremely shabbily dressed in a hand-me-down tweed jacket over a frayed black sweater, jeans, and beat-up Nikes. He was a Mediterranean type of the sort usually called "swarthy," for darkness of skin, eyes, and hair, and perhaps eternal melancholy, except that if you could get him to smile, you saw that he was quite handsome. He had a mop of unkempt hair dark as any wine-dark sea; a vague sense of cof feehouse revolutionary to him; and quick, furtive eyes that missed little. He was one of those uncomfortably intense men most peo ple find a little unnerving, as if his rhythms were a little too rapid, or perhaps he was too quickly wired through synapse, or bore too many unforgivable grudges, or was too quick to haggle to the death over a nickel.

"It's the desert," said Rodriguez. "It changes continually."

"I know something about the desert," said Bilal.

"Then you know that the wind moves mysteriously and covers and uncovers rocks, reshapes cactus, sometimes seems to move— there it is!"

His flashlight beam penetrated the dirty windshield to illuminate a certain crack in the earth that widened eventually into a full gully. This time of year there was no water and even the mud had turned to crushed pottery. The gully would run like a superhighway for about two hundred yards, and reach the border fence and open a channel beneath it. With a little industrious snipping, the gap in the fence would be wide enough to drive the van under. Then it was another hundred or so yards of rough but not impossible transit to a long, straight road that ran to a major highway. A left turn at that junction and into the belly of America you flew.

"Hold on," said Bilal. "You, old dogs, cut the chatter. It's rough and dangerous through here."

Alas, Dr. Faisal did not hear him. He was making an exceedingly important point about the Greek myth of Prometheus, bringer of fire, and how he had been punished by Zeus. It was his carefully considered opinion that the tale was out of something the Jew Jung had called "the collective unconscious," and it wasn't really fire that Prometheus brought, it was the foreknowledge of the arrival of Muhammad and the fire was the destruction of the West.

Professor Khalid thought this rather a stretch.

"I agree," he said, "that many of their myths suggest that in their view of the ethos they are unconsciously aware of something missing, something yet to come, something yet to rule, something yet to proclaim truth, but I wonder, truly, if one can be so explicit in assigning meanings."

"Yes, yes, yes!" shouted Dr. Faisal. "You can! Have you read the original Greek? I have read the original Greek and I tell you there are meanings—"

"*Shut up!*" screamed Bilal. "It is very dangerous here. You fools have no idea what is happening. Keep those old yaps shut until we get across and up into Arizona. Then you can talk all you want."

"It's almost time to pray," said Dr. Faisal.

"Prayers are canceled today," said Bilal, "with Allah's permission. I guarantee you, Allah understands."

The van puttered shakily along the rough track, rolling over rocks, grinding through vegetation, knocking down this or that cactus. It was not completely beneath ground level, as the gully was only around five feet deep; a foot and a half of van top stuck out, and when they reached the fence itself, most of the lower strands had to be cut.

"What was that?" said Bilal.

"You are seeing things," said Rodriguez.

"Oh no," said Bilal. "See, there, there in—"

Something poked him in the ribs. He looked and saw Rodriguez had a shiny automatic pistol in his hand, pointing apologetically at Bilal's middle.

"So sorry," the Mexican said, "I must inform you of a slight change of plans."

Two men came from out of the dark, illuminating the van in their flashlight beams. They wore red cowboy bandannas around their heads, almost like turbans, and carried AK-47s with the easy grace of men who'd spent a lot of time with gun in hand. Bilal could see that each wore a shoulder holster under his jeans jacket, with another shiny gun. They had the raffish, ignorant insouciance of Israeli paratroopers.

"Out, you and the old ones, and we shall see what is so important that you must smuggle it into Los Estados instead of merely driving through the border posts."

"What is he saying?" said Dr. Faisal. "Why does he have a gun? Bilal, what is going on?"

The door of the van was slid open roughly and the bandits grabbed the two old men, shoving them to the ground.

"Now you," said Rodriguez, "don't make no trouble. I am reasonable, but my two amigos are locos. Bad ones. I think I can control them, but you must show them you respect me, or they will get very angry. And I know you have more money, señor. I know you would not be going for a long trip in America with these two geezers without no money."

"I have money," said Bilal. "Lots of money. I can pay. No need for anything unpleasant to happen."

"See, that's the attitude. My friends, the young man here will cooperate, he understands."

One of the two huskies came over, grabbed Bilal by the lapel of his decades-old sports coat, and threw him hard against the side of the truck.

He opened the coat, looked up and down, then backed off, nodding.

"You tell me where the money is," said Rodriguez amiably. "Emilio doesn't like to be kept waiting. He is an impatient person. You tell me where it is, and I will get it. Oh, and another thing. We must have a look at what treasure behind the curtain is so important to get into Los Estados. Oh, it must be something very interesting to go to all this trouble."

"It is religious tracts. Booklets on the true faith."

"Oh, yes, I believe that one. You must think I'm a fool. Besides, the true faith is our lord Jesus and his immaculate mother, heathen."

"Sir, I—"

Rodriguez struck him hard in the face.

"Money, then treasure, monkey asshole."

"Yes, of course, sir."

Professor Khalid called, "What is happening, Bilal? Why did he strike you? Who are these men?"

"Tell the old one to shut his yap," said Rodriguez, "or Pedro, I'm afraid, will kick in his teeth."

"Professor, it is not a problem. Just another few minutes and we will be on our way."

"Indeed," said Rodriguez, "now tell me where—"

Bilal hit him with five bunched fingers in the center of the throat, crushing the larynx. He began to make unpleasant sounds and quickly lost interest in his firearm. Bilal pivoted, way behind the two AKs coming up, but he had hands faster than Allah's, it was said in the training camps. He got the .380 Ruger LCP taped inside his left wrist into his right hand and in the next second it became evident that the nasty boys Pedro and friend had yet to cock their AKs before firing, an amateur's mistake that Bilal or any of his cohorts would not have made, and each bolt was at the halfway point when Bilal fired the tiny pistol twice, putting a .380 into each head. He was a superb shot, even with so small a gun having all but nonexistent sights. The bullets were so tiny they didn't deliver much impact, that is, other than the instant animal death they generated by pulping the deep central brain, and one of the men began to walk around strangely, blood pouring down his face, as if he were trying to remember how a chicken dances. He disappeared into the blackness, clucking. The other merely sat down disappointedly and sagged off into an eternal nap.

Rodriguez sat against the wheel of the van. He was coughing blood as well as expelling it copiously from his nostrils, holding his ruptured throat as his lungs and all other available vessels filled with liquid, drowning him. Bilal had not been trained to recognize any kind of mercy, as the camps were not an environment that emphasized mercy as a value, but the look of pain was so extreme that without willing it, he shot the man in the temple.

Professor Khalid came racing over.

"I have to get away from him! If he tells me he read the myth of Prometheus in the original Greek one more time, I will strangle him, and then where will we be?"

Dr. Faisal was not far behind.

"What can you do with the uneducated? The fool knows nothing. He is all hot air and opinions without a single reliable fact. I cannot continue this trip with such a fool!"

Somehow, Bilal got them into the truck and on their way.

Anything would do. Did they still sell breakfast at this time of night? Maybe eggs and bacon. But eggs and bacon wouldn't work without coffee, and he couldn't drink the decaf and he couldn't afford a sleepless night in the motel, even if, on the FBI per diem, the Hilton was an upgrade from many of the places he'd stayed.

Swagger had a headache, the beginnings of a cold, and a serious case of exhaustion. This "investigating" was debilitating. You had to be "on" all the time, your mind alert. And even after fifteen hours of it, you got nothing.

"Have you decided?" asked the waitress.

"Double Jack neat, please, with a side of water."

"Sir, we don't—"

"I know, I know, my idea of a little joke, ma'am, peculiar, I know."

She smiled. She had the look of some kind of marine wife or girlfriend here a couple of miles off the main entrance to Lejeune, and maybe her husband or boyfriend was deployed somewhere and she needed the dough, serving old coots such as himself to keep going with two kids and not enough allowances. It was sometimes harder on the ones left behind, and there were no guarantees the man wouldn't come home in a box.

"Okay," he said, "I guess I'll have the Caesar salad and this grilled fish special." No meat; that would make Julie happy.

"Anything to drink? We do have wine and beer."

"Ma'am, water's fine."

She left, and he pulled his briefcase up to the table. It contained the notes he'd taken today during a full day of interviews on Camp Lejeune in 2nd Recon Battalion headquarters, a Xerox of Cruz's career-long 201 file, and preliminary reports from field agents and NIS canvassing of previous duty stations for information and background, still woefully incomplete.

He got his yellow notepads out from today, recording his conversations with Colonel Laidlaw; Lieutenant Colonel Simpson, his successor as 2nd Recon commander; Major Morton, former S-2 of 2-2, now at Division S-2 while he waited to get out and head off to law school; Sergeants Kelly and Schuman, both snipers who'd served in Sniper Platoon with Ray Cruz; and Lance Corporals Sigmond and Krahl, who'd been friends with Lance Corporal Billy Skelton.

It was pretty much the same all the way through. You couldn't find a bad word about Ray Cruz on this planet, much less the South Carolina sector of it.

Colonel Laidlaw: "I didn't know Cruz except by report and reputation. I'm not one of those meet and greet leaders. I just can't stand it when the boys get hurt or killed: I keep my distance so I can do my job. I'm way too old for combat, I know. Anyhow, I found him to be a quiet, intense professional. I was aware of the many times he'd been offered commissions and his opportunities outside the corps but I understood his commitment to his job. He was one of, hell, maybe he was, the best."

Lieutenant Colonel Simpson: "At any time, he could have written a ticket out of there. He didn't have to keep going on the missions. I said to him, 'Look, Sergeant Cruz, I'm getting tired of writing commendations and listening to you call me sir when I should be calling you sir. Will you go be the next commandant or something?' He'd smile, and say he was fine with it the way it was. He liked *saving* people. He believed that's what a sniper does. If some unit got in a firefight, Ray was the first one on the track to get out there; he'd work his way around, taking incredible chances, and bring fire on the hadjis, and after he dropped two or three, they'd be gone. It must have happened a thousand times. A sniper dings a kid and Sergeant Cruz saddles up and slithers out. A few minutes later we hear a shot and a few minutes later, Cruz is back, checking on the kid. And note: we didn't have to go to Hellfire and blow up a house or go to Apache and blow up a neighborhood or go to F-16 and blow up a town. One shot, one kill. Everybody's happy."

Morton, the intelligence whiz: "Look, I'll be frank with you. When you brief or debrief these guys, you do become aware of the limits of their minds. Some aren't what we'd call 'smart' in an intellectual way, but their strength is doing exactly what they're told and then reporting back exactly what happened. Not Cruz. He was smart *smart,* if you know what I mean. He got it. He'd seen through all the follies of the corps, he knew Simpson was sucking up like a whore to Colonel Laidlaw to get the battalion, he knew that Kelly was smarter than Schuman but that Schuman was more reliable under fire, he knew that Skelton was one of those college guys in the marines who hide from some issue in civilian life but was still the smartest and the best of the spotters. Cruz knew what was bullshit and what was real. Yet still: he risked. He risked so much, even knowing that in the end it would all be decided by assholes in suits sitting at tables. To me, to have that kind of IQ—what was it?"

"One hundred forty-five," Bob had said.

"Much higher than mine. But to have that kind of IQ and understand that it was all a kind of bullshit and yet still believe in it and still go out, day after day, that was something."

Sergeant Schuman: "Ray was, you know, *Oriental* in his ways. He was kind of zen, you know? Never got excited, never raised his voice, never had to, because he never made a mistake. Everybody knew he knew a better way, a faster way. Even under fire, never any panic in his voice, never a wrong move, and if you got hit, he'd stay with you until evac. Ray would never leave anybody behind. If we'd had a mascot, Ray would have stayed behind with the pooch, putting down hadjis to the end."

Lance Corporal Krahl: "Billy hated the corps but he loved Ray Cruz. He'd never let Cruz down. Cruz was the mythical sergeant. He seemed like he was out of the movies or something. In the end, I wish he'd loved Ray less because he wouldn't have worked so hard to impress him and to become Ray's spotter. Loving Ray got him killed. I hate to say it, but that mission was a major fuck-up from the start, sending guys way out in bandit country with no air, nothing but fucking *goats* as cover, help two hours away. But if anyone could do it, it would have been Cruz, and if Cruz was going, Billy had to go. God, I miss Billy. Such a good kid, deserved so much more than a facedown in some shit hole full of people with funny hats."

Swagger'd also watched videotape of the ambush over and over, this under the guidance of the S-2.

It took a while to make out, the angles so grave, the visual information so sparse: the men were, viewed from the top down, just glowing jiggles of light against the multihued dark of the landforms beneath them, the goats faster moving, longer. Still, in time, it became clear. You could watch the ambush team setting up. You could see them checking maps, and whoever was in charge put his security people exactly where any experienced soldier in any army in the world would have put them. He set up his big gun, squirmed behind it. Next to him had to be his own spotter. They held to good ambush discipline, no fucking around, utter stone stillness, no excess motion, men hunting hard and well.

"The colonel wanted to put a Hellfire into them. Would have blown the mission, I think, but would have saved our guys. But there was no way we could get an Apache in close enough in the time frame. We just had to watch and hope the bad guys didn't shoot, but they did. It was horrible in the bunker, watching it all happen, not being able to do anything about it."

The major froze the video image of the ambush team setup and still, the targets moving in along their goddamned goat track a distance calculated to be 841 meters out, completely blind to anything except the bleating of the goats.

"Did you request Reaper coverage from the Agency?" asked Bob.

"No, sir. It involves going through a lot of protocols, and no one really trusted that the info would stay private. It's one thing when a big unit moves out—everybody already knows everything—and another when an outfit is under fire and you can bring Reapers in fast, so there's not an issue of security. Here we wanted to run as tight and quiet a ship as possible."

"Major, how do you figure these guys knew where Ray and Skelton were, and set up so perfectly? I mean, if I had to textbook an ambush, I'd use this tape."

"I don't know. A leak? Maybe. More likely these hadjis were on some mission and they saw targets. They had a new toy, a .50 Barrett they'd recovered somewhere. They're not the most mature individuals, are they? So they set up to take the goatherders down, to test the weapon, to spread the word, maybe to blame the Americans. Only, one goatherder gets away, so they follow him, because he's no longer a random victim, now he's a witness and maybe if he makes it out, he gets them in trouble with their own command. I don't really get how their minds work. I don't know how they can kill so much and think it's moral. It's baffling to me."

The food came, jarring Swagger back to the real world. He shoved his notepads to one side, ate sparingly, not really paying attention, trying in his mind to find something that would tell him any little thing. Was there a Ray Cruz explainer in there? A little anecdote that revealed an insight, if indeed it was Ray Cruz on the other end of that radio message? The one thing that stood out had come from the sniper Kelly, when Bob asked him, "Tell me about his shooting. He was, for sure, an excellent shot. But was there anything peculiar or unique about his shooting?"

Kelly thought awhile. Then he said, "There wasn't a shot Ray couldn't hit and a position he couldn't hit from. He was like a machine, mechanical, unhurried, classic by the book. But, this is strange, we never shoot standing in battle. No one stands up in a battlefield. Good way to get your head chopped."

Bob nodded. It was true.

"Ray decided he needed that shot. I thought it was a waste of time and ammo, but he didn't even bother arguing the point. He just put hours in on the range on his legs, used up crates of Match 7.62, until he could put three in an inch offhand from a hundred yards. He was slim, but very strong, very tough, much stronger than you'd think for a guy like that."

"Offhand?" Bob wrote.

"I don't know if he ever had a use for it. He just didn't want no holes in his game, no matter how small."

He saved the picture for last. It was an official Marine Corps promotion shot, on the occasion of the last stripe, couple years back. He didn't want to stare at it, let it become a blur of dots and shadows. It lost its voodoo with overconcentration.

Bob just stole a glimpse, trying not to bore too hard into it. It seemed so straightforward: white sidewalls, the face smooth, the eyes with that slight Asian cast, the cheekbones prominent, the lips thin, maybe Cruz's father's Portuguese aquilinity to the thin nose; Swagger also picked up on the sniper's wariness, his quickness and depth of vision. Or maybe he didn't, maybe he was dreaming things. After all, it was just a picture of a marine NCO on what was nominally a good day professionally, a souvenir utterly banal in its lack of meaning.

He put it back in the file, wondering about only one thing: why was the sensation it generated so connected with the idea of loss? *Losslossloss.* Why did it cause an ache so deep and inconsolable?

He thought maybe in Cruz's face there was a trace of a first lieutenant named Bill Go, Japanese-American, his first officer in Vietnam, 1965. Great guy: smart, fair, calm, steady as a boulder in combat, judgment superior, a real superstar. Bill didn't make it beyond month six. Some meaningless firefight, some worthless jungle 'ville, over in a second, a spatter of shots from them, a spatter in response from us, and only Bill Go didn't get up because he'd been shot just under the lip of the helmet in the right eye. So much loss, so much grief. It fell to Buck Sergeant Swagger to get the boys back humping, to finish the job, to make it back to the compound. His first "command," as it were, and he got through it by going into hard NCO mode so no one could imagine how much he felt the loss of Bill.

Or was it Bill? There was another, an Army master sergeant with SOG, second tour, Russell Blas, a Guamese, great guy, pure guts in a fight, captured on one of the hatchet missions he so loved to lead, and never heard of or seen again. Poor Russell, probably dying of malnutrition in some shit hole . . .

He didn't want to go there anymore. That's what had eaten a decade of his life away in a wash of bourbon and rage and self-hatred. He told himself that the picture had no connection with anything. *It's just a new marine. It has nothing to do with Bill Go or Russell Blas or Vietnam.* Those memories were too hurtful and could not be entertained cavalierly, in schlock restaurants on jobs set in the real, the new, the only world that counted.

UNIDENTIFIED CONTRACTOR TEAM

It's gotta be him," said Crackers the Clown. "Check it out. Right age, thin, rangy, sniperlike, discipline, dignity, seems to have a limp, he's looking at data, he's on the wagon."

The three of them sat in a nice black Ford Explorer. They looked at Bob through the window, each with a pair of high-end European binocs.

"Plus," said Crackers, the unit intellectual, called "Crackers the Clown" because he had the demeanor of an Iowa mortician, "the time matches up. We caught him out of the main gate at 1950, he'd been there all day talking to folks, now he's tired out, he's reviewing his shit, he's eating a little, and he's going to go back to the hotel, send out e-mails, call the wife, and go to bed. Tomorrow, the same thing again."

"On the other hand," said Tony Z, the cynic, "he could be the guy trying to sell Lejeune on a new brand of trash masher for the enlisted dining areas. He's here trying to make a fucking pitch. He works for Grinders-R-Us dot com, out of Gomerville, Indiana."

There were no pictures of this Swagger, that was the problem. Everything was theoretical and judgmental and the theoretical and the judgmental were slightly beyond Bogier's areas of competence.

"I hate this shit." He stewed. "I'm an operator. I break things and kill people. Now I'm supposed to be some kind of James Bond super-agent bullshit performer. Man, I hate this shit."

Crackers was pro IDing the john as Swagger; Tony Z, despite his cynicism, was leaning toward pro, but still a little unable to commit.

"It should be him, it has to be him, nothing else makes any sense, but when you make an assumption, it always bites you in the ass."

"Is there any way you could test? Maybe call the restaurant, ask for a Mr. Swagger, see if he gets up?"

"I think this guy would see through it," said Bogier. "I don't even like eyeballing him from here; guys like him, they have radar, they can sometimes feel it when they're being watched."

The binoculars went down.

"So do you want to move, Mick?" said Crackers the Clown. "We may never get another chance like this."

"But we've only got one card," said Tony. "If we do get it planted and it's planted on the wrong guy, then we've got to get it back and still find the right guy and plant it again."

"Agh," said Mick.

The card was the latest in high-tech bullshit James Bond spy craft. It was a red BankAmericard made out to Bob Lee Swagger. The idea was somehow to sneak it into Swagger's wallet under the theory that few men examined their wallets carefully and would notice the addition of a new credit card. Except it wasn't a credit card. It was actually a miniature transponder called an "active RFID" for radio frequency identification device. It gave off a return signal when it received a recognized interrogation signal. It used 16 nanometer technology, a unique dual-layered nano lithium-cadmium battery that was actually part of the card itself, along with the molded-in single strand of antenna wire. It responded to an inquiry signal sent from a classified Aegon satellite that had the highest sensitivity and best signal-to-noise ratio of anything placed in space. When the satellite sent the inquiry, huge umbrellalike antennas began to look for the specific frequency and tone of the encoded response, which, diminutive as it is, still can be counted on to register. Of all this, Bogier, Crackers, and Tony Z knew exactly nothing.

The second part of the deal was a BlackBerry with software that could find the appropriate Google map and then would receive the satellite information and track the card on the map. Mick and his pals could easily track the bearer of the card from any distance, even over the horizon. There'd be no hassle over staying close in traffic or through sudden turns or accelerations. They could always stay in contact, until the moment Swagger recognized an extra credit card in his wallet, which would probably be never.

"Okay," said Mick, finally. "Let's do it. If it ain't him, we can get it back in a more direct way than we have to plant it."

"Ooh, cool," said Tony Z. "I like that part."

S wagger finished the meal, sat back, tried to relax a bit, yearned for booze, daughters, wife, a simple life, and an endless amount of time to sleep, and lied to himself harmlessly about a deep and rewarding platonic friendship with Susan Okada as well. Why not dream about having it all? But none of that was apparently in the off- ing. Worse, this late, his hip sometimes ached a bit. It seemed to have gotten better in the past few months, but if he put a lot of weight on it over a long day, it could become inflamed and begin to declare an unhappy memory. Now, it felt restive, as though in the pre-pain stage.

He signaled the girl, gave her a twenty, waited for change, left too big a tip, grabbed the receipt, dumped it into the briefcase, and stood, favoring the good leg. A wave of stiffness came but he shrugged it off, went out the front doors and looked for his car in the lot. Hmm, a rental, what was it again, oh yeah, a Ford Taurus on government con- tract from Hertz. He spotted it, and walked toward it down the half- full aisles, behind a screen of low bushes that marked the roadway, the whole thing red-gold in the neon of the big TGIF sign up on top. He reached his lane, and turned down it to the car.

When the guy hit him, he hit him hard, crushing him against the car rear, not hurting him so much as completely de-coordinating him.

"What the—!" Swagger felt himself blurt out as the muscular energy of his assailant nailed him hard against the trunk and he slid down. Flashbulbs, pinwheels, Roman candles ignited behind his eyes at the impact as his optic nerves shot off, but then he came back—an instant too late. A heavy knee went on his back, another on his neck, and between them they bore the weight of a big man.

"Keep your fucking mouth shut, mister, or I'll crack you good."

The guy had total leverage, pinning him by weight and power. Bob squirmed under the assault, but knew he was way outmatched. He turned his head sideways, felt as his robber ripped up Bob's sports coat, pulled the wallet out, then grabbed the briefcase and began to pry it open.

"Hey, you!" came a shout from across the parking lot.

"Fuck," his assailant said, rising.

He turned to run, and Bob watched as he sped out of the parking lot, leaped the low hedge, and started down the road. But an athletic-looking guy intercepted him from out of nowhere with a superb open field tackle right at curbside and the two of them went down in a tangle. The robber was a tough motherfucker and managed to get a driving right-handed blow into the Samaritan's ribs, knocking him back, and enabling the thief to squirm to his freedom. He was upright and gone and last seen hoofing it down the street, disappearing behind a strip mall a little bit farther down.

Bob got there just as the good guy was picking himself up.

"You okay, mister?" he asked.

"Ah," said the guy, "my mother hit harder than that."

Bob saw a rangy guy, midthirties, completely athletic, like a ball-player, who just picked up and put back on his Yankees cap then wiped sweat off his face.

"Hey," said Bob, "no kidding, you were great, but you really shouldn't have done that. Guy could have had a knife or a gun."

"You know," said the guy, smiling, "it happened so fast I didn't even think about it. I just reacted. You want to call the cops or anything?"

"Well," said Bob, foreseeing an hour giving a report that would yield absolutely nothing, "not really. I'm not hurt. Oh, my wallet. Shit, he got—"

But the guy said, "Wait, I saw something drop off him as he ran. Let's check."

They walked a few steps ahead and there was the wallet, splayed out on the sidewalk.

The guy picked it up, opened it, peeked in, and said, "Are you Mr. Swagger?"

"That's me," said Bob, taking the wallet.

"I doubt he had time to take anything," said the hero.

Bob did a quick check. His stack of ATM twenties was still intact, and paging through the plastic card display, he saw nothing missing.

"Looks okay," he said.

"You sure you're okay?" said the guy. "Physically, I mean."

"I have a few scrapes, and maybe a bruise or two. But nothing particularly traumatic."

"I could call an ambulance."

"Nah," said Swagger. "Who's got time for that?"

"Okay," said the guy. "I guess I'll go on in and get myself some food. You sure, now? No assistance necessary?"

"No, and thanks again. You must have played football."

"Years ago," said the guy with a laugh. "Baby, I thought my tackling days were over."

They had a good laugh, Bob offered his hand, and they shook. Then Bob went back to his car, thinking, *Strangest goddamn thing.*

UNIDENTIFIED CONTRACTOR TEAM

Y ou're sure?"

"I guarantee it," said Crackers. "It said 'Bob Lee Swagger,' plain as day, on the Idaho license."

"And you got the card in," Mick asked Tony Z.

"I did. Between two cards in the card thing, you know, the plastic thing. Meanwhile, the Clown is punching me in the fucking guts."

"Hey, you whacked me pretty hard too, goddamnit," said Crackers.

"Damn right. After you fucking laid me out like Ray Lewis."

"You didn't know I was all city?"

"A pussy like you—"

"Easy, little girls. I'm going to call MacGyver. This is good news, we did this part, I don't want any screwups. Let's go over it again."

They sat in the SUV across from the Jacksonville Hilton at the edge of the city, near the freeway, seven miles from the main gate to Lejeune. It was in a zone of fluorescence, chain restaurants, car dealerships, fast food joints, all gleaming plastic and chrome. Each guy went over the event again, slowly, step by step.

Finally Mick accepted the reports. He picked up the satellite phone, pushed the magic button, and in a few seconds the control came on.

"Okay," Mick said, "good stuff to report. We got the RFID planted, he didn't suspect a thing. We followed him a mile off, no visual contact, all the hardware is working A-OK, and he's gone to bed for the night. No matter what, from now on we'll know where he is."

"Like actual professionals," said MacGyver dryly.

"We'll just stay with him, far back, we won't push anything. If he can find Cruz, we'll be there and we'll take them down."

"You boys and your toys. You love the toys. It's your favorite part. What did they get you? I don't even know."

"M4s, an MP5, plenty of mags. SIGs and Berettas. A .338 Sako. Best of all, another Barrett. This one's much better than the last. I wouldn't mind an RPG. We couldn't miss with that."

"Don't be ridiculous. We can't have you blowing shit up in Hometown, USA."

"Anyhow, I can do him with the .50 from a mile out or the .338 from half."

"You missed the last time, Tex."

"No, I hit. I just hit the wrong guy because I didn't know which one was the right guy. The guy I missed was already on the move when I zeroed him. Tough shot. Nobody could make it."

"Cruz could. Swagger could. Make sure you're never in their kill zone, Bogier. They won't miss, I guarantee you. And don't you miss again."

"I won't, goddamnit. Now we're going to settle down here for the night, and follow him. I'm guessing he's going back to the base tomorrow for more meetings. Nothing's going to happen tonight."

"Oh shit," said Crackers the Clown, on the BlackBerry in the front seat. "He's moving."

MCDONALD'S

A clown stared at the three rather scruffy men. He had big eyes, a huge red nose, puffs of crazed red hair, and lips the size of cucumbers. He was 100 percent polyurethane. Blond children made up like cats and dogs ran around his legs. A crusader father tried to keep order. Two of the kids, a boy and a girl, got in a fight over a milk shake and the girl seemed to be getting the better of it, until the dad adjudicated on behalf of the shorter, weaker boy.

"You are an infidel," said Dr. Faisal.

"Alas," said Professor Khalid, "it is true."

"You must be destroyed."

"Surely, I will be," said the professor.

"You will not go to heaven."

"My belief insists there is no heaven."

Dr. Faisal turned to Bilal and demanded, "Did you know? He is a traitor, he is a monster, he is a heathen."

"Yes, I knew," said Bilal. "I read his important essay in the Islamabad *Islamic Courier.* But he is not a Christian, if that's what you think. If I understand it, he is an atheist."

"I would say a realist," said Khalid.

"Realist, atheist, what's the difference? He is not of the true faith."

"It is not a matter of faith," said Khalid. "It is a matter of political will."

"Again," said Bilal, taking a gulp of his chocolate shake, "if I understand him, his political will is strong, possibly as strong as your faith. So you both go on this enterprise, you both risk all, you are both martyrs. What private nuances transpire between each set of ears, it is of no matter."

"I am shocked," said Dr. Faisal.

"By realist," said Khalid, "I mean tribalist. I am of the tribe that is culturally Islamic. The god at the center is meaningless, a delusion. Moreover, I happen to have been educated in the West—"

"I was educated in the West too, do not forget. It did not affect my faith. It made it stronger."

"Hear him out," said Bilal. "I have fought many times with men of indifferent faith. They were just as good as fighters as the devout. Some drank alcohol, ate pork, some were actually of the homosexual perversion, some lacked hygiene and spat at God, but under fire were as willing to die as any."

"Why then," asked Dr. Faisal, "would you face death, believing that beyond is nothing but oblivion? Could I have another milk shake?"

"No," said Bilal, "no more milk shakes. We must go, we are behind schedule, I have many more miles to drive and we do not have immense quantities of money."

"If you would let me explain," said Khalid. He let his face compose itself, he sought the dignity of the earnest student encumbered with the truth and the need to spread it, and he leaned forward in piety and humility, even as the red-nosed plastic clown examined him like an interlocutor. "Although these people around us seem very nice, they are actually devils. Not in their daily demeanor, which as you can see is moderate and full of love of family and fun, but in the economic implications of the resources they require to live in such invisible comfort. They have no idea what crimes are committed in the name of this monstrous pillow of comfort, and if you tried to show them logically, they would not be able to process it. It would seem a delusion, a bad dream. If they looked at the cesspool of the camps and the degradation and depravity visited upon those children, they would say, 'Oh, it's so sad,' and perhaps even give a dollar or two to some charity and feel good about themselves for a day. And yet they are as responsible, in their addiction to the great comfort—the cocoon of pleasantness, not sensual pleasure as you can see, but the pleasantness of driving down the street and buying their child a milk shake exactly like the one you so greedily desire, Dr. Faisal—they are responsible for the war against our people, for our suffering, for our pain. They are as responsible as Israeli paratroopers or helicopter assassins or Hindu missile designers—"

"This is very troubling," said Dr. Faisal. "Please, Bilal, I am begging you, another milk shake."

S wagger drove through darkness, having long since left any trace of the suburbs. He was in some rural zone, off main highways, on ribbons of blacktop, coming now and then to stop signs but rarely to streetlights.

He'd gotten to his room, unsatisfied. What a wasted day. Nothing but banalities regarding the strange case of Ray Cruz and his threat to take out the new hope of the Afghan political scene, Ibrahim Zarzi, once known as "the Beheader." Opening his laptop, he'd sent an e-mail more or less summing up the day to Memphis at FBI HQ. Then a late e-mail registered, stating only that no sightings of Ray Cruz had yet been confirmed, that the NIS canvassing of marine bases or other spots where he might be tempted to go to ground had yielded no new information, but that some new stuff had come in from various parts of the background investigation of Cruz, and photocopies had been FedExed to Swagger. He called the desk, the package was located, and he went down to pick it up.

Not much. His eyes ran over the reports from various agents who'd been interviewing Cruz associates at marine bases the nation over, all of it confirming exactly what the men of 2-2 Recon had been telling him today. It seemed to add up to nothing. But . . . there was a curiosity. It seemed that someone had dug out a letter Cruz had sent to the Energy Department upon returning from his second tour in Iraq in 2004. The Energy Department was known to deploy extremely sophisticated SWAT teams at nuclear facilities the country over, and Cruz, evidently a little worn down from a year's hard combat in and around Baghdad, dodging IEDs and seeing the effects on those who did not manage to dodge the IEDs, had succumbed to the generalized despair of the presurge environment. Who could blame him? Everybody had. So Ray, in a moment of weakness, had thoughts of leaving the corps before his twenty and taking up as a firearms and tactics instructor with Energy. The pay was said to be high, he'd come in at a high GS grade, and he'd be in one place for a long time doing what he loved to do, without anybody attempting to blow him up with a bomb disguised as a pile of dog shit.

The Energy people, anxious to get someone as well qualified as Ray on their team, had written back enthusiastically and invited him to contact this officer at this number for further discussion of employment opportunities. Evidently Ray never had, had resigned himself to another few years, and then Bush's surge kicked in and morale soared as the killings went down. Final score: Us 1, them other guys 0. He'd gone on to another tour in Baghdad before the tour in Afghanistan, which had been terminated under such unusual circumstances.

But included in the xeroxography of the correspondence was a curriculum vitae in which Ray listed his accomplishments and his credentials. It was clearly meant for civilian eyes only. It indicated that he was investigating something, on his own dime, that was heretical at that moment to marine doctrine.

Ray listed courses he'd taken under the heading "Civilian Schools Attended," and they included such learning adventures as Advanced Sniper Techniques and Team Entry Techniques and Team Communication Techniques at several companies, including Graywolf, which had a training division in Moyock, North Carolina, and others such as the confusingly titled Gunsite and Frontsite training facilities in Arizona and Thunder Ranch in Oregon under an ex-marine of excellent reputation named Clint Smith. But the one that leaped out at Bob was a week-long course in Urban Sniper Operations, offered by Steel Brigade Armory, of Danielstown, South Carolina, under the tutelage of a Colonel Norman S. Chambers, USMC (Ret.).

That name was familiar, and so Swagger did a quick Google on Chambers. What he learned provoked him: Apostate! Heretic!

Defier! Enemy of the Jesuitical code of the Marine Corps Sniper Program! Chambers actually had not come out of the program at all. Instead he'd been straight infantry with time at the Command and Staff School at Leavenworth; he was a combat leader, not a sniper acolyte, which meant he wasn't bent double under its doctrine. He was the critical outlier, the Billy Mitchell of sniping, who felt free to scorn the doctrinaires, at the same time risking the reputation of bitter wannabe, failure, whatever. Among his apostasies: he hated the M14 and thought the idea of welding up the old battle horse of the early sixties into a sniper rifle for the war on terror was a waste of time. He had been right on that one, and the corps, though it dug a great many of the old beauties out of mothballs for accurizing and scope fitting at the dawn of the war, soon learned the hard way that the zero on such a jerry-built assemblage would go wrong, and would never consistently deliver the accuracy at long range that would justify the careful and expensive training a sniper would get. Chambers also saw the M40 system—an iteration of the Army's M24 system, which was a highly accurized Model 700 Remington with a Kreiger barrel and Schmidt & Bender or U.S. Optics on top—as stopgap at best.

Chambers was an exponent, outspoken and sometimes brutal and mocking, of the SASS, or semiautomatic sniper system. His weapon of choice for general issue to marine sniper teams was the Knight's Armament SR-25, as derived from the original ArmaLite AR-10. In fact, both the SR-25 and the common infantryman's M16/M4 rifles had common ancestry in the AR-10, which, designed in the late fifties by Eugene Stoner and some aerospace hotshots at Fairchild Aircraft, had seemed like some kind of plastic ray gun from outer space. But its profile—the straight-line design, the rakish pistol grip, the magazine well just forward of it, the need for high sights either optical or concealed in a carrying-handle assembly, plastic foregrip with ventilations, triangular front sight and flash hider at the muzzle—had become the basis of the Western combat small arm of the last half of the twentieth century. Chambers pushed hard for the adoption of the SR-25, once it had been proven in competition, courtesy of the Army Marksmanship Unit in the nineties, signifying that a semiauto or full-auto weapon was capable of the accuracy a bolt gun routinely produced.

Chambers argued, generally within the pages of arcane publications like *Precision Shooting, The Infantry Journal,* or *Defense Review,* that the advantages of an SASS far outweighed the advantages of the bolt gun. It allowed the sniper to engage multiple targets in near simultaneous real time; it allowed for fast follow-up shots when windage or mirage caused a miss; it gave the squad another fire point in a fight, should one develop; and it also allowed the sniper, using battle sights appended to his scope in the form of a diagonally mounted micro red dot, to become essentially a BAR man, bringing heavy volume of fire if the hadjis got inside the wire, where the bolt gun was all but useless. Moreover, the Russians had proved the system in combat since 1963, when they first fielded their Dragunov SVD in Vietnam against American troops—the CIA had somehow obtained an early one—and later, very successfully, in wars in Africa, South America, Indonesia, Afghanistan, and Chechnya.

Against that he chalked up only minor disadvantages: one was that the ejecting brass case, sailing through the air, was a tell as to the sniper's position, but Chambers could find no actual evidence that such an ejecting case had ever given away a sniper's hide in combat, much less with any regularity. The second was the gun's ungainliness: unlike the bolt gun, it was fairly deep and denser for its size. It had to be monitored constantly as, fired heavily, its zero was subject to disengagement. It would tempt commanders to deploy it as a kind of squad automatic weapon instead of allowing it its full tactical potential as a long-range—out to a thousand or so meters—precision instrument.

Perhaps it was that Ray saw the future; clearly, he'd wanted to study and learn at the feet of the master, following the smaller, more aggressive SEALs committed to the SASS/SR-25. He'd taken sabbaticals to study with Chambers and to master the intricacies of the weapon, when on his first three tours he'd been strictly the bolt gun guy. Such an agnostic's move would certainly be something to hide from the corps' Jesuits.

So that intellectual connection between the apostate Chambers and the pure sniper Cruz was extremely provocative to Swagger. The more he thought of it, the more it seemed to suggest possibilities. If Cruz was back, and serious about the mission he'd set up, he'd need to mount it from someplace. Initial FBI thought was that he'd draw on his connection to the marines or possibly to ex-marines, but no one had made the link to Chambers before.

Swagger had seen that the "Steel Brigade Armory," out of which Chambers ran his little sniper think tank and mail-order empire (high-end tactical goods, such as Badger Ordnance rings, Nightforce scopes, reinforced recoil lugs, sniper data books, and so forth), was in rural South Carolina, within forty miles of Jacksonville, just across the state line. He guessed it might be an informal marine sniper hangout where the guys could cluster off duty and tell war stories and theorize about possible futures (for example, the latest info was that Chambers was running an exhaustive R & D program on the new .416 Barrett to see how it matched up against the .308 of fifty years' service duration, and the big .50 boomer now used for those very long engagements so common in Afghanistan). Before he knew it, he was in his car, roaring through the dark down these country roads, aiming for the Steel Brigade Armory complex.

Was he going to sneak in? No, but he had to see it, make an initial recon, see who hung out there, what the milieu was. He had to figure out how to approach it: as an anonymous FBI investigator requesting answers, or as the Great Bob Lee Swagger, hero and celeb in this little-bitty world, expecting the royal treatment but also aware that if he wasn't honest about his Bureau affiliation, he was somehow dishonoring the bond between long-range life takers.

Thus, well after midnight, he pulled through a tiny rural burg called Danielstown, turned right down Sherman at Main, and just when it looked as though he would run out of town, came across a surprisingly unimpressive recent building, aluminum siding under a flat roof, with two or three garage doors at one end, minimal landscaping, unfenced, and with a gravel parking lot out in front. It might have housed an infirmary, a battery warehouse, a software firm, but instead wore the nondescript sign STEEL BRIGADE ARMORY.

A light in one window was on.

They pulled off the road out of town and, looking at the Google map of Danielstown, calculated where under the nest of trees and buildings, at the crossroads just ahead, Swagger must have stopped and now sat in his car, unaware that the tiny transponder in his wallet was broadcasting his position.

"Okay," Mick said, pointing to Crackers, "you cut through backyards and you get a night vision look-see on him. Tell me where he is, what he's doing. You do not scare the neighbors, arouse the dogs, watch the widow lady jacking off nude in her shower or Jimmy Dick fucking Sally Pussy on the couch of the Pussy mansion. Remember, you are secret agent man."

Too bad Crackers had no sense of humor. He didn't even fake a grin. He adjusted his see-in-the-dark apparatus—a head harness that supported a single battery-controlled optic called a dual-spectrum night vision goggle, new to the inventory, fresh out of a box—fiddled with it to bring the world into the greenish focus of intensified ambient light, then slipped out, silently. He was a pretty good operator, after all. Soon he was gone.

In seven or eight minutes, the radio crackled, and both Mick and Tony Z stirred and picked up their handsets. Through a gravy of static, Crackers's voice came in, sans radio protocol ID games, as it was a small net and only the three of them were on it.

"This thing is really cool," said Crackers, noted gearhead. "You can switch between intensified ambient and thermal, or you can combine 'em and get a real good picture show."

"Save it for your column in *Soldier of Fortune,*" said Mick. "What have you got on, you know, what's it called? Oh yeah, our mission."

"Okay, I'm prone in the bushes of a house about two hundred yards out. He's sort of waiting or something in the parking lot of some kind of low cottage-industry-type building, you know, like where an air-conditioning supply house would be—"

Both men knew instantly the kind of building.

"Can you ID it? Does it have a name or anything?"

"Yeah, bright as day on the NV. It's called Steel Brigade Armory. It doesn't look like an armory though."

"Okay," said Mick. "How's your secure?"

"Total. I was invisible and I low-crawled the last hundred yards through some lady's garden. No bowwows, nothing."

"What's Swagger doing?"

"That's the funny thing. Nothing. He's pulled off the road but not quite into the parking lot. He's just sitting there."

"Is he on a phone?"

"Not from his profile. I think he's just trying to figure out what to do next. There's one light on in the building and there's an SUV parked in the lot, so I'm guessing someone's at home."

"Okay, stay in position, give me any changes ASAP."

"Got it."

Even as he set down the unit, Tony Z handed over the Thuraya satellite phone. Bogier pushed the preset button and in a few seconds, a voice spluttered on.

"What the fuck? Do you have any idea what time it is?"

"This is a twenty-four/seven gig," Mick said, glad, for once, to have a little leverage on the normally unflappable MacGyver.

"Don't lecture me, Bogier. I know a little about this business."

"Okay, okay. I have Swagger at some place in a town called Danielstown, South Carolina, maybe twenty miles southwest of Henderson. He's pulled up at a nondescript low-threshold industrial facility that seems to call itself Steel Brigade Armory. We need a quick read on it."

"I'll call back," said MacGyver.

The two men sat in the quiet car, listening to the southern night wind around them. Bogier looked at his Suunto and saw that it was getting on to 0300. What the fuck was this guy doing out here at this hour?

The radio crackled.

"Okay," said Crackers. "He's going in. He went to the door and knocked."

Nothing. He knocked again, louder, heard some kind of stirring inside, the sound of someone on metal steps.

"Get the hell out of here," a voice said through the steel door.

"Colonel Chambers?"

"I said, get the hell out of here. Come back tomorrow. I'll be here from eleven on, friend."

"I have to talk to you."

Even through the door, there was no mistaking the heavy clack of a shotgun slide racking.

"Don't push it, friend. You don't want to come through that door. You'll be a sorry pup. Come back tomorrow, goddamnit."

"Sir, I'm going to push my driver's license through the mail slot. Then I will back off a few feet while you decide whether to see me."

"Goddamnit, I said—"

But Bob peeled his license out of his wallet, slid it through, and backed off.

No noise came from the building.

Finally, a door opened, to reveal what you'd expect a marine infantry colonel (Ret.) to look like: burly, crew cut, lots of weight training under the plaid shirt, late forties/early fifties, shotgun in hand, glasses on square face.

What you might not expect on that square face was love.

A flashlight spot-lit Bob in the doorway.

"Goddamn," said Chambers. "You are him, aren't you?"

"I seem to be," said Swagger.

"Jesus fucking Christ."

The colonel, now transformed into a fourteen-year-old girl at a Justin Timberlake concert, ran to him and almost hugged him. He was both utterly impressed and awestruck. He seemed to have some trouble finding words. Then a torrent of garbled Bob-love came out, and he grabbed and hugged the old sniper.

"Colonel Chambers," said Bob uneasily, "I'm very appreciative, sir, believe me, but I'm not here because of old times. I'm here for these here new times. I'm on a job for the government people."

"You're with the FBI now?"

"In a manner of speaking, sir."

"Okay, come on, come on up."

They went into the building, the colonel locking it tightly behind him, resetting a complicated alarm system. Then he led Bob up some metal stairs to a drywall hallway that displayed the flimsy, haphazard construction of the building. At the end of the hallway lay the colonel's office, a nave dedicated to the religion of the sniper. A walk-in gun safe dominated one wall, and on the others, from racked rifles of a highly evolved nature, to bookshelves full of memoirs, military texts, and battle histories, to a computer station, to well-punctured targets, to photos of several of the great ones, including Carl Hitchcock and Chuck McKenzie, to say nothing of the picture of a twenty-six-year-old Staff Sergeant Bob Lee Swagger, of Blue Eye, Arkansas, on the occasion of his victory in the Wimbledon Cup 1,000-yard national match in 1972, the colonel's obsession was well demonstrated.

"Looks like a hall of fame or something," Swagger said.

"*My* hall of fame," said the colonel. "Drink, Gunny? May I call you Gunny?"

"Friends call me Bob," said Swagger.

"Then let's be friends," said the colonel, full of dumb love. "I would consider that a great honor. Drink? This calls for libations and salutations."

"No, sir. Actually, I wish it were social, but if it were, I'd be here at a decent hour. As I said, I'm here in a kind of semiofficial way. I hope we can be friends after the business is done."

"Well," said the colonel, "let's see if we can manage that."

"I'm on a temp contract with the FBI to advise and consult on the case of a marine sniper named Ray Cruz, thought to be killed in Afghanistan six months ago, but possibly here in this country with mischief on his mind, tragic mischief in my humble opinion. But I have just learned that you have an association with Cruz."

"Ray," said the colonel, his face jumping to life. "Alive! Jesus, would that be a trick! Now, I would drink to that, believe me. Hell of a guy. You'd like him, Bob. You and him, you're brothers of the high grass and the long kill."

"Sir, that may be so, and what I've learned of Sergeant Cruz suggests it is. But if he is alive, he has got himself on the government's shit list by making certain threats, if it's even him."

Bob kept his focus on the colonel's eyes, trying to read them for sparks of hidden knowledge. He'd already noted that the colonel had done a nice Ray-is-risen act, and it seemed spontaneous enough, so that was a plus. On the negative, the colonel hadn't had a nanosecond of private grief when the death of Ray Cruz was mentioned, as you might imagine if the pain was still considerable. The colonel hadn't even reacted. Then he did, as if catching up to his own character in the drama.

"When I heard he was dead, it broke my heart. So many good men gone in a war half the population doesn't even know we're fighting and the other half hates. So wrong. But don't get me started."

"What I've said about Ray going his own way. That's the Ray you knew?"

"Ray had his own ideas, certainly. He was one for doing the right thing. But it was quiet, not loud. He wasn't a yeller or a crusader. He was a doer. And he just didn't stop coming."

The colonel told a story about Ray working an early version of the then-unadopted Stoner SR-25. He'd worked it all night in the shop, taking it apart, piece by piece, putting it together, trying somehow to divine the religious essence of it. Wanted to know the zen of every last screw and spring. Just wouldn't stop coming.

"Maybe it's the Filipino in him," Chambers added. "We had to invent the .45 ACP to stop the Filipinos, you know. They didn't stop if they'd set their minds to do something until we invented a big, fat bullet for them, did you know that?"

"I think so, sir. Sir, I came across your connection to Ray Cruz about two hours ago. As far as I know, it's completely new information, as no one else understood the significance. But tomorrow I am formally obligated by contract and duty to notify the people I work with. I ain't got no choice on that. By noon, an FBI task force will be here, with forensic investigators, assistant attorney generals, subpoenas, and search warrants. They will take this place and you apart in their hunt for Ray. Your files, your phone records, your credit records, your accounting, your business dealings, it'll all be gone through. So I'm here unofficially ahead of that tidal wave. Probably shouldn't be, may get yelled at on account of it or some such. That ain't important. I felt I owed you something for your service to us grass crawlers and long-shot takers. So I'm begging you: if you have any knowledge of Ray, of his plans, of his survival, you'd best give it to me now and go into the records as a cooperating witness. These federal people have a job to do and they mean to do it, and if you get in the way, it don't matter to them, they'll crush you."

"I appreciate the warning, Gunnery Sergeant," said the colonel, his voice going official marine. Then he said, "Do you mind if I pour myself a glass of bourbon?"

"Please do," said Bob.

The colonel opened a drawer, pulled out a half-full fifth of Knob Creek, dispensed a shot into a small glass, and downed it in one swig.

"If Ray was back," Bob said, "and he was in fact going to try to hit a certain fellow available in Washington starting next week, he'd have to mount a mission out of some logistical base. Our working theory was that he'd use old marine contacts, maybe at Two-Two Recon. I was down here to look at that. But he could just as easily do it out of your shop, using one of your custom builts, your ammo, scope, laser ranger, the works. It would be logical, and I bet you think so highly of Ray, you'd pull in with him without much rigorous thinking. If he'd have come to me, hell, I might have. You just have to know— well, if you're involved—you're playing with very hot fire that can burn down everything you've built in just a few days. It ain't worth it, sir. And it would be a real hard tragedy, the saddest, in my book, if Ray thought he was doing something noble and right and he was just setting himself up for the rest of his life in some shit-hole pen. That would be such an injustice."

"On the other hand," someone said, "maybe Cruz is playing the only card he's got the only way he's got and he thinks he's doing it *for* the corps, not in spite of it."

Swagger turned to face Ray Cruz.

Mick was now an up-to-speed expert on Steel Brigade Armory and the life and times of its founder and presiding genius, Colonel Norman Chambers.

"So," he explained to Tony Z, putting down the phone after his callback from MacGyver, "this guy's some kind of sniper guru."

"I think I read a piece he wrote in *Precision Shooting*. He's not a bipod guy. He doesn't think sniper rifles ought to have bipods. Cause more trouble than they're worth."

"Try shooting a Barrett without a bipod," said Mick. "See how far into the next state it gets you. Anyway, Swagger may have somehow come across something suggesting that Cruz the sniper at one time knew Chambers the guru. So Swagger decides to come hell for leather across South Carolina in order to have a chat with Chambers."

"At three in the morning?"

"Swagger's an action hero. He can't sleep on a twitch. He's got to go check it out."

"He thinks Chambers can lead him to Cruz," said Z. "God, I wish we had a mike in that room."

"Now, when Swagger leaves, what the fuck do we do? Do we stay with him? I guess so. I mean, we got the plant on him, right? We went to all that trouble. But if we switch to Chambers, maybe he's the magic ticket to Cruz. Maybe he goes to Cruz tomorrow, to tell him about Swagger, and we can put the Barrett on him, blow him out of his boots, and go back to the pool much richer than we are."

"Mick, it's tempting, but it ain't orderly. As you say, we have Swagger in our pocket. We can stay on him out of sight, no rush—"

"Hey hey hey—" came the sudden crackle of Crackers the Clown through their earphones, "hey, I got another guy in the room."

"What?"

"I just discovered it. This thing, this optic, you can go ambient light, you can go thermal, you can go combined ambient/thermal, which is where I've been, but I just went all thermal."

Mick wanted to strangle the guy. He didn't care about this shit. Who was the third man?

"So I flick on thermal, reads heat, you know, cool night, that building's pretty much an aluminum eggshell, plus they're in an outside room with only one wall, and goddamn I got *three* body heat signatures. Three. I don't know where the other guy came from. He wasn't there when they went into the room."

"Was he hiding?"

"Maybe there's a dead zone, a strong room, another entrance, I don't know. I'm just telling you what I see."

"Jesus," said Mick.

"If it's Ray," said Tony Z, next to him, "we could maybe go for the kill tonight. Now. In the next ten minutes."

"*If* it's Ray," said Mick, thinking.

"How can we find out?"

"We can't," said Mick.

He was right. Without some visual or at least aural penetration of the room, there was no way of knowing from outside if indeed the third man was Ray Cruz.

What to do now?

Bogier's mind ratcheted through possibilities.

1. Nothing. Maybe Swagger'd convince Ray to leave with him, they could ID him in the car, and do a drive-by on the two of them, spray-paint Swagger's car with 5.56, get two, good, confirmed kills.

2. Nothing also. If Swagger had led them to Cruz this time, he'd do it again. If he leaves alone, we stay with him. We can't stake out in this little town in daylight, because by 7:30 A.M. everybody's going to wonder who's in the black SUV parked on the roadside. That's

the way small towns are. That gives Ray Cruz, if he's there, plenty of time to make a good E & E and they might never get him again.

3. Nothing a third time. The mysterious third man is Colonel Chambers's son or an employee, his wife, his ho, whatever, and came in to join the conversation. It means nothing, and tomorrow they'd be hard on Bob again and maybe he'd strike pay dirt then. Maybe that would be the smart thing, though of course it went against Bogier's nature, and as he considered that nature, he came upon—

4. Go in hard now. Blow the door, hit the steps, kick in the office, dynamic entry SWAT style. Could probably make it up there in twenty seconds. If it's Ray, blow him away and the witnesses as well. If it's not, kick the shit out of them, rip out the phones, steal some rifles and what cash is on hand, and then disappear and try and disguise it as a gun robbery. Or maybe kill them anyway, what did it matter? Well, it mattered in that it informed whomever that another team was on the field and that would cause a stir, raise questions, start investigations that couldn't be controlled, lead to all kinds of unforseen questions. Agh.

And that led to another possible outcome of 4. That Swagger, the colonel, and the third man were just as much spec op superstars as Mick and his guys were, and in the twenty seconds after they blew the door and began the big rush, the targets got all gunned up and went to total war and instead of, like moron citizens, being behind the action curve were actually in front of it, and so Mick, Tony Z, and Crackers the Clown found themselves on the wrong end of a 5.56 shitstorm and bled out eight seconds after they hit the ground.

And then there was 5.

5. Hmm.

5. Oh yeah, number 5.

5. Oh, he liked it.

Mick toyed with it, savored it, tried to look at it from a batch of directions to find a flaw and found none.

"Phone," he said.

"Mick, I see a tiny gleam of piglike intelligence in your eyes. Are you cooking with gas?" said Tony Z.

"Just listen to daddy, little amoeba, and learn something about how we adults go around blowing up shit and killing people, but not in a bad way."

He punched the button. MacGyver was quick to answer.

"Well?"

"We have a situation," said Mick, and laid out the scenario.

"But you are not sure it's Cruz?" said MacGyver.

"No, sir. But who else could it be?"

"A tinker, a tailor, a candlestick maker. The man in the moon. Barack Obama, Michael Jordan, Ernest Borgnine, David Nix—"

"And suppose someone mysteriously kills David Nixon? Actually, I think you mean David Eisenhower. Suppose someone kills David Eisenhower? We took a risk, we didn't get a payoff, but are we any worse off than if we let David Eisenhower live?"

"Yes," said MacGyver. "Because you've informed the world that you exist."

"But nothing would connect the bodies with Ray Cruz and an Afghan politico. The forensics here are still in the Stone Age. It would just be some local crazed trailer-camp murder spree. And down here all's you got is Barney Fifes on the case and no evidence. We're out clean."

MacGyver's silence told Mick he'd gotten the control's attention. So he laid on the rest.

Unlimber the Barrett and rest it on the window ledge of the SUV, just like a Chicago gangster's tommy gun in 1927. Full ten-round magazine of 750-grain warheads moving out at about 3,000 feet per second. Mick's on the big gun, crouched next to him in the seat well is Crackers the Clown with his thermal imaging instrument, and Tony Z is driving. Pull around corner, take road to Steel Brigade Armory in its flimsy tinfoil building. Halt when distance to the building was shortest and the angles flattest, about thirty yards from the roadway. Crackers goes to thermal, which would be even stronger at the closer range, and gets a fix on the three living bodies behind the aluminum walls. He indexes Mick on the body locations using the window as the baseline, as in "two are clustered in same line about three feet to the right of the right line of the window, and one is two feet farther right." Hell, maybe he's able to throw a SureFire circle of light at the wall position.

Mick fires ten times in four seconds. He's that good, he can be depressing the trigger even as the beast is setting down from its recoil impulse. The bullets shear through the metal, almost without deviation, and they whack the citizens so hard they are fluffy puffs, gossamer unravelings, oozy twists of pink mist before they know it.

The car pulls off into the night. And though the gunfire racket is terrific, it takes a good forty-five minutes before any serious cops can get there. Best part: the Barrett ejects its spent casings into the SUV, leaving no evidence at all.

Three dead for sure. No links, no tracks, no evidence, no forensics because the .50s are moving so hard that after passing through metal, flesh, and more metal they fly out into the countryside. Best of all, there's no sense of high-tech professionals at work. It could be any gun guy with a Barrett, and in this neck of the woods, there were probably dozens of them. It was big-bore territory.

The sum of the parts: if it's Ray Cruz, end of problem. If it's not, it's somebody else's problem.

"Bogier, you are clinically insane. I had no idea how insane you were. Really, you should be studied by Harvard. Someone there would surely win a Nobel Prize in medicine."

"Okay," said Mick, "it's a little *loud*. It could be called *messy*. But consider: we may never get a shot like this again. Ever. If we let it slide, we will look back on this minute and hate ourselves into eternity. I say, fuck it, it's here, let's do it."

"Note to self," said MacGyver, "do not invite Bogier and his insane crew of mongoloid sociopaths to daughter's wedding. Okay, do it, Mick. And hope that God favors the incredibly brutal."

"He must," said Mick. "Look at how much fun he has with earthquakes."

STEEL BRIGADE ARMORY OFFICE
DANIELSTOWN, SOUTH CAROLINA
0305 HOURS

Cruz, my name is Swagger."

"I know who you are, Gunny," said Cruz, thin, intense, almost feral under a thatch of black crew cut. His eyes were, as promised, exotic, even Asiatic, but his face was white in its prominence of cheekbone, thinness of nose and lip. He wore jeans and a hoodie and a pair of New Balance running shoes and a purple baseball cap with a crow on it. He had a Beretta in his hand, but wasn't pointing it at Swagger.

"Is that pistol for me?" Swagger asked.

"No," said Cruz. "It's for me. There's a lot of people who want me dead. I'll have a piece close at hand at all times, thank you very much. Nothing's faster than a gun in the hand."

"Cruz, you sound a little paranoid."

"Bullets cutting your spotter in half will do that to a man."

"I know about losing spotters, Cruz. I also know how it can fuck up your mind. I've been there."

"Nobody's been where I am now. And nobody can get me out but me."

What was it? Who was he? The information was rushing in on Swagger so hard he had trouble staying with it. He was talking to a ghost. Bill Go, all those years dead in that anonymous little 'ville? Maybe. Maybe not. It wasn't an aura, a vibration, a tingle in the blood, but something was leaving tracks in the snow and Swagger knew he wasn't smart enough to read them. What? *What?*

"Cruz, I don't know what game you're up to, but you have a whole lot of important people upset. They'll stop you to the point of killing you. That would be so fucking wrong, Sergeant. We can end this tonight and get you back on duty next week if that's what you want."

"You were the best. You were a god to all of us. But you don't get it, Gunny," said Cruz. "If I go in and we all kiss and make up, in a day or maybe a week, I'm dead. They won't stop now. And whatever it is they're up to, it goes on and it finally happens."

"Cruz, you—"

"I saw a very good kid named Billy Skelton torn in two by some motherfucker on a Barrett. A hadji? Uh-uh, that would have been war. No, I hunkered down for a look and the guy with the big gun and his buddies were white. Contractors. I've seen enough of 'em in the zones to know. These guys were sent to hit Two-Two. It wasn't war, it was murder."

"Maybe Russian mercs. Maybe Iranian advisers. Maybe Chechen volunteers. It's only skin."

"These were American party animals. I could tell."

"I'm not convincing you, I see. But I am on contract to the FBI. You say the word and I go to my cell phone here and in two hours, maybe less, you are under protective custody. Whatever you charge, it will get a fair hearing. I'm working for a very good guy who's an assistant director, and I've known him a long, long time. I can guarantee you safety, that fair hearing, and a follow-up on your charges. It's the best way and this is the best offer you'll ever get."

"Everyone says you're the best, Gunny. Love to trust you, but I only trust the colonel because he's completely outside the system. You may not even know who's pulling your wires. So I will—"

In the hundredth or so of a second before he lost consciousness, Swagger was aware of the wall exploding inward in a great demonstration of the physics of high velocity and, insanely, the big steel desk behind which sat the silent colonel leaped off the deck as if it weighed an ounce and its leading edge hurled at Swagger, striking him so hard it knocked him into instant oblivion.

O h, this is going to be so fucking cool," said Crackers.

Z drove, turned the corner, headed down the two-lane; the building, low and unprepossessing, was a few hundred feet ahead.

Mick, curled on the backseat, was on the big gun, which was supported on the window ledge with a combat jacket scrunched under it for padding. The weapon was an oar, a wheelbarrow, a ton of fun—close to twenty pounds of semiauto rifle, unwieldy in any but the strongest of hands and arms, looking like some kind of steroid-engorged M16. He crushed its butt plate into his meaty shoulder and with his strong right hand tense on the grip and his strong left hand tense on the comb, guided the thing deftly, as if it were a child's .22. He was magic on the rifle. He squirmed to locate the right eye relief to the $4,000-worth of U.S. Optics scope on top of it, then cranked down to 4 power for the short-distance shots to come. He hard-tapped the magazine to make sure it was well seated. That thing alone weighed about six pounds, stuffed with the missilelike 750-grain cartridges, immensely heavy for their size.

"Hey," yelled Tony Z, because everybody was wearing earmuffs, "you're shooting without the bipod, just like the guru said. He'll be so pleased."

"We like to leave 'em happy," said Mick.

The car slowed, then halted. The black wall of the building was less than thirty yards away, one window blazing but, because of the upward angle from the vehicle, showing only ceiling.

Crackers the Clown squirmed into position from the seat well behind Z, next to the heavy forearm, ventilated for cooling. He put the NV monocular to his eye. He was already in thermal.

"Much better," said Crackers, "big as life. Okay, I got one guy separated from the two other guys by about five feet. All are seated. I'm guessing the guy out of the group is the guru guy, behind some sort of desk, because I'm not getting a full-body signature on him. The other two guys are directly facing each other."

"Index me off the left line of the window," said Mick.

"I'm estimating five feet; I think you should hold a little low on center of mass because you're shooting upward. You do the first guy, rotate maybe six inches farther right, and do the second guy. Then come back and do the colonel."

"I'm two feet low of the window left line," said Mick, rotating the heavy rifle to the right a bit as he held a solid cheek weld and a solid eye relief to the scope lens, "and I'm coming right, damnit, Tony, give me another foot or so."

Tony took the foot off the brake, and, easily, the vehicle slid forward.

"Good, good, good, okay, I'm going to shoot, tighten up, three, two, and—" He felt the trigger break and then it was as if a comet had smashed into Earth, a flaming ball of destruction to suck up the oxygen and flatten the vegetation and scorch the earth in the exact moment that something hydraulic unleashed full force against his heavily muscled shoulder.

The rifle rose in recoil, having sent a nuclear flash into the air along with its 750 grains of pure mayhem and a sonic boom, then settled, and Mick rotated just a bit, cheek and eye relief still perfect, fired again, producing the same assault upon the senses by flash and bang, sending another hot spent casing flying from the breach, which itself was in the process of ratcheting and clacking in the bolt blowback sequence.

He waited for recovery, rotated back left, and fired at what should have been the colonel. Three shots, in under two seconds. Took a good, trained man to do that on a Barrett.

"Rock and roll!" he shouted, while up front Tony Z was going, "Whooooooaaaaahh, mother*fucker*!"

Reindexing on the zone of his initial targets—he could see two craters spewing pure illumination where the big slugs had bludgeoned through the aluminum and wallboard—he really put the pedal to the metal. He fired six more times, trying to hold his strikes within the parameters of the first two penetrations, and with each arrival a blast of fragmenting metal and spewing dust and streaks of flaming debris snapped off the wall in supertime.

"Fucking A," said Crackers—he'd ducked to the floor during the shooting, to save his eardrums and his night vision—"look at that!"

The burst of .50s had literally ripped a slash in the wall next to and a little beneath the building. It looked like the hull of a ship that had caught a torpedo full on, a twisted mass of metal, bent struts, sheaves of tormented wallboard, all in a haze of dust and smoke.

"Ma, we won the war," said Tony.

Mick pulled the big rifle back into the truck, awkwardly got it into the back space over the edge of the seat, and said, "Okay, punch out. No, punch out slow, no howling. No more than fifty-five. Just drive, son, drive into the dawn."

"Fuck," said Crackers. "I didn't get to see any of the hits."

"It looked like a fucking movie. Man, did those suckers kick ass."

"It would have been cooler," said Mick, connoisseur of destruction, "if we'd had tracers."

"Oh shit yeah," said Tony Z. "Man, what a fucking show that would have been."

"Should we go and check—"

"Yeah, and run into Barney F with his double barrel who happened to be pissing behind the gas station? Punch it."

They got so far so fast they never even heard any sirens.

Ray didn't know his reflexes worked in that science fiction time zone. He was on the ground before the desk, lofted mightily into the air by the first shot, crushed Swagger hard in the head, putting him over backward in his chair. Ray squirmed into the fetal as another big hammer punched through, and hit his own chair—the one he'd just vacated—and sent it spinning crazily through the air as well. Nothing stood against these heavy hitters and he knew without putting it into words that it had to be Ma Barrett and her half-inch, 750-grain progeny, atomizing all that lay in their way.

The next shot hit flesh and it could only be the colonel's. The sound of bullet on meat is instantly knowable and completely unforgettable to those who've heard it: a kind of *whap!* of vibration being quieted by the density of flesh, a sickening wetness implied under the abruptness of the noise. Either in that second or the next, the back of Ray's neck felt a shower of warm droplets and mist.

He got his eyes opened for the next six big hits. Whoever was shooting was damned good. He kept the recoil in check and put the six in a neat pattern, almost a group, between the first two holes with but half a second between, and each, hitting the wall, blew it asunder in a cascade of vibration that lifted Ray from the floor and sent shards of supersonic metal spraying into the atmosphere but, following the laws of physics, on a slight upward direction and thus mostly missing him.

Dust jetted everywhere, as did debris of mysterious origin, flaming chips of wallboard, chunks of metal from the struts of the structure, all of it illuminated in the fluorescent light up above: it was an image of a turbulent universe. Would they reload and fire another mag? Would they now rush? He had the Beretta and knew he'd go down hard, taking many along on the trip.

But it stayed quiet, even though his ears rang like alarms. It was through an actual hole in the wall that he spied a flash of motion that told him the shooters had been in a vehicle and had now taken off.

Shakily, he stood, turned to see the colonel against the far wall, the impact of the huge bullet unkind. Metal does things to flesh, as no one knew better than Ray, and he deduced in a second that no first aid was capable of fixing the colonel. He felt a stab of pain: old friend, good guy, sound advice giver, supporter in time of need, really a true believer in the Church of Ray. And for that he'd been taken down hard by assholes on a .50. That goes in the book, he thought. Ray will deal with that when the time is right.

He then turned to the old sniper. Swagger, a dry stick of a man, all ribs and bones and sinewy grace, under a butch-waxed moss of gray, was either dead or unconscious. The edge of the flying desk had opened a bad, deep cut along his cheekbone, and it was oozing blood, though the lack of squirt action suggested no arteries had been cut. It ran down his still cheek, caught in his nostrils, then sluiced to the floor, forming a lake. Ray touched him, felt a heartbeat. Quickly he lifted the desk off the bottom half of the fallen man and dragged him to the wall. Had to get him upright so he wouldn't drown in his own blood.

Ray peeled off his hoodie, wrapped it around the broken head, and secured it with his Wilderness belt. Maybe that would keep the crotchety old bastard alive until the medics arrived.

Having done what he could do, Ray turned and zipped out into the hallway. Knowing the building well, he got to a rear door, unlocked it, and slipped out, and set out across farm fields and backyards, even as sirens were finally beginning to sound, as firemen and officers tumbled out of bed. Ray knew exactly where he was going; he was far from unprepared.

He'd loaded his equipment in the trunk of a clean, legally pur-

chased, and unstolen Dodge Charger, parked behind the Piggly Wig-
gly in town. He popped the lock, got in, and quietly started up, turned
left and headed out. As far as he could tell, no one had seen a thin,
athletic man in jeans and a UCLA T-shirt with a Baltimore Ravens
ball cap up top. He disappeared—it's the sniper gift, after all—into
the night.

HOLIDAY INN MOTEL
ROANOKE, VIRGINIA
1730 HOURS

The phone awakened Bogier. It was Tony Z in the next room; he and Crackers were up now, and were going to start drinking. Did Bogier want to come? No, Bogier did not want to come. Had Bogier heard from MacGyver? No, Bogier had not heard from MacGyver. He would wait until he did and then join them.

Bogier lay naked in the dark room, under clean, crisp sheets. His massive, beautiful body was a god's, though he'd been a week out of the gym and yearned to get back to the discipline and purity of the heavy-iron dead lift. He could tell; the ridges that defined the tectonics of his delts were a little less precise, the knobs that represented his abs a little less jagged, the bulge of his veins a little less prominent. It was, ever so slightly, beginning to soften. He was still doing this shit.

He'd been up for forty-eight straight, the last twelve of it driving mad-assed across the mid south, monitoring radio stations for news on the incident at Danielstown, South Carolina, where it was said a deranged ex-sniper had opened fire on the offices of Norman Chambers, a former marine and some kind of sniper warfare expert, who had been killed in the incident. But no other news was forthcoming.

So when they hit Roanoke, it was nappy-nap time. A Holiday Inn just off the interstate would do fine. He hit the sack, and drifted into thick, dreamless sleep. Now, he was awake, hardly feeling perky. Agh.

After a while, he got up groggily, took a shower. The Suunto showed him it was close to six. What to do, what to do? When would that bastard call? Was it over? Had they—

The satellite didn't ring, it buzzed. He picked it up, and hit the button.

"So?"

"So you didn't get him."

"Shit," said Bogier, feeling disappointment bite deep and hard. He knew what would come next. Asshole MacGyver would ream him hard and he'd have to sit there and take it like a schmuck.

"He was there all right. You got that part right. His prints were all over the place."

"Christ," said Bogier.

"That's the bad news. The good news: you also didn't get Swagger. You conked him hard on the head, and he's out like a light in some hick hospital, but expected to recover. You did, however, blow a hole the size of a football through Colonel Norman Chambers, USMC, retired. Congratulations: you managed to kill the one man in the room who had nothing to do with this shit."

"Fuck him if he can't take a joke," said Bogier. "Collateral damage."

"Yeah, well, be careful you don't 'collateral damage' your way into the gas chamber, sparky."

"It's war. It happens. Nothing personal. You go for an objective and a shell lands in downtown Shitbrick City, population, people seventy-five, chickens two hundred forty. Sorry little brown people, but important personages put our nation's values over Shitbrick City."

"I forgot. You're a patriot."

"You forgot. You okayed the hit. You're pretending like I went rogue."

"Bogier, your job isn't to outsmart me in debate. Remember, you never got higher than master sergeant. I'm the guy in the officer's tuxedo eating pheasant at the post club. If I want, I can arrange a nice duty detail for you—stables to be mucked out, garbage cans to be scrubbed, grout on latrine floors to be scraped out with toothbrushes. Your job is to outsmart Cruz, another sergeant. You're both mud crawlers, sentry knifers, bridge blowers, laser painters, macho action jocks, so you ought to be up to that, or at least I'm betting you think you are. So let's concentrate on what's what."

In Bogier's mind: an image of this ponce, with a goatee and a cigarette holder, wire-frame glasses, an ascot, as he crushed his head in his bare hands, spurting gray matter out of the ears and nose before the eyes popped like Ping-Pong balls from a toy gun.

"Good idea," said Mick, grinding his teeth.

"Okay, what we have to worry about now is whether they shit-can Swagger."

"Why would they?"

"Duh, went in without backup or informing HQ. If he were a special agent, his ass would be grass. Maybe they let him slide but keep him on a tight leash because he's fundamentally an amateur who happens to know a lot about the bang bang."

"Don't forget, that 'amateur' found Cruz in twelve hours his first day on the case while everyone else was jerking off."

"He's a smart guy, no lie. That's why we have to hope they keep him aboard. Assuming he hasn't found the magic credit card in his back pocket. So let's assume next they still want to use his brain in scoping out the sniper. So they move him to DC, does that make sense?"

"We're on our way."

"My guess is, you'll pick up that RFID response at the FBI building on Pennsylvania. You stay on it. He'll figure out where Cruz is sooner or later. Maybe you can get a hit on Cruz that saves Zarzi's life and be a big hero. Mick Bogier, the new Bob Lee Swagger. Then you and your new best friend Bobby Lee can go on dry-drunk rages together."

MacGyver insulted Mick for another few minutes and then let him go. Mick checked the Suunto and headed toward the bar to drive out the image of MacGyver roasting in flames to the laughter of all the fellows in the grog-and-wench shop called Sergeants' Valhalla. Tonight would be a big night for getting drunk. Tomorrow: Washington, D fucking C.

INTENSIVE CARE UNIT
BRIGHTON COUNTY GENERAL HOSPITAL
HOPKINS, SOUTH CAROLINA
1642 HOURS
THE NEXT DAY

The first time he awoke was when some doctor was pulling up his eyelids and shining a flashlight into his eyeballs. That hurt. The second time, someone had given him a shot. That hurt. The third time it was Nick Memphis, poking him. That really hurt.

His eyes came open. It felt as though a camel had been licking his face for a month. His limbs were dead, his fingers dead, his legs and feet dead. Consciousness was a thick sludge, and he fought his way through it, struggling for focus and breath.

"Oh, shit," he said, his voice evidently not dead.

"He's coming out of it," Nick said, and the next person who leaned in was Susan Okada, beautiful and untouchable—why had she come back, damnit?—and looking at him as, say, the shogun's executioner might look at someone whose neck he would in the next second split.

"Hello," she said uncheerily, "anybody home?"

"Yeah, yeah," he replied and found that his body did move, he wasn't quadded out. He had a headache that only a dozen Jacks in an hour would justify, and the right half of his face was swaddled in bandages, the eye occluded by pouches of something—his swelling, he guessed—pressing against it from all sides.

"Water, please," he said.

She poured it for him from a bottle.

"Our hero returns from vacation," she said.

"How do you feel?" Nick said.

"Like shit."

"Funny, that's what you look like," said Susan.

"Oh, Christ, what happened?"

"You were smashed in the head by a flying desk. You have a concussion. Your cheekbone for some reason refused to break, but it took thirty-one stitches to close up the slice beneath your eye. The swelling will go down in November. You look like an abused grapefruit."

"Agh," he coughed. "And what about, um, that colonel, and Cruz."

"The colonel's dead, Cruz is gone. Total catastrophe."

Bob swallowed the water. Goddamn, his head hurt. The news about the colonel hit him hard. The guy was just—

But what was the point?

"Tell me what happened."

"Sure. Then you tell us what happened."

Nick explained: ten .50-caliber slugs through the wall of Steel Brigade Armory, a fluke of ballistics that the first one hit and spun the desk through midair instead of blasting Bob into particles, another one zeroing in on Colonel Chambers—"You don't want to see the crime scene pictures"—and the others generally ripping the hell out of the place. Cruz's prints were all over, but the lack of blood samples suggested he'd gotten to the floor in time to just miss getting jellified, then slipped out the back after the shooters pulled away. There were no forensics on the shooters except a partial tire track near the edge of the road that pointed the way to sixteen million Goodyear Wrangler P245 tires.

"Oh, hell," said Bob.

"Now, your turn. Excuse me for asking the sixty-four-thousand-dollar question, but what the hell were you doing in a conversation with the object of a federal manhunt and why oh why oh why didn't you call for backup, for guidance, for anything?"

"Oh, that," said Bob, and he searched feebly for a joke, almost saying, "Backup is for pussies." But he didn't. Nobody seemed much interested in his sense of humor.

He told it as simply as he could. He explained it, then justified it.

"I just went out there to get the lay of the land. I knew I'd be back the next day, I didn't want to go in cold. A recon, that's all. When I seen, excuse me, *saw* the light on, I figured, what the hell? I thought it was going to be another old geezer who probably knew who I was and I could get more out of him on my own, man to man, than if I was part of a goddamned invasion force. I didn't know Cruz was there. I had no idea someone was going to start blasting with a fifty. I didn't plan on taking a ten-thousand-caliber desk in the head."

Nick was silent.

Susan said, "Tell us exactly what Cruz said. Can you remember?"

Swagger tried to re-create the conversation in his own head.

"'Nobody's been where I am now. And nobody can get me out but me.' That's the line I remember. He had an idea people were trying to kill him. Seems like he was right on that one, or maybe these stitches on my face came from my imagination. But he's a serious man hell-bent on a course. He's burned bad because of the death of his spotter. He thinks he's the only one who can figure it out because all of us are in 'the system' and can't be trusted or are being manipulated by shadowy forces. Wasn't interested in coming in. I played that line hard, but he wasn't having none of it, any of it."

Nick let a melancholy ton of air escape his lungs.

"So, basically, we're nowhere."

"We do know it's him. And we know that somebody wants to kill him. We do know that," said Bob.

"We don't," said Susan. "Excuse me, but this colonel knew a lot of snipers, he ran courses for snipers, and among them are sure to be some unstable people. Maybe one had a grudge against him. You just can't jump to the conclusion that it was an attempt on Cruz's life without a thorough professional investigation. Maybe he was in a love affair, a business crisis, a lawsuit, any one of a dozen mundane reasons—"

"They'd go for him with a Barrett? His wife's boyfriend goes for him with a—"

"Barretts are civilian legal," said Nick. "If you wanted a safe way to kill a guy who was known to work very late in an aluminum building, a Barrett semi would be number one on your wish list, especially if you knew a little about guns, as anyone who knew the colonel probably did."

"So you're not going to—"

"Go on a witch hunt, no," said Susan. "I know how conveniently the Agency fits all manner of paranoid fantasies, justifies any interpretation, satisfies any mandate of evil or conspiracy. We will not use this as an excuse to probe in areas that are off-limits unless we develop hard evidence, and I mean hard, that suggests Agency personnel were involved. Unknown gunmen shooting up a building in the night in rural South Carolina doesn't cut it."

"High-level gunmen. You could tell because he fired so fast and he kept his shots tight. He'd ridden that recoil before in dusty places full of guys with tablecloths on their heads and daggers between their teeth. Do I need to point out that it was almost certainly a Barrett that the guys in Afghanistan used on Whiskey Two-Two? Coincidence? Sure, the world's full of them. Anyhow"—Swagger coughed, in the grasp of a phlegm-throated oxygen debt—"who are they, what are they doing here? What's their interest in Ray?"

"Nothing ties them to Ray," said Nick. "Sorry, but Okada is right. Without hard evidence we have no license to poke our way into Agency business. No one at the Bureau wants that. This temporary truce is something everybody wants and I can't endanger it on the evidence of nothing."

"You people and your rules," said Bob. "It's like dealing with kindergarteners at a goddamn ice-cream party. 'I want the ice cream!' 'No, no, it's *my* ice cream.' How do you stand it?"

"The system is the system, Swagger," said Susan. "Look, there is indeed a schism in the Agency: those who believe in Zarzi, those who don't. The disbelievers have been exiled because the Administration also wants to believe in Zarzi."

"Is it possible some of the pro-Zarzis have gone overboard in their protection of him?" Bob said. "They want the Zarzi ice cream, they're crazy for the ice cream, and so they've gone around the bend to make sure it don't melt?"

"These are professional people. They don't go around bends. I will make certain delicate inquiries, but my accessibility itself has been threatened by this episode. They'll all know we had a shot at Cruz and whiffed. That doesn't help, Swagger."

Delicacy! Swagger wanted to say: Are you here for them or for us? Is your job the truth or is it to protect your bosses? But he couldn't. She had stood hard for him and gone into battle with swords for him. She had brought him the rest of his life in the form of his daughter, Miko. She had nothing to prove to him.

"Susan, I will obey any policy you say. I'm sorry if I suggested otherwise. You can count on me not to betray you or disobey you."

She nodded. Then she said to Nick, "Look, let me talk to him alone."

"Sure, but no necking on company time."

"Ha-ha," said Susan, "count on the Bureau for laugh riots."

But she turned to Bob once they were alone.

Her gaze was steady, as it always was, her face annoyingly perfect. Her hair looked a little mussed, and of course that made her seven or possibly nine times more attractive.

"Look, this isn't easy," she said. "I am well aware that they put me here because we worked together before and I get a sense, once in a while, that you seem to like me a little. They know that, they're using that, just as they're manipulating me through the fact that I never met a cowboy with brains before until I met the old dog. Cowboys are cheap, but the smart ones are one in a million. So don't think I don't feel whatever it is we're not supposed to talk about. But, Bob, I have to cover for the Agency. I married it, it's my husband, everything I ever got I got from it. It's my Marine Corps. I know its follies, its pretensions, its weaknesses, how many of its people are self-infatuated fools. But it is necessary and it is the only one we've got, so no matter how many times I remember when Samurai Swagger kicked in the door and faced off with that creepy Yak and sent his head in the direction of Sevastopol, I have to pull back to my loyalty to the Agency. Okay? You have your code, Semper Ho and Gung Fi and all that, and I have mine."

"I'm hearing you, Okada-san. You were a hell of a case officer."

"Get some sleep, cowboy. We need you on two legs and a horse."

He smiled—a little—through cracked lips.

Nick stepped back in.

"Okay," he said, "old friends' time officially over. Bob, we will forward any info we develop to the state police detectives—they're waiting for your statement, by the way—who have to solve this case. In the meantime, we will continue our pursuit of Ray Cruz. We need you in Washington to read the possible shooting sites. Be on our team, be our friend, okay? As Ms. Okada says, rest a few days, wait till the ringing stops and you only look like a tomato and not a grapefruit, and come back to work. Is that clear?"

Bob said yes, knowing secretly that he would never leave this case till the end, if it killed him—or anybody else.

He had to find out: who was trying to kill Ray Cruz?

BALTIMORE, MARYLAND

I t had to be Baltimore. The thinkers at the various agencies, offices, bureaus, and departments all agreed. They discounted the *Meet the Press* site because, although the studio had a transparent rear window to show the dome in the background, the material was high-strength ballistic glass through which no bullet could penetrate and the only shooting location would be in public, somewhere on Capitol grounds, even up a tree, impossible to hide. The White House was also a no-go, as security was extraordinary, and that night, the Secret Service, the FBI, and the Washington Metropolitan Police would be out in abundance. No sniper could get close enough. The speech at Georgetown was in the center of buildings that could be easily controlled for access.

Just as important, the three Washington sites were terra firma for security people, who knew every nook, cranny, crack, and fissure in the zone. It would be extremely hard to penetrate without an elaborate set of false documents that were almost certainly outside the reach of lone gunman Ray Cruz, who was a singleton, without elaborate intelligence professionals backing him up. The cordons in all three cases would be tight with choke points everywhere in a city that was used to and unfazed by choke points and presidential security.

That left Baltimore, and a neighborhood of aspiration called Mount Vernon, after the square that dominated it. The site centered on a civilian restaurant on a main thoroughfare, plenty of ingress and egress, hundreds of windows. Baltimore was terra incognito, open ground, untested, just as new to the Secret Service as it was to Ray Cruz. It so happened that Ibrahim Zarzi's brother Asa owned an extremely successful restaurant much favored by the city's many academics and medical personnel, where lamb kabobs, rice, red wine, and squares of unleavened bread were served; colorful knit garments hung on the walls; and the photos of wily, craggy Pashtun faces gave the place a touch of the Hindu Kush without the danger of an IED, which was for marine L/CPLs to face on MREs in unarmored Humvees. So if Cruz was going to take the fatal shot and send Zarzi to his next destination, it would have to be somewhere along Charles Street, two or three blocks each way from the restaurant, as the Great Man was hustled into or out of the building.

Bob walked the street with two Secret Service snipers, their supervisor, the Baltimore police SWAT commander, and Nick. The swelling blowing up the left side of his face had subsided and left a dappling of pinkish-red-yellowish bruise, and a jagged strip of bandage tracing the severing of his flesh on top of the cheekbone. Enough, already, with the "You should see the other guy" line of patter from the guys, though he took it in good spirit, and settled on the comeback, "That was no lady, she was two hundred pounds of steel desk." Ha, ha, and ha. But all that ended with the initial discussions at the Baltimore FBI offices in a nondescript building just outside the beltway. Now, by caravan, they had reached the prime zone.

It was one of those new urban American paradises, a reborn street in a once crummy zone that had found life hoping to mimic the European model, with low old buildings of stone turrets or copper wainscoting, each with a shiny set of retail opportunities at street level, trees in full leaf, sidewalk cafes, restaurants in various ethnic flavors besides Afghan, including Mexican, Chinese, gay, Indian, sushi, and snarky boho. It was very la-di-da, maybe even a little tra-la-la; it looked a lot like Paris, if you'd never been to Paris. At one end, a block from the Zabol's facade, was Mount Vernon itself, a cruciform city park with trees. Each of the arms of the cross shape extended a block and offered a meadow, a line of trees, walkways, and benches. At the center of the cross rose a 200-foot-tall marble pedestal, and on top of it a man, also of marble, stood and looked the other way.

"Who's the general?" asked Bob, noting the marble figure's tricorn hat.

"Washington," said the SWAT commander. "This was the first monument to him, 1820 or something. The joke is, he's extending his arm, and from a certain angle, if you look up, he's got the biggest dick in the world. Father of his country."

All the security pros laughed.

"Great shooting spot," said the Secret Service sniper, "but I'm guessing we'll seal it up real tight on game day."

"Nobody goes near it."

"So the normal drill," Bob said, "is control over street and vehicle traffic, countersnipers on rooftops, all windows sealed, airborne surveillance, all tied together on one channel?"

"That's it, Gunny," said the Secret Service supervisor. "Do you want to see the maps or read the mission plan?"

"No."

"This guy is really good, huh?"

"He can shoot a bit."

"What's your take?"

"He's got something you've never been up against and he'll use it against you."

"And that is?" asked the supervisor.

"He's got a great standing offhand. Not many do. What that means is that unlike anyone you ever heard of, he don't need a 'lair,' a 'hide.' He don't need a long look at the target, a ranging laser, ballistics tables, wind gauges, and the time to compute all the dope, followed by quiet to gather, concentrate, and deliver, as every sniper everywhere in the world does. Even with a top-of-the-line iSniper911 he'd be slower than with his offhand. He don't need a calm zone. Nope, not him. He don't need to be at a bench or prone on bipod. He's much more flexible and unpredictable. His main thing is concealing the weapon, and he might even go to a short barrel, I mean abnormally short—"

"What about a scoped handgun?" asked the Baltimore commander.

"I'm sure he's damn good with a handgun," said Bob, "but he spent last summer working hard on his standing. He can probably set himself, go to rifle, fire, slide the rifle back undercover, and make any shot out to two hundred yards, all in one second. Any one of these folks could be the shooter." The streets were not crowded but were steadily negotiated by people of all ages, shapes, costumes, and inclinations, and it didn't take too much imagination to see an old man, say 150 yards down Charles, as a guy able to whip out that short-barreled rifle, put the one shot into Zarzi as his guards hustled him out, full of lamb and wine, to the armored limo. It would be a near impossible shot for even the most trained sniper, but Ray's extra abilities, his hard operational background, his intensity, made anything possible.

"Is he a suicide guy?" one of the Secret Service snipers asked.

"Nothing would indicate that," said Bob. "He's a sniper, marine style, trained to execute, yes, but to survive too. We don't train our people to give it up for the kill. The point is to kill the other guy."

"Yet what would he get out of survival? We know who he is and even if he makes the shot and all of us lose our jobs"—they laughed—"and he escapes, what has he got? A few days before he's run down, then either the rest of his life in jail or some legendary last-stand gunfight that gets him in the history books, but also the ground. He might see that as a glory ride."

"He's not a glory boy. He ain't looking to get his name in the papers, like some mall psycho," said Bob. "He's raised a good Catholic boy by good Catholic parents, on an American naval base in the Philippines, and to him suicide, like betrayal and murder, is a sin. He's not no Moro, he ain't high on hemp, he's not no run-amok guy with a machete; everything he does is controlled, calm, graceful, quiet. He's still following orders. You don't notice him until it's too late. The kill would be enough, and in his mind, he's executing the perfect counterterrorism operation, he's a hero preventing something else much worse from happening. He'd shoot, then surrender. Then he makes his case in court. He goes into everything he believes about his team being betrayed, he gets a high-profile attorney who'd lay subpoenas on the Agency and the National Security adviser's office. He's probably already made his notes and contacted his big-deal lawyer."

"What all this suggests," Nick said, "is that if he makes it to Charles Street, we've already lost. We have to find him before he deploys that day. We have to find him where he's gone to ground."

FOUR SEASONS HOTEL

The Great Man arrived, by limo, from Andrews. Cops on Harleys; Secret Service gunboat SUVs; Army aviation overhead butter-knifing through the air, scaring off the news choppers; Agency handlers, gofers, commo experts, and upper-floor reps, the whole train about a mile long, tying up traffic for hours. Too bad for the unsuspecting citizen caught in it.

Ibrahim Zarzi, warlord and patriot, boulevardier, seducer, smiler, toucher, gourmand and oenophile, clotheshorse, called by Page Six the "Clark Gable of Afghanistan," and possible Our Man in Kabul, got out, accompanied by a number one factotum and two Agency functionaries, and was immediately surrounded by the Secret Service Joes from the following Explorer who were designated to take the shot meant for him. And they would too, because that was their job, even if this shady character had once been known as "the Beheader." All that was in the past, everybody hoped, in a different lifetime, in a different world.

Flashes strobed, suave TV reporters oozed against the ropes that restrained them, attempting to look cool and hot and concerned all at the same time, but Ibrahim Zarzi was rushed by them with no time to answer the shouters.

He was an extremely handsome man, about fifty-five, with a thick head of dark hair, nicely graying temples, a brush-cut Etonion's mustache, and piercing dark eyes that showed off his blindingly white teeth. Omar Sharif, anyone? He looked like, among other things, a polo player, a bridge champion, a scratch golfer, a man who'd killed all five of the dangerous game species at record trophy size, caught some really big scary fish, a man who had bedded many a blonde in his pied-à-terre in Paris and in his rooms in London, shrewd, ruthless, narcisisstic, and a total watch slut.

Today, he'd gone with the Patek Philippe Gondola, in gold, muted, with a black face and roman numerals, as well as a single black sapphire cabochon on top of the winding stem. It was about an inch by an inch, secured by a crocodile band. It set off his blue, pin-striped Savile Row suit, immaculately tailored, his crisp white Anderson & Sheppard shirt with Van Cleef & Arpels cuff links in tasteful onyx, and his black bespoke oxfords from J. Cobb, one of White Street's more discreet custom shoemakers. His face was brown, his tie was red (solid; he knew when to stop), and his watch was black. He dressed from the watch out.

"I think I will change to my gold Rolex for dinner," he said to Abba Gul, his assistant. "And, since it will be informal, my blue blazer—"

"The double breasted?"

"Hmm," said Zarzi, contemplating the choices, "yes, and an ascot, the red-gold-blue Seventeenth Royal Hussar, I think. A blue shirt, the gold Tiffany cuff links, gray slacks, and that nice pair of cordovan Alden tassel moc loafers. White silk socks, of course."

"Yes, my lord," said Gul, who never had to write anything down, who never made a mistake, who understood the Great Man's moods, needs, pleasures, agonies, ups, downs, wants, and occasional squalls of self-lacerating doubt. "It shall be done."

Zarzi did not acknowledge the man, who was from a family that had served his own for 250 years, after the first Zarzi, Alazar the Terrible, had swept down from the mountains with his band of fierce Pathans, said to be descended from the fierce Shinwari tribe, driven out the people of the flatlands and all their pretty poppies (or executed them by hanging them upside down from trees and cutting an incision from this hip bone to that nipple), and taken over Zabul, making Qalat its capital. The Guls made themselves useful to the Zarzi clan and were allowed to prosper.

A hotel personage said, "Sir, this way," after the man had been vetted by the Secret Service, led through the phalanx of Agency goons, and passed muster with the two bodyguards trained to give up their lives in an instant for the Greatness of Zarzi, "and I hope you enjoy your stay."

"I'm sure I will, Mr. Nickerson"—he'd noted the nameplate, part of his conspicuous charm being that he learned names quickly and never forgot them—"and I love the hotel. Please tell the florist"—he gestured to the sprays and waves of flowers decorating the lush central corridor of the place—"that he has done well, and please have a thousand dollars' worth of flowers sent to my rooms today and every day."

"It has already been done, sir," said the oily, professionally obsequious Nickerson, known to the others on the hotel staff as "the Greaser," "exactly like last time."

"Most excellent," said Zarzi.

"You have the entire floor, sir," said his Agency gofer, a minor handler with the Afghan Desk named Ryan, "and please, please, stay away from the windows. I can't emphasize—"

"Mr. Ryan, you forget that Allah in his justice protects me and shall not permit any mischief to befall me. That has been decreed, as it has been decreed I am the one to lead my people out of darkness. I am a river to my people and I must—oh, dear, I believe I'm quoting Anthony Quinn in *Lawrence of Arabia* again. So easy to get caught these days with every peasant dog tied by tether to the horrors of Google and able to produce instantaneous correction."

"Ain't it a bear?" said Ryan.

"A bitch, in fact," said the charmer.

"You have a couple of hours. Then cocktails with three senators on the Foreign Relations Committee at Ms. Dowd's place at the Watergate."

"And how is Mo? Is she still writing those delicious pieces twice a week?"

"Of course."

"Good for Mo! She's a jolly spitfire, that one! And tomorrow?"

"The Agency all day, with Mr. Collins and our staff in Afghan."

"I hope the catering is good," said Zarzi. "Burger King, double whopper, no fries. I prefer the McDonald's French fry to the less-textured Burger King product. Surely some young CIA killer can be dispatched to McDonald's for that."

"I think so, sir."

"A future president does not consume substandard French fries," he said majestically. "So vulgar."

"I'll see to the catering, sir," said Ryan.

"It will be such a pleasure before eating at my brother's restaurant in Baltimore tomorrow. It will be so nice to see him, but the food! Ugh, I cannot fathom how he sells it. You could find better in any village main street, cooked on a stove the size of a portable television by a barefoot old hag without teeth. Yet he has made a good living. Your press thinks me a scoundrel, Mr. Ryan. My brother is a true scoundrel!"

"I look forward to meeting him, sir."

"I look forward to seeing him, Mr. Ryan. I loathe the idea of *dining* with him."

"It humanizes you, sir."

"Could we not have met, say, at a nice Popeye's? Now *that's* an advance in civilization!"

He had napped, he had showered, he had deodorized, he had prayed—or had he? hard to remember—he had refreshed with several Dexedrine and felt ready as a tiger. Gul had laid out the clothes. But now, before leaving for Mo's, came his favorite moment in any journey: the winding of the watches.

"Sir, the servants are ready."

He sat down, barefoot, poured himself a glass of water.

"They may proceed," he said.

The factotum muttered a command and one by one a half dozen servants came in bent and reverent, and placed an odd object on the bureau, the coffee table, the mantel, the bedside table, any stable surface in the bedroom of the vast, plush suite. Since there were by far more odd objects than servants, the procession took a while until each had put his object exactly where it should be and gone back for another one, then gotten back in line. When they were finally done, the factotum Abba Gul made certain that all were equidistant in space, all aligned perfectly.

They were watch winders, elegant boxes that opened to reveal velvet, er, whatchamacallits—*things* maybe?—protrusions, protuberances, armatures, whatever. If there was a word for it, Zarzi did not know it. In effect, they were artificial limbs, wrists actually. Then came the watches, removed from their travel cases. Rolexes, Patek Philippes, Blancpains, Raymond Weils, Vacheron Constantins, Bell & Rosses, Breguets, Chopards, Girard-Perregauxs, Piagets, Cartiers, Omegas, Fortises, and so on and so forth, more than eight dozen of them, all mechanical analogs, all clicking away in perfect time, all second hands indexed exactly to the second designations on the faces and not between, as happens on cheap quartz movements, all elegant, all expensive, all shiny. One by one, in a certain order, a servant slid the watch he bore onto the artificial wrist of the opened box until the room resembled the discreetly expensive private viewing arena of a high-end Parisian jewelry store. It then developed that each box also sported a discreet cord, which was now unrolled by servants and each plug inserted into a lengthy socket box, which was in turn plugged into the hotel's electrical system.

"Sir?"

"Yes, proceed, Gul," said the Great Man.

Gul pressed the main switch on the socket box and each of the velvet wrists began a slow, methodical revolution, describing a circle about four inches in circumference. Thus, the watches, all self-winders, the culmination of the watchmaker's art, received their two hours of energy to keep them running perfectly. No longer was the space a jewelry showroom, but rather a kind of ghost hall full of apparitions rotating the watches to precise life, in soundless synchronicity, a symphony of gently moving disks of numbers. As it was dark, the radiated digits gleamed more brightly, but the many gold pieces had their own organic process by which they magnified what little ambient glow their surfaces caught and reflected.

It was like a slow-motion pyrotechnic show and behind each watch face, Zarzi knew, was a galaxy of gears and shafts and pins and jewels, set together with inexorable logic driven by extraordinary imagination and discipline, traceable back to the original *verge escapement* device created by who knows what forgotten genius in the European Middle Ages. It was, of course, the West: not computers or skyscrapers or women with bulging thighs and naked, painted toes; all that came later. But this was its core, its essence, and he loved it so and he hated it just as fervently, all the gear wheels, the tiny springs, the rotating winder weights, the hands sweeping inexorably around, measuring not time, as so many thought, but only the tension within their mainspring. That is what the watch calibrated; time was a metaphor against which it was applied. There was no time, not really, not that could be touched, weighed, licked, tasted, felt. The watches ticked against their own winding and the imagination that had designed the winding mechanism; it was magic, it was profound, it was touching, he loved it so much in all its glory and damnation.

Six meetings, and at each, Bob had given his little speech on Ray Cruz's standing offhand capability. Twice to Agency people, to the Baltimore metropolitans, the Maryland State Police, and two Secret Service meetings and at each positions were marked, radio frequencies verified, aviation coordinates laid in, the parade of intricate planning and counterplanning gone over a third, a fourth, a fifth time.

Everybody was exhausted. But nobody was going home.

Bob sat with Nick and several others—ties loosened, jackets off, sleeves rolled up—in the special agent in charge's corner office in the bland office building the Bureau had rented, and then decorated in the mind-numbing scheme known as Nineties Bureaucracy. One touch stood out: one of the office's bosses had been female, and she'd supervised a witty Dick Tracy toy and comic strip exhibit in the foyer, behind glass. None of the men noticed it and none of the subsequent male SAICs bothered to take it down.

The occasion was a situation report, sitrep in the jazzy vernacular. A special agent had just summed up the day's efforts in locating Ray Cruz, which included a sweep of all motels and hotels, rental apartments, trailer parks, homeless shelters; monitoring all local law enforcement reports, all speeding and misdemeanor charges (idiotic, Swagger thought; Ray Cruz wasn't about to get in a bar fight); and so forth and so on, including employee canvasses of all retail and eating establishments, review of postal activity, delivery by private carrier, garbage pickup, road crew work, traffic light maintenance, meter maids, et cetera. All telephone tips had been checked out, all the unglamorous clerk's work that is the essence of law enforcement.

"Nothing."

"You're the expert," someone said to Swagger. "Where's a marine sniper go to ground?"

"Right now," said Bob, "he'd be in a hole covered with leaves and branches. His face would be dark green and black; he'd be ready to shit in the hole, piss in the hole, eat in the hole, and die in the hole. He crawled a long way to get to that hole and he ain't about to give it up."

There was a little laughter, mostly of a tired sort.

Nick asked a special agent Travis, "Anything new from Washington?"

"More stuff on the Cruz background investigation."

"Sergeant Swagger, take a look at it, see if it's anything, when you get a moment."

"Sure," said Bob.

"Hey," said the Baltimore SWAT supervisor, "Sergeant Swagger, I remember you said yesterday 'good Catholic boy.' I'm wondering if Cruz could get hold of a priest's garment and get into that steeple in the square that way."

"Raymond Shaw in *The Manchurian Candidate*," someone else said.

"We've canvassed the church, but it's a very good suggestion," said Nick. "And Cruz seems to have the self-effacing low profile of a priest, so he'd fit right in. I'll detail some extra men there tomorrow."

Bob said, "Camouflage."

"I'm sorry, Sergeant?"

"Camouflage."

"You're thinking he'll disguise himself as a bush? Or maybe he's already there, disguised as a bush?"

There was some laughter and even Bob had a grin from the agent's wisecrack.

"No," said Bob, "I don't mean in that way. Despite what I just said, he ain't going to paint his face green and glue twigs to his head or wear no suit that looks like a swamp. But *camouflage* is at the center of the mind-set. That's what the mission was about in Afghanistan. Camouflage. Blending in. Okay, not with the ground but with the local population. So . . . what would he camouflage himself as?"

There was silence.

"Put it another way; where would he locate so he wouldn't be noticed? What is his first quality? What is the first thing about him?"

"He's a marine."

"He's a sniper."

"He's a hero."

"He's gone crazy."

"All that's no help at all," said Nick. "Bob, what are you thinking?"

"First of all, he's Filipino. He was raised in the Philippines. He speaks Tagalog without an accent. With other Filipinos, his features blend in; he ain't what we're calling 'exotic.' He becomes more Filipino in a group of Filipinos. They probably accept him on faith. He knows you guys ain't penetrated them because there's so few of them, a stranger would stick out, and you probably don't have too many Filipino special agents."

"Where is this going?" said Nick.

"I'm trying to think how he'd think. Here's what I come up with: maybe somewhere there's a Filipino who's already passed our once-over lightly. He's got a kitchen job, something in food service, maybe delivery, in the shoot zone. He's a recent immigrant, don't speak the language too good. It's a low-level job, but he's been on it a batch of months, so it's okay. So I'm thinking Ray, in that calm, methodical, focused way of his, has found him. He's befriended him, he's offered him some money, he's earned his trust as a Filipino, speaking the language. This guy don't know nothing, but the money's for the people back home, how could he turn it down? So Ray takes over that identity tomorrow. He gets in under that name and the people he fools don't even look close at him. He's one of the little folks who carry out the shit and scrub the toilets and wipe up the puke and wash the piss off the sidewalks each morning. Ray goes in as that guy, his ID and his name on the list gets him through our security. Nobody's looking close at faces in photos and faces on people. And he's Asian, they all look

alike to any busy cop at a checkpoint. And remember, he don't need
an escape route. He's not trying to get out, and that makes his penetration much easier. So tomorrow he steps out of the kitchen across the
street or down the block, and he's got a way-cut-down 700 with scope,
maybe just a good red dot. The package is maybe sixteen inches long,
enough to get a good shoulder brace and cheek weld, you could do it
with a hacksaw. He can see the hubbub, and when the agents come out,
out comes the rifle, there's Zarzi, he goes to target and ticks off the shot
offhand standing in one second and you've got brains all over the sidewalk. Whiskey Two-Two, mission accomplished, over and out. That's
what he's got to work with, that's what he'd do."

"Is that what you'd do?" asked a police officer.

"I'd have to find a white trash cranky old sack full of hot air and
bad breath, but it's the same principle."

"We don't have any evidence," someone said. "He could also paint
his skin black, buy a wig, and go Afro into the shoot zone, knowing
that we're hesitant to confront Afros."

"But Afro falls apart if he's confronted. One second of close examination and Afro goes away. Filipino doesn't go away, and if he's got
the right easy-to-come-by docs, he's in," another argued.

"All right," said Nick, "let's run this and see where it takes us.
Maybe nowhere. Maybe there are no Filipinos in the area and Swagger's been smoking that weird pipe again."

"Wouldn't be the first time," Swagger said, to some laughter.

Nick ordered, "Check the lists of the already vetted. See if you can
come up with any names of Filipino nationals, or immigrants. Maybe
we get an address, and if so, maybe we raid. Maybe we nab the guy
before he gets out of bed."

It took an hour. The run-through of the hundred-odd vetted
workers in the shoot zone for tomorrow indeed included four of
possible Filipino derivation, an Abated, a Batujong, a Ganaban, and
an Ulat, working at three different restaurants, an Indian, a Chinese,
and a barbecued rib house known to be popular with gays ("Boy's
Town," as it was called, was the next district north of Mount Vernon).

Calls to Immigration produced data on three of the four, who were not citizens yet. The fourth, a citizen, was a seventy-year-old sous-chef at an upscale place just marginally in the zone. He was discarded.

Immigration faxed the paperwork. Of the three, only one fit the profile. His name was Ricardo Ulat, from Mindanao originally, thirty-six years old, a dishwasher at a popular Indian restaurant just across the street and down half a block from the Zabol. He had been in the country a little over six months. But it turned out he lived at the same address in a suburban town bordering the city called Pikesville as one of the other, older immigrants. Possibly they were uncle and nephew or cousins? There were no legal problems, though the house had been raided once in 2002 in a search—futile, as it turned out—for Filipino illegals.

Pikesville wasn't in Baltimore but some other entity called "Baltimore County" with a separate police force. New phone calls, new introductions, new arrangements had to be made, but ultimately, the county police input showed no complaints against the house, no altercations or police visits or calls, no trouble. The Filipinos were very good visitors. A traffic ticket for the older Batujong, that was all. The cops put Nick and Bob and the team in touch with the commander of the county police station, responsible for Pikesville and an old hand there, and he gave them a rundown on speakerphone.

"The neighborhood used to be Jewish when Baltimore was the Jerusalem of the East Coast. Lots of big old homes, built by prosperous business owners, bankers, furriers, restaurateurs, that sort of thing, at the turn of the century through the twenties. It's now what you call a 'changing neighborhood.' It's about sixty percent black, forty percent what we'd call 'mixed ethnic.' Real estate has been depressed for a few decades as the rich people move farther out. One of the things we've seen is a kind of 'rooming house' phenomenon. A restaurant guy, who depends on cheap labor, some of it possibly illegal, will buy one of these big old arks at low cost, do absolutely nothing to fix it up, and turn it into a kind of dormitory for his low-end labor force. With some of these, you've got continuous problems that generate a lot of complaints, fights, drugs, parties, noise, trashed property, sometimes a killing, which requires a lot of police activity.

"The Filipinos, though, are different. Never a fight, never a party, no drinking hardly at all, very tidy, lawn is always mowed, no rubbish anywhere. You'd never be able to tell that 1216 Crenshaw has ten occupants, all single. These are usually rural guys; they're not from the big, crazy cities like Manila or Cebu, they're not sophisticated and criminally inclined. What they do, they get the visa, they sign up with an employer, a restaurant guy who needs the cheap labor, and they come over here for seven years. It's pretty awful, living four to a room in a country whose language they don't speak and whose culture they don't even get. But they work hard, live very simply, and manage to send home a pile of money. They're really helping out their families. After the seven, very few of them jump and go illegal; they go back, having done their duty, and another family member comes over. So what you've got at 1216 is just that, a houseful of very quiet, hardworking guys without English skills at any level who just want to go home."

Nick said, "Captain, we may want to raid tomorrow morning at dawn. These guys work late, and our best bet to nab all of them is early morning. I've got people at the federal level trying to get a search warrant, I may have to bring Immigration in, but I'm wondering if you'd provide perimeter security for our team, and if we need it, I'm hoping you could make a phone call to a local prosecutor on our behalf, and we'd go in under your flag. It's not a hard bust, a kick-ass raid. I don't want to disturb or harass these guys, but I need to contain them totally, and run a careful search for a possible terrorist suspect of Filipino heritage. This seems like our best possibility for apprehending him, if he's there."

"Sure," said the commander. "Happy to."

"I'm going to give you over to Special Agent Matthews," Nick said, "for further coordination and logistical requirements."

He handed the phone off.

"Okay," he said, "Swagger and I are going to drive out there discreetly and take a look. You guys get on with the planning; again, let me emphasize, this is about containment. I don't want any battering rams or flash-bangs, I don't want any SWAT monkey suits or MP5s and Ninja Commando Force 9 bullshit. I want a lot of people in civilian clothes, wearing comfortable shoes and FBI raid jackets, I want to flood that zone, I want it all to go smooth and quiet and I don't want any of these subjects to have cause to complain of police harassment, is that clear?"

B ob and Nick sat in Nick's government-issue Crown Victoria, across the street and four houses down from the big dwelling at 1216, which just sat there in Gothic splendor, a many-turreted old beast of a house that had to have been built by a jeweler or a dry-cleaning magnate of the century before. Trees overhung the streets, and the houses, all of them big and most of them dark, were smothered in landscaping—though it was shabby and overgrown, as the original owners, with their American dream of success, had long since moved on, and the inheritors didn't pay as much attention to the details. It was actually only a few minutes' drive from the FBI office via a one-exit trek on the beltway. But Bob didn't like sitting there.

"I don't advise parking here."

"I want to see if there are any surprises. We have the house plan, we have satellite photos from National Reconnaissance satellites, but I want to make sure no doors or windows are boarded up, or there are any new entrances. Relax. It's dark."

Nick was examining the property through his own night vision binoculars, and taking notes.

"This guy has radar for aggression," said Bob. "That's how he's stayed alive so long. If he's in the house, he'll note that we pulled up and nobody left the car. Maybe he's got binocs on us right now."

"Okay, okay," said Nick, "almost done."

"Suppose one of 'em comes home about now and sees the two white guys in the big black sedan spying and tells the others."

"I hear you, I hear you," said Nick. "All right, I'm going to pull out, pass the house, turn right on Dickens, and you run a check through these from that side. I'll go slow."

"Don't go slow," said Bob. "He'll notice if you go slow. He notices shit like that. He's a sniper."

"You mentioned 'radar for aggression.' You've got it too, I know. Some buried ESP synapse left over from reptile days. All you tactical people have it. Maybe that's why you become tactical people. But do you feel anything now? You seem jumpy and I've never seen you jumpy."

"I'm worried that this ain't right. It's a big gamble."

"It's smaller than it seems," Nick said. "If he's here, ball game over, we win the Oscar, our class gets the Bible. If he's not, so what? It's not as if we're overcommitting to this. I'm not taking resources that would otherwise be deployed as countersnipers tomorrow. The same number of guys will be on the street. What I'm doing, frankly, is a little management-level ass covering, that's all. I have to work it hard so no one sitting on the fifth floor with four martinis in him says, 'Oh, if only you'd done *that*.'"

Bob was quiet as Nick pulled out. The car glided down the street, took the right, and Bob got a good ambient-light view of the southern and the western, that is, the right side and the rear of 1216, seeing nothing out of the usual, no movement, nothing but a big old house dozing in the night, probably looking better because its shabbiness was veiled by the darkness.

"Okay," Nick said as the car pulled away, "now tell me why you're *really* jumpy. What came up on the Swagger aggression radar?"

"Ahh," said Bob, "you FBI guys, you don't miss a damned trick, do you?"

"I'm Dick Tracy, didn't you see my picture on the lunch box in the cabinet?"

"Well, it ain't nothing," said Bob. "It's just . . . something."

"Nothing, but something. Yeah, I get it. That's perfectly clear."

"Don't know what. Like a hair tickling me somewhere, like somewhere someone's watching me. Maybe it's because I'm so goddamned tired and a little over a week ago I got whacked in the head by a flying desk. I got nothing I can point at and say, now, yessiree, that's it, that's the thing. It's just an oozy feeling I used to get in the bush when bad hombres moved in. I'd say it's my imagination, except I don't got no imagination."

"You need some rest."

He got some rest, three hours' worth, on the SAIC's couch. He was awake before they came for him, and stepped into general chaos. He followed the swell of personnel down the hall to the elevator, down that to the entrance to the parking lot where, as if lit for the movies and oh so SWAT-team dramatic, the raid was staging. Special agents buckled on body armor, then pulled raid jackets with FBI emblazoned in huge yellow letters across the back. Most wore jeans, athletic shoes or assault boots, carried their Glocks in cowboy-cool tactical rigs that held them to midthigh, below the extension of the body armor beneath the waist. Everyone had a radio and the air was alive with the crackle of static as call signs and nets were checked. Nick talked earnestly to Matthews, his raid commander, and when it seemed everybody was done being dramatic, Matthews turned, gave the whirlybird rotation with his fingers, meaning "Guns up," and everybody piled into the six SUVs.

Matthews led, followed by the five SUVs, and last came Bob and Nick in Nick's sedan. No need for flashing lights at this time of morning, as Beltway traffic was nonexistent. To the east, over downtown, just the tiniest glaze of a pinkish blur colored the sky. The parade roared its one-exit hop, got off on Reisterstown Road, and turned inward toward the city. Now the red-blue dance of the flashing lights began, as the few motorists on Reisterstown yielded to the federal convoy as it blazed through the three stoplights, and into what comprised "center-city" Pikesville, and at the corner of Reisterstown and Crenshaw turned the hard right.

Bob could hear the radio chatter between the feds and the on-scene county police locals.

"Baker-Six-five, this is Twelve-Oscar, we are inbound."

"Roger, Twelve-Oscar."

"Be there in a minute or so."

"We are set to cover your perimeter, Twelve-Oscar. Area is cordoned off."

"Very good and appreciated, Baker-Six-five."

Dramatic spurts of color splashed against the trees and houses as the convoy, lights flashing, passed down the corridor of old big houses that was Crenshaw, and came at last to the corner house, 1216, where they halted, then turned spotlights inward to illuminate every turret and gable of the old place. Bob watched as the raid theater continued.

The men piled out, no long guns among them, but hands resting comfortably on or near their holstered Glocks, and went to assigned doors and windows, making egress impossible. That took a minute, as the federal team was well trained.

"One, in position."

"Two, I'm set."

"Three? Three, where are you?"

"Sorry, Command, my radio switched off as I was pulling it from the holster. I am in position."

"Four, I'm ready too."

"Okay, let's open her up."

With that, Matthews, carrying a radio unit but no sidearm and two other agents with drawn pistols but nothing exotic, walked swiftly up the front walk, and pounded.

And pounded.

And pounded.

"Oh, shit," said Nick. "I wonder what's wrong."

Matthews tried the door. It opened to his turn of the knob.

He disappeared inside and came out in a few minutes. He yelled something to the other men, who started to put away their pistols and file into the house. Then Matthews walked straight to Nick. His face was grave.

"I don't like the looks of this one fucking bit," said Nick.

BALTIMORE, MARYLAND

S ee," explained Crackers the Clown, "I'm just not that into this. I'm an operator, a rock star, an action-Jackson guy. I blow shit up and kill people. I learned from the best."

"You learned from *Soldier of Fortune* magazine," said Mick.

"Mick, no, I wasn't SEAL or DELTA but I was forces, just like you. And I did some shit for an outfit I can't talk about."

"The Boy Scouts of America," said Tony Z. "He got his merit badge in Advanced Paintball."

Laughter.

"Hey, paintball's *tough*. Tougher than Airsoft!"

More laughter. The three of them sat in their by now rather-well-lived-in Explorer. Ahead, the only large building in this zone of cottage industry and light manufacturing, the one whose three floors comprised the Baltimore FBI office, loomed against the sky. As it was somewhat creamy in complexion, though undistinguished architecturally, it was easily visible and its burning lights made it all the simpler to mark.

"I don't like this shit either," said Mick. "I don't like sitting on my ass like some vice cop outside a Korean massage parlor, waiting for a politician to show up. Give me a nice torture interrogation or a shot at laser-designating a Sadr militia warehouse for the Mavericks, that's my preference. I also really like that big gun and watching them toss when you knock them off at a mile."

"That's so cool," said Tony Z. "I like that part too."

"But we are stuck on this sucker until we make it go away," said Crackers.

"I think he has a morale crisis," said Z. "I'd make an appointment with him for the chaplain."

"My morale improves with pussy. Any suggestions?"

"We kill this guy, and go someplace with a lot of pussy."

"You have muscles, so you get chicks who give it out easy," said Crackers.

"Plus, you're a psychopath, a great advantage in fucking chicks. Me, I'm a rather nice guy and I always empathize with them. They like me. They don't want to suck my cock, they want to tell me about their mothers. I have to go someplace special."

"By 'special' he means 'whorehouse.'"

"Can I help it if I'm not sexually competitive?" said Crackers. "I thought going forces would get me laid more, but so far it hasn't panned out that way."

"I thought that's why you got married."

"Funny, that hasn't panned out sex-wise either."

They laughed.

"Okay," said Tony Z, his eyes drawn to the BlackBerry in his hands, "got movement."

Crackers made a doodley sound along the lines of the 7th Cavalry's famous "charge" bugle call. All three men tried to shake off the dreariness that had turned them to putty over the last few hours.

Mick, behind the wheel, started the SUV and nudged it out into the road. He did not turn on the lights.

Up ahead, advanced by its own blazing headlights, a sedan exited the FBI parking lot and turned right, then left, toward the close-by beltway entrance.

"He's in that car," said Tony. "I have him clear."

"Have they sent him out to get doughnuts, I wonder," said Crackers.

"Not likely," said Mick.

They had worked the following technique out well, having learned to keep Swagger in any car within a mile and a half, but not within a mile. Maybe a little closer during daylight, but now, late at night, Mick knew to keep his distance. Only when he verified that Swagger's car had hit the beltway did he go to his own headlights and approach the giant roadway superstructure at a modest pace. He went up the ramp, merged into a very thin traffic stream, and progressed at just under fifty as the faster vehicles buzzed by on his left.

"One exit," said Z. "Well, two if you count 795 West, but one actual city exit. Reisterstown Road."

Mick followed the directions, not really seeing the ratty neighborhood into which the ramp to Reisterstown Road deposited him but rather locked hard into the hunt.

"He's turning right, third street past Old Court."

They counted too. Mick doused his lights before the turn so that a psychic voodoo sniper mojo motherfucker like Swagger wouldn't pick up on the sudden disappearance of light behind him, found Crenshaw, and turned. He followed the roadway through big, softly quiet houses, and eased to the curb two blocks behind the car in which Bob and whoever had parked.

"Now what the fuck is this?" Crackers asked.

"Maybe it's your whorehouse. Maybe the great Bob Lee Swagger has a bone on, and he's come down here to Chinatown to get it off. Clarifies the thinking."

"I'll take sloppy seconds, no problem," said Crackers. He didn't mean it as a joke.

"Okay," said Mick, "Crackers, on the night vision, you stay low, you move ahead, you find solid cover, I'm guessing between cars, you set up and you keep them in surveillance."

"Yo," said Crackers, "action."

He slipped out.

Mick watched the man, one of those scrawny, thin types with a lot of surprising strength in his narrow arms, slip down the road, low, under the cover of parked cars. A few minutes passed.

"Okay," came the call over the radio, "I got him in the car, they're just eyeballing this big corner house."

"Can you get me an address?"

"Ah, let's see, let's see, yeah, 1216, 1216 Crenshaw."

"What is it?"

"Big dark house, that's all."

"Great. Otherwise . . . ?"

"They're eyeballing, they're talking, that's all."

"Okay, hold tight."

Mick picked up the satellite phone, sent the call out.

"This better be good, Bogier," said a groggily irritated MacGyver.

"Don't know why, but Swagger and an FBI guy are now parked outside a house in a town called, ah, Pikesville. Address is 1216 Crenshaw. But there's no team here, it's not a raid or even a real recon. They're just, you know, studying on it."

"Crenshaw, 1216. Okay, hang tight."

"This has just developed, I don't know how long they'll be here."

"I will get back as fast as the system allows," said MacGyver, somewhat annoyed.

Mick sat back, thinking.

Has he found Cruz? Is Cruz in the house? Why would they be here? But if he's here, why don't they have a raid team? Why aren't they pouring in?

"Whoa, now they're pulling out. Starting up, heading out."

"What do we do?" Tony asked.

"Fuck if I know," said Mick. His head ached. He hadn't been to the gym in a week. Z and Crackers were driving him nuts. He could feel his body melting along with his mind. He wanted it over. This was the worst shit. He didn't sign up for this cop shit. He was Special Forces, cross-trained in sniper and demolitions, plus he knew a good bit about radio. He had worked all over the world and here he was sitting in—

"Miiiiccccckkkk," said Tony, slowly.

"Yeah?"

"Don't jerk, don't move fast, but I got a guy across the street, walking toward the house. Or maybe to another house. But he's an Asian guy, I think, thin, strong, looks sniper to me."

"Jesus Christ," said Mick, understanding in a flash why the feds hadn't raided.

They didn't know if he was in there either. And if he wasn't but might be, and they raided now, they'd blow that deal. So they'd hit the place at dawn, figuring the stragglers might come into the house all night, whatever it was. The image of drunken college kids, from any of the six or so schools he'd been kicked out of, came to his mind. From there the connection was easy to Alabama, the big one. Number one recruit, best high school linebacker in history. Great six games, then Auburn, a legendary game, nine solo tackles. Got drunk. Mary Christian DeLaux, the only girl he'd ever loved. The yellow Corvette from Mr. Bevington, the Chevy dealer. Bevy's Chevys, biggest outlet in town. How 'bout a 'Vette, Rhett? The crash. He tried to push it away. He thought it was gone. But it wasn't. The word "dormitory" flashed to him from some file deep in his cerebellum.

He turned his head just a quarter of a degree, and a man, thirty-five feet away, directly across the street, walking forward briskly, came into view. In profile he was Asian with a thick bush of stiff hair, very muscular, maybe a little tall, in jeans and a sweatshirt. He gave no sign of noting two men sitting in an SUV across the street; he was intent on his progress, just churning ahead.

But, goddamn, Mick hadn't gotten a good look at the face.

He picked up the radio unit.

"Guy coming, your five o'clock, on sidewalk, I need you to get a good visual on his face with night vision, but don't give your position up. Move real slow."

"Got it," said Crackers.

They watched. The walker passed the end of the row of cars in the street, diverted across the lawn, opened the unlocked door of 1216, and disappeared. No light came on, he didn't go to the kitchen for a beer, or kibbitz with his frat brothers in the TV room. There was no TV room, no frat brothers, just darkness.

Crackers appeared in his car window.

"You get him?"

"Yeah. Asian, thirties, muscular, tall, thick hair."

"Could he be forties? Cruz is forty-two."

"Hey, I'm no expert. They don't age like we do. He could be thirty, he could be sixty."

Mick rooted around, came up with a briefcase, pulled it open, and pulled out a xerox of a photo of a marine sergeant in dress blues in a formal promotion shot. But the duplication had eroded its subtleties and it flowed weirdly toward the generic.

"That him?"

"Hell, Mick," said Crackers. "It could be. I couldn't say for sure."

"God, I wish I'd hear from that motherfucker MacGyver. Where is he when you need him? Look again, goddamnit, tell me it's him."

Crackers examined the flimsy photo first in the dark, then in a bright cone of illumination from his SureFire. "Mick, maybe. I suppose. You know, some of them have distinctive faces, round, square, fierce, dumb, fat, thin, whatever. This guy looks like all of 'em, with some white thrown in."

"Mick, let's roust 'em," said Tony Z. "Do it fast. If he's there, we pop him, we leave. They won't know what hit them. The fucking door isn't even locked."

"That'll never work," said Crackers. "We don't know how many there are, how do we control 'em, we don't have cuffs or blindfolds, we don't have balaclavas, we leave prints, man, that is all fucked up. Plus, even if we have him full frontal in the flashlight, how can we be sure it's him? We just won't know."

"Okay, junior," said Tony, too intensely, "what's your bright idea?"

"Sit, wait, and see."

"Negative," said Mick. "The feds may raid at any second, and when that happens, if he's there, we have failed, we are screwed, all hell breaks loose."

Both the team boys were silent.

"I don't like it either," said Mick. "But I'm not here because I like it and neither are you. This is what we do. The hard thing. For the right reasons. It sucks, but there you have it. I am open to suggestions for the next five seconds."

Silence.

"Look at it this way," said Mick. "You call in artillery, you get a coordinate wrong, a shell lands in a village. Too bad. Our war, their village. You don't feel good about it, but that's the price of doing business. Collateral is to be expected. We've all seen it."

"Mick, I don't know if I can do it," said Tony Z.

"Sure you can," said Mick. "You're a cowboy. You're a trooper. You're a one hundred percent life-taking, throat-slitting, mother-fucking rockin', rollin' operator, baddest of the bad, meanest of the mean. You're Ming the Merciless, got it? How 'bout you, laughing boy? I know you're in."

"I don't like it either, Mick."

"It ain't about liking," said Mick. "It's about doing. Give me the fucking night vision. I'm in the lead, I'm on the gun."

UNIDENTIFIED CONTRACTOR TEAM

Nobody liked it. It wasn't a thing a soldier would ever brag about. It involved no heroics at all, just suppressed pistols. Mick did all the killing. They slipped into the house, Crackers in the lead with the night vision monocular. Mick just behind, with an untraceable M9 Beretta and a Gemtech suppressor. No kicking in doors, no shouting, nothing. They crept to the first floor and began to edge down the hallway, coming to a bedroom. Crackers pushed the door in, Tony Z, also with a suppressed M9, covered the six o'clock. Mick stepped in, target acquired, and fired.

One or two stirred when Mick hit them. The impacts puffed up little supertime geysers of fabric debris, maybe some blood misting into spray in the force of the considerable subsonic velocity. Mick shot for midbody. Nobody screamed. There were no scenes. Room to room to room. Crackers cupped his hand right at the breech of the weapon, so that each ejected casing struck his palm and was deflected downward. After the shooting in that chamber was finished, he scooped them all up. He also counted rounds. And he handed Mick a new mag. Room to room, floor to floor. The smell of men living together, of showers used a lot, of cigarette smoke. The sound of the heavy breathing in sleep.

One man looked up and Mick shot him in the face. He got to see the details, though not in Technicolor but in the muted tones of ambient light, by which the blood that coursed voluminously from the hole in the cheekbone was dead black.

·　　·　　·

It didn't take long.

"You get 'em all?" Mick asked.

"You fired twenty-two times. I have twenty-two shell casings," said Crackers.

"Okay, let's extract."

They left the house and walked to the car. Across the street, a smear of dawn was beginning to ooze across the sky. The air outside smelled fresh and clean.

"You drive," Mick told Crackers.

"Got it, boss."

"I feel like shit," said Tony Z.

"Guess what, nobody cares what you feel like," said Mick. "You did your job. That's the important thing."

CRIME SCENE INVESTIGATION

M ost of the drama was over, though forensic technicians from both the Bureau and the Maryland State Police were still working inside the house. The bodies, ID'd and photographed in situ, had been moved to the morgue. Nick had released most of his team to change, chill, and then move to duty stations in Mount Vernon for that 2 P.M. to 5 P.M. ordeal. The convoy from DC into Baltimore was about to leave, but its trek from one city to the other was in Secret Service's bailiwick, so Nick hadn't yet begun to focus on the real business of the day.

He leaned against his sedan fender, across the street from 1216, numbly watching the action at the big house, whose lawn was jammed with law enforcement vehicles and clots of Baltimore county detectives smoking, joking, joshing as they broke it down. Meanwhile everything seemed draped with yellow crime scene tape, like a Christmas celebration. The press was cordoned off down the block and there was more activity there, with all the on-the-scene standups going on, than here.

Next to him, Swagger also leaned, a dull look on his face. He had the thousand-yard stare of the man who'd seen too much.

An agent came up to Nick.

"The last ID came through," he said.

"And?"

"Dionysus Agbuya, thirty-nine, born in Samar, the Philippines. Employed at Johnny Yang's Chinese Delight in Columbia, dishwasher, never missed a day of work. That's it."

"No Ray Cruz?"

"Not on the prelims. Maybe there's a fake ID in there, but I don't think so, Nick. One guy maybe looks—looked—a little like him. Maybe they made that one and thought they had a go."

"Or maybe one of them hadn't paid off the Manila syndicate that got him into the country. And this was a message it was sending to its other clients. You pay us first, then your family."

"Maybe, Nick."

"Thanks, Charlie. Didn't mean to snap."

"It's okay, Nick. It's been a long night for all of us."

Nick took a sip of coffee, found it had cooled beyond the drinkable stage, and flung it out on the pavement.

Swagger said, "This is all wrong."

"Murder is always wrong."

"No, I mean the way this is happening. There's a leak. In your outfit, in Susan's, somewhere in the Bureau. These assholes keep showing up on us."

"We don't know that. It looks that way, but we don't *know* it."

"Come on, Nick. Everywhere I go, they're there, either ahead or a little after. They're pros. Barrett .50s, suppressed 9s, someone even has the thought to collect the brass."

"Maybe they were using revolvers."

"You can't suppress a revolver. All the shooting, no noise complaints, had to be suppressed fire. And you wouldn't do a job like this if you had to fumble through revolver reloads in the dark. This was a kill team. They'd done it before, they knew what they were doing, and they were trying to put down Ray Cruz. They were the same boys who blew up the Steel Brigade Armory offices in Danielstown, South Carolina. And then as now they had a fucking tip-off. We weren't followed, not through dark city streets at night with no other traffic on the road. We'd have seen it, just as I'd have seen it on dark country roads ten days ago."

"It's fabulous stuff, just what I've come to expect from you. You're operating on a level way beyond what I've got. That's your job. But I have to be practical and responsible. That's my job. We have to collect, catalog, analyze evidence before we proceed to conclusions. We picked up some forensic markers. When the shooter slid through one of the doors, he brushed it with his head, left sweat traces. We'll run that, and then, maybe—"

"There's only one conclusion. Well, two. You have a leak. And I'm an asshole for coming up with some bullshit thing that got nine guys killed for absolutely nothing."

"You're an asshole because that's your nature. You can't help that. All you hard macho door kickers and life takers are assholes. Your thinking was A-one, solid, deductive, top-of-the-line law enforcement creativity. I told you, you have the gift. Nothing wrong with it. Don't hold it against yourself. As for the 'leak' stuff, the time element argues against it. We hadn't even heard of this house until eight o'clock last night. The requests for subpoenas, the reports to higher headquarters, all that stuff didn't go out until much later. If something did get out or if there was a mole, how'd the other team put it together so fast? Man, that would be footwork."

"The team is here, all set, with all the tools of the trade. All they needed was an address."

"I say again, not likely. Nobody's that good. They had to follow us, know we'd left—"

"They couldn't have followed us. We'd have seen them."

"You yourself 'felt' something last night. You have the operator's weird nerve system that's unusually tuned to aggression. They had to follow us."

"Okay, then. Satellite. That's the only way. If it's satellite, then it's CIA. CIA wants Ray Cruz dead before he tells his story and a bunch of people are assigned to look into it. CIA wants Ibrahim Zarzi to be the next president of Afghanistan, no questions asked, forget all that 'Beheader' stuff. He's our man in Kabul. And CIA will want to protect him, even if it means targeting our own guy."

Nick ceased being Nick. Instead, he became an assistant director of the FBI, in full dignity and severity, posture improved, face drawn into upper-Bureau solemnity.

"I am not making accusations against the CIA," he said in policy-announcement voice, "until we have something to go on other than your theories. Going against the CIA means opening a big goddamn can of worms, and once the worms are out, you may never get them back in. We have to see where the evidence takes us. There aren't any shortcuts."

He looked at his watch and the old Nick came back.

"Come on, cowboy guy. We're due on station downtown. In all this terrible bullshit, we're forgetting: Ray Cruz is still out there."

UNIDENTIFIED CONTRACTOR TEAM
JUST OUTSIDE THE SHOOT ZONE
THE 900 BLOCK OF MARYLAND AVENUE
MOUNT VERNON DISTRICT
BALTIMORE, MARYLAND
1650 HOURS

The boys had the blahs. They sat grumpily, without talking. Where was the banter, the wit, the snappy retorts, the fabulous esprit de corps of Special Forces operators? Wherever it was, it wasn't here today.

Mick was in the off-driver's seat, his big foot on the dashboard as he sat back against the seat. Man, he could use some shut-eye himself. This was, what, hour number forty-eight without sleep?

Crackers, in the backseat, said, "I am about to pass out."

"If you do, I will kick your ass all the way to Washington. I need you on game, fully alert, concentrated. We don't know what breaks next."

"Easy for Superman to say. Superman has all the answers. Superman has no weaknesses, flaws, human foibles, neurotic conditions. But I am not Superman. I am Mere Mortal. And Mere Mortal needs to go to bed, sleep late, read the Sunday papers."

"Drink some more coffee," said Tony Z behind the wheel. The car was parked near a church with a red door and a steeple, one block west of Charles, that is, one block away from all the hubbub of the fabulous Ibrahim Zarzi's visit to his brother's restaurant, the Zabol, on Charles Street. From where they were—a block over, but with a parking lot's emptiness granting a clear view of the shoot area—they could see the convoy of Secret Service Explorers parked in the street's left lane, their blue-red gumball flashers spitting out blink-fast blasts of light, their windows darkened to hide the gunned-up agents just inside. Meanwhile the street was cordoned off by Baltimore cops;

Secret Service, FBI, and news aviation orbited noisily in the ether a few thousand feet up, cops and Bureau boys in raid jackets with big FBI letters, snail cords leading to their ear units, and tactical holsters pinioned to midthigh were up and down the street, looking this way and that.

"The coffee lost its charm sometime yesterday. Anyway, he'll never get in," said Crackers. "If he did, he'd never get out. Which means he'd never go in in the first place. So I say we hit a motel and crash for a thousand or so hours."

"Swagger's still on the case, so we're on the case," said Mick.

He held the BlackBerry, and on its screen, with the map of Mount Vernon glowing as its template, a pulsing light that signified Swagger's transponder responding to interrogative requests from satellite, blinked away brightly. The guy was less than a quarter mile away.

"He's another Superman," said Crackers.

They were low because the victim list from last night's episode had just been released. Nine names, none of them being Ray Cruz's. Nine guys taken out, no home run. A complete waste of energy and lives. Not a good day in professional-killer land.

Tony flashed his big tactical Suunto and read the time.

"It's almost five," he said. "This party's breaking up. Where do we go?"

"We'll stay with Swagger. When he beds down, we'll bed down. He's still our best—"

The satellite phone buzzed.

"Oh shit," said Mick. "Now this guy is going to crap all over me for ten minutes. Man, when this is over, I would like to . . ." And he trailed off as he wearily hoisted the heavy communication device.

"Talk to me," he said.

"Genius Bogier. You've heard, I assume. You missed him again."

"Yeah."

"You killed nine men who had nothing to do with anything."

"No kids, no women though," said Mick. "No suffering. It's not like we tortured them."

"How reassuring. What a humanitarian you are. Now tell me your thought process."

Bogier went through the whole thing.

He lamely finished up with, "Sometimes you get the breaks, sometimes you don't. Last night, we didn't."

"A massacre. No one authorized you to massacre anybody. When this is over, I am getting you out of the country ASAP and I don't want you back for twenty-five years."

"Hey, there's no forensics on us. No witnesses. The pistol's in a river. No DNA, no hair samples, no footprints. We wore rubber gloves. We were clean, we were professional. Nothing leads to us from our end. Your end I don't know about."

"There was some DNA and I hope yours isn't on file somewhere."

"It isn't."

"Memo: you always leave DNA. *Always.* Got it? My end is secure, don't you worry about it. What's the sitrep now?"

"We are off the shoot zone, but still on Swagger, who's put himself about a hundred feet north of the restaurant. He's just another street pair of eyes, that's all. But I don't think Cruz is going to show because this place is flooded. He couldn't get in, he couldn't get out. We're just waiting. When Swagger goes off duty, we need to crash. We're on our third day without sleep, which isn't helping matters any."

"Good idea. And here's a little something to improve your morale. Your decision? To hit those people. It was the right decision. It was a good risk. I don't think it cost us anything. I'm sorry about the collateral too, but it's a tough-luck world. As I say, after action, you are so gone no one will ever know you existed."

"We want a beach, a gym, lots of chicks and dope, a really profoundly corrupt law enforcement establishment, and indoor plumbing."

"You want *Gilligan's Island* with porn stars. Really an original fantasy. I can't guarantee the plumbing. You stay on Swagger, and we all believe he will lead you to—"

"Oh fuck," interrupted Mick. "I hear shooting!"

THE SHOOT ZONE

Getting him in was a bitch. Getting him out would be a bitch and a half because it took place after everyone had been standing around collecting blood in their feet for three grim hours.

Swagger felt like a ceremonial soldier at some state funeral for a distinguished old general. He stood, not at attention but in the uniform of the day—FBI raid jacket over shirt and tie, black cargo pants bloused into black tactical boots, a radio unit in his hand wired to his ear, along a street, doing nothing but yawning and watching. The only difference between him and the many other boys and girls thereabouts was the absence of a Glock .40 strapped to his thigh in a Nigel Ninja tac holster.

His sniper eyes darted about, looking for . . . well, what? A straight line where there shouldn't be one? No, that bromide didn't work in a city full of straight lines. The glint of sun off a lens? Cruz was too advanced for that. A figure on a skyline? A chopper would catch a rooftop shooter before any ground Joe would make the ID. A speeding black 1937 Cadillac with a Cutts compensator on a Colt tommy gun muzzle sticking out the back window? That made as much sense as anything else. He just watched, waited, looked around, eyes lighting on nothing, more or less committed to the single idea of movement, because if Ray Cruz moved, he'd move fast, and that might be the only way you could spot him, and then only if you happened to be looking at the small section of the universe through which he moved at the precise moment. But try as he could, he could not spot an uncovered area, that is, an area not already on someone's regularly assigned observation schedule.

"Boring, huh?" said Nick, standing next to him.

"Not fun," he said.

"I could use some sleep myself. I'm hoping to let everyone go when this guy—"

"BREAK-BREAK, ALL STATIONS, COMING OUT, COMING OUT!"

The Secret Service incident commander from inside the restaurant alerted all that the moment of maximum risk was about to occur, as the principal was about to move to the limo and would be on the street and vulnerable for a few seconds. If Ray was here, this was when he would act, unless he had an RPG capable of blowing through armored limo glass, unlikely.

Along the street, all the drifting watchers tightened up, reasserted control over their dozing nervous systems, put hands on pistols, blinked crud from eyes, went to balls of feet for a few minutes of maximum concentration. Above, the choppers came down a few hundred feet, their rotor wash stirring up flecks of grit from the rooftops they were putting the binocs to, all the Secret Service sniper teams in various designated windows locking hands to comb, cheeks to stock, eyes to scope for serious examination of their shooting areas.

Bob sensed, rather than saw, the flurry of motion as Zarzi, his brother, two children, and about ten Secret Service agents and bodyguards spilled from the restaurant in a sloppy formation, the two brothers chatting animatedly, as if none of this security drama were surrounding them. Ibrahim, of course, had to show off. He dawdled in plain sight, holding the hands of two of the younger children, laughing at old memories of childhood with his brother Asa. He refused to move, out of some polo athlete's macho instinct by which he dared the universe to destroy him if it had the nerve, while around him the Secret Service people ground molars to powder, looked feverishly this way and that for signs of movement or action, saw only the pedestrian and the banal, the expected, the normal, the dreary: a homeless man far down one block, a flock of pigeons on the park lawn, a hip-looking couple across the street, a garbage truck pulling out of an alley in the next block, a cab on a cross street, nothing to—

Bob thought: *Wrong. Something wrong. What is wrong with this picture? What is—*

Jesus Christ, in thoughts so fast they defied the words that tried to catch up with them, *what the fuck is that garbage truck doing there?*

BACK ALLEY

Romy Dawkins lifted the can to hoist it into 144's dumper bin, and that's when he saw him.

"Hey," he called to Larry and Antwan, "hey, there's a guy here."

The man lay behind the row of cans, facedown, evidently passed out or dead.

Antwan came over, and then Larry climbed down from the cab. As crew supervisor and driver of the big truck, this was not welcome news. They still had half the route to go, there was some big traffic tie-up in the blocks ahead, and now they had to deal with a drunk.

"Fuck," he said. "Kick 'im, see if it gets him up."

Antwan drove a heavy boot into the figure, who groaned, stirred, then settled back.

"He's out, boss," said Antwan.

"Okay," said Larry, "nothing we can do. I'll call the cops, and we go on. We got a route to finish."

"He could—"

"Let the cops worry about it," said Larry. "It's their job."

At that point, the collapsed man rolled over. He held a dark automatic pistol in one hand.

"Okay," he said, "I will hurt you if I have to, but that's not the point. You do what I say, you get out clean. You fight me, you go home in a box."

He was sort of Asian, semi-Asian you might say, with no accent whatsoever, very hard, sharp dark eyes and a demeanor that suggested he meant what he said. He connected with a lot of kung fu and Hong Kong shoot-'em-ups most of the trashmen had seen on DVD. He looked like Chow Yun-Fat in *The Killer,* only for real and really pissed off.

"You guys, you haulers, you drop to your knees, fast, come on, *fast!* You, driver, assume the position against the fender."

All obeyed.

"Never heard of no garbage truck robbery before," said Antwan. "You must be one dumb motherfucker you think you gettin' any change off us."

"Just chill, trashman," said the Chinaman.

He knelt and deftly looped a set of flex-cuffs—high-strength, plastic, disposable handcuffs—around each set of big wrists. With a yank, he tightened both of them.

"Ouch," said Romy. "Too fucking tight."

"You wanna be tied up or dead, big guy? Okay, get over here," he said, gesturing with the pistol. He led the three of them to the rear of the truck.

"You two, you climb into the scoop, you lay flat, you don't breathe, you don't shout, you don't yell, nothing. You give me up and before I go, I'll take you down. Don't disappoint me, don't disappoint your widows and orphans."

Larry the driver helped the bound trashmen into the scoop, which was big enough to conceal the two.

"Don't fall in love and come out of this engaged," said the gunman.

"Motherfucker," said Antwan.

"Throw some shit on them, Larry."

Larry lifted a can and shook its contents over the two bodies.

"Larry, man, that's *rank,* goddamnit," Antwan protested.

"Okay, Larry, into the truck. You're going to turn left, hit St. Paul, go right, pass beyond Eager and Read, and turn right in the alley before Madison."

"Man, they got all that blocked off."

"Not for this crate they don't. And if a cop stops you, I know you can talk your way by him."

Larry got into the truck cab, while the gunman, keeping him covered, moved around, came in the other door, and settled low in the well under the dashboard.

"Chinaman," said Larry, "this is all fucked up. This is going to cost me my job."

"You tell 'em I had you at gunpoint and, as a matter of fact, I do have you at gunpoint. You do what I say. This isn't about you. You're just a little part of it."

Larry threw the big truck in gear, ground down the alleyway to his cross street, turned left, then right at St. Paul.

"You're just a garbageman doing your job. Keep your face still. I can read it like a paperback and you don't want to get hurt over nothing that concerns you. Believe me, this is not worth dying for unless you lost a son in Afghanistan."

At the alleyway, Larry turned right, but halted at a policeman's signal.

"Closed down, big guy," the officer said. "Some security thing a block over."

"Officer, I am so behind schedule. I ain't going through, but I got to get in the alley, collect, then I'm backing out and getting on with my route. This traffic done messed me up bad, bro."

"It's not my problem," said the cop.

"Five minutes," said Larry. "No shit, then I'm out of here."

The cop shook his head, seeing a conundrum that could only be solved by mercy. "Don't nose out onto Charles," he said. "You get yourself and me in big bad trouble."

"Got it, Officer."

Larry geared the big truck into motion, and it lurched, then began to creep forward over the cobblestones, between the looming profiles of old mansions turned into apartment houses, whose perspectives dampened the sunlight away.

"How far?" said Larry.

"Right to the edge of Charles Street. But don't go out. Not yet."

Larry eased forward a bit.

"Now what?"

"We wait."

Helicopters gnashed overhead, their black shapes scooting across canyons between the buildings, and Larry, looking out, could see figures of policemen on roofs.

"What you waiting for?" Larry said.

"When the action starts, the birds will descend. As they descend, their pilots will be changing the pitch of the rotors. I'll hear it. Then you roll this crate out another five feet, turn it off and put your hands through the wheel, and I'll cuff you. You fuck me by gunning into the street, I will kill you and you would be dying for nothing on this earth that can be weighed or counted, you hear?"

"I hear you, man. Ain't dying today, no way."

"That's the spirit."

"Man, them guys got a hell of a lot more guns than you, Chinaman."

"Can't be helped," said the gunman.

"You gonna get so fucked up."

"Wouldn't be the first time," said the gunman, and then even Larry heard the helicopter engines begin to alter the speed at which they churned out their message of fuel consumption, exhaust, and brute energy.

"Go, goddamnit," said the Chinaman.

Larry eased out till his cab cleared the edge of the building. About two hundred yards to the right, he could see a convoy of black Explorers, blue-red light flashes blinking out from their interiors, before and aft a great black Lincoln limousine. A gaggle of people seemed to be emerging from the restaurant.

"Wrists," said the Chinaman.

Larry put one wrist through the wheel and the other around it, felt the loop go over one, then the other, then yank tight as the Chinaman pulled hard on the flex-cuff strap that locked in place, even against the power of his strong arms.

Larry watched as the man shifted in the seat, reached under the old overcoat he had on, and rotated out what appeared to be a toy gun with a thick, short barrel. It had a telescope too, and appeared to be cinched somehow to the shoulder under the coat.

"You a fucking terrorist?" he asked.

"Not quite. Now shut up."

Carefully the Chinaman braced himself, bringing his right leg up, crossing it and forcing it under the left leg, locking it tight, at the same time locking himself against the seat back. Larry understood that he was tightening himself up for a shot.

Holding the rifle in his right hand, he rolled down the window just halfway.

Quickly the rifle came up and Larry understood that he was in the presence of some kind of artist, for the move had the grace of an athlete, that sure manipulation of limbs and torso in liquid syncopation, and Larry knew that whatever he was aiming at was a dead man walking. It *was* Chow Yun-Fat.

But he didn't shoot.

What the fuck, Larry thought. Conditioned by a popular culture that rode narratives to completion and left no gun unfired, he felt a secret urge slide into his bloodstream, along with a quart or so of chemicals. *Shoot the motherfucker,* he couldn't help himself for thinking.

Swagger's eyes saw nothing; he had a frozen moment. But then he saw some kind of blurry movement on the truck cab, took another second to relate it to his own knowledge and discern through his fading distance vision that the window had come halfway down, had another thought arrive so fast it came as a rebus, not a sentence: window half down means shot/window full down means curious watcher. Then forces he'd never figure out took over.

He threw himself hard against Nick, shoving the astonished FBI agent against a parked car, reaching simultaneously to the .40 Glock secured against Nick's leg, nimbly popped the security latch, and pulled the gun skyward. He pulled the trigger five times fast.

"What the fuck?" said Nick.

"Gun, gun, gun," screamed Bob, "over there, that garbage truck."

But by that second, everything was lost in chaos, as the radios all shrieked and ten people started talking at once, signifying the confusion on the ground.

"Break-break, shots fired."

"Principal down."

"Call a goddamned ambulance."

"Where is the fire coming from?"

"North, north, a burst of fire north, about a hundred feet up—"

"Negative, negative, that was an agent returning fire. I can't see a sniper."

"All units, all units, stand fast, go to glass, get me situation reports fast. What is story on principal, Ground One?"

"Fuck, it's a mess, we got agents all over him, the kids are crying, I don't see blood, but I can't—"

"Did you take fire?"

"I don't know, I can't verify."

"Somebody tell me what the fuck is happening. Air, any air, do you have a visual?"

"Negative, negative, I just see crazy shit around the principal, I see agents and cops racing toward him, I see no—"

Cops were thundering toward Nick and Swagger as well, drawn by the sound of the pistol. Nick held up his hands, waving them off, and went to the radio.

"This is King Four, Memphis, goddamnit," he said. "My guy fired because he saw sniper activity, 700 block Charles, sited on the garbage truck that's halfway out of the alley, get people there fast, be very careful, suspect is extremely dangerous, I say again, armed, extremely dangerous."

"Principal is okay, there was no shot, we have no evidence of bullet damage, no sound of report."

"Get people on the truck, get people on the truck."

Bob relaxed, handed Nick the gun.

"They have no bullet damage," Nick said, incredulously. "And no sonic. He didn't get the shot off, because you grabbed my gun and started the parade."

"Fuck," said Bob, feeling a sudden terrible weariness flood his limbs, coupled with a need to sit down before his knees melted and pitched him onto the sidewalk. He staggered to the car, and set himself against the bumper. *I am way too old for this shit,* he thought.

"You saw it? You *saw* it? It must be two hundred yards away, for Christ's sake."

"I saw the truck move out, caught my eye. I saw the window come down, or I *think* I saw the window come—"

"All units, all units, we have principal in Charlie One, we are out of here, we are out of here, secure area."

But by the time they got there, they found no sniper. They found a city sanitary crew flex-cuffed in its own garbage scoop and cab, they found an unconscious policeman judo-chopped by a lithe Asian martial arts expert but otherwise undamaged, except that his car was stolen. That vehicle was found one hour later, in East Baltimore, a neighborhood named Canton. But no one saw how it got there, there were no prints, and there was no sign of the sniper.

UNIDENTIFIED CONTRACTOR TEAM

Bogier pressed it hard, but finally saw that nothing was gained by remaining on the scene.

He used the satellite phone to run his decision by Mr. MacGyver.

"We're not doing any good here and we're running totally on fumes. Swagger will be tied up for hours; he's not going anywhere. We're going to check into a motel, crash, and pick up Swagger tomorrow at the FBI HQ."

"Are you sure, Bogier? Swagger has ways of—"

"It's just *CSI* bullshit, without the chicks. Measuring, interviewing, collecting, all that cop stuff. The area's a complete mess with downtown shut down. We'll be in traffic for an hour even getting out of here."

"What's the latest?"

"I have nothing inside. I'm just listening to the news. Someone—Ray, we know—pointed a gun at Zarzi, but Swagger—I'm guessing it was Swagger—picked up on him and fired pistol shots at him, and the shots set off a Chinese fire drill. Ray never pulled down, Swagger missed, the cops went into crazy-town mode, sirens, ambulances, SWAT team, choppers, the whole nine yards. Somehow Ray got away in the confusion. He conked a cop and slipped out."

"Shit."

"So near, so far. He was just a few fucking blocks away from us. But who knew; we had to park where we could find parking."

"I'd stay with Swagger."

"Goddamnit, my people are about to collapse. Nothing will hap-

pen here for at least twelve more hours. Tomorrow will be press conference bullshit. You can watch it on Fox. I've got to get these guys
some shut-eye. It's my call, that's how I'm calling it."

"All right, all right, rack 'em out. Come back tomorrow with
renewed zeal and exuberance, that renowned Bogier touch you're so
famous for."

"You have to let us know if they cancel the Washington events.
If they do, if there's no Zarzi to bring Ray out, I don't know what's
going to happen."

"I'll keep you informed," said MacGyver, and with his normal
arrogant rudeness hung up.

"What a prick," Mick said. "Okay, let's head to the 'burbs and sack
out. We'll be back on station 0630 tomorrow."

"I'm so tired I wouldn't know what to do if some bitch started
sucking on my cock," said Crackers the Clown, not as humor but as
an earnest statement of fact.

"Well, you don't have to worry because it ain't about to happen.
And we ain't about to cap Ray Cruz either; he is one slippery little
yellow bastard, I'll say that."

"I wonder why he didn't," said Tony Z. "First time I ever heard of
him not shooting."

He didn't shoot because you scrambled the zone on him. He lost his sight picture because six Secret Service guys jumped on Zarzi. That's why he didn't shoot."

"You're not getting it," said Swagger. "He's much faster than that. I saw the window go down. I whacked you—"

"A little enthusiastically, I might add."

The other agents in the meeting laughed through their own fatigue. They'd been on-site for hours after the incident, this after the raid in the morning. Everybody was ground down, the coffee was cold, the rats had already carted off the doughnuts, and the Snickers bars had ossified. They'd been going over it for eight hours, and yet no one had said anything intelligent.

"I grabbed the gun," continued Bob, "I raised it, I fired. That whole thing goes at least three seconds. I'm old, I'm not fast anymore, I didn't get a clean grip on the pistol, I had to fumble with the release button, I got it out, I got it up, then I fired. All that takes time. Three seconds. Minimum. Maybe more. What's he doing in that time?"

"Waiting for the target to clear. There's agents all over the place. He's shooting into a crowd, he has to get a good sight pic on Zarzi. Zarzi never cleared, then the shit happens, he has the discipline, knows he doesn't have a shot, realizes this one's a bust, and beats it."

"When we get videotape, I'm betting you'll see that Zarzi was clear. He held when he could have wasted the guy. I know it."

"There's no evidence," someone said. "It's fine to just *say,* but there's no evidence, so why even bring it up?"

Bob ignored the comment. "I don't see no theory by which he don't shoot. He's fast, that's what's different. On target in a split second, perfect trigger control, it's over in less than a second. Yet he had three, and never pulled. Very hard to figure."

"You raise provocative points," Nick said. "But maybe you have a natural empathy for the sniper. You want him to be running some game on us, as opposed to simply trying to kill his target out of some twisted sense of vengeance for Whiskey Two-Two, which he thinks was betrayed and targeted. I have to play your insights off against what the evidence says."

Bob shook his head. He was blurred too, his thinking fuzzy, his reflexes gummy, his tongue tied up in his mouth.

"Okay," Nick said, "I'm calling it. Get some sleep, everybody. Let the investigators continue to gather info, and the cops to look for Ray, fat chance. I want everybody on duty by 0630 tomorrow, we'll go over this stuff and get it into a presentational order, I'm under great pressure from DC to hold a presser, so that's scheduled at ten. Maybe something will break. Maybe Ray will turn himself in."

The laughter was desultory.

"Nick, we've got solid IDs from the garbage crew guys. Are we going to go wide with the Cruz photo tomorrow?"

"I haven't decided yet. If we do, then we have a thousand reporters digging into Ray Cruz and all that info just floods everything, it's more bullshit between us and what we have to do. We don't talk to anybody who hasn't already been on *60 Minutes*. We make him the most famous man in America and what do we get out of it? I don't think it helps us find him, because he's too clever. And it dumps a huge screen of smoke on everything. Let me run it by the Agency, see what their cool, giant, Martian intellects think of it. We may want to keep it quiet, hope we can make it go away without much more disclosure."

The agents stood, began to file out.

Bob leaned close. "Sorry, I'm tired. Do you want me to can it with my doubts? I see it ain't helping you much."

"Nah, everybody knows you're crazy. Plus, you're the big hero. You get to do what you want. What you're doing, questioning, prodding, bringing your unique skill set and IQ on to this stuff is very helpful, believe it or not. The kids on the team love you, so it keeps them working hard without complaining. It's a win-win, but just don't go mouthing off to any reporters."

"I hate those bastards."

"Get some sleep. You're not Superman anymore."

"Don't tell no one, but I never was."

TIMONIUM HOLIDAY INN

He slept the dark sleep of the dead, dreamless and heavy, gone far away from the world. Then a dream began to nudge him. It seemed that one of his hands was bound, he couldn't move it, it stymied him and he twisted against it, beginning to come up through the various levels of consciousness and REM until he arrived hard at the insight that his hand *was* bound to the bed headboard and it then occurred to him that he was in fact awake and that he wasn't alone.

"I'm in night vision," a voice said softly. "I can see everything you do. Take the other hand out from under the covers and lay it out in front of you, wide open. Keep it there. Otherwise don't move. I have a gun on you, but I don't want to kill you. The bullet would probably bounce off, anyhow."

Swagger knew the voice. It pulled him to full alertness.

"Cruz! How the hell did you—"

"I can get into and out of anyplace. I'm a Ninja assassin from the planet Pandora. I am the trees, the wind, the planet itself, white man. My face is blue."

He laughed a bit, dryly, at his own twisted sense of humor.

"And I'll ask the questions."

"Man, you are crazy coming in here like this."

"Just answer. What was with all those poor Filipinos who got wasted last night? Does that have a connect to this sordid little game?"

Bob said nothing.

"Come on, Gunny, I don't have all night. Don't make me use the blowtorch on you."

"It was my fuck-up," said Swagger, then explained briefly how it had happened.

"And the Bureau doesn't see any tie-in?" Cruz asked.

"They're not saying that. They're saying no evidence."

"They don't want evidence. They don't want to go into some cesspool of national security bullshit where a faction of CIA is trying to take out an American sniper team to save an Afghan scumbag from the headshot he so richly deserves, and the whole thing spins out of control in some kind of sick mission-creep phenomenon."

"They say the guy is clean. They've gone over him a dozen times—"

"If he rises, they rise. That's how it works. It's politics and ambition, there, here, everywhere."

"Cruz, maybe you're overplaying it in your mind. The weight of combat operations, all them tours, the kills—"

"I saw a building in Qalat I'd just exited turned into a crater and thirty-one people thermobarically toasted. I saw Billy Skelton torn in two by some motherfucker on a Barrett .50. I saw Norm Chambers with a hole in him the size of a football."

"You have too many people working against you."

"As long as I'm on the loose, as long as you think I'm going to cash out the Beheader, you guys have to ask questions. The more questions you ask, the harder you look, the more likely it is to become unraveled. That's my game. You want to stop me? Figure out what they're pulling off with this guy Zarzi—"

"Everything you say sounds like you're psycho about the Agency. You're implying the Agency is after you. You should know, the Agency is cooperating with the Bureau. I'm working for an Agency officer I've known for years, and she's smart, tough, fair, and decent. She wouldn't be party to some scam that targeted our own people."

He was totally aware that he had become Nick. Now he was the guy saying "no evidence" and "stuff like that doesn't happen" and "it's all subjective." Yet the theater of the moment forced him into his supervisor's shoes, because if he just dumbly agreed with Ray Cruz, where did that leave him? Not on this side of the law.

"Think about it," Cruz responded. "At our level, we take out a double-0 license on a warlord. Off Two-Two goes. Halfway there we're intercepted by contractors who classic-ambush our sorry asses. I discover they've been tracking me by satellite transmitter implanted in my SVD. I pull a switch on them and get away. I make it to Qalat, tell my people I'm setting up the shot as planned. I enter the building, then I depart the building, because I know somebody in the system is talking. And they *knew* which building. A fucking missile totals the building. Much more than a Hellfire."

Now he became Susan, speaking for the Agency of mystery and endless games, with objectives so shrouded no man could view them. Again, a feeling of rootlessness hit him: if you could change perspectives so quickly, then who, really, were you?

"You don't know it was a missile. Lots of things blow up in that part of the world. And if they wanted you to abort the mission, they could have simply ordered your battalion CO to issue the withdraw. The Agency has that kind of power. It's a phone call, that's all. You're saying they hired contractors, ran an ambush in tribal territories, finally called in a missile shot, when they could have reached the same ending with a phone call. Sergeant, it doesn't track."

"Think harder, Swagger. That's all I've been doing for six months. If they go through channels, through the leaky, penetrated, cheesy-security chain of command, then everybody in country knows the Agency's got game with Zarzi, and pretty soon everybody everywhere knows. Maybe his own ex-friends behead him. Maybe the newspapers blow it all over the front page and his political future is shot. Langley couldn't have that. To protect their boy, they had to double-tap Two-Two, and once it started, they couldn't stop it. So whatever they're doing, it involves Zarzi. Zarzi's the key. That's the end of the—"

He seemed to run out of gas. He, clearly, was exhausted as well.

Finally he said, "Either you stop him or I will."

"Sergeant Cruz," Swagger said, "I'll make you a deal. You go underground. You don't try no more attempts on Zarzi; I will see what I can see and learn what I can learn. I will get people to help and to talk. I'm their big hero now, I've got a tiny amount of juice. You check back with me, and I will have something for you. Just trust me a little. If I discover what you say is true, we will go in together, sniper all the way. Fair enough?"

Again he was aware, painfully, that the deal he offered Cruz he was basically offering himself as well. *I will consider it. I will put it on the table and look into it, because in its way, it coincides with my own doubts as well.*

The pause told him Cruz was listening.

"You have a few days," said Cruz.

Bob felt a tug on his wrist and the flex-cuff was cut.

Then the sniper was gone.

ON THE ROAD

C an we stop?" inquired Professor Khalid. "I have to go to the bathroom again."

"Ach," said Bilal, "you old men. You have to go to the bathroom all the time. We have a schedule."

"But I can't do what I must do pissed up. One does not martyr oneself with urine in the underpants."

"Martyrdom is a week away," said Bilal, "if this van doesn't break down or I don't go mad listening to you two argue all the time."

"Do you not think," said Dr. Faisal, "that the boys of Palestine feel a pee drop or two dampen their trousers before they detonate? Yet they detonate, nevertheless."

"No," said Professor Khalid. "They are too insane. They feel nothing. Besides, their penises are probably engorged at the prospects of sexual activity in the next world, just seconds away. No pee could pass. Their dicks are hard, their pants are dry, and ka-boom, imagine the surprise when the next world turns out to be a blind walk through eternal blackness, if even that. No breasts, no cunts, no oral enticement of the members, nothing."

"*He cannot say that*!" screamed Dr. Faisal. "Apostate! Infidel! He must be beheaded, as the text states clearly! He cannot say such things!"

"Dr. Faisal, if I behead him, then the whole point of the trip is destroyed. You will not have your martyrdom, you will not have your many women."

"He does not believe in the women thing," said Professor Khalid. "He cannot let himself state it as such, but in his mind, he does not believe in anything any more than I do. He clings to his faith as a prop to get him through this last ordeal."

"Is that Disneyland?" said Dr. Faisal suddenly.

"No," said Bilal, "that is not Disneyland."

"I would like to see Disneyland," said Dr. Faisal.

"That is Las Vegas," said Professor Khalid. "You can be forgiven for mixing up the two. It's all the same America. Pleasure domes, games, stupid distractions, and the pursuit of ecstasy. No rigor or discipline anywhere. Spiritual torpor. Meanwhile, in his faith, it's all memorizing bad poetry written seventeen hundred years ago by a psychotic charismatic high on drugs. That is what he thinks is revealed truth."

"Tell the apostate," said Dr. Faisal, "that his musings are pornographic. He denies the true faith and his afterlife will be a forever of torment and pain in flames on a spit. He should check 72:23 for a sense of what lies ahead."

"Who would prepare such a dry, tough dish?" asked Khalid.

The press conference had not gone well. The pressies seemed enraged that the man the Administration was touting as the Answer to the decade-long war in Afghanistan had almost been shot to death on a Baltimore street. Who was at fault? When it turned out to be the infamous Nick Memphis, who at one controversial point in his career had seemed to utterly foul up the investigation of the death of Joan Flanders and three other martyred sixties peace demonstrators, their anger only grew. Not even Susan Okada, who represented the CIA in this issue and was, incidentally, quite beautiful, could mollify the snide hostility in the questions, even as she expressed thanks from the Agency for the superb job the Bureau had done in protecting the principal. Even the Secret Service rep's insistence that it was one FBI agent who had foiled the hit did little to quell the emotion. "The system worked," he maintained. Tough sell. And when the only real news that could be announced was the bland insistence that "we have some suspects and some leads, but this appears to be a very tricky, dedicated individual," it only pissed them off further.

By contrast, the press conference that Ibrahim Zarzi held in Washington the same day was some kind of lovefest. Declared a hero by the Administration for his refusal to yield to a murder attempt against his personage, he was magnificent: generous, brave, noble, handsome, sexy, cosmopolitan. He specifically singled out the nameless agent who had foiled the attempt, wishing that this brave man would come to visit him in Kabul and see the hospitality of the Afghan people. He expressed his admiration for both the FBI and the CIA for their dedication to his safety. He said he feared nothing, as Allah had given him a destiny and he would fulfill it or die trying. What was death? When so many of the brave have died, what was death? Yes, he agreed that it was indeed ironic that once he had been called "the Beheader" and now his survival was the key point of statecraft of the United States. He promised more for our two great countries, a future of peace and prosperity and so forth. He really laid it on. They really ate it up.

"Not that it matters," Nick told his inner circle a short while later, "but if we don't get this guy, I am so gone it'll make your noses bleed. I will be lucky to end up in Alaska investigating the Fairbanks garbage scandal. But enough about me."

The overnight reports contained no breakthroughs. The only new piece of information was trashman Larry Powers's description of the rifle he'd briefly seen in the cab of the truck, a very short bolt-action rifle with a thick barrel and a thick scope.

Bob was asked at the meeting for his opinion on the weapon.

"I'm betting it was a sort of Remington bolt-action rifle, short action, maybe in .308 or even .243 or .22-250. So I'd advise the people in South Carolina to try to find records for a transfer of that rifle in that caliber to Colonel Chambers's shop. I'm guessing he did the work, or his smith. I'm also thinking a new barrel with an integral suppressor rather than the 'can' type that screws on, again for the shorter size. I see a gun that's mostly suppressor and action, without a lot of barrel or stock. He carries it looped to his body at the shoulder, under a coat. He just reaches in, pivots it upward and it's already set against his shoulder by the loop, goes to scope, maybe a red dot because, remember, he said it was 'thick.' Then he fires, slides it back under his coat, and wanders down the street. You'd never know he had it."

"Is that legal?" asked someone, and there was laughter because some thought it was a joke, but Bob answered it anyway.

"You'd have to get ATF to clarify, but I'd say no on two counts. The suppressor is classed as a Title III item, like an automatic weapon, meaning it has to go through the legal hoops for private ownership. Did Chambers's outfit have the legal classification to manufacture and sell such a thing? As for the rifle itself, if it's less than eighteen inches in barrel length, it cannot have a shoulder stock."

"Why don't we turn the whole thing over to ATF," somebody said, again to laughter that was simply to express the fact that the agents had very little to go on: their own law-enforcement-only distributed picture of the suspect, his habits, his background, and very little else. It looked as if the only chance for an arrest would come if he made another attempt.

"He won't," Bob told Nick a few minutes later in Nick's temporary Baltimore office. Susan was there too, in the usual pantsuit, her hair unusually mussed, and of course the more it got mussed the more Swagger got mussed. She was long, tall, thin, mostly leg, with high cheekbones and some kind of mean intelligence behind her bright eyes that would always keep you from confusing her with your mama. Thirty-eight, going on twenty-five, face smooth, wise, serene, perfectly colored in nuances of lavender and off-pink, like some kind of ancient vase behind glass. She knocked him out every goddamned time.

"How do you know?" she said.

Maybe he said it because it was his job; maybe he said it just to see a flair of response in those dark eyes.

"Well," Bob said, "because he told me so last night."

FOUR SEASONS HOTEL

I'd like to follow up, sir, on the irony theme if I may," asked David Banjax of the *New York Times,* recently exiled from the Newark Bureau and on a very short leash back in the Washington office, trusted only for a one-on-one setup by State Department flacks. "Do you consider it ironic to visit this city, with its monuments, its marble vistas, its statuary, as the center of a state visit in light of the fact that at one time you were sworn to destroy it?"

"Oh, Mr. Banjax," said Ibrahim Zarzi, a fraught look on his handsome face, his dark eyes pooling with melancholy regret, "I am afraid you have been misled by early press reports which ascribe to me activities in which never ever did I participate. One has enemies. Enemies fight with more than bombs, they fight with unpleasantly inaccurate information. This is exactly such a case."

They were in a room on Zarzi's floor in the Four Seasons immediately after the news conference and all around Banjax, watch faces undulated gently. Square, round, black, gold, white, vivid, subtle, encrusted with jewels, screaming of Special Operations by dark of moon, or seductions in the dining room of the Ritz, it seemed like some kind of slow-motion museum on the theme of time passing. It was hypnotic. He thought of a common scene in a certain kind of movie that always seemed to take place in a field of reeds or wheat things (wheat *fronds?* wheat *leaves?* wheat *staves?* wheat *puffs?*) weaving rhythmically in the wind. Wasn't it the one where the girl first gave her heart and her body to her lover? And wasn't that sort of what was happening now, as it was his job to be seduced by the charisma of this man, whom the *Times* already supported editorially, and to give him his say about his colorful past? And on top of that, it was making him a little bit sick. In the pit of his stomach, he felt uncertainty.

"Well, sir," said Banjax, "it is true you were once known as 'the Beheader' for the unfortunate death of Richard Millstein, which was videotaped and shown around the world."

"I am so glad that at last I have a chance to address that tragedy. In fact, no, I was not to blame, nor in any way responsible for Mr. Millstein's death. That I swear. That I attest, with one hand on the holy Koran. Sir, I am rewarded in my patience that I will make my virtue and my innocence clear once and for all in this matter, peace be upon you."

He smiled, teeth glittering. He had changed for the interview and now wore gray flannels, Gucci loafers (no socks), a white shirt open to the midchest and displaying bronzed, toned muscularity and a frost of hair, some kind of massive black military watch on one wrist that set off the many gold rings his fingers sported. He was lean, muscular for his age, and bold with macho vitality. Polo later, perhaps? A brace of grouse? Perhaps a ride aboard Jumbo in the forests of the night after a tiger, burning bright, and if the Jeffrey .500 didn't put the big cat down and he made it up the elephant's back, then there was always the double-barreled howdah pistol to drive two .600 nitros into the animal's open jaws and jackhammer him to earth.

"Mr. Millstein fell in among thieves and brigands, alas. In their apostasy, they used my name in order to give a cover of political animus to what was basically a kidnapping and ransom operation. They represented not the Muslim street or even the groups that are called 'terrorist' but the simple universal greed of human corruption, as prevalent in our culture, alas, as in your own. It is tragic but it is inescapable. Wars bring out rogues and rascals, opportunists, the like. It was Mr. Millstein's bad luck to encounter such. You believe me, of course?"

It was hard not to believe everything Zarzi said, for he said it with such earnest conviction. But Banjax tried mightily to offer some resistance, even if the unease in his stomach was mounting.

"Well, sir, it's easy to say, of course, and you are very convincing. However, some sort of objective proof would—"

"Proof? Proof? What proof would I have? A note from a teacher? Possibly the statement of a wife? My best friend's testimony? Sir, you require that which does not exist. Had I it, you now would have it. I have only the humble power of my—oh, and one other thing."

Banjax leaned forward.

Ticktock ticktock went the thousand watches, each in a hulu gyre, reflecting this way and that against their orbit as they rotated slickly through the light patterns. Banjax felt sweat pop on his brow, a wave of wooziness pass, pass again, and pass a third time.

"Of course I ask your forbearance in linking it to me."

"Of course," said Banjax, if barely.

The elegant man reached into his briefcase and pulled out a sheaf of documents.

"This is the original report, not by Afghan officials, but by the Pakistani Directorate for Inter-service Intelligence, into the incident. It is, of course, in Urdu. You will have it translated, I'm sure."

"Yes."

"Certain elements of ISI are sympathetic to revolutionary movements in Afghanistan, as you know. Thus, it is important for them to know exactly who did what to whom when. They may even be paying certain funding. It is my hope, with the presidency in my control, to engage them and dissuade them from such activities. But the more immediate point is that their agents found no evidence of either my own or revolutionary groups'—terrorist groups', you would say— involvement in the tragedy. It cost a great deal of money to deliver this from their hands to yours through mine. It is my gift to the West. It is something not even your Central Intelligence Agency has laid eyes upon yet."

He handed the papers over to Banjax, who took them greedily.

Ah, he was thinking, *a scoop.*

He remembered his great run of them during his last shot at Washington and the big leagues. The pleasure was intense. He looked up to make his next brilliant point.

And then suddenly it hit him: all those undulating watches, the thickness of the man's cologne, his closeness, his earnestness, his warmth, so cloying. Banjax felt woozy, then blurry, then defenseless.

He fainted.

O h, Christ," said Nick.

"Bob," said Susan, "this is not good. You can't be consorting with the object of a federal manhunt."

"If he approached you," Nick continued, "you should have grappled him to the ground, screamed bloody murder, and we'd all be home free now, and I'd break my long-standing rule never to have a martini before noon. Jesus Christ, this is a mess. You may even have broken the law."

"Nobody knows better than the man who wasn't there. Are you done?" Bob said. "Okada-san, got any more shit to pour on me? Nick, I'll bend over and you can whack me a few times or kick me. Oh that's right, you've got a bum hip. Bring in some young guy."

"This isn't getting us anywhere," said Nick. "So tell the story."

Swagger did, point by point, tracking Cruz's revelations: white contractors, planted satellite transmitter in SVD, pursuit by satellite surveillance after first ambush, pursuit after evading second trap, radio contact with 2-2 Recon, missile strike on hotel.

"It's nothing if he doesn't give himself up now," Nick said.

"And I'm telling you," said Bob, "he doesn't buy into your ability to protect him. After all, there've been two attempts on his life so far by a real hard-core professional team."

Swagger faced his own absurdity: when he was with Cruz, he argued for Nick and Susan. When he was with Nick and Susan, he argued for Cruz. He realized he had no future in Washington culture, because he couldn't even keep his own sides straight, much less anyone else's.

"As for me," said Susan, her face mandarin and remote and official, "I see where this is leading and I don't like it. I told you this and I don't get why you're not listening. The Agency will not stand still for an outside investigation of its operations in Afghanistan, which are undertaken in good faith and under great danger. I'm here to help you stop Cruz, not lead a witch hunt."

"It ain't about a witch hunt. There wasn't no witches, right? But maybe Cruz does have enemies. And maybe they're our enemies too. I don't have no dog in this fight, I ain't here to steal turf from any outfit called by its initials. I'm here for the truth, and I'm going to find it or look for it until you put me in the bag."

"God, he's a stubborn man," said Susan. "In Tokyo, he went and fought a master swordsman who should have sliced him to shreds. No one could talk him out of it. You cannot talk to the man when he's like this. It's like arguing with a forest fire!"

"I want to work this angle, and I gave him my word."

"The truth is, your word means nothing," said Nick. "You were not authorized to make commitments. You don't represent the Bureau."

"My word means nothing to you. It means everything to me, especially to another sniper."

"You are so fucking stubborn!" screamed Nick. "It's like beating your head against a gun stock."

"It's a sniper thing. You wouldn't understand."

"This is the real world, not a Boy Scout jamboree."

"Listen. Cruz ain't going to go again," Bob argued. "I got that from him. That's his concession. The next public outing is Sunday, Zarzi's run of talk shows in DC. He ain't going to try nothing then. He gave me his word. I gave him mine. So get me out to Creech."

"Creech is off-limits," said Susan.

"What's Creech?" asked Nick.

"It's an Air Force base north of Vegas where they run the drone war," said Susan. "It's where our snipers go to play life-and-death video games with terrorists, gunmen, IED teams, high-value targets, and the like. It's where the real hunting and killing take place."

"Nick, get me out there with some smart partner agent to cover my rough edges and let me sniff around. Say an American asset was killed in the explosion in that hotel and some outfit is bringing heat on our asses. They'll let me on, strictly pro forma, give me the tour. They ain't going to tell me nothing, not up front. But if I'm there and it gets out what's being looked into, something may shake out of the trees. Then I can find out if in fact they did put a missile into that hotel."

"Agh," said Nick to no one.

Then he said, "Susan, I don't see how I can say no. He's a hero. They like him upstairs. And he has found Cruz twice and neither of us has even come close with all our resources. And sometimes he's right."

"Been known to happen a time or two," said Bob.

"You are *such* a bastard," she said evenly to Bob. "You are taking this exactly where my orders are to prevent you from going."

"But you know it's the right thing."

"I told you. I went over the records very thoroughly. This shooting off of missiles isn't casual, you know. Everything is recorded, everything is documented, every shot is noted as to operator, intel validity, time frame, and result. It's not like the Mexican revolution, bang bang bang, with everybody shooting everything at once all over the place drunk on tequila."

"Yes, ma'am," said Bob. "But there may be secrets within secrets. Black ops so black records don't exist. Skunk works shit, black bag shit, wet work, all that ugly crap that spy outfits been doing for four thousand years. It's in the Bible, even. I'm no expert but maybe I can find something somehow, some way. Maybe you could too if you tried again."

"You're telling me I should start prying in locked drawers in Langley," she said. "I should spy on the spies. I *am* a spy."

Swagger was filled with doubts. Maybe this was all bullshit he'd dreamed up to engage her and from there make the leap to something else. It was how the cunning male-sex mind sometimes worked. Goddamned Asian women, he couldn't get over them, and that brought up a long-dead, bourbon-soaked ache best not addressed now or ever. He also knew he was still fundamentally exhausted, the confab with Cruz who'd caught him cold was upsetting to say the least, and this whole Washington game was more complex than he'd imagined. He'd been the lone gunman, the tall-grass crawler, and now he was exactly where he didn't belong, in a soup of confusing loyalties, some of them even within his own mind.

So: when in doubt, press ahead blindly and pray for luck and God's delight in the reckless.

"You know these people. You go to backyard barbecues with 'em. You could ask around."

She shook her beautiful head.

"I don't know anything. I never had this discussion, I don't know a thing about anything."

"But you won't rat me out?"

Her silence meant that no, she wouldn't rat him out, but it also meant that she hadn't remembered until that moment what an asshole he truly could be.

V egas?" said Mick Bogier.

"Yep. Him and this chick. Pretty gal. Maybe the old coot has some Pez left in the dispenser after all. Off to Vegas for a weekend of whoopie. Been known to happen."

It was Crackers the Clown who'd dogged Swagger, watching him check in with the young woman, head through security and on to a gate. Crackers had pulled a Baltimore police detective badge and gotten through security without a hassle from TSA and followed him all the way to the gate. Now he was on the cell to Mick and Tony Z.

"Unlikely," said Mick, "this guy's too duty-crazed."

"I hate that kind," said Crackers. "All work and no fun. What, he wants to be a saint?"

"Let me make a call."

Even before he put the cell down, Tony handed him the Thuraya phone.

"This better be good news," MacGyver said. "I'm about to make myself a martini."

"We followed Swagger to the airport. He's about to fly to Vegas with some young agent. I don't know what it's about."

MacGyver considered.

"We could get the next flight out," said Mick. "Then we pick up the signal in Vegas and we follow him there. But I don't know what Cruz would be doing in Vegas or what Vegas would have to do with Cruz. Cruz is here, we know that."

"I can find out," MacGyver finally said. "But that's going to take a while. No, I'd stay in DC. I'd set up somewhere in the vicinity of the talk show studios this Sunday and get ready to roll if there's an incident."

"Sure, but that's thin. This Sergeant Cruz is really good. I mean, he's fucking big league all the way. The chance of us nailing him before he nails Zarzi without Swagger bird-dogging him first are somewhere between thin and negative one million. Since he's riding the action curve and we're trailing it, we'll be lucky to get there when the smoke is still in the air. And don't forget there's going to be about ten thousand cops in the area, somewhat complicating things."

"I understand," said MacGyver. "I don't know what else to tell you. I'm out of answers."

"MacGyver, your show's going to be canceled if you can't do better than that."

"Hey, asshole sergeant, if I'm canceled you're canceled, so you better pray for me. Oh, and I make the smart comments, I get to do the sarcasm, get it? Don't go all Mick Bogier on me. Cowboys are cheap in this world."

Bogier enjoyed lighting up the asshole like that. He knew it was expected that he would now apologize and show contrition, but he would not do it. Fuck him and the horse he came in on.

"Okay, here's what you do," said MacGyver. "Monitor the Four Seasons and the Afghan embassy. You guys have seen Cruz in action, you know his walk, his moves, you know what he'd have to wear to conceal a weapon. You may pick him up on a scouting mission, a recon, just from the way he moves. Ask around, see if anybody's suddenly started showing up at those places. Meanwhile, I'll find out what Swagger is doing in Vegas and when he's due back. He's still our best bet. After all, he's found Cruz twice and nobody else is even in the game."

Which was stonier, the desert landscape or Agent Chandler's remote personality? The desert was desolate, rocky, filled with crusted hills, ugly spiny things that appeared to be vegetable in origin, lit by a merciless sun and drifting off to a horizon that was a forever away. She was extremely attractive, eyes beaming with intelligence, but face held in disciplined dullness and disinterest. She drove. She was the special agent. He was a consultant with the rank of brevet investigator. She called the shots. She commanded, in silence and concentration on the road. He sat there, in his off-the-rack suit, hoping for something a little more cooperative, but finding it not forthcoming. He knew she was a Nick mentee, one of the talented young ones Nick liked to work under him, that she was married to a CIA guy, that she had a reputation for "creativity," whatever that was, and that she'd been a big player and winner in the Tom Constable dust-up of a few years back. He knew her nickname was "Starling" because she reminded people of a movie star who'd played a memorable FBI agent.

They'd eaten lunch separately and were headed out for a two o'clock with Colonel Christopher Nelson, USAF, CO of the 143rd Expeditionary Air Wing (UAV), which is to say the Air Force CIA headhunter outfit at a desert air base called Creech, whose ugly name foretold the ugliness of the installation.

"Okay," she finally said. "Talk to me. I'm open for business."

"Ma'am, I follow your lead. You just tell me what you want to know and I'll answer straight up."

"I know you're a gunfighter, an action guy. I know you dusted some very bad people in your time. I like that, I get that. But this is different. It's interrogation. It demands suppleness, intellectual agility, concentration, patience, a deeply fraudulent charm. Can someone as direct as you work at indirection?"

"Don't know about indirection, but I do know about fraud. Ma'am, I am a completely fraudulent individual. Too many people think I'm a hero when I'm a total coward. All the brave men died in the war, only us lucky yellow rats made it out alive."

"Utter bullshit from a man who took down a pro hitter with a subgun at close range, time of engagement three seconds."

"More like four. He wasn't as pro as he thought."

"I guess not. Okay, I will take the lead. We agree on cover upfront. You are looking for signs of weakness, for twitches that indicate untruthfulness, for signs of prevarication and mendacity. Do you know what they are?"

"Eyes mainly. He'll look up or away if he's lying, because he's reading a script in his head. He'll swallow a bit hard if he's lying. His lips will dry. He's foursquare military, he ain't used to lying because their system is about no bullshit. If he's got this big command, he must be an up-and-coming guy in the new robot Air Force. He'll be nervous because the last thing he wants is to screw up his career chances. He'll pause before answering. He knows the best lie is only a few degrees from the truth."

"You cannot do anything extralegal. You cannot peek, disappear, misrepresent. All the time you have to be thinking and noticing. Are you capable of that?"

"I'll sure try," he said.

"Cool," she said. "You're not as dumb as you look."

"I do look dumb, don't I?"

"My dad was head of the state police in Arizona. You look like any oldish, unpromotable trooper sergeant, tough as hell, good man in a gunfight, steady, and hopelessly obsolete. My poor dad had to get rid of a bunch of those guys, though he loved them all."

"Never said I wasn't no dinosaur," said Bob. "And I thank you for indulging me against your better instincts."

They reached Indian Springs, not that they really noticed. It was a trailer park, a convenience store/gas station, and a one-room casino in a glade of barely green scrub trees. The town abutted the base, which looked more like a prison complex than an airfield. A motley collection of brown corrugated-metal buildings, it spread across a desert basin, the same color of dry heat as everything else the sun bleached. It lay behind a barbwire fence and the two security gates were like Cold War border crossings. It was large and flat, disappearing over a ridge at least a mile or so out. In the far distance, on one of the short runways, some kind of white aircraft could be seen, something of a cross between a Piper Cub and a kite, and Bob realized that it was either the Predator itself or its killer progeny, the Reaper, which patrolled the skies of Afghanistan, looking for something to kill.

I 've directed my people to cooperate fully," said the colonel, a solid linebacker guy with one of those square jaws and short, all-biz haircuts the upper-field grades favored. "And I will open any documents or records you require. I just have to tell you up front that a) we *are* very busy here fighting a war, and b) this matter was previously investigated by an Agency officer and she found no traces of anything handled incorrectly. But you say it's a criminal matter, not a national security matter."

The three, plus the Wing Executive Officer and a secretary, were sitting in the commanding officer's office, a well-lit room decorated with pictures of himself in various stages of his career, standing proudly before beautiful pieces of stainless steel sculpture that also happened to be supersonic jet fighters, all F-somethings, sleek and dangerous looking, like machined raptors hungry for a kill. In a few, as armored as a medieval knight, he sat in a cockpit under a raised plastic bubble with a winner's wide grin while holding up a thumb as if to say "Mission accomplished" or even "Bogie downed."

"No, sir," said Chandler, "we are not alleging criminal misconduct. We only say that it's a possible criminal matter and that as a neutral agency, we have been asked to look at the data points again. You know the basics. On a certain date seven months ago, a hotel in Afghanistan was obliterated, possibly, but not certainly, by a missile. We have no forensics on the case because it was in tribal territory at the time, meaning an area full of bad guys. Subsequently, the site has been razed. There was a cursory investigation by Dutch security forces repping the UN, mainly photos. It tells us almost nothing except that something made a big hole in the earth. The reason we are here is that of the thirty-one Afghani nationals killed, one was an informant for the DEA. His loss set back one of their infiltration programs a great deal and that is a heavy poppy-growth area, and it ships product that shows up on the streets of, well, Indian Springs, for one, and Vegas, where I'm sure most of your staff and pilots live, for another. DEA says that other informants in the area claim the hotel was detonated by a missile. These reports are persistent, and it's only a matter of time before they show up in an American newspaper. It would be a black eye if someone accidentally whacked a civilian structure, though of course it happens, and it would be an even bigger black eye if a DEA informant was among the killed, and the worst thing of all—I make no accusations here, but simply state fact—if it turned out a cover-up tried to obscure some second lieutenant's honest mistake in the heat of battle. We have to be ahead on this one, not behind it, sir. And that is why we are here."

"Fine. By the way, does the guy who looks like Clint Eastwood ever talk?"

"No, sir," said Bob, "not since I shot Dillinger."

Everybody laughed, letting a little tension out.

"All right. Here's what I've set up for you. In the next room, you'll find our complete documentation of air activities for that eight-hour duty shift. You'll find a TV monitor and all our fire missions from that shift on tape, and you can look at them. We took sixteen shots that time, at all levels of permissibility. You'll learn what a 'level of permissibility' is shortly. I have my battle manager from that shift on hand, and he can go over each mission separately with you if you need to do so. I also have seven pilots, that is, seven operators who fly, and I mean literally fly, the drones from our op center here at Creech. They're the real heroes, and I'd hate to get any of them in trouble. They took the sixteen shots among them. I have one missing, First Lieutenant Wanda Dombrowski, whose term of service expired last month and who opted to end her commitment to the Air Force. She was great and I'm sorry to see her go. Anyhow, I have her next address and phone number, and if you feel it necessary to contact her, then you're of course free to do so."

"All right," said Starling. "Then let's get to work."

"But first, just so you understand the situation we deal with in our duties, I want to walk you through our op center. I want to take you into the heart of combat, even if you're in an underground room in a Nevada desert. Either of you have any combat experience?"

"He's been in a gunfight or two," Starling said.

"He looks like it. Well, Agents Chandler and Swagger, you're about to see how the wars of the future will be fought. You won't have to do as much ducking, Swagger."

CIA HQ

S o is it true," asked Jared Dixson, Afghan Desk number two, handsome dog without conscience or tremor, eye-power seducer, and all around not-so-great guy, "that you were in a sword fight?"

"I was, yes," said Susan. "I held a guy off, until someone stronger stepped in and cut the head off the guy who was about to take mine."

"Wow. So what does it look like when a guy gets his head cut off?"

"It's very moist."

"They should call you 'the Beheader,' not Zarzi."

"Well, if the *Times* is right, he's no more a beheader than I am."

Dixson laughed. "Well, between you and me and the woodwork, the best three words to describe Ibrahim Zarzi are 'guilty,' 'guilty,' and of course, 'guilty.' We call him 'Dishonest Ib,' but only when we're drunk. The *Times* bought that phony Paki intel report hook, line, and sinker. We had great fun drawing it up. It's Afghan Desk's most profound moment of theater, up until the bastard gets the Freedom Award from the president next Saturday night."

"He's an asshole?"

"You have no idea. A watch queen with the sexual appetites of a Warren Beatty. He'd seduce the meter maid if you let him. But he's *our* watch queen and that's the point. So we'll get him all the meter maids we can and let him cut off the odd journalist's head if it gets us some sort of stability in Crazyland."

Dixson was assistant to Jackson Collins, who was, in the argot of the joint, the actual Afghan Desk himself, though no one ever called him "Mr. Desk." They called him "MacGyver," as he was an ex-SEAL, and had actually blown up a lot of stuff in the way-back when he was operational yet had a kind of too-serious-for-the-ironists quality that rendered him faintly ridiculous and thus earned him the nickname of a fatuous TV jerk from the eighties. Even his serious creds couldn't make the joke go away: he was an Annapolis grad, Hopkins Institute of Foreign Studies star, former Brookings Fellow, and epic drinker, and under this Administration had become the senior executive in charge of running the Agency's missions in Afghanistan in coordination with policy goals set by the Administration through the National Security advisor's office, if not the president himself.

"So," she said, "are you getting along with Jack 'MacGyver' Collins any better now?"

"Oh, yeah," said Dixson. "He used to call me 'Pussyboy.' Now I've been promoted to 'Dr. Vulva.'"

"Wow, that's progress. I had a guy like that in Tokyo. Office was like a destroyer bridge. We called it 'the fo'c'sle.' He was as dumb as a screwdriver. No moving parts whatsoever."

"These Annapolis guys, what's with them? They think if you don't know which one is port and which one is starboard, you're worthless. By the way, which one *is* port?"

She laughed. The guy *was* funny, just the tiniest bit upper-class swishy with a face that was too lively with emotional information. Reputedly brilliant, clearly resentful, Jared had run hard into the Agency's ancient military cerebellum. But then she said, "Look, you know why I dropped by."

"Of course. You're using your appointment to the FBI liaison committee as an excuse to come visit your long-time crush object Jared Dixson. I'm glad that you've finally made peace with your abiding love and intense sexual longing for me. It was so *wrong* of you to play hard to get for all those years. Think of the motel time we could have logged."

"Gee, another married guy who wants the cookies but doesn't want to pay for the bowl to mix them in. Oh, that's right, you'll be married to—what's her name, Buffy? Jennifer? Gigi?—forever because she's got all the money. You can't divorce."

"Why, what would one do without three houses, six cars, a stable, a really big sailboat, and a very fine collection of vintage wines? Her name happens to be Bunny. No, Fluffy, no, no, now it's coming back, *Mimsy*."

"You're such a bastard. Anyhow, I want to go through our missile and munition records for that day when the hotel blew up. One more time. Maybe I missed something."

"I doubt you ever missed anything in your life."

"Well, the near-kill in Baltimore has got people asking about Cruz's motives again. I just have to make sure that base is covered, that we are in the clear. It would prove so embarrassing if Afghan Desk were taking shots at our own people to save the Watch Queen's ass."

"You know, that stuff's way classified. I know you're cleared most of the way, but how about all of the way?"

"I'm cute, it's allowed."

"Okay," he said. "MacGyver's a big-foot asshole, but he's not that big an asshole, I guarantee you. I will get you everything," he said, "except of course Pentameter. You understand, Pentameter can't be compromised."

"Sure," she said, thinking, *What the hell is Pentameter?*

PART THREE

PENTAMETER

Here was war. In glowing screens that sent gray-blue shafts up to the ceiling of a smokeless bunker in a room that could have been full of insurance adjusters, or newsletter writers, or catalog telephone operators, the young people of the 143rd Expeditionary Wing (UAV) hunted and killed and blew shit up extremely well.

"You've been briefed on MQ-9 Reaper?" asked the colonel as he led them through the large, hushed room, ultra-air-conditioned, almost like a religious space occupied by intensely filled confessionals.

"More or less," said Starling.

"Let me recap. It's our primary hunter-killer system. It's the Mitchell bomber of the war on terror, the do-anything, go-anywhere airborne sniper. It can hang in the air low or high for fifteen hours at a time and the kids who run it develop an almost mystical feel for its handling capabilities. They meld with it somehow, as an old fighter jock like me might say. It has superb optics and target-guidance systems. It has weapons hard points for up to twelve missiles and two guided munitions, as smart bombs are called. It's a big thing too; you think 'drones' you think little buzzy kites with motors. Uh-uh. It's the size of a Warthog, with a 950-shaft horsepower turbocharged engine. It's nothing but wings and streamline and gizmos, and one of the reasons people assume it's small is because it has no features, not really, to give it a sense of scale; no personality, no eccentricities, no pizzazz. It's just white streamlined death. We think of it as 'deadly persistence' in the way it hangs around while it hunts. It's got all the bells and whistles, including a Raytheon AN/AAS-52 multi-spectral targeting sensor suite which includes color and monochrome daylight TV, infrared, and image-intensified TV with laser range finder and target designator. You could broadcast a talk show from it."

"What're you shooting from it?" asked Swagger.

"Primarily, Hellfire AGM-114. And we are talking some kind of precision. They say 'Hellfire' is an acronym for *hel*-i-copter launched *fire*-and-forget. Sounds weak to me. I think it's just some Baptist general's Old Testament imagination for hellfire and brimstone, raining down on the evil and depraved of Sodom and Gomorrah and Afghanistan. For the record, it's a laser-guided rocket with a twenty-pound warhead, initially developed to burn red tanks rolling through the Fulda Gap. No tanks here, so we put what we call a blast-and-frag sleeve on that twenty pounds of explosive so that when it goes, it sends out a hundred-thousand-piece spray of supersonic steel. It's primarily for killing people or blowing up vehicles. It can take out a small building too. For those hard-to-reach spots, we have a little treat called 'thermobaric,' which means that in a nanosecond before detonation the explosive atomizes, that is, turns to droplets of mist that fill the air. Then it goes and it really rips a hole in the wall of the universe. We can put it nearly anywhere. Hellfire can fly about three miles, top speed 950 miles per hour, so time in flight is minimal. Originally it was to be TV guided but they couldn't make it work. They switched guidance systems to what is called soft laser; our operators lock on the target from here and download that info into the guidance system of the weapon itself and then engage, and the bird follows the laser signature down to the end of the ride. It goes hot in a few hundred feet and then it's very reliable. It's a nasty bitch; it comes in at a low angle, a little over treetop level, and depending on how accurately it's been aimed, it can go through a window, pass the Coke machine and the water cooler, stop and use the men's room, knock on the door, go into the imam's anteroom, wait until he's ready, then go in and blow him up."

Swagger got the joke, if Starling didn't quite.

"But it's a tank killer, basically, right?" asked Swagger. "Suppose you've got something bigger to whack?"

"That's our Paveway Two," Nelson said. "It's a smart bomb, a TV-guided, five hundred pounder, thermobaric for enhanced destructiveness. The camera's in the nose, the operator can switch to it and actually ride it down. That's our crater maker, and each Reaper carries two, in case we need to wipe out a building. It happens. Now how do we decide to use these beautiful little toys? That is the question, isn't it?" Nelson said.

"That's why we're here, sir," said Starling.

"Fair enough. We have very strict policies on when we can and when we can't fire. There are three levels of permissibility. The first is called Tango, mil-speak T, for tactical. Normally, all the tac jobs are handled by service aviation. A marine company is pinned down, they call their own command and get a marine Apache and he Hellfires the crap out of whoever's shooting at the marines. Doesn't concern us, but sometimes for whatever reasons, the Apaches aren't able to get there fast enough and we have a drone in the area, our people will take the shot on a Tango license to shoot. They can communicate directly in real time with the grunts. I'm somewhat prejudiced here, but I think the marines would prefer a drone shoot over an Apache or an F-15, because our people are so much better. I mean this is all they do, day after day, and some of them get an almost zen feel for what the aircraft can do and what it can't, and they can turn on a pin, change angles of attack in a split second, Immelmann turn to the deck, do amazing things with those little aircraft and really put some hurt on the bad guys."

Swagger watched: in one of many similar cubicles, a young woman in the smart uniform of an Air Force officer, but for her pink flip-flops, sat at a console. She had one hand on a joystick and one hand on a lever to her left. Before her, a black-and-white television screen mounted in a wall of switches and buttons displayed a landform sliding underneath her from ten thousand feet, plus all sorts of technical readouts. Her ears were muffed with earphones, and a prong mike curved around her cheek to her mouth. She was talking, flying, searching, and hoping all at the same time.

"Lieutenant Jameson represents our second level of permissibility. It's called Oscar, that is O, the O standing for opportunity, as in targets of. Using intel developed by on-the-ground CIA assets, she knows where there is likely Taliban activity. Her battle manager vectors her onto the area, and they're both looking hard for signs of men with weapons. They may or may not represent any direct threat to coalition troops, but our rules of engagement won't let us just pop anyone. We have to see a weapon. Sometimes we'll stay with a truck or an SUV for hours waiting for a glimpse of an AK muzzle. Then we spend ten minutes trying to get permission, first from whoever's area of responsibility it is, then from the Agency, first on the ground in Afghanistan, then from an agency coordinating committee, then from AF command, and they have a legal officer sitting in on all Oscar operations, and all of them have access to the same battlefield visuals. Then and only then do we shoot. That's most of our shooting."

Lieutenant Jameson seemed to have come up with a possible target. Now she was really flying the aircraft ten thousand miles away, and Bob watched as her body language indicated the torque and concentration she was putting in as she delicately played the two controls against each other.

"The stick," said Colonel Nelson, "is vehicle manipulation, stick and rudder in the old days. Up, down, left, right. The rudder pedals are now part of a computer program, so she's not pumping away with her feet at the same time. Meanwhile, the lever on the left is throttle, controlling airspeed, engine pitch, that sort of thing. When we're close to the ground and engaging targets, we're operating right near the stall zone, so the trick is to find the equipoise between the stall and the maneuver. As I say, these folks develop an amazing touch for it, I mean I've seen them do things I couldn't even dream of in my F-15."

Jameson was good. Just a few feet from her glowing, lit-by-screen face, in black and white and flickering with the technical monitors that, in a river rush of cascading integers, told her the speed, direction, health, and mood of her unmanned aviation vehicle, the ridges of Afghanistan slid by. After one of them, she banked hard left, tilting her wings to forty-five degrees to match the incline of the slope beneath, then jacked into what felt like a left hand so harsh Swagger could feel the imaginary Gs in his stomach as she skittered over a village, twirled again, until a cruciform was on a single house. She rotated in low orbit, the house staying locked in the cruciform reticle.

"Jameson's our new ace. They call her New-D, which she doesn't like, but it's a tribute to her and to Old-D, Dombrowski, who was the best until she left. Now watch: Jameson could take it out with the snap of a button," the colonel said, "but not without permission. You can't hear it, but she's on the horn this very minute, extremely intense conversations with a variety of sources, not only her battlefield manager"—he pointed to an officer on a platform in the center of the room, bathed in gray light as he was following several dramas of interception at once—"but the other sources I mentioned. She's even reading the license plates of the vehicles to see if they match any affiliated with the Taliban or Al-Qaeda."

"And if she gets a signifier, she'll shoot?" asked Chandler.

"With approval."

But this wasn't a good one for Diana the Huntress. That goddess would have to wait for her blood offering from her young acolyte Jameson as her unseen collaborators and supervisor decided against pulling the trigger, and she climbed from the area, locked on a steady course, riding the grid this way before she rode it that way.

Nelson led them onward, talking as he went.

"The third level of permissibility is what we call Sierra, S for strategic. That's polite terminology for assassination. That's when the Agency develops a high-value target opportunity, specific to time and place. A big bad guy, in other words. It's rare enough to be fun and a highlight in a duty week. We will intercept him, just like we did Yamamoto in World War Two. We'll know where he will be and we'll be there, real high or real low. All the permissions are already in place, legal has signed off, we're just looking for one of a dozen preselected descriptors. Maybe an on-ground asset will be communicating with us. All the folks involved generally tune in; it's everybody's favorite TV show. But it's really up to the battle manager and the pilot to bring it off, and the other people usually keep their mouths shut. That one's all flying, just waiting for a moment when Mr. Big is in the car, there aren't any school buses or ambulances or trucks full of violin prodigies nearby, and they drop the hammer. The Agency is very strict on collateral, particularly in a Sierra shoot. It's one thing to blow up a school when you're trying to save a platoon from getting overrun and another to blow it up to kill one guy whose presence you're not a hundred percent clear on. Anyhow, you'll see a good one when you look at the shot tapes. We got a Taliban assistant commander in Kandahar province on that shift, I've already checked. Poof. Instant vapors. My people like those a lot. They're the shots that'll end the war sooner, rather than later."

"There's no other 'level of permissibility' as you call it, nothing beyond Tango, Oscar, and Sierra?" asked Starling.

"No, ma'am. Not at present. Not seven months ago. Now, if we find ourselves in a fall-of-Vietnam scenario, that might change. Or if Al-Qaeda goes belly up if we get the tall man, that might change too. I can't forecast the future. But those are our standards, our rules, and as you will see, we document everything and nothing is left to chance."

"And drones aren't run out of any other base?"

"No sir. The Air Force flies the drones, the CIA provides the intel and co-ops on the supervision. The CIA and the Air Force have a very good operating relationship, at this level anyway. Everybody's on the same page."

"And you tape all your shots?" asked Starling.

"Yes, ma'am. Partially to learn from them, but also to cover this eventuality so that we can answer any questions quickly and honestly."

They walked on through the center, seeing Jameson's scene played out by a dozen other pilot operators, some in Air Force officers' uniforms, some in shorts and T-shirts—civilian contractors, the colonel explained—passed under an archway, and came to a corridor. The colonel led them to a room.

"This is where I've set you up. We're at your disposal. You see before you duty logs, and the sergeant here will call your operators and battlefield managers for interviews. You can go through each operator's shifts in real time—well, you won't want to do that—or on channel two, you can see all the shots. You can talk with Captain Peoples, who was the battle manager that shift. I'll have meals brought to you, the bathroom is down the hall, and call me if you need anything at all. As I said, I want it noted that our cooperation was one hundred percent."

"Thank you," said Starling, and she and Swagger got to work.

Nick was in records on the second floor. It looked about as law enforcement as a midsize software company, with a lot of intense people locked into their computer terminals. He went to the duty desk and waited for someone to notice him. He could have sent someone, for as an assistant director, he now had a fleet of staff, as well as endless extras assigned for the duration of this task force emergency, but somehow he felt it best if he handled it himself. He also could have had a clerk dispatched to his office, but he'd never adjusted to the perk thing. It was something you didn't want to get too attached to or you'd really miss it when it went away.

"Yes, Mr. Director?" one of the clerks asked, having rushed to his side. ADs were big news in this part of the building, on this floor, and assisting one could always lead to some kind of break in the career climb.

"Hi," he said, squinting to see her nametag, "Doris, how are you? How're the wife and kids?" he joked, playing the sincerely-insincere card that was always good for an ice-breaking laugh.

"The kids ran away with a motorcycle gang and the wife is divorcing me for a bull dyke in Latent Prints," the girl said brightly, and both laughed. He liked her spirit.

"Okay," he said, "here's the deal. I'm not sure how you access this, but I'm thinking that in some way you ought to have records on a certain kind of guy."

"You don't have a name, a crime, a booking number?"

"Only a category."

"I'll try my best."

"Okay, you know these guys who work overseas for these big security firms on government contracts? Graywolf is the biggest, but there must be more."

"Yes, sir."

"I know we looked into Graywolf in 2005 on the issue of illegitimate or indiscriminate shooting in Baghdad."

"I remember it."

"The guys they hire: they seem to be called contractors, they're tough, hard guys, with a lot of military, even Special Forces, experience."

"Yes, sir."

"I need a list of the ones who've gotten in trouble with the law."

"I can cross-reference by affiliation against conviction. What sorts of infractions?"

"Gosh, I'm guessing assault, second-degree murder, maybe extortion, maybe rape, the kinds of crimes you'd find in a war zone. Wouldn't be crimes against property, but excess violence, a tendency to shoot, things that would get someone in trouble even in a wild and woolly town like Baghdad or Kabul. Maybe cross-reference with the authorities there, maybe check with State, Department of the Army, the marines, and so forth."

"Okay. I'll get right on it."

"And maybe also check with State as to whether or not any of them have recently reentered the country. I'm looking for a hard-ass guy with lots of combat experience, a real operator who's shady on the criminal front at the same time. I'm sure a lot of these guys are straight-on professionals, doing a very hard job in a crappy piece of the world. But the guys capable of that sort of thing over the long term, the guys who enjoy the action, who love to carry the black rifles and wear the watch caps low over their heads, the tactical freaks addicted to the rush of pulling the trigger—there's got to be a kind of pool of them available for various odd, dirty jobs in those towns. The washouts, the screwups, the just fired, the embittered. Those are the guys I'm looking for, and I'm real curious to see if any Tommy Tactical heavy hitters have come back recently."

"I'll get right on it, sir," she said.

"And this is just between you, me, and the bull dyke who stole your wife."

HIGH DESERT

S he drove listlessly if proficiently. The desert slipped by, unre-
markable in its repetitiveness as the rental ate up the miles
between Creech and Vegas and the hotel beds that would give
them a few hours' rest after an all-nighter talking about and watching
missiles blow up vehicles mainly, the odd mud shanty, now and then
an unidentifiable gun position, a spot on a ridge, a copse of trees, a
wall off the road.

It was the same. The missile hit too hard and fast for even the
highest res camera and the slowest slo-mo to catch it. What one saw
was only the release of an energy bolt in the severe constraints of
the black-and-white camera work, first a blinding smear of illumination, then unleashed, boiling coils of smoke lit from within, tumbling
tumultuously, almost with anger and vengeance as their propulsion,
while at the margins waves of dust whipped outward in supertime
and anything unobscured by the blast wave rippled against the sudden pressure spike, people, furniture, junk of any sort, all of it airborne and deposited elsewhere in a second.

And the shooters. The same. Earnest techies, some civvie, some
young Air Force officers, all polite and to the point, like a Boy Scout
patrol dead set on a high merit-badge count. They were so decent
you couldn't really play them, somehow, so eager, having been clearly
instructed by command to give it up to the feebs, all with bleached-
white teeth. Maybe the civvies were a little more loosey-goosey, but
not much, and in all their eyes Swagger read only commitment to
duty, pride in warrior skills, the lack of self-consciousness of the best
fighters (no intellectuals, no ironists, no wise guys among them).
They were a one-way street.

The drive rolled onward, low energy and without seeming purpose except getting there and getting to bed. At a certain point, Bob checked the messages on his cell, then settled back into the silence that pretty much defined his relationship with Starling when they weren't trying to nudge a young officer into explicating more precisely on the nature of this or that hit and the protocols that determined it. It had been exhausting, and only the work ethic of Spartans had gotten them through it despite jet lag and the need to return to DC and the actual mission at hand as soon as possible.

It wasn't until the comical cityscape of the strip, that mile or so of fantasy money-trap architecture that comprised tourist Vegas, revealed itself that she spoke.

"Not much, I'm afraid."

"No, ma'am."

"So I'm going to e-mail HQ a prelim. I'll account for our time, enumerate our IVs, and report our conclusions, which would be, correct me if I'm wrong, zilch, zappo, zip, nada, *rien*, and, of course, nothing. Do you disagree?"

"No, ma'am," said Bob. "Nothing we didn't know before."

"I'm going to ask to fly back tonight, tomorrow earliest. What day is it, again? All that time underground, you lose a sense of time."

"It's Sunday, it would be one-forty in the East."

"Okay, give me a minute."

She flipped her phone open one-handed, punched in a preset number, waited for the answer, and spoke quickly, listening more. Then she snapped it shut.

"He's been to the Sunday talkers under that heavy security, no difficulties, no emergencies, so Cruz has gone to ground for the time being and I think we're okay. I do want to be back before the next outing, that speech in Georgetown."

"Yes, ma'am," he said.

"Anything to say? Any disagreement with my conclusion? For the record, I was impressed. You handled yourself very well and you slipstreamed nicely with my lead on the interrogations. Hard to believe you aren't a trained agent."

"Thank you, ma'am. Just trying to be helpful."

More silence.

Then she said, "What did you mean?"

"I'm sorry?"

"You said, 'Nothing we didn't know before.' But we didn't know anything before. We still know nothing, or am I missing something?"

"Well, I would say we learned that a) there *is* a secret CIA program, and that b) we know what it does and how it's structured and who mans it and what its task is, and c) that Dombrowski took the shot on the day in question, though it wasn't a Hellfire, it was more likely one of the big boys, a Paveway Two."

Starling was silent for a while, then she guided the car to the shoulder. Cars buzzed by loaded up with prospectors, hungry to reach the promised land just ahead and, as promised, lose all their money. The comical town with its pyramids and space towers and Renaissance castles set against a crusty rim of low mountains lay bleaching in the sun. It looked like an idiot child's creation.

"All right, Swagger. What are you seeing that poor dumb Chandler isn't? What does the cowpoke Svengali have up his sleeve?"

"Yes, ma'am. First, the milieu. Hey, ain't that a fancy word? Can't believe I used it. I must have read it in some book or something."

"No attitude, please."

"I'm just funning you, Agent Chandler."

"Since you seem dead set on destroying my entire interpretation of the last sixteen hours, why don't you call me Jean. Or, I suppose, 'Starling,' since everybody else does."

"The milieu. If you looked carefully—"

"I suppose I didn't."

"You saw a lot of tape strips. Meaning there were a lot of banners taped up in that op center that they took down. It had been sanitized, you know, like a toilet in a motel with a paper ribbon around it. I'm betting the banners said things like 'Kill Towelheads!' and 'Go Git 'Em, Tigers.' All that fighter pilot macho kill-the-bastards stuff. See, that's that colonel. He's a fighter jock, he brings fighter jock mentality to the job, his thing is get in close and blow the bastards away. That's the spirit of the room, not the hum of techies. All those kids, they was suppressing, they was holding it in. They're young killers and they're proud of it. And they compete. That's why they have nicknames like New-D and Old-D and I bet the rest have 'em too, like Saxon Dog and Red Hawk and Bravo and Lionheart. They don't want us to see that but that's how people who kill operate, because they have to stay close to their high so they're together when the shit is in the air. I know. Three tours, 'Nam, one as a sniper."

"I know you've done some killing."

"Way too much."

"So what does that tell us? That's not—"

"No, but it sets up the climate of the place and it tells us it ain't as 'professional' as it seems and in that kind of a joint, things are sloppier, wilder, crazier. The stars have latitude, the bossman wants his kids to perform, he doesn't want to override them with ridiculous rules and bullshit, so he relaxes the regs. But he tightens it up for us and Jameson almost got with the program, but she couldn't say no to her comfy flip-flops today and go with the short little heels the women officers wear with that duty uniform. She probably normally hunts in jeans and a T-shirt or a tank top, and she loves it and they love her for it, because right now she is at the top of her game. But what that tells me is: there's room for something to slide by the Air Force monitors."

"I'm listening."

"Second thing: her battlefield manager, Captain Peoples. Remember him?"

"He was the dullest of the dull."

"He did seem like an IRS agent, didn't he? He is the key guy. He had to be in on it, and he probably reports directly to the Agency in certain circumstances. His console is so complex he could have all kinds of communications circuits the brass know nothing about."

"That doesn't prove—"

"I watched him extra hard. Remember when you asked him, 'And there's no other category of permissibility except Tango, Oscar, and Sierra?' And he said, 'No, ma'am, absolutely not'?"

"Sort of. I think I asked Colonel Nelson that."

"You asked everyone that. But only Captain Peoples was interesting when he answered. You know why?"

"Obviously not."

"Because unlike Colonel Nelson or any of the others, Captain Peoples leaned forward in his chair, fixed his eyes on yours, and did not blink. They all blinked, all through their chats, it's human to blink. You don't blink if you're concentrating on controlling your eyes because you don't want to give up the lying tell signs, the sideways or upper look to the script you're trying to remember. He had been professionally coached on how to get through an interrogation, how to lie without no tells. They trained him too good and he overdid it."

"Okay," said Starling. "I missed that. You didn't. Good work. It's thin but it's not without its compelling element. But you said you know what this program does."

"Think about what Tango, Oscar, and Sierra *don't* do. Think about the possibility they *don't* cover."

"Just tell me. I'm too tired to play games."

"Tango is urgent, tactical. Oscar is longer in duration, involves hunting, obtaining permission, checking with legal. Sierra is longest in duration, requiring preengagement permission requests and acceptances. But suppose . . . suppose they get a big guy in their sights and they have to make up their minds fast. In minutes?"

"All right. I'm supposing."

"They don't have time to go through committees and permission protocols or to haul a junior partner in from legal. So there's got to be an ultra-override program where somebody of senior judgment

and experience can make a fast read on intel and authorize an immediate shot. You get a good ground Joe who reliably sights Osama in
a tent in some province. He calls it in to his Agency case officer, and
that officer trusts him, sees the shot, and he calls Langley to get a
fast, fast-shoot permission. It's built on speed, no time for arguments,
assessments, ramification surveys, tallying the yeps and the nopes,
nothing like that. He goes to a big guy. This guy, whoever he is, he
gets to say shoot or don't shoot. He says it, the code word is sent to
Creech, not to Colonel Nelson or the XO or whoever, but directly to
the battle manager who goes to his best shooter and speaks the code
word, delivers up the grid location, and she puts a big, smart bomb
on it ASAP. From first sighting to delivery of ordnance, probably less
than three minutes. And who knows? The shooter, for one. The battle manager, who immediately erases the tape and makes no document entry, for another. And then some Air Force crew at the fly-off
base in Afghanistan who maybe notice Bird Twelve done come back
shy one of its two Paveways. It don't go no further, because the point
is, in certain instances they will miss and they don't want to answer
no questions in case they take out that school or a hotel with thirty-
one traveling salesmen in the bar. It's self-sealing. It's deniable. In the
instant it happens it ceases to exist."

"There's no proof."

"There will be tomorrow. When we see Dombrowski."

"I'll tell DC, we'll get her service records and bio. You run the
interrogation."

"I will."

"But if she stonewalls, I don't know where we'll be."

"I have the key to unlock her. Susan Okada left a message on my
phone. She found out there is just such a program and she found out
the name. It's called Pentameter."

FBI HQ

TASK FORCE ZARZI WORKING ROOM
FOURTH FLOOR
HOOVER BUILDING
PENNSYLVANIA AVENUE
WASHINGTON, DC
1750 HOURS

D oris in records must have worked overnight, and she was
very good. By late the next afternoon, she'd come up with a
list of possibilities, based on the investigation into Graywolf
run by the Bureau some years back on the issue of illegal shootings
during security operations in Baghdad. That shook out seventeen
names. Of the seventeen, she ran down and accounted for fifteen; it
was the last two who seemed to have disappeared and she'd run each
for known accomplices, and cross-referenced those to come up with
a third. She researched them all, made the calls, put the packages
together, and got it to him fast.

He thanked her, and retreated to his office while outside agents
ran down Ray tips or just relaxed after the stress of playing security
guard while Zarzi was doing his fabulous TV bits. Nick didn't want
it known what he was looking into, because people talked to people
who talked to people. He opened the files.

Faces. One of the great mysteries of law enforcement: what do
faces tell you? Do people look like their characters or look unlike
their characters? Nick tried to read the faces. But the faces, so common to men of high vitality and action orientation, were blunt, mute,
almost flat. Zemke, Anthony, was feral and quick, but well muscled,
an ex-Ranger with combat in the Raq, a street cop in Sausalito, Cali-
fornia, after his time in the service finished. Four years with Graywolf, three in Baghdad as a security specialist, cashiered over certain
irregularities in expense accounts. Last know address "c/o Black Cat

Cafe, Kabul," evidently the spot where the mercs hung and drank and looked for odd pickups from the town's many intelligence shops.

Then there was Crane, Carl, twelve years U.S. Army, Airborne Ranger, Fifth Special Forces, demo, commo, and first aid, aka "Crackers the Clown" for his stony, humorless demeanor, just a medium-size guy with enough combat in his background to have won a war, any war, single-handed. Silver Star, DFC, Bronze with two combat valor indicators, CIB, three tours in the Raq, one in 'Stan. It came apart on allegations of rape, him married, with two kids and a loving wife in Jupiter, Florida. The next three years were Graywolf, then again a whiff of scandal and separation. He was interviewed twice, deemed uncooperative on the issue of indiscriminate shootings while commanding a Graywolf security unit but, as he pointed out, none of his principals ever got his hair mussed.

Finally, Adonis. Or maybe Hercules. This one was really interesting. Michael C. "Mick" Bogier, considered his senior year the number one or two high school linebacker in America. Heavily recruited, he settled on the football factory at Alabama as the straightest road to the pros, but six games into a stellar freshman year he got drunk at a fraternity party, took his high school girlfriend on a ride in the yellow 'Vette some alumni "loaned" him, wrapped it, himself, and her around a tree. Neither the car nor the girl survived, the tree was also totaled, and Mick left school. He tried juco, Divisions II and III, Canada, played some pickup ball, got into drugs and partying in L.A. while trying to become "an actor," and finally enlisted after 9/11. For a while he'd found his niche: fast-tracked to Special Forces, he was sniper qualified, demo and commo cross-trained, a natural combat leader, a real Sergeant Rock. Decorations up the wazoo and it seemed he'd stay Green Beret for his twenty and morph into security consulting. But then along came Graywolf and their $200,000 sign-up bonus and Mick, who'd never been rich, and thought the NFL would make him so and was thus bitter about vanished chances, couldn't say no. He should be running the joint now, the poster boy contractor with the lean face, the thick burr of blond hair butch-waxed to crew cut attention, the god's body, the smarts, the guts. But he too had let his shooters go wild on the streets of Baghdad protecting various bigs. He was quietly let go, though with a bonus, and stayed in the Green Zone, where he acquired a reputation. He was suspected of a number of things, selling drugs and guns, trying to export dope (interviewed twice by DEA in Baghdad); that town finally got too hot for him and he took the picture show to Kabul, became a go-to guy for a number of drug lords with security problems, supposedly banked $4 or $5 mil in Switzerland, knew everybody and everything, and if you absolutely positively needed it done in Kabul by Tuesday, Mick Bogier was your guy.

Why did they bail on Kabul? War was their business and business was good. The three had entered the U.S. five months ago, via Miami International after taking the soft way home via Istanbul, then England, then the hop to Florida. State noticed and flagged, DEA noticed and flagged, and now and then Miami Vice checked up on them but just found three rich bruisers having fun getting drunk and laid. They disappeared from Miami just about the time . . . the Zarzi thing started up.

These were guys who could blow the shit out of a building or cut down nine unknown men, not for fun but because that was their job, they were being paid nicely for it. But who would hire them? They worked an exclusive world, mostly servicing intelligence agencies, international criminal entities, the odd billionaire who could buy his way in and needed some dirty deed done dirt quick and to hell with the expense.

Question of the day: who are they working for?

Wouldn't it be nice to talk to these gentlemen and see what they've been up to? he thought, and tried to figure out how to do it. What tales they could tell . . .

But he had nothing, except some vague confirmation of Swagger's claim of "contractors." He didn't have enough to book them, he didn't have enough to APB them, he really didn't even have enough to look for them. But he could put out a low-priority law enforcement request for any and all information regarding them to be forwarded to this headquarters, and maybe that would turn something up on the three stooges of death.

HENDERSON, NEVADA

I t was a small house, with gravel for a lawn and a cactus for a bush. One story, flat roofed, one of dozens like itself in a huge subdivision of Henderson, itself a subdivision of Vegas, laying out under a baking, bleaching sun. A Honda Civic was parked in the driveway and a half-scraped-off AF AND SOAR! sticker curled off the bumper, which, intact, had presumably declared JOIN THE USAF AND SOAR!

They knocked, and a young woman in a pair of gym shorts and a tank top answered the door in a bit, a pair of recently removed earpieces hanging around her neck from an iPod clipped to her shorts. Her hair was cropped short, naturally blond, and her skin beautiful, although, unfortunately, she was not. But she was certainly pleasant and looked kind without the intimidating beauty that scared so many off.

"Ms. Dombrowski?" Chandler asked, flashing her badge.

Badges are always bad news, even when they're not. Dombrowski stepped back as if hit, blinked, lost all confidence, and said, "Uh, yes?"

"I'm Special Agent Chandler and this is Investigator Swagger. We're with the Federal Bureau of Investigation. We're looking into events in the 143rd Expeditionary Wing ops center at Creech a few months back. May we speak with you for a bit, please?"

Chandler had the warm but no-bullshit, no-refusal part of policework down pat, and the young woman, her face closing off even more darkly, stepped back to admit them.

"I'm sorry I'm sweaty," she said, "I was on the bike." Then she launched into a pointless explanation of how she was due at Borders at eleven, then at the Center at eight, and she didn't have time to exercise except in the morning except it was getting harder and harder and . . . but she didn't really care and neither did they.

They sat, she in a chair, the two interlocutors on the sofa. Coffee? No. Juice, water, any sort of liquid, no. Now what was this all about? And finally, "Do I need a lawyer?"

"No," said Chandler. "We're simply being thorough. Allegations have been raised about a certain missile shot. Maybe it wasn't even that, just a random explosion in a city full of them. But another agency has requested we examine, and so we have to. We were in the ops center yesterday and spoke to all the pilots on duty at the time in question, Colonel Nelson, and the battle management officer, Captain Peoples. You were the only one not present, and as you were in the area, we decided to complete the interviews for the record. You are not a 'person of interest,' nor at this time is any legal action contemplated against you. Possibly that will change, and if it does, you will be duly informed and given the opportunity to retain counsel."

She nodded grimly.

She swallowed.

Then she said, "I can't tell you anything."

"Well, that's not a good start," said Starling, stagily disappointed.

"If there are any infractions or any crimes or any anything, they are my doing alone and I am guilty of them and nobody else is. I will not testify against any colleague or superior officer. If you have evidence against me and are going to indict me or subpoena me or anything, I will not testify or offer a defense. If I have to go to prison I will go to prison. I've thought this through carefully and that's all I've got to say. You seem like nice folks and I don't think you're here to hurt me but that's the way it has to be."

"Whoa," said Swagger. "We're not here to bust you, Ms. Dombrowski. Ma'am, nobody wants you in jail. I already handed out my share of parking tickets, so I met my quota, and I shot a couple of rustlers in the driveway, so I don't have to bring nobody in today. We just want to talk informally about events of that duty tour and see where that leaves us."

"It will leave me in jail," she said. "I killed thirty-one people that day for nothing, and it's something I'd like to forget, but if it is determined that I'm to be punished, then I will be punished. That's all I have to say."

There was silence in the room.

Chandler looked at Swagger, nodded, and got up and left.

The older man and the young woman were alone.

"Why are you here?" the young woman said. "I'd think you would have concluded it might work better with a female interrogator. Empathy, gender identification, feminine bonding and understanding, all that."

"Well, you and I have something in common that cuts much deeper than gender or any of that other stuff. And that is that we killed for the king. We were the royal assassins. We loved it, we enjoyed how special it made us, we liked the way the room quieted when we walked in. But there came a time when we looked at it, and thought, why? Why did that have to happen? Did it do any good?"

She shook her head, not in denial but in recognition.

"What were you?"

"Gunnery Sergeant, USMC. Sniper. Vietnam, seventy-three to seventy-five, until I was hit bad. Ninety-three kills on the record, many more off the record. Like you I put a crosshair on something and sent a package into it and watched it die. Like you I said it was for the good of the country, or at least each man I killed wouldn't kill an American kid, and like you, at the end, I thought to myself, well, what the hell? Who am I? Why was I so good at it, and if it was so right, how come I see faces every night? You ride an exercise bike, I crawled up in the mountains of Arkansas and stayed drunk for twenty years before I finally came back to the world."

She just stared at him.

"I wanted to fly fighters," she finally said. "I wasn't good enough. So I ended up with the next best thing and I never knew the price I'd have to pay."

"You killed some people. So it goes. The world can be a wicked place, you and I both learned that the hard way. So let me tell you, for what it's worth from a fella who's faced the same bad demons as you, they don't go away, but over time they soften and over time you realize that yes, there are boys who grew to be men and fathers and citizens because you done your killing. You can say, well, what about them people you killed, they might have grown to be men and fathers and citizens and made their contribution to their place too, and I say, I can only worry about so much, and I chose to worry about other marines, just as you did. No, it ain't easy, and those of us who take the responsibility to press the trigger and fire the bullet or the missile, a little of us dies each time, but it does mend, heal, soften, go away, and you do get your life back slowly and are capable of contributing again."

"Yes, sir," she said. "I hope so."

"And if you're not talking about it because you think you have to 'protect' some people, let me tell you, that cat's out of that bag. We know about Pentameter. We know about the top-secret, possibly illegal, fast-shoot leader-killing program that can be called up and executed in seconds and then ceases to exist. We know they used you to put a thermobaric Paveway into that hotel and that thirty-one souls went wherever they went, and no big bad leader died that day. But you didn't kill them people. You lived up to your honor, your tradition, your family's tradition"—Swagger knew Dombrowski's father had been a lieutenant general in the Air Force and a Phantom jock in Vietnam, her grandfather a one-star general who'd done fifty (two tours) over Europe in the Sixth Air Force in World War Two, she'd graduated third in her class at the academy—"and you acted in a warrior's good faith. You were used, but it happens, and you have to go on."

"But," she said, "in war, collateral happens. Wrong place, puff of wind, your finger slips, you misread a map, anything, and innocent people die. You live with it because that's the process of war and it's big and sloppy and cruel and you put it behind you. This was different. I was told to shoot, I rode the bomb down because Paveway isn't a fire-and-forget system, so you have to actually fly it into the target. You're in the nose. I saw that roof get bigger and bigger and bigger and then disappear in the flash. It happened because of me. And I checked the papers, I checked with everyone I knew: no, no leader went down, the intelligence was wrong, so let's pretend it didn't happen. You know, if the Israelis send a missile through the wrong window, they pay off and apologize. Here, we just pretend it hasn't happened and we walk away from it. It's not right."

"And that's why you left the service?"

"And broke my parents' hearts and ended up selling books at Borders and working a rape hotline at night."

"I'm betting you could get back in. They need people like you. You're the best, and you make the service and the nation better for your participation."

"Are you a recruiter?"

"No. I'm after whoever ordered a Pentameter hit that day. Someone high in government did it for reasons we haven't figured out yet. Yes, he killed those thirty-one but he done some other killing too, for some policy goal that he's the only one who's aware of. He's the bastard I'm hunting."

"I'll tell you everything," she said.

The state trooper's light flashed red-blue, red-blue and he hit some kind of klaxon device, an unpleasant sound not unlike the Israeli antiriot psy-war technologies. Bilal guided the van to a halt on the shoulder.

"What is it, Bilal?" asked Professor Khalid.

"I don't know," said Bilal. "You two sit there and keep your foolish mouths shut. This man does not want to be engaged in your dialectics. He is beyond enlightenment. When he sees that I am Muslim, he will want to arrest me and impound the vehicle. He will find what is in the back and we will be put on trial and treated like amusing dogs for the infidels. Then you will spend the rest of your lives in a Western prison and you will have contributed absolutely nothing."

"Oh, dear," said Dr. Faisal. "That would be most unfortunate. I would not go to heaven. Although it is meaningless to the apostate, as he is not going to heaven under any circumstances, the circumcised dog, and I—"

"Faisal," said Khalid, "your hostility is pointless when directed at me. Save it for—"

"Be quiet, the both of you. Worthless, yakky old men, all the time with the yakking, I almost hope he does arrest us so I can get some peace and quiet."

"I have to go to the bathroom," said Faisal.

"Use the jug," said Bilal.

"It's not that one. It's the other one. A jug is of no use."

"Then just hold it. That's all we need, shit all over everything for this big American hero to smell."

He tried to gather himself. The Ruger .380 with a Velcro strip adhesived to its slide was held in place by another Velcro strip wrapped around his forearm. He could draw and shoot in a second. Yet what would that accomplish? Broad daylight, highway, the middle of America, top speed sixty-two mph. They certainly weren't getting away with anything, much less getting away, period.

Finally, presumably after checking their Arizona plates with HQ, the trooper lumbered out of his vehicle, stopped to hitch up his belt, then ambled forward to the van window. Bilal watched him advance, placed his wallet out on the empty seat next to him so that the officer could watch him reach for it, then set his hands at ten and two on the wheel, and concentrated on holding still.

"Good afternoon, sir, may I see a driver's license, please?"

"Yes, Officer."

He reached over and picked up the wallet, held it deliberately out front so the cop could watch both hands—this was a trick he'd learned as a child when the Israeli Security Forces detained boys en masse—and plucked out the license, a very good fake linked to an actual license holder in Tempe, Arizona.

The officer took the license, took a brief look around the van, giving the two old men a once-over, then said, "I'll be right back, sir."

He went back to his vehicle, now to run the license against watch lists, APBs, wanted circulars, other security checklists.

"I have shit myself," said Faisal.

"Praise be to Allah," said Khalid. "When you need Him, He comes to your service."

"Infidel. Apostate. Fiend. Demon."

"Stop it, you two. I will find a place for you to purify, if we get out of this."

"I am trying to be rational."

"The text is all the 'rational' you need—"

"Please, I can take no more," said Bilal. "Silence. He returns."

The officer came to the van window again.

"All right, Mr. Muhammed," he said, handing the license back. "The reason I stopped you, your right rear tire looked wobbly to me.

I think you should pull in at the next highway rest area and have a mechanic look at it. Maybe the lug nuts are loose, or maybe you have a worse problem and it'll need some looking after. You could also help whichever old fellow had an accident get cleaned up. Sorry to detain you and cause an unpleasantness, but your safety is our most important concern."

"Thank you, Officer," said Bilal. "I will have it taken care of."

"Good luck on your trip now."

"Thank you, sir."

Bilal started the engine again, waited for a space to open up, and reentered the traffic.

FBI HQ

**DIRECTOR'S OFFICE
HOOVER BUILDING
WASHINGTON, DC
1000 HOURS
THE NEXT DAY**

S o let me get this straight," said the director, "your job was to apprehend a man who'd made a threat against a high-profile diplomatic visitor to this country. You haven't done that. You really haven't even come close and he's come closer to doing his job than you have to doing yours. But you say you have uncovered a secret CIA killer program that in at least one case has targeted American servicemen in Afghanistan. You've decided that case is more important than apprehending Ray Cruz. You now want latitude to widen the investigation, bring in the U.S. Attorneys' Office, begin subpoenaing high-ranking Agency officers working in the most secret and sensitive of national security areas. Hmm, Mr. Swagger, it seems like every time we hire you as a consultant, we end up in a completely different pea patch than the one we thought we were going to end up in. Is that a fair assessment?"

Bob said, "Yes, sir, that is fair."

The three sat alone in the director's big office overlooking Pennsylvania Avenue with a nice view of the Capitol dome. The man himself, pink and glowing in his dark suit like so many of the DC bigfooters, had his legs up on his table and his body language communicated the "friendly talk" mood as opposed to the "you are so fucked" mood. He liked Nick, and had more or less "supported" (best not to look too carefully at it) Nick during the twisted investigation that had led to the still controversial murder-one four times conviction of Tom Constable some years back. But he was also putting out a message that maybe this time, Nick was asking a little too much. He was a genius at sending messages with layers and layers of subtext.

"Mr. Director," said Nick, "the evidence is pretty incontrovertible. We have a former drone pilot willing to testify that she was ordered, via secret CIA protocols, to destroy what turned out to be a nonmilitary target. We can tie that by time frame to the destruction of the hotel in Qalat where a U.S. Marine sniper had told his headquarters he would be setting up his mission. It connects to almost the minute. No, we don't know how the Agency got into the marine communications net. But we'll find that out. The marine was set to go Afghan time 1700, the missile, smart-bomb hit actually, was set up fast in real time, enabling an on-ground spotter to relay the info to whomever that the sniper had indeed entered the hotel, and the shot was ordered at about 1658.30 Afghan time. That gave the pilot just enough time to vector her Reaper vehicle to the exact grid location her battle management officer had given her, acquire target, launch the Paveway, and guide it down so that it hit at 1559.38. The time is on record at Two-Two Recon, Cruz's battalion, outside Qalat. That fact won't go away."

"And you believe that operation continued in the United States?"

"I have the entry into the U.S. of three extremely proficient 'contractors,' last known locality Miami, Florida. After they disappeared, things started happening: a building was shot up in Danielstown, South Carolina, and a man killed. Mr. Swagger here just survived the incident by chance and you can still see the scar on his face where he was hurt in the gunfire. Second, four days ago, nine Filipino temporary workers were killed in Baltimore by a highly proficient team utilizing silencers and extremely developed raid craft. They had, we believe, followed Swagger and me to that location and meant to wipe out its inhabitants as a way of nailing Ray Cruz, whom we thought might seek shelter there. They're still around, they're still trying to kill Ray Cruz, and they won't be leaving any witnesses. Since we believe they have satellite assistance in all the tracking they do, there is a good chance they are working for elements within the Agency."

The director nodded. But then he said, "And the fact that Ray Cruz is still out there, that he tried to make his kill in Baltimore, the fact that he has not been apprehended, that seems not too important to you."

This was the time to put it on record, Bob realized, that he had been in contact with Ray, that Ray had agreed to back off while the scandal was sorted out, and that he had not attempted any operations on Sunday last against his supposed target.

But knowing that was the only card he still had to play, Bob kept it to himself. Instead, he said lamely, "He did not make an attempt this past Sunday. Maybe he's backing off. Maybe he's letting us dig into Pentameter and that's the point of his game, not killing this Zarzi fellow. He actually never pulled the trigger in Baltimore. His supposed 'attempt to kill' Zarzi certainly did lead us to Pentameter. Maybe that was the original idea."

"Maybe it was, maybe it wasn't. Maybe you're giving him too much credit. Maybe you like him too much."

"That is a possibility," said Swagger. "I hope it ain't the case, but maybe it's working that way in my mind."

The director sighed.

"I will take your findings to the U.S. attorney general and we will see what will exists in the Justice Department to continue and widen the investigation. I suspect very little, and I warn you of that. If this Ray Cruz has evidence to give, he'd better turn himself in. That would make everybody's job a lot easier."

"Yes, sir. I'd like to emphasize that time—"

"Yes, time is of the essence. I've got a crew of attorneys on their way over and their Administration overlords too. This will be political, you understand. Politics will have its way, maybe more than truth and justice. You have to get, especially you, Swagger, that we can't have any Marshal Dillon stuff this time or the hammer will come down in very hard ways on all of it."

"I won't do no Marshal Dillon, sir," said Bob. "Way too old for it."

FBI HQ

**OUTSIDE THE DIRECTOR'S OFFICE, CONTINUING
INTO ELEVATOR, AND CONTINUING TO NICK'S
OFFICE IN TASK FORCE ZARZI WORKING ROOM
FLOORS 7 TO 5
HOOVER BUILDING
PENNSYLVANIA AVENUE
WASHINGTON, DC
1028 HOURS**

O kay, we will see what we will see," said Nick as they waited for the elevator. "I told you, I'd give it my best shot and he will too. You have to prepare yourself for the fact that some things won't happen."

"Such as?"

"They are not going to give Ray Cruz a Silver Star and his old job back and erase the several crimes he has committed. He will do time, no matter what."

"Don't seem right," said Bob.

"Can't have one law for heroes and another for us normal folks. Although, yes, you can have one law for corporate presidents, elected officials, congressmen and lobbyists and Wall Street bankers, and one for the rest of us. I'm sorry about that and if I ever get any juice in this town, I will try to change it. But it doesn't change reality: Ray will do time and his marine career is finished. Assuming he doesn't kill Zarzi."

"He won't."

"And I don't think we'll get a case out of it. I think what we'll get is nothing but the satisfaction that the Agency had to explain itself and back way down and a lot of heads will roll and maybe Susan Okada will get a big promo and maybe when she gets it she will run off to Idaho and iron your Jockeys for you for the rest of your life."

"Unlikely," Bob said.

"Well, you're probably right about that. Okay, I'm going to bump up my inquiries about these guys Bogier, Zemke, and Crane to 'Detain for interrogation. Approach with caution.' If we get them off the field, then maybe Cruz will be more cooperative."

"Them bastards may not go easy. You could get some cops killed."

"I will also add a 'Caution, presumed armed and dangerous.'"

"Real good."

"And I want you to go to Georgetown today and make a site analysis, just like the last time. Then it'll be the same, a round of meetings with our good friends from Secret Service and metro police and we'll lay out our plans for Friday."

"There ain't going to be no hit on Friday."

"Let's hope. Meanwhile, we'll wait for our callback to the director's office."

"Sure," said Bob, "I'll get right on it."

"Starling says you did really well."

"The gal pilot and I had a lot in common. I don't want to see her getting in any trouble over this either."

"I don't see how she can. There isn't going to be any case, you have to be ready for that. The Administration is too in love with drones to let anything happen to the program. Okay? *Comprende?*"

"I get it."

"Now go, do your job. Or someone else's, anybody's job."

"Yes, sir," said Bob, knowing that first he had to get his car washed.

Y ou are so beautiful," Zarzi said. "Your eyes, black diamonds. Your skin, the touch of satin. Your limbs, smooth and grace- ful as poems. Your throat a golden vase of supple nuances. But it is your mind that is remarkable, more remarkable than your beauty. It sees, it penetrates, it isolates the actual, it understands the play of history and tradition. It is the most extraordinary of your many, many gifts."

He put his hand on her shoulder.

"Sorry, sir," said Susan Okada, "but just out of curiosity, does that stuff ever really work?"

"You'd be surprised," he said. "I could make you a queen."

"Queen of Afghanistan!" she snorted. "Please, are you trying to be funny?"

"I will make you queen of Washington. I will make you queen of Bloomingdale's."

"Hmm. What about Saks?"

"Well, I—"

"No, not even for Saks. And anyway, you're lying. You lie most sincerely. You're at your best when you lie. But we both know you wouldn't make me queen of anything. And we both know I don't want to be a queen. I'm already a princess, why would I want all the responsibility?"

"Such wit. But you think yourself too good for me."

"I think no such thing, sir. Thinking doesn't enter into it. I *know* I am too good for you. It's simple fact."

The watch faces on the winders undulated all about her. Was this

his seduction technique? Maybe it worked with idiots, but it just made Susan slightly nauseous and she'd arrived knowing the bastard would probably throw some moves on her. It was his nature. Ugh, he was handsome and charismatic in an extraordinarily uninteresting way. Yes, the technical aspects were all in place, but he seemed to lack a coherent center to bring it all together.

"So, I assume we're finished with the Cary Grant–Doris Day aspects of the interview and now, if I may continue?"

"Certainly."

"Around five P.M. that day, a hotel across from your compound explodes."

"Most ferociously."

"I have been tasked by the Agency to look into it. We are concerned that it represented an attempt on your life by Taliban members or even Al-Qaeda."

"No, no," said Zarzi. "The brotherhood would not have missed. If they decide I must die, then I will die. I happily sacrifice myself for the good of my country. I yearn for martyrdom not to get to paradise but to inspire our young to stand against the forces of evil arrayed against us. Why would I want to go to paradise? I am already in paradise."

"Well, if being surrounded by watches is your idea of paradise."

"And the flesh of beauties. You turn me down, that is the right of a Western woman, but I must say, not many do. I have, what do you call it, oh yes, according to Page Six, that 'Omar Sharif–Dr. Zhivago vibe' going. And I think a young man from the *New York Times* fell in love with me some days ago. Such a puppy. Why, he even fainted. We had to call a doctor."

"Journalists," she said. "Attention sluts, all of them."

"You know, young lady, to return to the subject of the explosion, there is much narcotics trafficking in that area. I believe that the explosion was related to narcotics trafficking. The money in that business is capable of corrupting even the holiest of imams."

She knew of course that he had banked about $90 million in a

Swiss bank from his control of certain vast poppy field holdings, but she ignored the subject and veered off in another direction.

"It has been reported that the explosion was instrumental in your decision to envision an American future for your country, 'our two nations entwined and facing a bright future ahead.'"

"I believe I did say that, yes. Another lie, of course. I cannot help myself, the West is so eager for another thousand or so *Arabian Nights*. And, as you say, I am at my best when I lie. See, that is another remarkable thing about you, your perception. So precise, so in depth."

"Possibly we should not focus on the ethical, the psychological, the political, but merely the practical. What sort of blast was it?"

"A blast like any other blast. *Ka-boom!*—that is all. Rather big, I suppose. Bigger than normal, if explosions can be called normal. Rubbish and body parts rained into my courtyard for days afterward. A head dropped in on the Tuesday following. Most astonishing."

"Heads falling from the sky are only amusing when they belong to other people."

"My head will stay where it is until Allah calls it to be placed at his right hand," he said, too merrily.

"If I thought you actually believed that, I'd be horrified."

"I do sometimes exaggerate. It is my way. I'm of the impression your legs may be the most extraordinary thing about your body. They appear to be quite long for an Asian woman. Yet you hide them in pants. You should enjoy the Western freedom and wear short, tight skirts and very high heels, black leather, I think, and I am undecided as to stockings, black of course but still rather sheer, or bare, with the shine of the skin so . . ."

It went on, until finally she acknowledged that Ibrahim Zarzi was immune to blandishment, refusal, shame, threat, or pressure. He was a self-sealed system, utterly impenetrable by the West, hiding efficiently behind an armor of superciliousness and clichés copped from bad thirties movies. She ended the interview, endured a rather long, warm handshake, almost a sexual act in itself, gathered her stuff, and exited as graciously as possible with the vague promise of having a drink with him sometime, and knew what had to happen next. This is what she'd been playing for. She looked around, saw some Afghan Desk handlers, a few cops, and had started to think *Oh, shit* when a presence rushed through the door, slightly frazzled, slightly flushed, no less than Jared Dixson, assistant to the Afghan Desk. It was the only time in her life she'd ever been happy to see Jared Dixson.

"Hello, hello, hello," he said.

"Good-bye, good-bye, good-bye," she said.

"Susan, please, it has to be fate that I ran into you."

"Does it? I bet when you found out I was here, you blasted off from Langley and made it in twenty minutes."

"Susan, you overrate my love for you. I didn't have a police escort, I drove myself. It was a full thirty-two-minute ordeal, and I only ran six reds. Look, nothing is going to happen here. He'll sit in there among his watches and think of new lies to tell and which reporters to tell them to. That's his job, after all, and he's damn good at it. Let's have lunch. I want to hear the latest manhunt news and I have some very funny stories about Jack Collins's real war, which isn't against international terrorism but against international Jared Dixsonism."

"No let's-have-an-affair bullshit. The answer on that front now and forever will be no. I don't feel like going over it again."

"Got it. I'll prove to you I can play by your petty, bourgeois rules."

"And no martinis either. Two and you're sticking your tongue in my ear. That's so attractive."

"Sure, we'll just go downstairs, talk shop, drink Pellegrino, and eat those little shrimpy things they have here that are so good."

"If you touch my hand, I'll stab it with a shrimp fork."

"You're so damned good at playing hard to get!"

HOWARD COUNTY, MARYLAND

G reen country hurled by outside. Swagger drove, passed a town called Laurel where somebody had once tried to kill a presidential candidate, and closed the distance to Baltimore. In his pocket was an envelope. It had been delivered to the hotel suite that was his living quarters in Rosslyn that morning. He'd opened it to find nothing but an ad ripped out of a newspaper that read "Best Car Wash in Baltimore/Brushless Wash/Professional Detailing and Waxing/Howard Street Car Wash at 25th/Rain Check If the Weather Is Bad Next Day."

The cell on the next seat rang.

Who knew his number?

"Hello?"

"Swagger?"

It was Susan Okada. He felt a little spurt of something. Not big, but not small: something.

"Hi," he said. "What's up?"

"Listen, I'm in the ladies' room of the Four Seasons. On your behalf I've just spent too long with a bitter asshole named Dixson who's high in Afghan but wants to be higher."

"You poor thing."

"It wasn't easy. And it's not done yet. But I want to get this to you. I think, from several things he's said, I've figured out the meaning of 'Pentameter.'"

"I looked it up. Some kind of measure of verse, ain't that it?"

"Shakespeare wrote in 'iambic pentameter,' yes, which has to do with the number of 'feet' or beats to the line. That number is five. That's really what Pentameter means: five."

"Like the sides of the Pentagon?"

"That's it. Or, in this case, five senior intelligence officials who are vested with the power to call a Pentameter shot. One of them had to order the hit on that hotel. One of them wanted Ray Cruz dead in a hole in the ground. It could be no one else."

"Do you know who they are?"

"Not, surprisingly, the director. He's a political appointment and he showed good judgment in declining the offer because he didn't want to make a real-time call without the background. So: the three in the Agency are the assistant director, the director of plans, i.e., 'Operations,' and Afghan Desk himself. Outside the Agency, in the Administration, are the National Intelligence director and the president himself, though Dixson says the president doesn't seem really engaged on the issue and probably wouldn't let himself get involved."

"Okay. Four guys. Great."

"I'm going to work on ways to smoke out one of these four guys."

"Well, we'll see if we have an investigation. We went to the FBI bigfoot and he said he had to share with the Justice Department and he fears they'll close us down."

"Maybe we can at least get Ray Cruz out of the hot seat," she said.

"That would be something, I guess," he said. "Anyhow, thanks."

"Anything else?"

"Okada-san, as usual, you are terrific. Sorry I've been a jerk. For some reason I'm too close to the edge on this one and I'm all cranky and smart-ass, quick to go mean and rotten. It's just me. It don't mean a thing. Sorry I'm such a jerk."

"Some are born jerks" she said, "some have jerkhood thrust upon them, and some mature into rich and vibrant jerks. You are all three." She hung up.

He drove on, watching the skyline of the city reveal itself as he hit the beltway, looking a little like Omaha, without the fun parts.

He was totally unaware that a mile back, a Ford Explorer carrying three men and a lot of guns followed quietly, like a Reaper drone, silent, deadly, watching.

HOWARD STREET CAR WASH

S wagger sat in the sunlight under a crisscross of flapping pennants strung on wires, as if at some kind of medieval fair, while the rented red Taurus was shipped through a long tunnel, squirted, sloshed, rubbed, spritzed, steamed. Soon it would emerge into a kind of courtyard here just off Howard, and a bunch of third worlders, Mexicans, Salvadorans, a few blacks, a few Asians, would fall upon it with a kind of intense rub-the-paint-off thing going on, and theoretically the car would emerge a few minutes later shiny as new and smelling of whatever, God knows, wafer—chocolate, spearmint, lime, fruit punch?—they hung by string from the rearview mirror. He guessed Ray was among them, but the scene was complex, with vehicles of all sorts—beamers, Benzes, SUVs, pickups, cabs—moving in and out, a substantial number of car owners drifting into the courtyard to watch, then tip the men with the towels, some kind of white foreman acting like a landing officer on a flight deck, trying to keep the whole chaotic process moving and prevent the overenthusiastic towel guys from banging the cars together as they moved them through the steps.

He watched the dripping car emerge, he watched an ad hoc crew assemble around it, as one guy steered it to an empty space and the others pounced. Like all the Mercedes owners and all the BMW owners but none of the cabdrivers, he drifted out to supervise, and bent in to point out one particularly loathsome rental car smear to a hardworking towel professional in an old Orioles cap, baggy jeans, and a Harvard sweatshirt, and the towel guy said, "So what's happening, Gunny?"

"I didn't recognize you," said Swagger. "But I guess that's the point."

"I just look like any other little brown man in this place. Tell me what's going on."

"Okay," said Bob, and summed up the last few days of investigations.

"I wish you'd quit this high-paying, prestige career, climb in the car with me, and we'd go to DC together now," he concluded. "It would save a lot of trouble."

"I'm not in this to save trouble. I'm in this to get some justice for Billy Skelton and all the other little people these motherfuckers stepped on, Sergeant. You know that, so don't even ask me."

"Stubborn bastard. Okay, you tell me. What's next? Please, please don't do nothing at Georgetown. You do that and I don't think I can help you. We are almost there, Cruz. I'm betting the time you do won't be nothing, you can have your life back, you can—"

"I still have a death sentence, Sergeant. For all I know, these guys could put a Paveway on me right now. They'd kill everyone you see here to take me out. Collateral means nothing to them. I'm appreciating what you've done, but we won't be there until I get some kind of solid assurance I am off the bull's-eye, that whoever set this thing up is the one doing the time, and that the contractors who filled all those body bags are somehow dealt with. In prison, preferably in the ground, but I don't care. It's not about me getting my life back, it's about payback."

"Jesus, you are a hard-case sonovabitch."

"Here," said Ray, handing over a cell phone. "Hit one and it rings me. You keep me in the loop, I'll keep you in the loop. I know you won't use it to track me. Now I gotta go. Saw a Benz coming through the line. Those guys are usually big tippers."

And with that, he turned back to his wheel-trim-polishing career.

Bob slipped the cell into his pocket, got in and eased the car through the busy yard, then turned onto Howard Street and headed back to DC. Hell of a long way to go for a car wash.

UNIDENTIFIED CONTRACTOR TEAM

There was no celebration. They were too coldly professional for that. It was simply time to get to work, and with this troublesome asshole, no chances could be taken.

Too chaotic a scene to snipe into. Too many bodies moving unpredictably here and there, the .50 Barrett on its bipod was more unwieldy than a plow, so tracking target movement under duress could be a bitch, and the .338 Lapua was only a little lighter; plus the courtyard was hemmed off from the street by a brick wall and all Cruz had to do was drop and he was under cover.

"Your basic raid deal," Bogier proclaimed. "Go in shooting, get up close, put the fucking mags into him. Then we get the fuck out of town."

"They'll get a read on the license plate," said Tony Z.

"That's why when we get suited up, we go somewhere nearby and steal a car. We take the car to the scene. I take the car through the line, get the car washed. You guys are down the street a bit. When I have Cruz marked, I will give the signal. Crackers ambles down to the courtyard. I give another signal and the thing begins. I will close on him and full-auto his ass to itty little bits. Crackers, meanwhile, will buzz-gun the shit out of the car wash wonderland of Baltimore—"

"Cool!" said Crackers.

"—and people will run like fuck. Tony Z pulls the SUV up and we jump the wall—"

"It looks like a pretty high wall, Mick."

"You're an Airborne Ranger, you can do anything."

"I'm an *old* Airborne Ranger. It's my knees. They aren't what they used to be."

"Just roll over it like an old man," said Tony. "You know, hit it, swing your legs over. You don't have to do any Hong Kong gangster shit."

"Yeah, yeah," said Crackers. "That'll work."

"May I continue?" asked Mick. "Or are there other important areas of discussion you two would like to examine?"

"Sorry, Mick," said Crackers. "I was just thinking about shit."

"I hate it when you do that. No good can come of it."

"But if I'm in the SUV, they'll still get a read on our license plate."

"Okay, okay. So . . . the car we steal, we trade plates."

"Actually, it would make more sense if we stole *two* sets of plates," said Crackers earnestly. "We steal SUV plates and we put 'em on our vehicle. We keep our plates. Wait, no, we steal SUV plates because they're *different* from automobile plates. We put them on our wagon. Then we switch back to *our* plates."

"Numb nuts, we have a .50 caliber Barrett in the backseat. I think that's going to—"

"Jesus Christ, girls, this bicker-bicker-bicker shit has got to stop. We steal SUV plates and make the change. Then we steal a car. One pair of SUV plates, one car. Then we do it as I have laid it out. I take the car in, Crackers wanders down the street to the yard. I do the dirty deed, Crackers burns off a mag or two making holes, breaking glass and blasting pennants out of the air, his own private Fourth of July, and off we go in the SUV. I'm guessing nobody gets a read because it's going to be thirty seconds of World War Three. But we do the plate switch just to be sure. Then, Miami Beach, here we come. Home free, a year's vacation, lots of pussy and dope, some new tats, the life of O'Reilly."

"Reilly. Not O'Reilly. He's a TV guy."

"O'Reilly lives plenty high enough for me."

Body armor. An entire 9-mm trousseau including MP5s and SIGs. Randall fighting knives. Black wool watch caps. Danner Desert warfare boots. So Tommy Tactical. They looked really cool.

FBI HQ

DIRECTOR'S OFFICE
HOOVER BUILDING
PENNSYLVANIA AVENUE
WASHINGTON, DC
1700 HOURS

The call came at five. Swagger was just back from a too hasty trip to the Georgetown site of Zarzi's upcoming speech. He joined Nick in the director's anteroom, and the two were beckoned in.

"Sit, sit," said the director.

They sat.

"You guys look all frowny. Why the frowny faces?"

"It's too fast," said Nick. "If you had good news, there'd be an Agency liaison, two or three guys from Justice, and probably an Administration overseer. I'm not optimistic."

"It's not as bad as you think it could be. The key is, Cruz has to come in. Cruz has to come in, he will be placed under our protection, and he will cooperate. All charges against him will be held in abeyance. He will be placed on administrative leave from the Marine Corps, seconded to the FBI TDY, and he will give his material, under oath, to us and to Justice. At that point a determination will be made between the players, us, Justice, the Agency, and the Administration, as to whether or not we will progress with the investigation. I'm promised a fair and positive chance to make our concerns known and to build a case, and the Agency will cooperate. Evidently, there's some in-house feeling over there that the Afghan Desk cabal has become too powerful policy wise, and this is seen as a way to take them down a few notches. You can have Okada on the team too, if that's what you want. But Cruz has to come in. Can he be reached? I'm assuming one of you is in contact with him, because your stuff has to come from him."

Silence, and then Bob said, "I may have a way to reach him."

"I thought so. Swagger, once again you impress. I love the way he takes over *our* investigations, changes their objective and content, and advances them in another direction—fortunately for us, the right one. Oh, and once this is completed, you are to go home to Idaho and you are sentenced to the rest of your life in a rocking chair. Nick, I'll get you another promotion if you agree to handcuff him to that chair."

Swagger and Nick looked at each other.

"It's pretty good," Nick admitted. "I thought we'd be bigfooted into silence, the investigation officially closed before it got started, and—"

"Can I say one more thing?" Bob interrupted.

"What would that be?"

"This just seems smart to me. The Agency people have got to feel a little on the spot by now, like we's hunting them. So I'm thinking we run a briefing for them. We reach out and give them some kind of palaver on our progress with Cruz. Get all the players there, all the big Afghan Desk people, all the Zarzi big believers. We're real smooth and assy-kissy."

"*You* could do 'assy-kissy'?" Nick asked.

"Not for long. Maybe fifty-nine minutes. Around minute sixty, you throw a blanket over me."

"I'd pay to see that. But is this really the time for a public relations offensive?" said Nick.

"No, no," said the director, "it is a good idea."

"Okada can give us a list by name," said Bob. "Get 'em in one room just to set them straight and settle them down. I'm thinking the deputy director, the head of plans, the head of Afghan Desk, and of course, in the Administration, the director of National Intelligence. We'll even bring free doughnuts."

"No doughnuts," said the director. "It isn't in the budget."

FBI HQ

CORRIDOR AND ELEVATOR BETWEEN DIRECTOR'S
OFFICE AND TASK FORCE ZARZI WORKING ROOM
HOOVER BUILDING
PENNSYLVANIA AVENUE
WASHINGTON, DC
1720 HOURS

D o me a favor," said Nick, "the next time you get a bright idea about doing PR, let me in on it. That way, I get the credit, it helps my career. Helping your career doesn't amount to much because you don't have a career."

"If you'd suggested it," Bob said, as the elevator doors opened, "he'd have turned it down. He only said yes to annoy you, to punish you for bringing me into this again."

"You're probably right."

"Anyway, I didn't do it to help the Bureau with its Agency problems. That don't matter spit to me. But one of those four guys pulled the trigger on Cruz. I want to see 'em, throw some business their way, and get a read."

"Uh-oh. You've been reading Shakespeare again."

"What?"

"*Hamlet.* 'The play's the thing, in which to catch the conscience of the king.' Old idea: if you put before the bad guy an image of his crime, he'll in some way react and give himself away. Shakespeare believed it, but it's bunk."

"I ain't never read *Hamlet*. Not in Polk County, Arkansas, in the fifties where I's educated."

"Whatever, it's based on a folk concept of the mind. The image of their crime sparks some kind of overt response. But it's bunk. We know now that people are complex, devious, sophisticated, practiced, and they don't go 'Boo!' when manipulated into such a confrontation."

"Still like to try."

"I know you have all kinds of sniper voodoo and eighth and ninth senses, but these guys are much smarter than Hamlet's uncle. These are all sophisticated, mentally tough, experienced, widely traveled, and brilliant men. You won't see anything they don't want you to see. If they've navigated their way through DC intelligence politics, plus survived in the field, they will have a little bit of smarts in how to handle an office meeting, even with the great Bob Lee Swagger."

"Everybody has tells, from eye rolls to breathing patterns to body posture. Everybody's his own landscape. And I will say this, if I have a skill it's at reading landscape. So let me look over the landscape and we'll see what I—"

They had emerged from the elevator, made it down the hall, and turned into the suite of working rooms that Task Force Zarzi occupied, and there to greet them was Starling, looking shaken.

"What's up?"

"There's been a huge shoot-out in Baltimore," she said. "World War Three at a car wash. And it involves somebody you put an APB out on, somebody called Crackers the Clown."

HOWARD STREET CAR WASH

T he glasses were the key.
    Check the glasses, he always told himself. Once every five minutes, *check the glasses.*

Cruz had fallen into that rhythm. Here, he worked anonymously, one of twenty or so invisibles who scurried for tips by drying, sweeping, polishing the drippy wet vehicles that emerged from the tunnel of spray wax, steam, jetting soapy water, and rubber strips like jungle fronds that hung from a mechanically contrived tube structure and somehow magically undulated the road grime off the cars. It saved him from brooding, it brought in money, it kept him active. Nobody asked questions, nobody took roll, nobody made friends outside their ethnic groups; the pay, usually about $50 a day, was in change and small bills. He was faceless in this crowd of hustling shiners and polishers, and he was the only one who looked at the shape of the sunglasses, for a teardrop that spoke not of Jackie O and her husband Ari, but of the sandbox, the 'Stan, the global war on terrorism.

He saw them while the fellow was still in the glass building laying out his $15 for the super wash.

Tear shaped, dark, held in place not by two arms but by a stout elasticized strap as insurance against vigorous action, with insectoid, convex lenses under polyurethane frames, the curvature of the lenses extreme so that the polarized plastic, strong enough to stop buckshot, also protected the wearer's peripheral vision, just the thing to pick up the approach of a fast-moving assaulter from three or nine o'clock. They were Wiley X's, of the style called AirRage 697s, big in Tommy Tactical contractor culture.

Ray slipped low, between cars, not panicking, but breathing hard.

Then he had a spurt of rage. *How did the motherfuckers find me again?* There had to be a leak somewhere, goddamnit, and he swore that if he got out of this, he would brace up old man Swagger so hard he shook his dentures out. Every fucking time Swagger showed, these goddamn bastards were right behind him.

But he got his war mind back fast. He pretended to polish a wheel cover of an already shining BMW convertible, and slipped a quick recon glance at the dude just as he emerged from the building and sat under an umbrella on a kind of patio where the owners waited and watched as the towel boys worked over their cars.

Guy was wearing a black baseball cap without insignia and some kind of bulky raincoat as if it was cold out and of course it wasn't. You could hide a lot under that coat. Cruz continued to steal seconds of examination, noting next that the Tommy Tactical made an obvious show of disinterest in the cars before him, not hunting for any particular one, not noticing his own car—it must have been that Dodge Charger, just coming out of the steam, its wet skin glinting in the sunlight—but adapting a quick posture of lassitude and sloth as he flopped casually in a plastic chair and began to examine his nails.

Cruz shot a glance at the man's shoes: Danner assault boots, though unbloused, the crumple of the sloppy hems denoting that they had been smartly tucked commando style until just a few minutes ago.

"Hey, guy, are you trying to win the Nobel Prize for that tire or what?" someone said, and it was the car's owner, impatiently leaning across the trunk to hurry the pitiful illegal onward.

Ray smiled obsequiously and backed off, waving the man onward.

As he turned to work on another vehicle, he let himself look down the one-way course of Howard Street and saw another guy whose face, though far off, appeared obscured by the tactical shape of the ultracool combat shades and that guy was coming along, and would be here in a minute or two.

Run? He could pretend to mosey backward, hit and roll over the wall, and head down the alley to—but he didn't know what was down the alley and cursed himself for the operator's most basic mistake: he hadn't had the energy to learn all the back streets, all the fast exits, the fallbacks, the shortcuts, the near invisible secret passages.

Besides, the guy on the street was drawing closer, ever closer, and now it was too late to make a sudden break. He saw how it had to go; they would wait a few more seconds, until the walker got right up to the courtyard, then he and the sitter would go to guns fast with whatever big mean black toys their coats concealed, and converge, catching him between fire from two angles, with nowhere to go but down.

He had a Glock 19 concealed in a Galco horizontal shoulder rig under his beat-to-hell Harvard hoodie and long-sleeved T-shirt, and two extra fifteen-rounders on the off-side, giving him forty-five rounds of 147-grain Federal hollow point. He turned his O's cap backward on his head, so its bill wouldn't protrude into the top zone of his sight picture. He reached inside the outerwear, unsnapped the Galco, felt the small, heavy automatic pistol slide into his hand and, under these circumstances, he took joy from its touch. It was found money, getting laid on the first date, all black on the range, a nice word from the colonel.

Okay, motherfuckers, he told himself with another deep, calming breath, going hard into his war mind, *you want me, you come and get me.*

Taking care not to directly confront or track his target, Mick Bogier eased into one of the plastic chairs sloppily, arms and legs all over the place, and tried to be a guy with no particular place to go getting it cleaned up real nice while sitting in the sun. As he oriented himself, he could see Crackers moving down the street, not rushing, not tactical, but—Crackers had a lot of combat and a lot of ops behind him— totally selling the pic of another innocent stroller shuffling along, maybe to the liquor store for a six of Bud and a lottery ticket, maybe to the library for a new thriller, maybe to the Mickey D's down the street for a Big Mac with fries and a Diet Coke. Crackers just walked along.

A plug ran from Mick's ear to a throat mike dangling just alongside his chin before the cord disappeared inside his jacket and linked to his cell.

"You got him?" he asked, trying not to speak loudly or even look like he was speaking.

"I saw him duck. Yellow baseball cap, maroon sweatshirt, he's behind that brown Galaxy, working the tires. Seems to be a tire guy, that's his specialty."

"How's he moving? I'm too close to look directly."

"Like any shine boy. A little monkey. He hasn't made us yet, he's trying to get the shine on that Galaxy wheel."

"When you get to the entrance, you slide into the lot and index on me. At that point, I'll head out there like I'm reclaiming the car, swing behind the Galaxy, yank the five and give him a mag. When I fire, you dump a mag high into the glass of that building. That should scatter the fuckin' ducks. Then we roll the wall and Z picks us up. You got that, Z?"

"Am pulling into street now," said Z, from his spot a block away. "I am watching you, you are watching him, any movement?"

"No, now that I'm close I can see him really scrubbing on that— oh, now he's moved to the front tire, other side from you. Still ain't made us, snoozing the day away. This is going to be easy."

Crackers veered in from the roadway sidewalk, slid on the oblique through the wide entrance in the brick wall which the customers pulled into as they edged their way to the payment booths and the vacuum station up ahead.

Close enough to make eye contact now, Mick nodded through his dark lenses at Crackers as the other man unbuttoned his coat with his left hand, slipped his right hand through the slashed pocket to grip the cocked-and-not-locked MP5, a dandy little subgun from Heckler und Koch that had delighted the spec ops boys for three decades now, and Mick said, "Fast and total. He's good, don't forget. Okay, peanut gallery, let's rock."

He stood, his jacket already unbuttoned, and with a smile and a nod to the phantom fellow who'd just finished drying his car, he beelined to the Galaxy, circled behind it, shivered to shrug the cloaking of the coat over his own German dandy gun, felt his hand grip it expertly—he shot well enough to fire one-handed—and raised it to discover his target had spun and was a split second ahead of him on the action curve.

Ray shot him five times in the chest.

That gunfire ignited screams, panic, crazed evacuation, a whole festival of human behavior at the furthest extreme of escape frenzy. People blew every which way, some to the wall to clumsy attempts to climb over it, some back toward the glass building as if it offered cover, some racing into the mouth of the torrential downpour that was currently frothing up an Escalade in the tunnel. For a brief moment, that perfect world of equality so longed for in some imaginations actually existed on earth as Salvadoran illegal and Baltimore hedge fund manager and energy executive's well-turned-out wife and Sid the cabbie fled outward with equal passion, though never quite ruthless disregard for the other. The good behavior and fundamental politeness of the typical Baltimorean was in play on the war field as much as the adrenaline-powered survival instinct.

Crackers was not concerned with surviving, however, but with killing. He had that rare gift of natural aggression that made him a god in battle, funnily unfunny with his buddies, and a nasty prick everywhere else. He just believed: if you weren't war, you weren't nothing. He rotated right, seeing Mick go down, looking for his target who was clearly among the abandoned cars gleaming and dripping in the sun. Bracing the gun against his shoulder via its stubby, compacted telescoping stock, he fired a short burst into the cars, seeing glass spider-web and metal puncture and dust and water fly, while the gun roared, the spent shells cascading free in a brass-glinting spurt like flung pebbles across a lake. Great special effects but to no seeming result.

His urge was to run to Mick, but he saw that Mick had spun, low-crawled out, and was now rising on this side of the Galaxy, reacquiring his German machine pistol, though moving stiffly from the bruising hits on his Kevlar.

"Converge, converge!" Mick was screaming. "Z, get your ass in here, goddamnit, and come over the wall on him, he is hot, live, and still moving."

Saying that, Mick raised the subgun above his head, angled it down, and squirted a long burst into the space where he thought the sniper Cruz should be, mostly tearing up dust and asphalt debris from the deck. Then he rammed through a superfast mag change, tossing the empty box—God, was Mick smooth!—seating the new one, throwing the bolt, and began to move through the corridors between the now bullet-dinged automobiles. At the same time, Z had arrived, slalomed off the road and up to the other side of the brick wall, only with a pistol though, and he too hunted for the sniper. They had him three on one, with no place to go . . . but where the fuck was he?

It's better to be lucky than smart, rich than poor, smart than dumb, but in a gunfight, best of all is to be smart and skinny. That was Ray, who had gone to earth after putting the five hard ones into the big guy from nine feet and slithered across the ground to, er, nowhere, and then, being quite agile, actually wiggle-waggled sideways under the dripping-wet pickup truck next to him. He came up in another aisle between cars, rolled, and popped up like a Whack-a-Mole game in a Toyland, two hands on the gun, oriented, as it turned out, slightly toward the oncomer, not the original assaulter.

In the naturally firm isosceles, triangles within triangles for structural solidarity, his hunched, tensed muscles controlling the pistol between his crushing grip, Ray shot that guy twice, high left-side chest, knocking him back and off stride, even as he was now catching on to the concept of *body armor* not in words but in an image that decoded instantly into all he needed to know. He felt things in the air nearby and cranked down, realizing that the other shooter, seeing him fire, had vectored on to him instantly and put a burst into him, but that between the two of them, unseen in the intense focus of advanced extreme pathological war-fighting Zeitgeist, neither had realized that the cab of a Honda Civic lay between them and so while that burst chewed the crap out of the windows, splintering, shivering, fragmenting them, the passage through two glass barriers also skewed the bullets mightily and they rushed off at one remove from their target. By the time that shooter realized and came around for an unimpeded shot, Ray was to ground again, crawling like a muskrat under the cars.

"Can you get a shot?" Mick yelled at Z, who had two-handed support of his SIG over the top of the wall.

"That way, that way," screamed Z, sliding northward down the wall, craning his eyes through his AirRages for a glimpse of something to shoot, but seeing nothing.

Bogier looked back to Crackers, who, though he'd never gone down, had been staggered and briefly stunned by the two bolts that had cracked into his body armor and would leave him bruised blue and purple for a month and a half.

"Close, close, close," yelled Bogier as he himself darted between cars, not quite having figured out that Cruz's tactical improvisation was to move under the cars, not between them, and that he was skinny enough to do it. It didn't occur to him to lean down and spray-paint the entire 180 to his front under the cars and thereby hit the guy if only once or twice.

There was a frozen moment. Bogier and Crackers, guns loose and fluid in their hands, faces sweaty and bug eyed with concentration, moved stealthily through the fleet of parked, shot-to-shit cars, spurting ahead now and then to unzip a blind spot, while from the other side of the wall, with his SIG like the mighty Excaliber, Z too hunted but also covered them.

A siren heated up, then another.

Then Crackers went down.

·   ·   ·

Ray froze. He was trapped. He was on his back under a Chevy cab, this fucking thing turned out too low to get quite all the way under and he knew that he needed to make a strong, wretchedly awkward maneuver to get himself out the way he'd come in. And he couldn't cover anything to his left, under his feet, or above his head. But he heard the faintest scuffle of tread to ground, and saw a Danner-booted foot just a few inches from his head. Without much thought, he shot it.

He heard the scream, saw the blood fly, and in a second, a man was lying next to him, almost parallel, not three feet away. It was Dodge City, only horizontal, under cars, with cool modern black guns, as the guy, seeing him, eyes bulging with fear or excitement, tried to wedge his MP under the car for the shot, while Ray had to twist, pivot on his shoulder, and bring the gun to bear in a new quadrant. Intimate, nasty, graceless, only speed mattered, and—*crak!* spurt of muzzle flash, jerk of recoil, drama of slide rocking back and forth in supertime, leap of spent shell—Ray got his shot off just a split second sooner and shot the man in the throat, causing him to jerk and vomit blood, then shot him higher in the face, just below the eye, hammering a black hole into it and imposing terminal stillness on the body.

Cruz dug his feet into the ground and propelled himself forward, expecting to emerge into blue sky and the sight of two armed men with submachine guns about to dump mags into him, but instead he was unimpeded. Sirens sounded.

He pulled himself up, knowing that he was cut, abraded, bruised, scored, ripped, whatever in about two thousand places, just to see the two survivors hit their parked SUV and gun it to life. Coolly, one of the guys opened the door, cantilevered himself half in and half out and fired a burst. Ray tracked the trajectory of the burst until it splattered into the hood and grill of a blue-white first responder, and that police unit tanked left, hit a parked car, jarred itself sideways, hit another, and halted.

Ray thought, *I should get a shot off,* but by the time that imperative made itself clear, he was too late, and the SUV had zoomed away.

Silence. Steam rose, automobiles still ticked or issued death sounds, but there were no fires.

Go on, move your goddamned ass, he told himself.

He ran backward through the car wash complex, came to a cyclone fence, and scaled it. He climbed a hill to a railroad track, rolled down the other side, climbed another fence, came out into a yard, cut between two tiny houses. He didn't remember replacing it, but the gun was back in the holster under his T-shirt. Now he did a neat thing. He pulled off his crimson hoodie and dumped it, to reveal a T-shirt, an orange-and-black long sleeved, proclaiming sans serif loyalty to a team named after a bird. He flipped his Orioles lid away and out of his back pocket came an all-purple ball cap, again with bird loyalty as its primary message. He strode on blindly, waiting for a cop car to pull him aside, but none did, though farther along, on a major street, he could see them rushing to the site of the gunfight.

At last he came to a bar. It seemed to be what you might call "old style," meaning it attracted old Baltimoreans who remembered the town as a nesting place of grim taverns filled with smoke and grunge, a five o'clock city that worshipped Johnny and Brooksie. Everyone in the joint was fat and neckless and looked like they wanted to fight if you made eye contact—even the women. But it was also the sort of place where nobody noticed a thing. He found a place at the rail, ordered a beer, and watched the game. The Orioles won, 9–7 with a late comeback. It was pretty thrilling. Then he took a cab to another neighborhood, had himself dropped at the wrong address, cut through two yards, and found his car, untouched, where he'd left it fifteen or so hours ago. He got in, started the engine, and drove to his motel in Laurel. After a shower, half an hour of watching the gunfight and baseball coverage on TV, he called Swagger.

FOUR SEASONS HOTEL

SUITE 500
M STREET NW
WASHINGTON, DC
2300 HOURS

Her neck was slender, her skin alabaster, her teeth brilliant and blinding. She wore jewels only a king could have given her. Tawny blond hair piled on top of her head in a cascade of swirls, torrents, and plunges, secured by pins and a diamond tiara. Her eyes were passionate, dewy. *Do you want me? Then take me. Make me do bad things.*

Too bad she was only in a magazine.

Zarzi put the thing down. He sat alone with his watches. He wore a silk dressing gown and an ascot, was freshly bathed, groomed, and powdered in all the delicate man places. Alexander's blood moved in his veins, that was the original strain. But it had mixed over the generations with a thousand injections of mountain warrior DNA, possibly a Mongol element or two, since the odd squadron of Genghis Khan's cavalry had surely passed through the valleys that nurtured his line, leaving memories of rapine and strapping progeny that combined with the odd brave European explorer's, and finally with the entrepreneurs who turned the Western need for the poppy into billions. And it all climaxed in him, he the magnificent, he the extraordinary, he the potentate, the seer, the visionary.

"I want my Tums," he called. "My stomach is aflame."

A servant stole in and laid the two wonder tablets before him on a silver platter.

"Ah," he said, delicately ingesting them, feeling them crunch to medicinal chalk beneath the grind of his strong molars. *R-E-L-I-E-F,* he thought, as the glow spread and the fires were quenched beneath the balm.

"Is that better, my lord?"

"It is," he said. "For this alone, the West should be spared. Though I'm sure, like the airplane, the oil rig, the missile, and differential calculus, the antiacidic is originally an Islamic invention."

The servant said nothing, the jest lost on him. Servants do not speak irony; they only speak obedience.

"Young man," he said, "how old are you?"

"Twenty-three, my lord."

"Do you fear death?"

"No, my lord."

"Why are you so brave?"

"I know that Allah has a plan and if he wills it, I will die for him. It is written."

"But suppose his plan is that you work in subservient positions until you are unattractive and all your teeth have rotted, and so your master sends you into the streets because you now disgust him. You become a bitter Kabul beggar and freeze to death in the mud and shit of an obscure roadway."

"I . . . I had not thought of that, sire. But if that is his plan, then that is the life I shall have."

"You young people, you assume glory lies at the end of every journey. But at the end of most journeys lie nothing but squalor and oblivion."

"If you say so, sire."

"Thus, given the chance, you would choose glory, no?"

"Of course, sire."

"What if in the glory there was also death?"

"It is nothing, sire."

"But you are nothing. I mean not to degrade you, after all, this is the West, one does not degrade another; but it is the truth, is it not? You, truly, are nothing. You live to bring me pills, flush the toilet when I have deposited, sweep up my toenail clippings, make sure my repellent underwear makes it to the laundry. That is not much of a life, so leaving it for glory would be an easy thing, would it not?"

Pain fell across the boy's handsome face. He wanted to satisfy but was clearly not sure where satisfaction lurked. And he didn't want to make a mistake. He said nothing, but looked as if he had sinned.

"Now I, on the other hand—exalted, gifted with beauty, wit, wealth, courage, the admiration of millions—which should I choose, glory but early death or banal but comfortable squalor unto forever? I have so much more to lose than you."

"I am sure you would chose glory, sire. You are a lord, a lion, a true believer. You would do the right thing."

The older man sighed. "The right thing." It came so easily to the youth's lips. At his simple age, "the right thing" was obvious and knowable. It was clear. But for the great man, as for all great men, too much wisdom and experience gave the meaning of "the right thing" a maze of filters and screens through which to negotiate. Thus, "the right thing" was not always so apparent.

"Here," he said, "come with me."

He led the boy to his bureau, upon which a hundred or so watches gently trundled to and fro.

"Do you have a watch?"

"Yes, sir."

"Let me see it."

The boy peeled off a rather unimpressive low-end Seiko, built on a cheesy quartz movement from Switzerland manufactured in a huge, dreary plant full of Turkish emigrés for about a nickel, shipped to Japan, encased in clumsy stamped metal and low-grade plastic, then affixed to a thin leather strap by a Korean immigrant for twenty-four cents an hour, thirteen of which must be returned to her parents in Korea.

"Pah," said the great one, "it summarizes your life: nothingness."

He tossed it into the wastebasket and turned and selected two watches.

One was a thick Fortis, with a leather band, the chronograph that according to advertising was the favorite of the Russian cosmonaut service. It cost about $2,700 and you could use it to hammer nails or plant bombs on submarine hulls in Sevastopol and it wouldn't lose a second. Ticktock, it was the inevitable vanity of materialism and glamour, possibly, or the fact that the snow will never melt in the Himalayas or that the West will never fall: it was destiny, strength, and beautiful design.

The other was a Paul Gerber. Gerber made twelve watches a year with his own fingers. When they were finished, they looked even plainer than the Seiko, except that they displayed the phases of the moon, the date, the day, the time in Buenos Aires or Cairo or London, the arrival of the next solar and lunar eclipse, and all in precise accuracy for 128 years, assuming the watch was kept running over that time period. The waiting list to get one was fifteen years long, and the cost over $100,000.

One was glamorous, sexy, fast, sleek: the West. The other was subtle, incredibly complicated, a symphony of wheels and gears and pins and diamonds. It represented the furthest reaches of the mind of man as applied to less than one square inch, and yet was impenetrable to those who did not appreciate its exquisiteness. Its maker had applied, even if he didn't know it, the harshness of sharia against his own mind, and through that discipline had created that which was absolute, unknowable, irrevocable, impenetrable, undeniable. To Zarzi, it was the East.

"Go ahead, choose one. Which appeals? Each is equally fine, but you must choose."

The boy pointed to the big watch.

"Of course. That is what I feared," said Zarzi. "You take what is beautiful over what endures. That is the problem. All right, go ahead, take it, it's yours, but do not brag of it or the other servants will be jealous."

The boy took it.

"There, now go and enjoy the new toy."

The servant hustled out and Zarzi was alone with his watch and his fate.

The boy had made the final choice for him.

It finally rang. Swagger had been staring at the folder for what seemed like hours. He imagined the young sniper Cruz shot up, bleeding out in a roadside ditch, losing consciousness, to be discovered in a few weeks by a convict cleanup crew.

He flipped opened the phone.

"Where are you?"

"As if I'd tell you, goddamnit. Every time you show up, a crew of gunmen shows up. I'm lucky to be alive."

"Are you hurt?"

"Nah. Cut, scraped, twisted, bruised, pissed, but they didn't quite finish the job, or even start it."

"Okay, good. Now here's what—"

"Hold on, goddamnit. Who the fuck are you? Are you being tailed? Are you stupid, sloppy, careless, unlucky? Are you the world's best liar and double agent? Can you look me hard in the eye and lie to me? How'd you last so long if you're this much of an idiot?"

"The answer to all them questions is no. I ain't a liar, a double, or nothing. I'm just a beat-up former sniper with holes everywhere, like a piece of cheese. I wasn't followed. I check. I have the discipline. Nobody was on me, not in sight anyway, and nobody has ever been on me, goddamnit. They must be using satellites is all I can figure."

"Oh, well then, it couldn't possibly be the CIA, could it? It's probably a Pepsico satellite or maybe McDonald's now has orbital birds."

"I never said the Agency wasn't involved. Clearly they are involved big time. But now we know it and we can use the satellites against them. Maybe there's a transponder in my car, that's the only way they could do it. I'll rent a new one tomorrow, just to make sure."

That seemed to quiet Cruz.

"Listen, it's time for you to come in. We took our suspicion and all our dope to the Big Man, and he got the Agency to acknowledge some things and pledge cooperation. It seems clear that there are some people over there who are overcommitted to this Zarzi. If laws have been broken—that is, if Agency people have targeted you or other marines—that will be dealt with. But it all turns on your coming in, giving your statements and your facts, working within a team structure, following the rules and so on and so forth. You can't be rogue no more. The rogue shit makes these people scared as hell and when they feel fear, they respond with violence."

"I come in and another mystery explosion craters a building."

"Cruz, it won't happen. I'm speaking for the Bureau. No, I ain't their number one boy, but I have Nick Memphis on the team and the director was—"

"The director was bullshitting you. Don't you recognize the signs? He was jiving you, man; get me in, and watch the promises disappear, along with me. And whatever the Zarzi people want to achieve, they do. Maybe it's for the good, but nobody can guarantee it, because it's a crap shoot. Maybe it's not."

"Think about it," Bob said. It was important to him to get Cruz through this for some reason. He didn't want to lose this guy. "Don't do nothing. Move tomorrow to another location. Do you need money? I can get you money. I think I can work on them about the time and maybe you won't have to do none. It doesn't seem nobody's linked you to the shoot-out in Baltimore because I never told them you were at that car wash and nobody else got hurt and it was clear self-defense, so I'm thinking you should be okay on that one. By the way, the sucker you busted was named Carl Crane, ex-Special Forces, ex-Graywolf. He hung with a crew led by another ex-forces guy, big, blond linebacker type—"

Cruz remembered: the big guy with the Barrett, ambling down

the crest of the hill after they'd checked out the kill zone that held the two parts of Billy Skelton. He remembered thinking: *I will hunt you cocksuckers down.*

"—named Bogier, Mick Bogier, who all hung out at a joint called the Black Cat in Kabul. Gun-for-hire types."

"There you go. CIA hires mercs for the dirty stuff and when the mercs can't make it happen, they laser-paint the hotel for the smart bomb. When they learn they fail, the Agency people go to the same team, for obvious security reasons, using people already part of it. The contractors hunt me in America. The Agency keys on you, plants a bug so they can tail you by a bird in the sky, feeding info to the contractors. When you locate me, they move in for the kill. In Pikesville, they *thought* I was in the house so they raided hard and killed every dishwasher in the place. They followed you to me at the car wash. They'll follow you to me if I turn myself in."

"It won't happen again. I got it busted now."

"And you still don't know why the fuck Zarzi is here."

"Cruz, damnit, for the first time, I'm thinking we're ahead of them. Tomorrow I go to a meeting. I will meet with the four guys who have the authority to deal a Paveway strike without raising no questions. I will eyeball them and see what I can see. I will report back to you tomorrow and we will see where we are. Think on coming over to us. Give it a fair shot. This rogue crap is just going to get you killed. Okay?"

Cruz said nothing.

"Get some sleep, Sergeant Cruz. I will bring you in, we will make this happen. I swear to you, sniper to sniper, it'll work out."

"I'll take you at your word, because I'm a fool and a dreamer. But only one more time," said Cruz, breaking the connection.

Bogier hurt everywhere. His nipples hurt, his toes hurt, his watchband hurt, the elastic in his underpants hurt. His mind hurt. But his chest was the worst. It was lit like the Fourth of July if that holiday was celebrated in fireworks primarily of the blue-indigo-violet range. Each of Ray's five shots had delivered about five hundred-foot pounds of energy to the Kevlar chest plate that prevented them from penetrating, but did nothing to halt the energy transaction that hammered his flesh like a drill bit driven by a sledge. A pink blood blister signified the actual point of the bullet strike and was itself the center of a radiant bloom of BIV swirls that unfurled like daisies in the summer sunshine. The wounds leaked interior blood as far as belly, biceps, and neck, so the flowers were as if displayed on a field of bluish velvet and wine stain. It hardly looked human.

"What happen, baby?" asked Kay. "You been in fight?"

Kay, wrapped in a flower-print strapless dress that showed what appeared to be cleavage to end all cleavage and a butt to end all butts, had a fifties sex-goddess vibration that was undeniable; she could have played bad girls in B pictures for a decade. Her doll's face was symmetrical but not quite approaching beauty in its flatness, her eyes were not without empathy but helpfully unencumbered by curiosity. The question was strictly pro forma.

"You should see the other guy," Mick said, the point of the joke being that it wasn't funny at all, and its lack of humor perfectly matched his black mood.

"You lie there. Kay take care."

"I can't shower myself," he said. "I tried, I hurt too much. You have to do it for me. Leave the backside alone, just do the front, under the arms. I stink of sweat. Go easy, stupid white guy is hurting bad."

She laughed in a way learned from cartoons. "Ha," followed by another "ha." Then she said, "You funny, honey."

"I'm a regular talk show host," he said.

She took his towel off, and if she was impressed with the MCGA equipage down there she said nothing. In her job she'd seen more dicks than a urologist, so nothing would surprise her. He lay on the table in a pool of hot water and she sprayed him three or four times, then smeared soap all over him—that is, *all* over him—and used her strong but gentle hands to knead some pleasure into his body. She was very good, the hands knowing and not shy, her concentration highly professional, up, down, around, slip-slop, squish-whish, in, out, here and finally there.

"Ah," he said, "that felt good."

"You big," she did say, finally.

"Big but dumb. That's how it goes."

"You come now."

She wrapped the towel around him and led him, quietly padding barefoot through the surprisingly clean hallways, to the room where the episode had begun. The place was dim, almost religious, but smelled of locker room disinfectants. Other dramas played out behind curtains sealing off rooms like the bland one into which she led him with its $8-a-night motel room art and lava lamp. There, she pulled off his towel, patted him down, and was surprised to find he was all ready to go again.

"Wow," she said, "what a strong fella."

"Strong but dumb."

He lay on his back. She turned the lights down, peeled out of her print dress to reveal that beneath the hypnotic cleavage lay two wondrous *Playboy*-quality breasts. She touched them for him because he could not touch them himself and discovering an avid audience for the exhibition, she continued with the touching theme in various private areas and in various unusual postures until he got very interested.

She rushed to him at that point, and with a mighty bolt, he emptied himself. Then she crawled up next to him and snuggled. He was not a snuggler, but tonight, her softness and warmth and uncritical if professional adoration were welcome.

"You sad, baby?"

"A good friend went away today," he said. "That's never fun, you know?"

"In same fight?"

"The very same. Can't be helped, it's the business we chose, but it's sad."

At that point something that couldn't have been a phone started to make a noise that couldn't be a ring, and he rolled from the massage table, went to his dumped clothes on the floor, and pulled out the big satellite communicator.

"Excuse me," he said.

He punched the button.

"Nice of you to answer," MacGyver said.

"I'm not in the mood to take any shit," he said. "From you or anybody."

"What happened? Three on one, he kills Crane, and you guys run like hell. Hardly up to Black Cat standards, much less Graywolf or Fifth Special Forces."

"What happened was, he outfought us. He read a tell, knew who we were, and jumped us instead of us jumping him. His first five went point blank into my chest. Goddamn lucky I was wearing a vest. The prick is world class, I'll give that to him. Any man who could take down Carl Crane is a hell of a man."

"They made Crane fast off prints from DOD. The FBI has a circular out for his pals Mick Bogier and Tony Zemke."

"You want us out of here? Are we too hot? You want your money back? I don't feel like calling Tony's mother like I had to call Carl's wife. Carl left her and three kids, he was a great dad, and he did what he did to keep them comfortable and because you told us it was for the good of our uncle."

"I wish I could afford to cut you loose. But it's too late now, I can't bring new people in. And since Cruz got out clean and nobody up there seems to have connected this with him, you still have to finish."

"Will do," said Mick.

"It's worth it. We're trying to find a way out and Zarzi's our best route. If this works, there won't be any more young kids dying in that shithole. Cruz, his spotter, the thirty-one salesmen, the Filipinos, whoever, they will have died for a noble cause, which is stopping the pointless slaughter of our people for no advantage whatsoever. You get that? Basically, we're trying to end the war and put you out of business."

"There'll never be an end to war, Nietzsche," said Mick.

"He was right, but maybe we can get ourselves a little downtime before the next one."

"Friday night. Georgetown?"

"That would be so nice. I may be able to get you security dispositions. Evidently this Swagger has some weird gift for figuring out where another sniper will shoot from. You don't have to be near Georgetown; with that Barrett you can be a mile away."

"A mile with ranging shots. No ranging shots. One shot, one kill, cold bore, twelve hundred yards would be the max. Then, Belize, here I come."

"Bogier, tough about your friend Crane. But don't stay depressed. Get this thing done, cover yourself with glory and honor and the thanks of a grateful nation. Save the sum of things for pay. What better epitaph could a mercenary want or get? Plus, all that dough."

"You get me the intel. More is better. And I will finally nail this little sucker, for Carl if for no other reason."

He turned, put the phone down. Kay was sitting naked on the table. Her eyes demonstrated her utter innocence as to the talk she had overheard. Her flesh was luminous, piles and piles of it. For some strange reason, unlike so many Korean women, she had permed her hair so it was frothy with curls. Her face was a happy pie. Her eyes were happy and shallow. He discovered himself tumescent and could tell that pleased her as much as him.

There were four of them, and various coffee- and briefcase-bearing assistants. They were serious men, pinkish, well dressed, in suits, though one outlier had a tweedy professional look to him in a sports coat and bow tie; he was the one without the assistant and he carried his own briefcase. Their faces, out of long discipline, expressed personality but little else, as if otherwise all nuances had been mastered and controlled. One looked fierce, two bureaucratic, the last one—the academic—kindly.

Swagger watched them come into the bland green meeting room. He could almost ID them by Susan's descriptions.

Walter E. Troy, "the Assistant," assistant director, longtime spook, thirty years at the Agency, specialist in counterterror, a mover and a shaker who was said to be disappointed that he didn't get the big boy job that instead went to an ex-congressman with big connections.

Jackson Collins, "Afghan Desk," the fierce one, ex-Navy SEAL, radiating hostility, face too red, hair too brusque, all mil-spec in body language, tiny pig eyes, a squid, and thus on Swagger's instantaneous must-fight list. Looked like trouble.

Arthur Rossiter, "Plans," head of clandestine operations, the guy who coordinated and produced all the actual dirty tricks, guileful, willful, yet almost faceless and without any personal eccentricities, no color at all, could have sold encyclopedias, collected child porn, written novels, painted bad pictures.

And finally Ted Hollister, the only outside-the-agency presence, the National Intelligence director, technically the boss and coordinator of them all, but also a man in a job that didn't exist until recently, so that no one had quite figured out what he could or couldn't do and whether they had to return his calls or not. Hollister had clearly been chosen to succeed a less successful NID because of his very inside-Washingtonness, his charm, tact, discretion, a creature totally of the foreign policy/intelligence/Washington circuit where he'd thrived for years, when he wasn't teaching at some prestigious university. Worked at the Agency for ten years, moved on to State, did Princeton, Yale, and Hopkins, then State again, well-known op-ed scribe for the *Post* and the *Times,* and now in the big job as the president's number one whisperer. In the movies, his kindliness would instantly make him suspect number one.

Yet they all had their finger on the trigger. Any one of them had the power to go to a computer terminal, a cell phone, enter a code number, say a code word or whatever the mechanism was, and order a hit halfway around the world, without justification, explanation, recrimination. A word from them and somewhere far away a First Lieutenant Wanda Dombrowski sent five hundred pounds of thermobaric HE into someone's back pocket and cratered a building, a mansion, a village, a hangar, a cave, even exploding the air around it. They were the real snipers.

"Good luck reading these Claudiuses, Hamlet," Nick whispered to Bob, before he stood to greet them with a peace offering from the Federal Bureau of Investigation.

Bob, in his off-the-rack suit and black tie, sat next to Nick at the head of the table as Nick stood.

"Gentlemen, thank you for coming," he said. "I know how busy you are—there is a war on, after all—and I appreciate your time. I am Assistant Director Nicholas Memphis of the FBI, chief of Task Force Zarzi, responsible for coordinating with you and with the Secret Service and with my own people on this issue. I'll try to be brief. I'm here for two reasons: first of all, since you're all involved in the state visit of Ibrahim Zarzi, I wanted to keep you in the loop about our efforts to apprehend the threat to him whom we have identified as Gunnery Sergeant Reyes Fidencio Cruz, USMC, currently AWOL from his service obligations, operating on motives unknown. And second, since I know rumors are swirling about our inquiries, I want to assure you that we are not contemplating a witch hunt against the Central Intelligence Agency, or any kind of examination of professional behavior in the crucible of the war on terror. Our investigation has brushed up against security issues, but the issues themselves are not germane. I will answer any questions you have, at length or in brevity, at any time."

He waited to see if he'd made a sale, and got dull eyes back at him. The assistants seemed to be the dedicated reactors; several snorted, rolled eyes, shook heads, issued semaphores of hostile intent. The Great Men just sat benignly, unmoved.

"Let me—"

But a hand came up.

It was the old man in the bow tie, the National Intelligence director, Ted Hollister.

"Yes, sir."

"Since I seem to be the only ancient mariner here," he said, "I thought I would take the opportunity to identify for my younger colleagues the lanky fellow sitting next to Assistant Director Memphis. When you all came to work this morning, you bypassed the first-floor Agency museum. Had you entered you would have seen a Russian sniper rifle, recovered from Vietnam in 1975. It was our first look at a weapon that had been tantalizing us for years. I was very new to the Agency then, but I was in Saigon at the time, and I know that the weapon came to us through the good offices of a marine sniper named Bob Swagger. I do believe we are in the presence of Mr. Swagger."

Swagger nodded.

"Sounds like you remember it better than I do," he said, and there was some polite laughter.

"I mention that because I want all the Agency people and all the Bureau people—I believe I speak for the president on this and I also speak in an official capacity as National Intelligence director, though of course I have no idea what that means—to remember that we are all on the same side and that we have the same goal. I know there's inevitable hostility between the entities, but I remind everyone, and that rifle in the museum should remind everyone, that we have worked together to great success in the past and if we remain civil and unconcerned with ego-driven issues like 'turf' and 'perks,' we can work this out."

"Well said, sir," said Nick, relieved that he had not yet encountered his first insurrection.

He then proceeded with the narrative: the threat, the response, the first encounter and death, the attempt in Baltimore—"That was Swagger," Nick said, "he saved Mr. Zarzi's life, no doubt about it"—on through the plans for the speech at Georgetown Friday night and the medal ceremony at the White House Sunday night.

"We have implored Mr. Zarzi to forego both these events. But he is a stubborn, brave man and insists on keeping to his schedule and living up to his engagements. The Secret Service has performed magnificently, I should add, providing the real manpower for the protection on the ground. We have helped, but our primary responsibility is to apprehend, not protect."

He outlined the investigation so far; all the man-hours worked by the number of agents, the field offices filling reports—"More arrived even late last night from the Naval Investigative Service in the Philippines"—on the life and times of Ray Cruz; the proactive attempts at apprehension, such as the raid on the house in Baltimore, the nationwide law enforcement circularization of the Cruz photo and particulars.

"Mr. Memphis, you still haven't released Cruz's name and threat to the public. He still has freedom of movement. May I ask why, sir?" asked one of the assistants.

"Of course. We have found that such enterprises are of declining value. This is the Internet era where there's such a profusion of information, it's hard to make an impression, so the widely circulated picture and warnings don't really justify themselves in terms of results, while the danger of overzealous reaction is magnified considerably. That's why we beat the drums to publicize 'most wanted people' very reluctantly."

"Can someone explain to me why FBI agents arrived at Creech Air Force Base in Nevada and interrogated Air Force Reaper pilots who are part of a joint Agency/Air Force program?" This was the hostile "Afghan Desk," Jackson Collins.

This time Swagger answered: "That one was my doing, sir. I learned from Second Recon's records that an explosion occurred in the city of Qalat in Afghanistan shortly after Sergeant Cruz radioed in that he was on-site. That explosion seems to be at the core of his motive, that and an ambush earlier that killed his spotter. It seems he believes the Agency used a missile or a smart munition to—"

If Swagger hoped for a *Hamlet* moment, the actors didn't provide one. Before he even got it out, Collins, the Afghan Desk, was overriding him with another argument.

"Are you aware that we had a very good officer, Ms. Okada, look into those allegations and interview all the participants, and she came to the conclusion that such an event was preposterous, given the security built into the system?"

"I have seen her report, sir. I merely wanted to double-check and see if memories had clarified over the passage of time."

"And you found nothing?" asked someone new.

"No, sir, not a thing at Creech," Swagger said, keeping his statement technically truthful.

His interlocutor was of course the colorless Plans, a sharp and focused prosecutor whose abruptness left no doubt as to his opinion of the investigation.

"We had to cover all the possibilities, sir," said Swagger. "So if any of you have any knowledge of any Agency connection to this mystery blast, I'd—"

"It sounds to me like this Cruz is suffering from battle fatigue," said Collins. "He's snapped and entered a delusional state. Unfortunately, his sniper craft has remained intact and he functions at a very high level. May I ask, will you shoot to kill if that opportunity presents itself?"

"Yes, sir," said Bob.

"This isn't just about my career," Collins said. "Even if everyone thinks it is. I will resign the day after Zarzi's election if anybody wants that, and never write a book or appear on a TV show. This man Zarzi, with all his flaws and his shady past, can help us achieve an important goal, so that all the marines, not just the snipers, can come home. I can't emphasize that enough."

"We are sympathetic, sir," said Nick.

But Collins could not leave the issue alone, even if his pretty-boy assistant was squirming with embarrassment. He was a burly, brusque man, 105 percent military, with his brush cut, his face red from what had once been long days at sea but were probably now long days on the golf course, a busted nose, and a boar's natural snarl. All squid lifer, and wasn't he a SEAL too, so maybe he'd actually had some mud time like a marine.

"You people, I know how you operate. You consort with scum, you grant immunity, you turn people and get them to testify against family and friends, you swear to hide and protect them. Well, this is exactly the same. We have to work with scum, we have to work with the people we detest. Zarzi was a drug lord, a beheader, a Taliban sympathizer, but because of all that, he is more, rather than less, valuable to us. He's the 'Sammy the Bull' Gravano of Afghanistan. It's a crime that he survives and flourishes and it affronts the moral order. But through him, we protect the moral order and we prevent even bigger monsters from surviving and flourishing. I just want that understood, so that you don't think we're nuts or that I'm riding him on some quest to get a bigger chair."

"I understand," said Nick.

Memphis then outlined the security arrangements for the Georgetown University appearance of Zarzi, the various liaisons with the Secret Service, the usage of air cover, and so forth.

"But, Mr. Memphis, it's also true, is it not, that Cruz is an extremely resourceful man. He is a testament to Marine Corps training proficiency. He almost succeeded in Baltimore. How can you be sure that despite your best efforts, he's not simply better than you?" This came from the assistant director, who had not spoken till this time.

"Well," said Nick, "he is a great sniper, but he's only the second best in the world. Mr. Swagger here is the best. I'd bet on us."

That was it, pretty much.

Nick sat back as his allotted hour was over. He watched the men and their assistants file out. Swagger had gone to talk to the National Intelligence director, the professorial Ted Hollister, and the two seemed to be enjoying an animated laugh about Saigon in the old days. They were the only ones who dated back to that ancient, lost war, and it looked like Hector and Agamemnon sharing a laugh in Olympus over a Hellene beer. Two old warriors, with their fading memories of the war of fetid jungles and 'villes and peasants in pajamas dying, dying, dying. Swagger leaned across the table and got old Hollister's briefcase for him, and the two walked to the doorway of the room. It looked like they'd be at it for hours, so finally Nick walked up and said, "Bob, we've got to go."

He thanked Hollister for the opening remarks, which he thought did much to mollify the mood in the room, and then there was a round of handshaking and Hollister set off, jaunty and alone, for the elevator and his car back to the Executive Office Building.

They let him go, and then their Agency escort came up and escorted them along the same path, from elevator to first floor, past the monument to the agents who'd lost their lives and out the door to the driveway where the car to take them back to the Hoover Building awaited.

"That place always gives me the creeps," said Nick.

"Me too," said Bob.

"You two old 'Nam guys have a nice chat?"

"Very interesting fellow. So smart. He remembers Vietnam much better than I do, but then I have to say, he probably didn't drink no six thousand gallons of drugstore bourbon to forget it, like I did."

"Anyway: conclusions, Dr. Hamlet? Was the king's conscience captured? Suspicions? Progress? Get anything?"

Bob shook his head.

"I came up bust, and that goddamn Collins wouldn't stop his spouting off. I do not like that guy. He is on the bull's-eye on this one and he don't like it one bit and most of what he said was for the other boys in the room, not us. Anyhow, all of them, they sure have their acts together. You'd need one of those 'behavior specialists' in the movies or on TV to get much out of that bunch. I thought Collins was a little too tough guy, the guy who scared me was 'Plans,' he didn't say much but he had that killer temperament without no give, always hard to work for, with, or be around, so he must be real good or he wouldn't have made it that high; the other two just seemed bureaucrat and policy monkeys of a higher order, and the old man was so goddamned charming and flirty it was hard to suspect him of anything except being your grandpop."

"Maybe that was his technique. To boost you, to flatter you, and in that way fog you on his real motivations."

"I thought of that, but I don't think so. Too obvious. It's an invitation to snoop. He wants us to snoop. No, I read it as utter confidence in himself, knowledge that he was, as a bigfoot, completely untouchable, so he could afford to be the life of the damn party. Them others all seemed to play their cards tight because they had something to lose."

"So as insight into your 'theory' of this situation, it produced nothing."

"Not a goddamn thing," said Bob.

"Good," said Nick, "because it gave me an idea."

"God help us all," said Bob.

D r. Faisal had disappeared.

"Maybe Allah showed him a new path," said Professor Khalid.

Bilal was too anxious to laugh.

Around them, the lights of the midway blazed. Odd machines that served no purpose but to sweep people around at exhilarating speeds and make them squeal and shout trailed neon streaks as they whirled about madly, going nowhere except around and around. The smell of cigarettes, sticky corn syrup, cotton candy, perfume, salted buttered popcorn, corn dogs, everything forbidden, filled the air.

"What should we do?" asked Khalid. "Drop to our knees and pray to Mecca?"

"Not an opportune place for a prayer break," said the ever-practical Bilal. Here in the heart of the heart of the heart of America, buffeted by crowds of cowboys and farmers and their womenfolk and chubby children, the three slightly disheveled and not terribly clean pilgrims had stopped in search of soft ice cream, under threat of another tantrum from Dr. Faisal. The man may have been a genius but he certainly had to have his ice cream.

"He was swept away," said Khalid. "Pfffft, like that."

It was true. They had stood, somewhat overwhelmed by the sight of the mysterious festival with its squads of whirling neon machines, its pennants, its odd play of colors unseen in nature against the dark sky, its crowds of flesh-packed Americans innocent in their simple joy at existence. They were looking for soft ice cream. They were not looking for hot dogs, funnel cakes, frozen Snickers bars on sticks, fried dough, nuts in a sugar glaze, doughnuts, hamburgers, bratwursts, gingerbread men, taffy, fried chicken, anything edible other than soft ice cream. Then Faisal took a step to the right and was swept up by a current of onrushers, and off he went. They soon lost sight of him.

"Can you pray standing?" said Bilal.

"No," said Khalid. "It is forbidden, plus I do not pray."

"Not to Allah but to some other god. I don't know, Jesus, Marx, Yahweh, Odin, something like that."

"You know about Odin, Bilal? Very impressive. A hard young man like you?"

"I was once a student, and not a bad one. I will pray to Allah, standing, believing that in this case standing is allowed. You pray to Odin or Yoda or another one, I don't care, just pray a little instead of making remarks."

"Oh my," said Khalid. "Another who has gotten tired of me. Oh well, it was bound to happen. I seem to estrange myself from everybody. It's something annoying in my personality."

The two stood there, slightly seedy men in baggy suits, unshaven and unkempt, looking a little too Levantine for the tastes of the local constabulary, unsure whether to move to hunt for the missing man or stay put and hope that he would find his way back.

"Do you see that clown?" asked Bilal. He pointed to a plastic giant with a red nose, red hair, and a red, white, and blue hat standing outside a tent that said, obscurely, B-I-N-G-O!

"Yes."

"You go stand next to it. Don't wander, don't start conversations, don't make eye contact, do not feel you have to reach out to the peasants we are pledged to destroy."

"You see, I am not sure I agree with—"

"Just stand there. I will, in the meantime, go up this avenue, find Faisal, and drag him back. But do you see, if you wander off, then finding Faisal has no meaning because you have become lost. And I will end up with either one man lost or, catastrophically, two men lost. You will soon be arrested, your patently phony ID will be seen through, and the whole thing has gone nowhere, a failure after all our tribulations. Do you see? Tell me you see."

"I see, I see, but if I may observe, it's hardly my fault that—"

"The clown, the clown of bingo."

"By the way, what would a bingo be?"

But Bilal had already set off.

He tried not to walk urgently, he tried to keep the fear off his face, he tried to emulate the loose-jointed walk of these Americans, he tried to blend in, to be invisible, a little man of no consequence. Mainly what he tried not to do was despise himself for his idiocy. Stopping at Dairy Queen: all right. Stopping at McDonald's: manageable if tense. Stopping at Friendly's: too intense, fraught with eye contact, demanding quick thinking in English and usually filled with suspicious white people who looked them over as if they were terrorists. Oh, wait, they *were* terrorists. Stopping at 39 or 41 or 57 Flavors? Marginally acceptable if during the daylight when not overcrowded. But stopping at the Williwaw County fair, just because it broadcast a rainbow of hues against the sky and weirdly reminded all of them, homesick and lonely and sticky and not unmindful of what lay ahead, of a mythical Baghdad from the old tales? Insane. He should be executed for so foolish a folly.

Would Faisal have ridden a Tilt-a-Whirl? It seemed unlikely. What about the Ferris wheel, more sedate for an elderly man—no sign of him there? Perhaps he'd gone into the so-called Fun House but then Bilal realized the stereotype swami in turban painted on the outside of the rickety canvas-and-plywood structure would keep him out. What about the Wild Mouse? Highly unlikely. It only battered you, and the point was to get Western girls and boys into squeezing distance under the pretext of fear. There was some vehicle roadway over which smallish replicas of cars from the 1910s rolled, but no, that was not—

He heard the whistle of a train.

He turned. It was a magnificent if miniaturized diesel, yellow, two engines pulling six cars just sliding into the lights of the "station," and indeed, there sat Faisal, quite happily sucking down the remains of what had to have been a giant soft-ice-cream treat, in the very last car. His face was a portrait of pure animal bliss.

Bilal ran to him.

"Sir, you cannot leave like that. You gave me a heart attack!"

"What? Why, it was most enjoyable. Come on, Bilal, I have tickets left. Let's go around again. This time I wish to ride near the engine. Look at the engineer. Now that is a job I would like to have."

The engineer was a slouchy teen boy who sat in a cockpit in the rear of the second engine. Bilal knew him immediately: one of those scornful Western ironists, too good for his job, his head full of dreamy ambitions. Pimply and anguished, yearning for something better than the Big Little Train.

"No, no, we have a schedule. We must get back."

And so Bilal dragged Dr. Faisal back through the crowds, on some kind of beeline, knowing exactly where the clown was. After all, he had navigated by starlight the forbidden zone between Jordan and Israel, dodging the lights and the radar of the Israeli border patrols, many times. What was the Williwaw County fair to that ordeal?

But when they got to the clown: no Professor Khalid.

"Agh," said Bilal. "You two, you will be the death of me. I told him—"

"Bilal!" came the cry. "Faisal!"

It was Khalid. He held a large golden pig with bright felt eyes and two happy fabric teeth sticking out from his open snout.

"I won a bingo! I won a bingo!"

FBI HQ

TASK FORCE ZARZI WORKING ROOM
FOURTH FLOOR
HOOVER BUILDING
PENNSYLVANIA AVENUE
WASHINGTON, DC
1300 HOURS

I t's a conceptual problem," Nick said. He and Susan and Swagger sat in his glassed-in office, while outside the two dozen agents pretended not to notice, even if these meetings usually produced policy shifts.

"We see this as a conspiracy. We want the big guys. We want action, attention, success. Sorry, that's the truth. Ms. Okada, Agency loyalist though you are, if you bring down 'Afghan Desk' and send somebody to prison for overstepping his authority and prevent the Agency from some major public humiliation, you're golden."

"I suppose I don't deny it."

"I want it too. It's my job, but if I can take down a major government illegality and put the Bureau ahead of the curve instead of behind it, I win too. And if we beat those press assholes to the punch, we prevent a major investigative Pulitzer from going to some mutt from the *New York Times,* that's only gravy. And what does Bob Lee Swagger get? He gets the satisfaction of being right, he gets the thrill of bringing in a marine sniper from the cold and seeing him recognized as a hero. That means more to him than our careers mean to us. So each of us, in his own way, has been seduced by pride, ambition, and greed."

"Not me," said Swagger. "I'm so damned perfect it's thrilling. Never make a mistake. Always guess right. I know it sucks being around such a great human being, but there you have it."

"Anyway," said Nick, "our ambition has seduced us into attacking the conspiracy from the top down, hence the little drama at CIA today where we could eyeball the boys to try and find a tell, a give-away. But you don't attack a conspiracy from the top down. Its top is too protected, too entrenched, its leaders are too smart and experi-enced. You have to attack it from the bottom up. We have to see this as a crime and we have to deal with it as a crime. And how do you crack a crime? How do you bring down the Corleone family?"

Well, everybody knew, but clearly Nick was riding this one for all its dramatic potential, so neither Swagger nor Okada said a thing.

"It's like Afghan Desk said. You bust the little guys. You turn the little guys. You plea them out, get them to testify, even if you have to immunity their scurvy asses. You use the littles to get at the bigs."

Susan wasn't quite with him. "I don't see where—" she started.

"The contractors!" said Nick, so pleased with self and idea, so excited. "We have to take them! It's our best move. Bust them, play them off against each other, get one or the other to break. Use that to go to the next level."

Swagger was a no-buy. "Nick, are you sure? Those boys are big-time tough, fast to guns, not afraid to kill or to die. Pulling them in won't be no easy thing. Scary guys."

"Well, if they scare you, then, yes, they are scary. But here's the move. First, you have to get some kind of commitment from Cruz to back off on Friday night. His presence completely fucks things up. If that's settled, we can get a good SWAT guy to play him and we can set up a scenario. A phony hit at Georgetown on Zarzi. We arrest our fake Cruz. We make a big deal of it on scene. But the point of the op is to lure the contractors in tight to make the hit on our fake Ray Cruz. We'll work out details and craft later, but when they make their hit—"

"What happens to the poor guy playing Ray? No body armor's going to stop a .50."

"We will handle that. The man will know the risks going in. Hell, *I'll* take that job if I have to. Anyhow, the deal is, when they make their hit, our real trap is sprung. We'll have stand-by teams hiding all over. We'll flood the zone, we'll apprehend the shooting team, and we'll go to work on them. These are hard-core individuals, as you say, rock and rollers, action heroes. They are not guys to like the idea of spending the rest of their lives in some cesspool of anal sex and boy-friends as girlfriends. They'll turn, I swear."

"I don't know," said Bob. "They might be harder to take than you think. You might end up with a Baghdad city fight on your hands."

"Swagger," said Susan, "listen to him. Cowboy, brave as you are and no matter how it kills you to put someone else in a kill zone, the truth is, we don't have another move. We cannot go directly against the Agency. We have been so ordered. We are stuck going around to legal back doors for months. This is a way of back-dooring the process."

"Are you aboard? I need you both aboard. I need you Gung Ho, Semper Fi, the truth shall set you free, all the way. Okay?"

"I guess so," said Swagger.

"What's going on? I can see the something in your eyes. It looks like fear to me. I've never seen it in your eyes."

Swagger said, "Well, it's fine for you to volunteer to play Ray Cruz, or get some guy to play Ray Cruz. But that won't work, you know it and I know it. These guys have been hunting him for months. They know how he moves, how he thinks, they've had him in their scopes, they see him in their nightmares, they fought him at muzzle-flash range in Baltimore. You ain't putting any stand-in into place for him and making it work. You know that, I know that."

Nick said nothing.

"Uh-oh," said Susan. "I see where this is going."

"So I'm the one," said Bob, "who has to sell Cruz on playing Cruz. I have to get him to trust us—me—not only enough to turn himself in but to put his ass on the bull's-eye with Mick Bogier's trigger finger six ounces away from sending him to hell."

Again, silence from Nick.

"And you know and I know and everybody knows that these things always break in odd and unpredictable ways, that you can plan till you're goddamned purple, and not plan right. And you can't say: 'Ray, you'll be all right. I guarantee it.' There ain't no guarantee."

"To some degree," said Nick, "it *is* his job. If he wants justice for Whiskey Two-Two, this is a risk he has to take. But you're right: no one says it's easy, it's safe, and no, no guarantees."

"It always comes down to one guy out there in the bush on his lonesome," said Bob. "Then, now, forever. Same as it ever was."

S wagger finally put in the call.

It rang and rang and rang. No answer.

Where was he?

But then came a knock at the door.

Swagger peered through the peephole, then opened up.

"Jesus Christ, you were here all along?"

"Nah," said Cruz. "I moved in this morning."

"How did—"

"A friend did some TDY for the Bureau some years ago. He told me they put him up here. I came, I sat in the lobby, I followed. You were careless. I came up in the elevator after you and saw you go into your room. Then I went to my room and waited. I like to know where the people hunting me are quartered. You never know what might come in handy."

"I'll say this, Sergeant Cruz, you are good in ways I never even thought of. Now sit down. We have some talking to do."

Cruz sat. He was in a polo shirt, jeans, some kind of running shoes, and wore the Ravens purple baseball cap. He could have been any slightly exotic early middle-aged guy who hit the gym a lot, kept the belly off, and moved efficiently, like a man in shape.

"Look," Swagger said, "this ain't my idea. But it's a good idea. I want you to listen to it and consider it. Don't say yes or no right away."

"I'm listening."

Bob laid it out, though he didn't cover the issue of who would play the fake Cruz.

"I have to come in, that's what you're saying."

"Yes."

"And suppose I do that, I'm off to a federal holding tank and the next thing you know I'm under arrest for any one or all of the dozen things I am guilty of. And they say to you, 'Thanks, asshole, you did a good job suckering the jerk in. Now get lost.'"

"It won't happen that way."

"How do you know?"

"I know Memphis. I've been in a gunfight with Memphis next to me. He's alive today because I made a fast shot on a real bad guy in a parking lot in Bristol, Virginia. He got his promotion to assistant director because I made some good shots on a quartet of Irish snipers in Wyoming. He wouldn't sell me out. It goes even further back, to the early nineties, not worth telling about. He's quality."

"How do you know the Asian woman won't run back to CIA and say this is happening and the Agency sets up some counterplotting to screw me? After all, I represent nothing of help to them and a whole lot of harm."

"Because I cut the head off a fat Yakuza bastard who was about to take her down. Then I fought the best swordsman in Japan and cut him near in two. Blood like a river, everygoddamnwhere. Worst fight I's ever in. Nightmares about it, every night. Anyhow, she got Tokyo head girl and now she's in line for deputy director. These people owe the old man a thing or two. I ain't bragging, I don't brag; but it's so."

"That was then. This is now. This town corrupts. The perks, the flattering press coverage, the access to and friendship with powerful people, the sexual opportunities, the glittery parties in mansions and condos overlooking the moonlit monuments: it's sweet poison."

"These two: no. That's all I got to say."

"So I have to take on trust what you take on trust."

"Seems like it."

"Okay, who plays me?"

"We'll get a guy who has the same—"

"No, you won't," said Cruz. "That's bullshit. These guys know me. They know how I move, what my body language is, what my size is. And this is for Whiskey Two-Two, so it's still my job. I'll go. If I get hit, well, it's nothing that couldn't have happened in the sandbox."

"Cruz, be sure. Think it over. There'll be a moment when Mick Bogier has you dead zero in his scope and his finger on the trigger and he's taking up the slack. Maybe we get there in time, maybe we get there one second late. No body armor's going to stop a .50."

"Just get him. Then break him. Then get the guy who set this up. Then find out what it's all about. That's enough. If you give me that pledge, then I'll go play the tethered goat."

"You'd make your grandfather proud," said Bob.

"My grandfather died in 1967. He was a Portuguese fisherman in Cape Cod, Massachusetts."

"That was Solomon Nicola Cruz, the father of Lieutenant Commander Tomas F. Cruz, who raised you with his wife, Urlinda Marbella, at the Subic Bay Naval Station in the Philippines. Lieutenant Commander Cruz was by all accounts a fine man and you were so lucky to have him and your mother too. He wasn't your real father and she wasn't your real mother and you're not half Filipino. They was stepparents. Your grandfather was a United States Marine who landed on five islands in the Pacific and was awarded the Medal of Honor on Iwo Jima. He was as brave and tough and good as they come and that's the dead-zero truth. He had one son, who married a beautiful Vietnamese woman who was killed in the Tet invasion in 1968. She was a fine, fine woman. Her husband never knew she had you, because he was in Laos attached to SOG at the time. When he came back, she was gone. And so were you. I don't know how you got to the Philippines. But sure as hell, and I see your grandfather's look on your face all the time, you're my son."

PART FOUR

THE LAST BATTLE OF IWO JIMA

H ere," said Bogier.

"Here?" said Tony.

It wasn't really an intersection. Basically, 37th bent to the right and became P, or, if you were facing in another direction, P bent to the left and became 37th.

"It has to be," said Bogier.

"Mick, I see a hundred other places it could be."

"Name them. Don't point to them, but indicate them."

"Any of those buildings on the campus," he said.

They were standing at the end of the wall that blocked off the public front to Georgetown University along 37th Street, the wall itself too tall to see over. But they knew what was there: several acres of campus lawn latticed with walkways and interrupted by benches, much of it shaded by the giant umbrellas of hundred-year-old trees, the whole maybe 250 yards long. From where they were, they could see an L formation of august Gothic buildings snared in vine over old stone, dormer windows, archways, whatever signifiers one can imagine indicating the solemnity of higher education. These sealed the north and west perimeters of the lawn and all faced directly or at a slight angle to the entrance, at the lawn's southern end, of Lauinger Library, itself an outlier in newfangled, cutting-edge, hip-to-the-max architecture that would be the site of Ibrahim Zarzi's upcoming speech before the American Foreign Policy Association. There, before assorted invitees mostly from State and the Administration, and several dozen reporters, it had been widely reported that Zarzi would make his formal announcement that indeed, he was a candidate for the presidency of Afghanistan in the fall election a few weeks off.

"Those buildings will be closed down," said Bogier. "No way he penetrates. The lawn will be closed down; no way he gets out onto it for a shot. And, you're not considering his skill set. He doesn't have to penetrate because, unlike you and me, he doesn't need a stable rest, a pedestal or bipod, a Kestrel weather station, a range finder, a computer, any of that bullshit. He's a super-offhand guy. He'll shoot from there," he said, nodding to indicate where his team boy should look.

Tony took the cue and saw the end of the wall where there was just a little space between it and a perpendicular wrought-iron fence complete with a line of black shafts and spearheads. Z realized that the sniper could wedge himself into that space and on the other side of the wall get a direct line of sight to the library entrance through which Zarzi, after the speech, would waltz in triumph, wave to his fans, pose for the cameras, and begin a walk to the limousine parked out on 37th. The range would be about 250 yards.

"Ray slides in there, out comes the rifle, *poof* goes the suppressor, and time in flight later, Zarzi, standing at the entrance, waving to reporters, supporters, and the world, has a crater for a face."

"Maybe he'll crash one of those houses on the left side of Thirty-seventh. Shoot from upstairs. Has a nice angle into the library entrance."

"Secret Service has it covered. Guys have or will have knocked on all the doors, spoken to all the people, asked them to stay away from windows during and after the speech. There'll be countersnipers on the roofs of the Georgetown buildings. Ray knows that and he knows his best bet is to kind of scuffle into the margins of the place, real late. Like I say, to just this spot."

"You don't think they'll have cops out here too?"

"Yep. They'll have P Street sealed off and Thirty-seventh as well. No car traffic. But it doesn't matter. You know why? Because he's already there."

"Already there?"

"Maybe even now," said Bogier. "That's how bad he wants this shot. Look over the wall on P. See what's behind it. Looks like some woods or forest, undeveloped, just waiting for Georgetown to build its new chem lab or something. He'll hit it tonight, slide in there in ghillie, probably up close to the wall. Then he waits. He waits through tonight, he waits through tomorrow. He waits through rain, snow, sleet, earthquakes, animal bites, bouts of depression, winning the lottery, cats and dogs living together. Thirty-six hours without a move or a sound or a shit. That's the zen of this bastard. They'll close this place down tomorrow, but he's already here. They'll run dog teams, but he's probably perfumed up with skunk piss, so the dogs'll steer clear. No human eye will pick him out. Tomorrow night, game time, he comes out of his hole. His move to his shooting site is probably no more than fifty feet. He has to get over a wall, no biggie to an athlete like him. He may run into a cop but he'll be on him and kung fu him down in two seconds, he'll slide along into that gap between the fence and the wall, the Great Man comes out, the red dot comes up, and that's the ball game. Ray doesn't care about getting away. Getting away isn't a part of the plan. And it doesn't matter if I put a hollow point into his brain a second after or if he spends the rest of his life in federal prison or rides the needle. Sergeant Ray Cruz, USMC, did his job, and by his Semper Fi code, by all that bullshit that he believes separates him from us and makes us shit to his noble goodness, that's what's important. It's moral vanity, his only flaw. He's got a code; we don't."

"And that's why you hate him, Mick?"

"I don't hate the fuck at all. I love him. I wish I was half as hung as he is. No way I'd be where he is now, not with all the shit we've put on his ass. I wish I could let him have his shot. I wish we could just go away. But we showed the greed, we showed the need, we have to do the deed. We took the dough, so we have to go. That's *our* code. It ain't much of one, but goddamnit, I will play it out, same as him, right to the end."

"Where are we, Mick?"

"Do you mean philosophically? Somewhere between Housman and Xenophon."

"No, Mick, I mean where are we space-time-location-wise. That kind of 'Where are we?'"

Mick pivoted, but did not point.

"Down P Street, almost to Wisconsin. Remember, the cops will have it cordoned off, so there won't be any traffic. It'll be a straight shot to his position. We park early to get a location. We go see a movie, then we come back, slip into our war gear, and set up. We've pre-lased the ranges, we've figured the angles, there's not supposed to be any wind tomorrow night. I've dialed in the scope setting, so there's no holdover. I'll go with the .338 instead of the .50, much easier to manipulate and shoot. I'm prone in the back, shooting through the rolled-down window. You're next to me, on the spotting scope. You pick him out, index me into him, and when I have him on the cross, I take the slack out on him whether he's made his move or not. Suppressor mutes our signature; the only thing anybody hears is a sonic boom six hundred yards downrange indicating nothing. I pull the rifle into the car, you scramble to the driver's. Then we just drive away, turn left on Wisconsin, drive to Baltimore-Washington airport and catch a flight to Florida. If we have time, we dump the guns and burn the car, but it ain't no big deal. MacGyver says all the firepower was obtained overseas for black ops and can't be traced, and the car is registered through a maze of shipping companies, holding companies, Cayman Islands banks, Mexican rental agencies, and what have you."

"Suppose you read him wrong, Mick. Suppose he doesn't show or he doesn't show at this spot."

"He will. He doesn't know why, but I do. He *has* to do the deed the sniper way. He has to complete Two-Two's mission, make Two-Two's shot. That's his thing. That's what's driving him, subconsciously. He'll be exactly where I say he'll be. It's his only shot."

"But I'm saying a lot can go wrong. He doesn't show. What then?"

"Well," said Mick, "I guess we commit hari-kari on the spot."

"Not me, Mick. Tony Z's not that much into the samurai thing. I'll just feel really bad for three full days, is that okay?"

"*Four* days," said Mick. "Minimum."

FBI INCIDENT COMMAND HQ

O'BRIAN CHILDHOOD DEVELOPMENT CENTER
BASEMENT
3614 P STREET NW
GEORGETOWN
WASHINGTON, DC
1530 HOURS
FRIDAY

I know you're a professional, Sergeant. But let's pretend I'm an infirm old man with short-term memory loss and I've forgotten we just went over this seven minutes ago. One more time, please."

Ray looked at the FBI executive hard, at the man Swagger who was supposedly—he was still trying to wrap his mind around this one—his father, at the beautiful Asian woman who repped the Agency, who were the stars here. Meanwhile, clerks, techies, SWAT cowboys, street agents, commo people bustled about, though all vehicles were parked a mile away.

"You're going to dump me off at Reservoir. My job is to infiltrate the mile or so down the hill, through the woods, and get to the other side of the wall that fronts P Street right at the point where P bends left to become Thirty-seventh."

"Do you think that's a good choice?" asked the woman. "It all turns on that choice."

"It's the only choice, ma'am. It's my only shot."

"Swagger made the choice," said Memphis. "He said it would be his choice."

"It was an easy read," said Swagger.

"I get in, I wait," continued Ray. "I'm next to the P Street wall. I'm hearing police activity outside, I know there are cops all over the place. We're hoping we have some bad guys down P Street, closer to Wisconsin."

"Another interpretation," she said.

"It's right. If I'm here, they have to be there. It's their only shot. We're both locked in by the geography of the site."

"Go on."

"I wait, I wait, I smoke a couple of cigarettes, I listen to Iron Maiden on my iPod, I watch the movie *Mesa of Lost Women* on my portable disc player, yadda yadda."

"He has a sense of humor," said Memphis. "I like that."

"Humor deflects bullets, though it didn't do Billy Skelton any good. Anyhow, the witching hour is 1915. At that point, I leave my hide, creep to the roadway that separates me from my shooting position at the end of the Thirty-seventh Street wall, check out the cop situation. I have to hop a wall. Maybe I can get across that roadway easy does it, on stealth, 'cause I'm a Ninja Turtle bastard from way back. Maybe I have to conk a cop. At any rate, I uncover, I move, and as I move into position, whammo, I'm hit, that is, by cops across the road. In ten seconds there are twenty cops there. I'm moving so fast Mick Bogier can't risk a shot, he's got no sight pic, or that's the theory, at any rate. But he's real into it, and he's got Zemke spotting the action for him, he's on me all the way. Anyhow, the cops wrestle me to the ground, a couple of cop cars pull up. I'm cuffed, surrounded by cops, and I'm dragged to the police car. I'm put in the back. And then I wait for the shot, head in profile through the back window. When he fires, I'm so fast, I can duck before it arrives."

"Ha, ha," said Nick.

"When I get in . . ." And he continued with Nick's plan, chapter and verse, crossing all the *t*'s and dotting all the *i*'s and Swagger more or less blanked out, having heard it so many times already.

"It's a good plan, I think," said Nick. "But then I thought it up, so I would think it's good. Sergeant Swagger, do you have any comments?"

"Sergeant Cruz, don't get cute out there. You are never standing still, you are never not moving erratically. You give the motherfucker a whisper of a chance, he'll put one right through you. And if he's shooting a .50 or anything heavy, the body armor don't mean a thing."

"I get it," said Cruz.

"You better get it. I'll kick your ass if you don't."

"My ass will be dead if I don't."

"Don't matter. I'll kick it anyway."

Cruz just shook his head at the man's intransigence. Once a sergeant, always a sergeant, no matter what.

"I know you'd feel better if you had your rifle, Cruz," Nick finally said. "But you know we can't play it like that."

"Sure," said Cruz. "I'll play your little game, even if it sucks. Me, I'd just call in a Pred and order up a Paveway Two crater. But your game is the only game in town."

INFILTRATION ROUTE

T he van pulled to the extreme southern edge of the woodland behind the Georgetown University Hospital parking lot. It halted for just a second, and Ray slipped out, crossed a walkway, launched himself over a low brick wall, and found himself on a wooded downslope that ultimately would bring him to the intersection of P and 37th with its interesting geometry of walls, trees, open shots across the green to the library entrance, the FBI trap, and a meet with Mick Bogier on the wrong end of a rifle.

Though encumbered by his ghillie suit and Kevlar body armor, he was unarmed, as per agreement. Through the trees ahead, he could catch glimpses of the twin Gothic spires that were the university's contributions to the skyline. He oriented on them, followed the incline, listening intently for human sounds, reasonably sure that in this twilight his slow movement and camouflage kept him invisible to whoever would be out here in this inaccessible parcel of undeveloped slope.

As he moved, he could not help but consider.

The story was simple. Swagger said it came from late-arriving NIS witness accounts. Someone in the Navy's investigative service, prodded by the FBI, had finally tracked down an elderly couple who knew Tomas and Urlinda Cruz on Subic Bay Naval Station in the late sixties and early seventies. The same investigator also found two other couples who had corroborated the story.

The story: Tomas and Urlinda had widely lamented their childlessness, particularly now that Tomas had retired and wouldn't be at sea anymore, and was running the Navy's Special Services department at a salary that by Philippine standards was quite generous. He grew restive; he could play golf, go to Europe, visit with his wife's relatives for only so long. They began to actively look into adoption.

But after Tet, with the upheaval in Saigon, he and Urlinda disappeared for a month. When they came back, they had a three-month-old baby, and the story they told, lame as it was, was widely accepted: Urlinda had taken some fertility drugs, the two had gone to Australia for medical care, the child was born prematurely, and now they were back home. An Australian birth certificate validated the process, and so Reyes Fidencio Cruz was accepted as the natural son of Tomas and Urlinda Cruz, of such and such an address in the rather nice residential section of the vast naval installation, really a small American city in the islands.

But State Department records had no mention of a trip to Australia. Instead, as an intrepid investigator found out, the Cruzes had gone to Saigon in the immediate aftermath of Tet. There, the inference was, they had been able to locate a black market mixed-race white-Asian baby for sale. They asked no questions, and even if they had, there would have been no answers. Presumably the aftermath of a major battle with massive civilian casualties would produce a bumper crop of babies for sale. The birth certificate, its fraudulence easily penetrated by the NIS investigators, must have been part of the deal, and in those days, who really cared? The Cruzes were happy, and the boy Ray grew up smart and lithe and quick, taking instantly to his dual heritage of American and Filipino, perhaps representing the best of both countries.

And that was the story Ray himself believed in until the man who called himself Ray's biological father told him another.

According to Swagger, he was back in country on combat tour number two. Already a superstar marine NCO with one spectacular tour behind him, he had returned as a loaner to the Central Intelligence Agency's SOG operation, the OSS of Vietnam, as it were, staffed by the best and the brightest and the bravest American NCOs and junior officers, most from Special Forces, some from the marines, some from the SEALs. Swagger made it sound like a KP detail, scrubbing pots away into the night. But Ray knew that SOG operators were incredibly brave men; they were the commando elite, going on long missions into Laos; they ambushed supply trains, they dared the VC to come out and fight; they did their share and much more. But on one mission, Sergeant Swagger had been wounded, and sent to Saigon for recuperation.

There he met and fell in love with one Tien Dang, the eldest daughter of Colonel Nguyen Thanh Dang, of the 13th Airborne Rangers, ARVN. It wasn't your wartime hayroll at all. He met her parents, he explained his prospects, he formally proposed and married her. He went to great lengths to arrange a visa so she could accompany him to the States when his tour was over; but the paperwork proved difficult, so he extended his tour and made arrangements for her to give birth in the naval hospital.

It all fell apart at Tet. Swagger was in Laos, leading what was called a hatchet platoon, whose mission was to serve as a blocking force into which other units would drive main force VC and North Vietnamese formations for heavy engagement. It was dangerous, productive work, and many believed that SOG showed how the war should have been fought and how it could have been won. But Swagger wasn't able to get back to Saigon for a month and when he did, the Dang neighborhood had been occupied by VC regulars and bombed out. Few survivors. No records. He never knew if she had the child or not before the war came and crushed everything.

The rest was unsaid, reconstructed by Ray as he slid through the darkening woods on his way to the wall at P. He inferred that Swagger lost his wife and child in Vietnam, and tried to imagine the anger and the bitterness and the sense of loss it would create. And maybe that's why he'd trained so hard to come back as a sniper and why he pushed himself so hard up in Indian country, and why he made war upon the enemy like few in the whole decade's doomed venture; and maybe that explained the twenty years of drunken, bitter solitude that followed before the man reinvented himself and somehow, some way, found a path back into the world, DEROS at last.

Swagger had insisted on a DNA test, but knew it to be so: he said, in certain lights, with a certain hard set of his features as viewed from a certain angle, Ray looked so much like his own father, Earl, it was a little startling. The way he carried his head, his hands, the way he squinted when he thought, his refusal to show anger, excitement, elation, anything at all with anything other than a dry chuckle and a wisecrack. All Earl, as Earl as any man could be, far more Earl than Bob.

Fine for him, Ray thought. *But what about me? Who am I? Am I American, Bob's son, Earl's grandson, am I Filipino, Tomas's son, or am I, all of a sudden, Vietnamese?*

Then he realized who he was: he was, taking after his father, sniper all the way through.

UNIDENTIFIED CONTRACTOR TEAM

They'd seen a movie. It sucked. They went to a massage parlor. It sucked. They had a nice dinner. It sucked. They'd taken a cab back to Georgetown. It sucked. They were nervous. It sucked. Now, crouched in the darkened car on the quiet street, two blocks east of the police barricade that cut off P as it headed to the bend in the road that turned it to 37th, they pulled on body armor over black tactical pants and shirts. They pulled on watch caps tight, covering the ears.

"Almost fucking done," said Tony Z.

"Z, listen up. If I'm hit, don't do anything stupid like coming back for me, or hanging around to give cover fire. Once we put this asshole down, it's ejection time and if you have to go one way while I go another, that's fine. If you make it and I don't, that's fine. We'll link in Miami."

"Nothing's going to happen, Mick. We pop him, the fuckhead cops wonder what the hell that sonic boom is, we drive to the airport, we leave a timer in the car so it goes bang tomorrow at noon, we fly away. The gardener finds him stuffed between the fence and the wall a few weeks from now. What the hell is that? everybody wonders. Who did Ray Cruz? Meanwhile, you and me, it's twenty-four/seven pussy, dope, and gin for a year or so. And here's the best part: the fucking universe was falling apart, the struts that hold it all together were cracking, we did our job, we lived up to our calling. What else is there? It sure beats teaching high school English or selling software programs."

"It does. Just so you know, you and Carl, you guys are the best I ever worked with. Too bad about him, but I'll be on your six o'clock any time you need it, bro."

"Same here, Adonis."

"Now let's do this sucker."

They slid back to the rear of the SUV. The spotting scope and the .338 Lapua Magnum, a Sako TRG-42 with a big-ass chunk of Nightforce glass up top, were already in place. They squirmed into position, and Tony Z worked himself to the scope, fiddled with it, while Mick set to rifle business.

"Wait," said Bogier. "Run a check on the BlackBerry on Swagger. See where he is. That might come in handy."

"You got it," said Tony. He rolled to his back, pulled the Black-Berry out of the pocket of his tactical vest, then squirmed back over and turned it on. Magically, a grid of the streets where they were operating opened up, and in a few seconds, the small, beeping light that always announced the satellite's astronomical opinion on the presence of Planet Swagger came to life.

"Yeah, he's on-site. He's at the library. That must be their command HQ."

"Good," said Bogier. "If they were on to anything, he'd be down here in this area. We got it locked. I am filled with confidence. The mission is a big go."

"Okay, Swagger's moving, not much, but there's motion." Tony looked at his watch. "Good, that means the speech is over, now Swagger knows it's the moment of maximum danger, and he's moving close to Zarzi."

"Go to scope, bro."

Tony put his eye back to the spotter. He saw the stone wall, an upslope of grass to it, the perpendicular wrought-iron fence, a sidewalk into the campus, another outpost of fence, then the driveway that presumably led to parking lots. Two cops stood together, talking casually, about thirty yards down 37th, their backs to the driveway and gate. It was six hundred yards out, and by now, it had darkened considerably. The range was too far for night vision, but the optics gave excellent resolution and there was enough ambient light from the campus lights and the buildings across 37th Street to illuminate the scene for him.

"I've got a good visual."

"Me too," said Bogier.

The rifle was a phantasmagoria of modern accuracy tricks, with a free-floating barrel, its action bedded and sunk into a green plastic stock that had accuracy enhancements 1 through 233, including a rigid pistol grip, a bolt grip the size of a golf ball, and infinitely adjustable potential, whole pieces and sides and hemispheres that could be adjusted inward and outward just so. It looked like a piece of plastic plumbing put together by a drunken committee of clowns, but it fit like a glove, and riding its bipod, Mick brought it readily to hand, eye, supporting elbow. The muzzle of the suppressor projected just slightly from the rear opening and the windows of the vehicle were so blackened that you'd suspect a sniper only if you were looking for a sniper.

Through the scope, which was set at a modest 6 power, Mick could see exactly what Tony saw, only smaller. But there was no jiggle, no wobble, no irritating tremble matched to his breathing, which is the great advantage of the lower magnification.

"I am so locked on," said Mick. "I can feel my heartbeats, I can feel my atoms shifting. Man, I am in a zen wave you would not believe."

"Me too, brother. Yes."

"Any second now," Mick said, and both understood the time for chatter was over.

They waited. It sucked. They waited. It sucked. They waited. It sucked.

"Uh!" said Tony, a little peep to his voice. "I have him. Jesus Christ, he just leaned out from around the iron fence at the entrance to the parking lot. You read it so right, Mick! He's twenty feet from his shooting position."

"Cops, do you see cops?"

"They're looking the wrong way, assholes. He's trying to decide whether to conk them, then go to the wall gap, or just go anyway, hoping they don't turn."

"I got him, damnit, he keeps pulling out and back in, I don't have enough of him long enough to shoot."

"You cool?"

"Like the hand of death, man. Just let him move, stay stable, and bingo, we got him."

Then the sniper emerged. He dipped across the entryway to the driveway, huddled at the foot of the separation between it and the walkway.

"He's going along the fence. Then he'll curve back into the gap. I'll take him when he's in place. I don't want to shoot through the fence."

"You cool?"

"I'm coolly cool, boy. High times ahead."

They could both see the sniper ease forward, but the problem was the wrought iron. From this extreme angle, the gaps between the metal would be tiny, and to risk a shot through them foolish. Let him slide along, get into position, and then whack him.

"He's almost—"

The lights cut into the scene like a madman's stab. The beams leapt from nothingness from the near building roof, three, four of them, crucifying the crawling sniper next to the wrought-iron fence. From nowhere it seemed, men rose from bush and from ground and closed the distance in split seconds. They had shotguns leveled and someone was screaming, if indistinctly, from this far out.

"Goddamnit! It was a fucking trap! Swagger must have set it up! Goddamnit!" screamed the angry Tony. "Oh fuck fuck fuck fuck fu—"

"Stay on the scope. Maybe when they move him, I'll get the shot. Be cool, goddamnit, be cool."

"They've got him now. Six of them. They're on him. Shit."

One of the cops broke away from the struggle and was talking on a hand unit. In seconds, a squad car, its lights beaming red-white pulses into the night, pulled around a corner a block down, and raced to the scene. It halted, and two cops got out.

"Okay, he goes in the car. Stay on him," said Mick. "I'm orienting on the car. Talk to me, talk to me."

"They've got him, man, he's fighting hard, oops, they knocked him down, he's cuffed, oh yeah, now they're dragging his ass to the car, I can't even see him there are so many cops on him, okay, they've got him there, pushing his head down, opening door, in he goes—"

"Dead zero," said Mick.

He had him. Cruz's head was silhouetted perfectly in the rear car window, the scene well lit by the pulse of the police lights. Mick more or less oozed through a slight correction, placing the exact and motionless intersection of the crosshairs onto the center of the head, knowing the .338 would not deviate an inch as it plowed through the glass so much more powerfully than a .308, and when it hit it would splatter whatever organic lay at the end of its long journey and in that moment of perfect truth and clarity, his finger independently squeezed gently into the trigger and he fired.

H e had them. Of course. They were eager to be had. They believed so urgently, so earnestly, so passionately.

"Finally," Ibrahim Zarzi said, "finally, I speak of honor. It is not much spoken of these days. It is an old-fashioned virtue that belongs, it is said, in books about Camelot or Baghdad during the great years of the caliphate. It is the bond between men of good faith, goodwill, and lion hearts that supercedes creeds, religions, sects, units, parties, any artificial human grouping you can name. It is not between groups, it is between men.

"Thus, standing up here in the blaze of lights, I do not see a group called 'American diplomats' and 'policy intellectuals.' I do not see uniforms, clothes, hair styles, skin colors. I do not see sexes. I see other men, and you will forgive an old fellow for not, briefly, indulging in the politically correct gender blur. The women in this room are men also, in that they are fierce warriors committed in the end to a world at peace, where the letters IED do not stand for improvised explosive device but for ice educational development, and those employing it work hard to improve the world's figure skating until even we Muslims can do a triple axel!"

He waited for the laughter to subside, luxuriating in the waves of love that washed upon him.

"As I say, this can only happen if men have honor among themselves. I look, I see men of honor. I see my new friend Jackson Collins who oversees his Agency's efforts in my country; I see my new friend Theodore Hollister who supervises all, I see Arthur Rossiter, sublime of countenance, yet as fierce a warrior as there is. And finally

I see Walter Troy, who makes sure that what must happen happens. These are men I love and respect. They believe in my country and in its future. They understand that our two nations and our two cultures must embrace and entwine and learn from each other. They understand that the trust between men is what holds us together and enables us to reach out and overcome our tiny, negligible differences, and in the words of your great moral reformer, overcome. One day we shall overcome, I swear it, my friends, my honorable friends, I swear it on my honor."

His eyes brimmed with a fervor that took the shape of tears, and the tears drained sweetly down his face.

"And thus it is my pleasure, my duty, my responsibility, but above all required by my honor that I declare myself a candidate for the presidency of my country and I will return on Sunday to begin to run to capture the hearts, the souls, the minds, and the love of my countrymen. Thank you, Americans, for showing me, a much fallen sinner, the path back to honor!"

The diplomats, normally staid men with dry eyes and the demeanor of undertakers, rose in unison to clap thunderously.

Dead center," said Tony. "Bing-fucking-go! Home run, three-pointer, *goaalllllll*! Now let's—"

"Shit," said Mick. "I hit a fucking TV. I saw it shatter. It's a fucking trap."

His bullet had struck the center of what was supposed to be Cruz's head, but wasn't. He realized, from the momentarily unperturbed image of Cruz sitting immobile after the hit, which a second later disappeared in a shattering collapse of transparent plastic and the sparks of electrical damage, that he'd drilled some kind of screen displaying a prerecorded image of Cruz sliding into the car and taking a seat.

From side streets along the five blocks of P to the target zone, heavy SUVs gunned into view, cranked east hard, and ramrodded at them.

It seemed that a fucking convention of special operators also began to spill out of bushes left and right with all the world's collection of submachine guns and black rifles, and spotlights came on them, as an amplified voice rose from an indeterminate point and said, "In the SUV, show us your hands, you are surrounded, this is the FBI." Choppers whirled in low overhead, sending their own beams of illumination down to penetrate through the elms above. The world had instantly gone to war.

Mick slapped Tony hard on the shoulder.

"Okay, son," he said. "Let's show these motherfuckers a thing or two."

"Hoochie mama," said Tony. "It's the big rodeo!"

Mick picked up his MP5, lying next to the big Sako sniper rifle, thrust its snout out the open rear window, and with one strong hand emptied a long burst into the darkness at the nearest men, watched them fly or drop. He heard Tony Z's M4 empty itself of thirty .223s in less than two seconds and saw the lead SUV vibrate in tune to his multiple hits as it veered left, hit something hard, veered right, and totaled itself and the car it creamed, blocking P street.

"Great shooting!" yelled Mick.

The night became magical with havoc. Their own vehicle began to shiver as bullets hit it, metallic clangs ringing in protest at each penetration. It sank on quickly flattened tires. The windows smeared with a spidery webbing of fissure and crack as the bullets sheared through them, holding for a bit, but as more came, one, then another atomized into a spray of shiny sparkles.

Mick got out first, left-hand side, curbside, as bullets plowed into the grass around him, kicking up superheated puffs of vegetable protein. He squeezed close to the car, seeking what little cover was available in its lee, as Z squirmed out next, fast and awkward. Mick saw targets, he gunned targets. He saw another SUV having squirmed around the wreckage and come down the sidewalk, he put his sight on it and lit it up, watched it waver as junk and shit flew off it, and then it collided with a tree and came to rest on its side. More lights came on, but Mick and Tony firing in a stack, one on top of the other in classic SWAT formation, each emptying a magazine at fast movers and vehicles with signs of motion in them, which seemed to drive back the agents. None of the badges wanted to be the only guy to die.

The shooting was fabulous, all you could want in the mad psycho surge of the moment, it was *Heat, The Wild Bunch, The Dogs of War,* the North Hollywood bank robbery, Babyface going hard at the FBI gunners, his tommy gun blazing, all of them, all at once, a world gone spastically into chaos and mayhem. Flashes danced at muzzles, the smokeless powder spurted its intoxicant, a devil's cologne so potent that the hair inside the nose became erect with pleasure, while the spent shells flew in a blur, like insects spiraling from the hive, the recoil was satisfyingly stern but not stout, and over that drama another one played out, the drama of men falling, windows shattering, cars veering, dust flying, things breaking, the fan exploding as the shit hit it by the ton.

Mick rushed through a mag change.

"You guys want a little war?" he screamed. "Okay, motherfuckers, we're gonna have us a little war, and guess what, we *like* war!"

Tony laughed. It was, really, mercenary heaven. It was all that mercs dreamed about, when they were honest with themselves. It was the final big ride with the devil, firepower, destruction, a great deal of ammo, an enemy who expected you to fold and was not at all anticipating World War Three here in sedate Georgetown.

"You good?" asked Mick, completing his reload.

Tony got a new mag into the carbine.

"I am so good," he said. "Man, am I good. I just wish Crackers was here."

Mick reached into his pocket, pulled out a handful of Dexies, and swallowed them dry. They banged off in his head like illumination rounds hitting stainless steel. Man, was he jacked. Fucking A, he was crazed with war lust.

He saw Tony swallow his share of the magic pills, and each flashed the other a cocky fuck-the-world grin, all macho death wish and lust, maybe the last look that passed between Matix and Platt behind the Suniland shopping center in Dade County, 1986, or maybe the Delta snipers Shughart and Gordon at Black Hawk UH-60's crash site in Mogadishu in 1993.

"Let's kill some assholes," said Tony.

Both rose, firing. Their rounds, splaying out in the night, plowed up debris, stucco, splinters, atomized glass, steel shrapnel, turning the weather to a 100 percent chance of death. They ran across somebody's front yard, while incoming rounds pulled up turf geysers all around them. A bullet smacked Tony down, but it was stopped by his armor, and he was up in a second, laughing at the wit of it all.

"Fucking guy thought he had me!" he said. "What a loser."

They got between houses.

Mick, changing magazine again, blinking to wipe the sweat from his eyes, looked up to see a little girl peering down on him through a window.

"Down, down, honey," he gestured wildly.

She smiled.

He smiled back, winked, and made the "get down" signal once again, and this time she obeyed.

"Good to go?" asked Z.

"Cocked, locked, hung like a stud horse, ready to rock, roll, and die proud and loud."

"I am so psyched," said Tony Z. "Man, this is so *Heat!*"

"It's the Auburn game all over again," laughed Mick. "Roll, Tide! Okay, on my lead, I'm reckoning we'll head to Wisconsin where we can really do some damage."

"Go on, you lazy bastard," said Tony.

They ran between houses, one with the MP5, the other with his M4, two armored, hulking terminators crazed on drugs and destruction, sweaty and doomed and loving every motherfucking second of it.

FBI INCIDENT COMMAND HQ
O'BRIAN CHILDHOOD DEVELOPMENT CENTER
CORNER, 37TH AND P STREET
GEORGETOWN
WASHINGTON, DC
2142 HOURS

Nick had gone to the scene, in full body armor.

All around, people talked on commo, coordinating incoming SWAT units, the air traffic overhead, the pileup of emergency vehicles, all of it made crazier by the Secret Service need to get its high-value target securely out of the way fast.

"I told him these guys wouldn't go easy," said Swagger.

"Jesus, get me a rifle, I need to get there," said Cruz.

"You stay put, Cruz. You're going nowhere," said Swagger in a voice that meant exactly what it said.

They could hear: "Suspects crossing Wisconsin, firing both directions. They are shooting up storefronts, they shot the windows out of a bus, there are people down everywhere, we need maximum medical personnel—" And then Nick's voice coming in, "This is Incident Commander, no, repeat *no,* negative medical personnel to move to site until suspects are apprehended, I will convey that information."

"This is DC SWAT commander, I have ten armed men good to go at the corner of Wisconsin and N, I need permission to deploy. Incident Commander, may I—"

"Hold still, DC SWAT, we have two active shooters, they are difficult to pin down."

"Incident Commander, this is Air Six, I have a good visual and a sniper aboard, permission to fire?"

"If you get him, take him, but be advised these individuals appear to be wearing body armor, so I am advising head shots, and if they are down, I am advising snipers to take brain shots on the body before approach."

"Maneuvering for shot, Incident Commander—Oh, he fired, I think he—" and the helicopter crew report exploded into chaos.

"This is Whipshot Four, I have one suspect down, I have the other suspect entered into convenience store, 2955 Wisconsin, I think he's going to barricade."

"Was that your shot, Air Six?"

"Affirmative, that was my shot," and Swagger recognized the voice of Ron Field, who had been involved in another event with Swagger some years back and ended up in charge of the FBI's sniper school.

"Good shooting, Ronnie, now listen to me, from maximum allowable altitude, I want you to put another one into his head. All units hold, let the sniper make sure the perp is closed down."

"Read you, Command, will comply."

The airwaves, still floating with static and crackle and dust, went silent for a few seconds and then a single crack went to all receivers.

"He's toast," came a call, then a dozen other confirmations.

"Good work, Ronnie," said Nick. "All teams converge on 2955 Wisconsin, we have a barricade situation. I'm releasing medical personnel to handle casualties on or near the five-block P Street corridor, but everyone else not in a SWAT team, stay off Wisconsin. DC SWAT, you are released to barricade position, 2955 Wisconsin, FBI SWAT be advised DC SWAT is incoming. We have a very dangerous individual."

"This guy thinks he's got the Bruce Willis role," someone said.

HERE-4-FOOD

Z was down. So much shit was in the air you'd never know who fired the shot. But he lay in the street, squirming, his carbine a few feet away, in a vast lake of blood. Still, he was trying to rise, and he kept waving at Mick, go back, go back, mouthing the word *no* even if blood had frosted his teeth and goatee.

Then the head shot blew his watch cap off, and he was still and that was it.

"Via con dios, amigo," Mick said, and felt a knife of pain that another good guy in a firefight had departed the earth. He took a deep breath, looked one way up Wisconsin, then the other. Each was a festival of blue-red flashes, and behind the screen of pulsing illumination, figures ducked and bobbed, dark men, bent double over their weapons, trying to find an angle to get the killing shot. Mick had been hit four times in the chest and lower back, the body armor saving him each time. He knew he couldn't stay put. Snipers, not the most mobile, would have finally caught up to the front lines and this very second be setting up over car hoods for the brain shot. As it was, rogue bullets pecked up dust puffs down the street, zinged through the glass windows of this place, shot up and withered the cars parked along the street. He could see creepers in the shadows trying to get close for that finishing round.

Fuck all you amateurs, he thought. *SWAT! Wannabes and never-weres. Do it where it's real, motherfuckers, where an IED may take you down any second or the nice lady selling pop will pull out an AK. Do it where the guy with the mild smile on his face and the gentle, empathetic eyes says Allah Akbahr and detonates himself and all pilgrims in a hundred-foot circumference. Hunt the motherfuckers on goat paths and in twisted arroyos and in little mud and wood towns where an RPG can turn you to barbecue at any fucking second. Lie in your own shit and piss for three days for a high-value shot. Raid the cave by moonlight, taking fire all the way to extract. Then tell me you're a pro.*

He turned, kicked his way into the store.

At first it seemed empty. But he ran to the rear counter, where four people cowered, one on top of the other.

"Hey," he said. "I'll take a six of Bud and a package of Camels. Also, got any 9-mil hollow points?"

He laughed at his own joke through cracked, dry lips, though his face was heavily wet with sweat, blood, crap, whatever. He caught a glimpse of himself in the reflection of the beer-cooler glass, a stocky figure in all black, watch cap low over the ears, face mottled, the sub-gun cradled in his hands, body armor, a SIG P226 in a mid-thigh tac holster, black Danner assault boots bloused, mags in pouches every-where. God, he was beautiful. He was war. He was Special Ops. He was Forces. He was the Real Thing. Nobody could stand up to him. Then he completed his turn, lifted his submachine gun over the racks of shelves that stood between himself and the door and win-dows, and fired the rest of his magazine in a sweeping blast that shat-tered all the glass into a spew of glitter until only a few jagged pieces clung to the frame.

He bent over. One of the women was a blonde, blondes are best. He came around, grabbed her by her hair, and pulled her up. He saw she was forties, attractive, the Washington party dame type, and he yanked her to the doorway of the walk-in beer cooler.

"You people," he yelled at the ones who remained cowering behind the counter. "You people, get the fuck out of here, make sure you go out hands up or these assholes will shoot you. I want to see the head FBI guy. Fast, or Diane Sawyer here gets it in the neck."

He pulled the woman by the hair into the vault and felt the frosty air against his sweating skin. He began to steam. *That* was funny. He dragged her to the rear, and forced her down.

"Please," she said, her face gone to dumb fear, "I have children."

He laughed. "So do I. About fifty. I just don't know any of them.

Here, have a beer." He pulled a big can from the shelf, and leaned over and handed it to her. It was a Sapporo, very good beer. Then he got one for himself, kicked her forward, and scootched down behind her, so that the wall was at his back and she was between him and anyone coming through the door. He locked his armored legs around her pelvis, drawing her near. He tossed the MP5 away, pulled her toward him, tight, intimate, sexual, and took out his SIG P226. He cocked the hammer, and laid his wrist along her shoulder so that the pistol muzzle nonchalantly touched her ear.

"Tell you what," he said. "I'm real close on you and you're thinking sex. That's your primal fear. But I won't do anything dick-wise, okay? I may kill you, sweetie, but I won't rape you, so you can relax. Now open my beer."

He handed the can to her with his other hand. She struggled with it, her fingers shaking, shivering with hysterical sobbing, but somehow got it open and handed it back.

He took a deep swallow, and lord, was it not the finest slug of beer he'd ever had in his life?

"Boy," he said, "did I have a tough day at the office!"

Again he laughed at his own bad joke. Then they sat for a few minutes, listening as various forces and entities got things organized outside.

In time, the beer-cooler door opened.

"Bogier?"

"That's my name, don't wear it out."

"Bogier, I'm Memphis, FBI. You don't need to do this. Let that woman go. It's not like you to put someone untargeted at risk. You're a pro."

"She'll get a book contract out of it and do the talk shows for a year. She'll become a star on that fat-black-chick TV show. She's in better shape by far than you or me, Memphis."

The woman shivered. Mick had finished his beer. He pointed at the one he'd given her, which had rolled a few inches away from her leg. She grabbed it obediently, opened it, and handed it back.

"Thanks, sweetie," he said. "Now just close your eyes and think of the happiest day of your life. When you got married. The birth of little Nicholas von Featherstone the Third. When you got that big divorce settlement. When you hit the putt on the eighteenth at Burning Tree to edge out Jennifer Tilden for the club bitch championship. Whatever, just think of it and it'll be over in a few minutes."

He took another swig.

"Bogier, you're not walking. You know that. No immunity, not after Baltimore and the Filipinos plus all the dead cops out there. But I'll get you off the needle, get you a good joint, maybe conjugals, no butt sex from the Blackstone Rangers. Give her up, give it up, walk out, testify against the assholes who put you here, everybody's happy."

"Sounds pretty crappy to me. I want a window, goddamnit. A guaranteed window and a cell next to Dr. Lecter."

He laughed again.

"Now I'll tell you the name of the game we're playing. It's called, 'Will Mick blow Lady Astor's brains out?' I think she's the wife of somebody important. This would be a very dark mark on your record, Memphis." He laughed again, at his own twisted, drug-cranked humor. Everything was pretty goddamned funny.

"Okay, here's the game. I want Cruz. Get his ass over here, send him through the door. Then Mrs. van Jackson gets to go home to her husband, the third assistant secretary of agriculture and mineral rights. I get Cruz, you get Lady Plushbottom. Oh, and do it fast. Like, say, in three minutes. Or I blow her fucking head off, and come out shooting, and in case you haven't noticed, I shoot very well and I will take a lot of SWAT bozos with me to hell. Nothing but head shots. Any trace of tear gas or immobilization chemistry and Lady Winthrop decorates a convenience store beer cooler with her cerebellum tissue and I know whose career goes into the dipsy Dumpster. Get me Cruz!"

The driver pressed it. He careened the wrong way down one-way streets, roared through power turns riding the brakes against the laws of gravity and physics, went to sidewalk blowing out shrubbery and small trees where emergency medical vehicles blocked the streets.

Outside, Washington gone to war sped past the windows: medics working on the wounded, gurneys, plasma units everywhere, men in battle gear with tense faces, lots of throat mikes in play, the roar of low-flying choppers, more guns than at the NRA annual meeting, all of it a kind of eternal D-Day in the half dark.

"I see where this is going," Bob said in the backseat. "He still wants his kill. Cruz, you do not have to do this. You don't have to do any heroic thing, do you hear me? Enough is enough."

Cruz said nothing. He was hunched in the front seat, breathing imperceptibly, his dark face tense and sweaty, his eyes gimlet slits. He gave no indication of having heard Swagger.

It seemed to take an eternity, but they reached the convenience store on Wisconsin, its windows shot out, fire trucks and ambulances standing by, a fleet of first-responder vehicles everywhere except the route out of which they'd been hastily pulled to admit the SUV. The lighting was intensified, the shards of glass everywhere seemed to pick up and reflect that already intense wave of illumination. Again, Kevlar-clad, helmeted commandos everywhere, crouching, weapons loose and ready, on balls of feet, with that go-to-war vibe so heavy in the air you could feel it.

As Swagger and Cruz bailed out, agents flew at them like butlers to push them into Kevlar vests and helmets, and they slid through the shattered doors, over glass and a thick gunk of soda, beer, cereal, canned peaches, gobs of yogurt, melting ice-cream lumps, burritos, cigarette cartons, squished doughnuts, a whole food fight on the floor, debris from the fusillade Mick had fired when he entered. A SWAT team, the Bureau's very best guys, all stacked up and ready for Armageddon, crouched against one wall. Nick and a fleet of commo assistants with radios up the ass were just off the entrance to the cooler, whose door was jammed open.

Swagger could see more evidence that Bogier knew what he was doing. The beer cooler: genius touch. No sniper could go for the head, nobody could flank, and a pro like Bogier wouldn't be fazed in the least by flash-bangs or any other distractors. There was only one way in.

Nick frantically gestured them over.

"Okay," he said, whispering hoarsely into Cruz's ear, "here's what it is. He has a hostage, some poor woman who happened to be in here. He says if you don't go in, he'll shoot her in the head and come out blazing. It's your call, Cruz. No man would say a thing if you say no. I have to tell you, your survivability in there is slim to nothing."

"I hear you."

"Memphis, you can't send him in there, goddamnit," Swagger yelled. "Bogier just wants his kill and he'll check out happy."

"It's his choice," said Nick. "Say the word, Cruz, and I'll send SWAT in behind a wall of flash-bangs. Maybe he's bluffing, maybe he's out of ammo, maybe in the end he can't drop the hammer on some innocent woman, and he goes down like Jimmy Cagney and it's a happy ending."

"You can't blow the vault?" said Swagger. "Come in from the outside?"

"Old building, thick walls. Enough explosive to get through the walls would kill them."

"Where's my little friend?" screamed Bogier from inside. "I want to see my little friend. We served together in Afghanistan, did you know? We're war buddies!" and his shout ended in a dry, harsh laugh, the laugh of a man who had the pedal on the metal and knew that his long-dreamed-of movie ending was just a second away.

"It's bitch-whacking time if little Ray doesn't come through that door," he yelled again. "Ka-pow, it's the end of Chatsworth Osborne's mother. I know Cruz is here. I heard the car arrive."

Ray stood, peeled off his body armor, tossed the stupid fucking Kevlar helmet away.

"Okay," he said, "I'm going in." He turned to Swagger. "Sorry, old guy. A world where she dies so I can survive isn't a world I choose to live in."

He turned.

"Bogier, hold fire. This is Cruz. I'm coming in."

Bob reached out to touch his son, thinking, irrationally but helplessly, *No, it's not right, I just found him,* and feeling a surge of pain and fear from a well so deep he never suspected it was there, but then Ray dipped in and was gone.

This was the worst hell of war, Swagger thought. He'd shot and been shot at, killed with blade, slithered in fear, ridden himself to exhaustion, seen boys following on his orders blown to pieces, been hit hard a half dozen times, felt the fear when the blood pooled out in lakes, ceaselessly, felt panic, begged God for life, clenched tight as incoming blasts searched him out, seen human wave attacks, done it all. But nothing was worse than sending a son off to die. He started, very quietly, to cry.

BEER COOLER

Cruz could see nothing at first. For some reason, a light fog lay across the cooler. All he saw was shoulder-high shelves and a glittery display of world beers. But he heard the breathing, followed it to its point of origin. Peering around a last shelf, he saw Bogier and the woman in a twisty heap against the back wall.

The woman's face had gone to stupor. She had given up and seemed barely conscious. Bogier had her in a tight wrap, his legs clamped around her pelvis. The SIG, cocked, was an inch from her ear. Bogier leaned out from behind her head, and Cruz saw him for the first time: an astonishingly handsome man, with a some-what grown-out thatch of blond hair, rugged, wide-boned face, thin cheeks under the bed-knob bones, and fierce or crazed warrior eyes.

"Bogier, let her go, goddamnit. She's—"

"Shut up, junior, this is my dance, I paid the band."

Ray froze, felt Bogier's eyes on him.

"For so much trouble, you're a scrawny rat. Goddamn you, if I'd have been a microsecond faster three separate times, you'd be among the permanently dead. You must have fucking reflexes like a cat. Think you can dodge this, sucker?"

The SIG came off the woman's ear channel and floated onto Ray, dead zero for his center chest. Bogier's finger teased the trigger.

"This isn't war," said Cruz. "This is execution. Some soldier you—"

"Shut up, motherfucker. I lost two very fine men trying to whack your ass. You know how hard it is to find men that good?"

"I knew one once. Billy Skelton, lance corporal, USMC. Some fucker blew him in two."

"It wasn't his day. You know what I fucking hate about you? I can feel it even now, at the very end. It's your fucking moral certitude. You sit there, knowing I'm going to blow your heart out in three seconds, and there's nothing you can do about it, and you still think you're so holy because you worship some bitch named Duty, and you don't get it that she's a whore and will fuck you up the ass any time she has a chance. Oh, yeah, you have a code. Duty, honor, country. Semper Fi, all that good bullshit, true believer, patriotism, Fourth of July, apple pie, all that war movie crap from the forties. Oh, you've got a code, Sergeant Cruz, that makes you morally superior."

There was nothing for Cruz to say to this mad barrage.

"Look at me! Look at me," Bogier screamed, and Cruz brought his eyes into total connection with the man.

"Guess what, junior. It's easy to die for something you believe in. I've seen it ten thousand times and it ain't that fascinating. You know what's hard? Here's hard: dying for a code you *don't* believe in. That's what the samurai knew. They died for the master they knew was corrupt, cowardly, venal, and pitiful. They died anyway. That was their code, and I'd say it was a hell of a lot tougher than that show tune you call patriotism."

Bogier's eyes bored into him.

"Here's our code, asshole. These in the day when heaven was falling, when earth's foundations fled, followed their mercenary calling, took their wages and are dead."

He smiled, raised the SIG to his own skull, and happily blew his brains out.

GEORGE WASHINGTON PARKWAY

At first, after the turn off the brown lights of the band of highway called a "beltway," they saw nothingness. Trees on both sides of the roadway, steep embankments, the hazy sense of lights, homes, civilization behind the screening, the traffic too fast, still too heavy, Bilal driving especially carefully, so tense he could hardly stand it now, so close, so soon.

But then the trees broke in the dark, the river was clear off to the left, and beyond it, lit like some kind of theatrical production, lay the city itself.

"It's no Paris," said Khalid. "The first time I saw Paris, oh, that was a sight. But it's nice. So white."

The city loomed across the river and two sources of reflection helped it shimmer, the river beneath, the low clouds above.

"Pah," said Faisal. "It is a city. It is not magical. Know its name or not, it's just another urban sprawl with a few monuments, more beautiful by night in its gown of lights than by day, which reveals its tawdry—are they expecting us? Look!"

He pointed. Something was indeed happening. They saw a high, arched bridge ahead, spanning the river, and beyond it to the left a ridge, on top of the ridge two steeples and a collection of Gothic buildings, and somewhere above the buildings or just beyond them, a swarm of circling helicopters, a frenzy of searchlights knifing upward; and on the ground, intermittently visible through a maze of streets, much commotion as illuminated by the presence of a great many police lights blinking red-blue, on-off in great rapidity.

"Perhaps it's a festival of some sort," said Khalid.

"No, no, not with all the policemen," said Bilal, at the wheel. "It's probably some kind of civic catastrophe, a fire, a crime, something banal like that."

"I hope nobody was hurt," said Khalid.

"You are *such* a fool," said Faisal. "These people bomb your country and kill your kin and occupy and defile your holy sites, they are infidel scum without souls, and yet you weep tears for a few of them caught in a brothel fire."

"Actually, they have never bombed my country, and I am not weeping, but I feel pain for anyone's loss. Loss is loss; it is degrading and debasing, no matter the faith of he who loses. You would know that, Faisal, had you ever developed any sort of empathy, but you are far too narcissistic for—"

"Narcissistic? Narcissistic! Do I spend an hour each morning patting my few remaining hairs this way or that? Do I secretly admire myself in every mirror, window, polished surface in America? Do I have a vocabulary of charming looks cultivated from debased Western movies? Khalid, give us 'slightly angry but secretly pleased,' please."

"You have seen a Western movie or two. You have lusted after the flesh they display so wantonly. I see your dried-up eyes in that ancient prune face as they follow a sixteen-year-old child in tiny shorts and undershirt. I see you make adjustments to your sudden erection, hoping that no one will notice. You're lucky you didn't get us all arrested—"

"*Old men!*" screamed Bilal. "Silence! I am so sick of your bickering. Bicker bicker bicker, all the way across America. You hardly notice America, except for the ice cream—"

"It is the buzzard who is obsessed with ice cream."

"I am no mirror-gazer, however, and my heart is true to Islam."

"*Stop it!*" screamed Bilal, aware that under the stress of the argument he had speeded up. He nervously eyed the rearview mirror for any sign of Virginia police, but saw nothing, and eased back well under the speed limit.

"Silence. Just look at what you have come all this way to destroy.

Face your destiny. Embrace your fate. Honor your God. Obey the text. And shut the fuck up."

To the left, on the other side of the river, the silver-and-white city sped by. It looked like a movie Rome. Its temples were marble with columns thick as old oaks, its rooftops flat, all of it lit by a genius with an eye for the play of light and shadow across glowing surfaces, all of it sunk magically into lushness, like the hanging gardens of ancient memory. It twinkled and blinked across the wide, dark, glimmering river, offering up its famous sights one at a time, the Kennedy Center, the Lincoln Memorial, the high needle of the Washington Monument, a glimpse of the president's mansion set in trees, just a smudge of white dignity in the dark, and finally that colossal dome, its flag rippling against the night wind, flashing blue-white-red signals as it furled and unfurled.

"Do you see corruption, decadence, blasphemy?" asked Khalid.

"Of course not. They keep them hidden. It is internal rot that threatens our world. But yes, they put on a nice show. It's a handsome capitol, I give you that, but its beauty expresses not love but power, not peace but war, and a hunger to obliterate. I see in its grace and beauty our doom, if we do not destroy it first. In fact, its very hugeness inspires me to what I must do, not that I ever had a whisper of a doubt."

Khalid sighed.

"Who knew the old buzzard with the horny eyes had a little bit of poetry left in him? Yes, Faisal, that is what I see too. I see and feel in my dreams the need to destroy it as well."

On that, and that alone, they agreed.

UNIDENTIFIED CONTRACTOR TEAM SUV

No interrogation.

"That's why he did it," Bob said. "He was telling us, 'I won't give up my bosses for anything. They don't deserve me,' he was saying, but he was doing it by the code of the mercenary, a lot harder to live up to, so he says, than the code of a marine sniper. He didn't seem to get that right to the end, Cruz outbraved him."

"Cruz is one hundred percent real, no doubt about it," said Susan Okada. "He's as real as Swagger."

"He's a lot realer than me," Swagger said. "He didn't make the mistake of getting old."

"But I will," said Cruz.

"And thank you," Susan said to Swagger, "for not jumping to the conclusion that these anonymous bosses were Agency," she said.

"I just learned how to stay on your good side. Maybe it's not the Agency. But it's someone with the power to do things and hide from the consequences. It's someone who gets to snipe without taking no incoming. He's the bastard I want."

"Maybe this is the night."

"If not tonight, tomorrow," said Bob.

"Swagger always gets his man," said Nick.

Now they were clustered at the Ford Explorer that the Unidentified Contractor Team had used on its mission. It was shot to pieces, with no window or door or panel unperforated, no tire inflated, on top of a puddle of leaking internal fluids and a spew of glass frags and twisted metal shrapnel.

"Looks like Bonnie and Clyde's last ride," somebody said. "And guess what's inside. The same swag. Look at what these boys were carrying."

The evidence recovery team busily photographed and tagged the loot: one Barrett .50 M107 rifle with Schmidt & Bender scope, four 9-mm semiauto pistols, one Sako TRG-42, one .338 Magnum bolt-action rifle with Schmidt & Bender 10× tactical scope and a custom Gemtech suppressor, two M4 carbines with Aimpoint or EO Tech optics, at least five thousand rounds of various types of ammo, a Schmidt & Bender spotting scope, dual-spectrum night vision goggles, any number of Motorola mini-radio units, several cells, a half dozen or so SureFire flashlights, some yogurt, some chewing gum, some prophylactics, several bottles of amphetamines, some—

"Look, Mr. Memphis," said Cruz, "I hate to tell you your business or anything, but I'm not seeing much urgency here. We're just standing around kind of laughing at all the crap these guys had. But doesn't that tell you something? Top-of-the-line stuff, all of it, the very best. The Marine Corps isn't that well equipped. And the fact that even this late in Zarzi's visit, whoever it is is still sending trained men with high-value tech at risk to protect him, because they don't think the FBI and the Secret Service are up to it. To me, it all points to the idea that something is yet to happen, and they are therefore locked into a total protective response, even one at some risk. So I see the seconds tick away and nobody seems to care."

"Earth to Cruz," said Nick, "evidence collection is the basis of any criminal case, and mistakes made during it can jeopardize the outcome of the prosecution. These evidence technicians are highly trained, methodical, the best in the world. They must be allowed to work, and when they clear what they recover, it will be turned over to us."

Cruz said nothing but was clearly not satisfied.

"Okay," said one of the technicians, coming up to Nick, "this is it, right? This is what you've been waiting for?"

"That's it," said Nick.

"One Thuraya SG-2520 state-of-the-art satellite phone. Tagged and printed, sign on the dotted line, your possession noted in evidence chain, scratch your initials into it with a key or something, and you will sign it in when you are done, according to regulations, right, Mr. Assistant Director?"

"Yep," Nick said. He looked over at Ray, then to Susan and Bob, as he scratched a crude NM into the plastic. "I think you'll find this interesting. I'll put it on speaker and cut all you guys in too. Folks, it's showtime!"

An assistant brought Nick a cell. He punched a button, waited.

"Agent Jeffrey Neal, Technical Support Division, Quantico," came the voice.

"Agent Neal, Assistant Director Nick Memphis, we've recovered, as you suggested we might, a highly sophisticated satellite phone. Care to open it up for us?"

"That's what I'm here for, sir."

"Tell us what to do."

"Describe what's on the screen."

Nick turned the instrument, which looked like a cell any kid in a mall carried, except that it had an aerial folded telescope-style inside. Like any cell, it had the small screen above the keyboard where a message glowed.

"It says 'Enter Unlock Code.'"

"Okay. Obviously we don't have the unlock code. So we'll be going back door, no offense meant to all you gay special agents out there in FBI land."

"Neal, I'm the head comedian. I'll make the jokes, okay? Your job is to laugh at them."

"Got it, sir. I want you to keyboard the number 667723 onto the screen and then hit the star button three times. Do it slowly and carefully. This number was inserted in the CPU by the subcontracted Israeli development team as a request from Mossad. Very few people know about it."

"Got it," said Nick, punching in the numbers and stars.

In a second "Unlocked" came onto the screen.

"Okay," said Neal, "now go to 'Dialed Calls.'"

Nick punched the choice on the screen menu.

"There's only one number here," Nick said. "It's got a 206 area code." Nick read him the number.

"Seattle," said Neal. "They have set up a few remote relay points. Need a sec to trace them. But first, I'm going to put you on hold while I call the U.S. Attorneys' Office in DC. They've been alerted. They will issue a numbered Federal Intelligence Surveillance Court warrant that will enable us to legally trace the linkages and come to the destination phone."

"Excellent," said Nick, listening as the phone went dead. "See, Cruz, this stuff can happen pretty fast if you know what you're doing."

"Okay, I was wrong," said Cruz.

"I'm glad you see the error of your ways and I don't have to have Gunnery Sergeant Swagger kick your ass."

"I may do it anyway, on general principles," Swagger said. "Dumb bozo goes into that icebox unarmed to face a man paid to kill him."

"What an idiot," said Nick. "Oh, and by the way, that's the bravest thing I've ever seen a man do in my life. I'm betting Swagger thinks the same and I bet these guys do too."

"Here, here," said a number of the clustered special agents and SWAT pros.

"He's got guts, he ain't got no sense at all," muttered Swagger.

"Somebody's sure cranky tonight," Nick said. It seemed true—all Swagger had said to Cruz on the way over was stuff like, "That was a really stupid decision. You risked your life for a hostage and endangered what we're trying to do. You don't own your life, Sergeant, the Marine Corps does. It'll give you permission to die, and it hasn't," and the younger man merely shook his head, almost in comic disbelief.

Neal came back on. "Okay, I've got the warrant, my next call is to Frontier Communications in Seattle, and with the warrant, they'll tell me where we're going. Give me a few minutes."

It went to silence again, and then—

346 • STEPHEN HUNTER

"Okay, Director Memphis, I'm finally through the bounces. It went from Seattle to Oklahoma City to Charleston before it arrived in Washington, DC."

"Good work, Neal."

"You haven't seen anything yet. Now we have some real magic coming up."

"Is he trying to get on the Comedy Network?" somebody asked.

"Typical IT guy," Nick said. "Smarts off to everybody, sucks up to nobody."

Neal came back.

"The phone number ties to an AT&T cell phone. Our FISC warrant means that we have full cooperation from AT&T and I have them working at level ten, the most dedicated and urgent level of compliance. Oh, I love it when a plan comes together. Now we're going to use a special program developed by the former technical head of a British security company. We can turn on our bad guy's cell from here in Quantico, going through AT&T. Once it's surreptitiously on, it not only broadcasts its GPS location but also sends a unique signature that we can track. The tracked signal is actually more accurate here in DC than the GPS coordinates and updates more frequently. Next call: National Reconnaissance Office and ask them—tell them—to direct their satellites to this area to listen for the signal and start a multilateration calculation to pinpoint the cell phone. They'll come back with a longitude-latitude that we can easily translate into an address. And there's your boy. Total elapsed time, seventeen minutes, a new record."

"Good work, Neal," Nick said, then turned to the crew:

"All right, people. Let's get convoyed up. We're going to make a big bust."

644 CEDARCROFT NW

I t was a big house, the kind in which most American kids dreamed of growing up. Secluded among trees on one of DC's most exclusive streets, it had turrets, gables, dormers, balconies, a screened-in front porch, a free-standing garage, a gazebo, a pool, formal gardens, the American dream.

"Security team, deploy," Nick said, and from the dozen or so unlit federal vehicles arrayed down the street, SWAT teamers slipped out and began to slide off into the trees and bushes to surround and control the dwelling.

"Do you recognize it?" asked Bob, looking to Susan's serene face as she took in the details of the house.

"Yes," she said.

"So which guy is it?"

"It's none of them."

Nick said: "You three stay put. I'll handle the arrest with my people. We'll repair to the Hoover Building and begin the interrogation. We'll go all night and through tomorrow if necessary. If he's lawyered up, it may take a while."

"I want to be there," said Cruz.

"Me too," said Swagger.

"I *have* to be there," said Susan.

"Marine guys," said Nick, "full frontal self-discipline. No anger, no unprofessionalism, no screaming, no punches thrown. I insult you by saying that, but I don't want any trouble with this bust. Do you read me?"

Silence meant they did.

Then a message came into Nick's earpiece, telling him the security teams were holding in place.

"Okay," said Nick, "now my people will make the pinch. Could you call him, Susan? Get him on the phone so he doesn't notice us pulling up. I worry about suicide in cases like this, or suicide by cop or something."

"This guy isn't committing suicide," said Susan.

Nick handed the phone over, got out of the vehicle, waving, as six agents from the car behind came out to flank him, and they headed up the walk.

Susan punched the button on the phone.

"Talk to me, talk to me," came the voice. "Did you make it out clean? I hear sirens and the TV is full of craziness. Did you get him? Where are you?"

"Hello, Jared," she said, "it's Susan Okada. No, they didn't make it out clean. They are in hell, actually. And no, they didn't get him. And we are right outside with a warrant for your arrest. Jared, don't do anything stupid. Get ahead of the prosecution and maybe somehow you can survive this."

"How about lunch tomorrow?" he said.

FBI HQ

**FBI INTERROGATION SUITE 101
HOOVER BUILDING
PENNSYLVANIA AVENUE
WASHINGTON, DC
0010–1900 HOURS**

Who would have guessed? Jared Dixson was a stand-up guy. He wouldn't budge. Handsome, diffident, supercilious in that annoying upper-class, so-Ivy way, heavily ironic; underneath, he was a steel ideologue. He seemed to be enjoying himself. He waived legal representation. He even went so far as to enjoy the claim that it was he who'd ordered the Pentameter shot using poor Jack Collins's computer codes.

"Jack's the jerk from World War Two," he said. "I mean, he thinks he's still a frogman. IQ, maybe thirty-five on a good day. Annapolis, old SEAL, all he-man Afghan Desk, straight out of the movies and Kipling before that. Hello, dummy! Wake up, smell the flowers. You need somebody with smarts, a view on strategy, a vision of what should be. Hmm, I think I described myself rather well there."

He wasn't bluffed by legal threats.

"Do whatever you want," he said to Nick and his assistant Chandler, as Okada, Swagger, and Cruz watched on closed-circuit TV. "Bring any charges you want. Subpoena anybody you want. I don't care. Some things are worth spending the rest of your life in prison for, and getting the guys out of Afghanistan is one of them. You can say: 'He tried to murder a marine sniper team.' I suppose it's true and I'll bet that marine sergeant would like to strangle me about now. Maybe that would be fair. But I would argue: national defense in the trenches is murky, bloody business. No way to recall the team. Nothing personal, but I could *not* stand by and watch our soon-to-be most valuable asset on the ground get taken out by a sergeant and a lance corporal. Ugly decision? Hell, yes. Hello, it's what we do. Ugly is our specialty. But consider this: since we had his unit's commo tent bugged and the team on satellite, I could have set Whiskey Two-Two up for capture by the Taliban. That would have been the easy way for me but not for them: interrogation, torture, eventual beheading. Instead, I opted for mercs who would do the job cleanly. No pain, no torture, no degradation. Why, I should win the goddamned Jean Hersholt Humanitarian Award. My only mistake: who knew that marine kid was Sergeant Rock and Superman combined?"

He quickly worked the political angle.

"Now, do you want to run a huge case against me? Do you want the dirty laundry in the world press for months? Do you want the Agency, the Marine Corps, and the FBI in a pissing match for all to see? Maybe you do, but you have to also see that it does nobody any good. I know the Administration doesn't want that, and I believe that by this time next week, once they've made their assessments, you will get orders to back off. I think you'll find I'm too big to fail. Tell you what: here's my offer. I will resign immediately and disappear even faster. You don't have a piece of evidence against me except the fact that my phone number happened to be on some gun-crazy screwball's satellite phone. How do we know I gave him that phone and all the equipment? You'll never prove it because, after all, we *are* the CIA and rather nimble at hiding stuff like that. Then consider the following: I actually succeeded. I put such pressure on your security teams that even if we didn't get Cruz, we made it impossible for anyone to get to Zarzi. Zarzi gets his medal"—he made a show of checking his watch to see the time—"in a few hours at the White House, which is impregnable, he's out of here tomorrow, and I won my little gambit. And as a special parting gift, I'll use my considerable influence to get Okada a promotion, though in my opinion she should be up on charges of treason. Her career will take off, she'll even get my old job, under a new Afghan Desk. Her life will be fabulous, except, most sadly, she won't be able to have that lunch with me, which would have been so much fun for her."

It went on like that. Meanwhile, Susan duly informed CIA, and a damage-assessment committee began to look into the charges, and meetings were set up to deal with potential public relations problems, while at the same time, arguments were broached at the White House and the Justice Department in favor of covering up the operation after accepting Dixson's resignation. The main worry appeared to be that some reporter would break the story, and then all havoc would come out to play.

"Sometimes I think these people lost all their goddamned moral bearings," Swagger said. "To me it's black and white, over and done with. The guy's a murderer. He killed Skelton, thirty-one Afghans, Colonel Chambers, nine Filipinos, and four cops. Put him on the needle. End of story."

"It's not that easy," said Nick. "In the Marine Corps it's Us, Them. In Washington it's Us, the Us who are with Us, the Us who are not sure about Us, and the many Us-es who don't care. The other team, our mortal enemies, are also Us, it's just that they happen to be against the Us that is Us; they're the other Us, and they have other Us-es who are against Us, then their own huge numbers of people who don't care one way or the other, and finally, between the two Us-es, there are thousands who aren't sure yet and are waiting for a signal from the Administration, from the pundits, from the blogosphere, from party headquarters or the union or the Internet message boards about which Us is really their Us. I should add, each Us is always one hundred percent right and has never, ever acknowledged a mistake in judgment, interpretation, execution, or public relations. Dysfunctional as hell, but at least you can say this—it doesn't work. Never has, never will. Bob, I told you this coming in. Sergeant Cruz, sorry to shock you, but political considerations will play a part. What I'm betting we get is a shake-up at the Agency—bye-bye Jack Collins and whoever was in his clique—and a compromise jail term on Dixson, maybe a soft five for conspiracy, which he'll use to write a book making himself out to be the smartest guy in the room. That's possible."

"What about the scandal?" asked Bob.

"Uh, today's press isn't eager to discredit this president. They backed him so hard they're invested in him. And anyhow, are you going to blow the whistle to your good friend David Banjax? I didn't think so. So it stays out of the papers and off the news."

"May I say something?" asked Cruz.

"Go ahead."

"Once again, it seems like you're accepting this at face value. It is what it is, it's a marginal triumph for the good guys, that is, what we've accomplished, there's some justice for Two-Two in it, but that's all it is, and now it's over. But maybe it's not over. Maybe it's just starting."

"Here we go again on the conspiracy merry-go-round," said Susan.

"Ma'am, I know how Zarzi operated around Qalat. I've seen young marines blown to ribbons by IEDs his people planted and then they went and hid in his off-limits compound. I don't see how he could have this 'change' that everybody says he had so fast."

"Sergeant Cruz," she said, "I have to tell you that our people went over Zarzi time after time, from all angles, using all technologies, from drugs to polygraphs to psychological evaluation to sleep deprivation. He volunteered, he got through it easily. If he's holding something back, it's beyond our science to detect it, which to me at least means he's not holding something back."

"Sergeant Cruz, you are an extraordinary man," said Nick. "Brave, resilient, the only man I've ever seen who's the equal of Sergeant Swagger here. But there's not a shred of evidence that anything is set for tonight. If it were there, I'd act on it, believe me. But I—"

The phone rang.

Hmm, Nick had given instructions not to be interrupted.

He picked it up.

"Nick, is that you? Jesus, you're hard to find."

"Sorry, Jim. I'm really in the middle—"

"I've got something for you on this guy Zarzi."

The Administration is to be congratulated on its heroic decision to continue business as usual with the Freedom Medal presentation to Afghan presidential candidate Ibrahim Zarzi. The violence that occurred yesterday in Washington when four police officers were killed and many more wounded by two as yet unidentified gunmen with a modern arsenal of assault-type weapons has not been allowed to stand in the way. This Administration's desire to bring peace, and with it American withdrawal, to a region much troubled by war, remains firm.

Though details are as yet unknown, the gunmen's modus operandi clearly suggests they were either far-right domestic terrorists or violent Zionists, possibly a combination of both. Extremists have more in common with each other than with the responsible middle-of-the-road adherents to their causes.

Mr. Zarzi himself must be singled out for courage and dedication. His selfless commitment to peace, his campaign to restore righteousness to a reputation much besmirched by political opponents who attempted to hang the nickname "the Beheader" on him, and his willingness to be a symbol of a peaceful, cooperative Islam are to be admired. The Administration is lucky to have him, he is lucky to have the Administration, and we are lucky to have both.

The suit—bespoke from Jay Kos, New York, dark gray light-weight Italian silk—fit superbly but with a muted elegance, too light for a funeral, too dark for a nightclub, perfect. Cuff links, gold, by Tiffany, thank you very much.

Glory to you, oh Allah, and yours is the praise.

The socks: Egyptian cotton, black, John Weitz. The shoes, again bespoke, from GJ Cleverley, Jermyn Street, London SW1. The tie, red, with small, subtle checks of gold, by Anderson & Sheppard, also Jermyn Street, London SW1. The shirt, bespoke of course, blindingly white, the white of movie star teeth, Anderson & Sheppard, Jermyn Street, London SW1.

In the name of God, the Infinitely Compassionate and Merciful, praise be to God, lord of all the worlds, the Compassionate, the Merciful, Ruler on the Day of Reckoning.

Cologne: Chanel. Mousse: Revlon cosmetics. Fingernail polish (clear): Revlon cosmetics. Underwear: 100 percent silk, Anderson & Sheppard, Jermyn Street, London SW1.

You alone do we worship, and you alone do we ask for help. Guide us on the straight path, the path of those who have received your grace, not the path of those who have brought down wrath, nor of those who wander astray.

Jewelry: gold diamond ring, Cartier; gold necklace with Islamic talisman in 24-carat gold, Jacques du Ritz; watch . . . watch? Watch?

I seek refuge in Allah from Satan, the Accursed. God is great.

The watch: black plastic, Casio DW5600E-1V G-Shock classic digital, Walmart, $37.95.

"Sir, the limousine to the White House has arrived."

FBI HQ

FBI INTERROGATION SUITE 101
HOOVER BUILDING
PENNSYLVANIA AVENUE
WASHINGTON, DC
1900 HOURS

Okay, Jim, just a second." He covered the mouthpiece. "Jim Stanford is head of counterespionage, DC. His people monitor, follow, infiltrate, tap, whatever, various 'diplomatic' initiatives here in the capitol." He went back to the phone. "Jim, I'm with my staff now trying to figure out what's going on with this guy. Can I put you on speaker?"

"Sure, sure," said Jim and waited while Nick tried to figure out the phone, couldn't, and a young agent came over and pushed the necessary buttons.

"Okay, Jim, you're on loud and clear, go ahead please."

"A week ago you sent out a confidential e-mail request to all coalition intelligence services with offices in DC embassies asking for any updates they came across on Ibrahim Zarzi, right?"

"I did. I got nothing out of it. But frankly, I expected nothing out of it, I did it to cover my ass in case later anyone said, 'Why didn't you blah blah.'"

"Understood. But of course Mossad got it from a dozen or so sources."

"They're pretty good, huh?"

"Not since the hot days of the Cold War and the classic KGB operators have I seen guys so good."

"Cool."

"You probably knew that. But here's what you don't know. The Israelis have a guy at the Four Seasons."

"Wow."

"He's contract, probably would work for anybody, but he's real good too, freelancer, keeps tabs on diplomatic guests whose policies might have a bearing on Israel."

"Got it."

"He told them, they told me, and now I'm telling you something that may or may not have some significance."

"We're listening."

"A week or so ago, Zarzi was in a very strange mood. This is a cosmopolitan man, mind you, with the tastes of a Saudi prince and the morals of an alley cat."

"We're aware of that."

"But he does this very odd thing. He offers a servant a choice between two watches. As a gift. Never done that before, never done that since, not known for that, a parsimonious man who tips the minimum and basically treats staff like cattle."

Nick looked around at the people in the room.

"These two watches were both expensive. But one was really expensive. It was one of these custom jobs, a Paul Berger—Paul makes twelve or so a year, the big richies love them, it takes a fifteen-year wait to get one, that sort of thing, and it doesn't keep time any better than a Timex, maybe even worse. It probably costs a hundred thousand or so. Of course the kid chose the wrong one, even if it was a nice watch, but the larger issue is: what the fuck?"

"Yeah," said Nick, "what the fuck?"

"Maybe it fits into a pattern, I don't know. Maybe it's just a tell on his psychology of the moment. But it's so out of character for this actor. That's all. Thought you should know."

"And you're sure on this?"

"I am. My guy is one hundred percent with me. He does me, I do him, you know."

"I got you. Thanks, Jim."

He put the phone down, faced a dozen bewildered faces.

"So?"

Nobody said a thing.

Then, of course, Swagger: "A guy like him only gets rid of wordly treasure when he's preparing to die. No other reason."

"Well, then wouldn't he dump it all?" said Nick. "Not just a selective, tiny percentage?"

"He knows if he did that, it would be noticed. This is 'symbolic,' or some crap that an egghead psycho nutcase like him would take as 'symbolic.' He's the kind of asshole who needs symbols."

"It's a reach," said Nick. "There's nothing solid there."

"He's dumping his shit because he's getting ready to blow himself up. And the president and the cabinet and the head of the CIA and all those generals, all of them, along with him. Tonight's the night, this is the hour, and the minute is very close."

"Impossible," said Susan. "Not merely because of the exhaustive psychological penetration we've put him through, but also because White House security is extraordinary and there's no way at all he can get an explosive beyond it. Even if he's swallowed it or, excuse me, had it anally implanted, he will be examined and x-rayed, he agreed to that. He can't be cleaner."

"Then why's he passing off watches to peons?" asked Bob. "It ain't a bit like him."

"Possibly he had an erectile dysfunction," said Susan, "and he couldn't find his Viagra and he was really depressed at his failure and in that vulnerable mood he uncharacteristically gave something of value to a servant. Been known to happen."

"It's not really actionable, Nick," said Chandler. "Provocative, as Mr. Swagger says, but not actionable. I'd hate to take it to the White House."

Nick glanced at his watch. "Practically speaking, there isn't time to take it to the White House. They're committed to this event, it's already starting, we'd only get the duty officer and it would never reach the president. Anyhow, Chandler, pick an office and make the call with our recommendation that the event be canceled. Just so we're on the record."

"Yes, sir," said Chandler, trundling off.

"Now what?" Nick said.

"Well, well, well," said Susan.

"What?"

She pointed to one of the many monitors in the room; this was a security feed from the White House, just beyond the 15th Street entry, where all guests were wanded, prodded, poked, sniffed, and inappropriately touched to make sure they weren't carrying any fizzing, bowling-ball-like cordite bombs.

"It's the man himself. Can you rewind and show the last ten seconds?" she asked. "Number 5, the center screen. Go back to 1745 or something."

Nick said, "Someone young, make it happen."

A couple of junior agents scurried off, and in seconds the images on monitor number 5 began to run backward until they reached 1745, at which point they froze, showing a blur, then lurched forward.

The crew in the room watched as an obedient Ibrahim Zarzi allowed himself to be probed, etc., etc.

"There. Stop," she cried, and the image froze.

It caught Zarzi with his hands up, his elegant suit momentarily drooping sloppily from the awkwardness of the position. His hands above his head as someone blurrily waved the metal-seeking wand across his body, his sleeves fallen back under the power of gravity. The angle, from slightly behind him, was such that his watch was displayed.

"Well, unless I miss my guess, that's no fifteen-hundred-dollar Cartier, much less a Berger hundred-thousand-dollar model. It looks more like something you'd pick up in a Seven-Eleven," she said, as if someone as elegant as Susan, much less Zarzi, had ever been in a 7-Eleven.

"Some kind of big, ugly plastic junk," said Nick. "Again, unlike him."

"Very unlike him," she said.

"If he's getting ready to do something nuts, the way his mind works, he wouldn't wear a good watch," said Bob.

"Very good catch, Ms. Okada. But . . ."

"But so what, you're saying? Maybe Swagger is right. It's an indicator."

"Nick," said ever-rational Starling, back from her call to the White House, "it is another indicator. But it sure as hell isn't actionable. This is very touchy stuff, seeing as he's an official State Department guest, under their protection."

"I don't see how I can do anything on that," said Nick. "Let's note it, and it goes into the CIA file, just in case this turns out real bad."

The monitor reverted to real time, and it now displayed the actual time, 1814.12 and emptiness at the security point. Other monitors showed something else: all the heads and swells were gathered in the Rose Garden in the warm late summer evening, and in a few minutes the president would come to the podium, make a few kissy-kissy comments, call Ibrahim Zarzi to the podium and present him with the Freedom Medal as a ringing endorsement of his commitment to America, to democracy, to the joint future of their countries, to the friendship of Islam and the West, to a bright and bloodless tomorrow. Then it was over. A few minutes and it was over.

Nick thought: *It is not going to happen. It is too fantastic. There is nothing he can do.*

And then he thought: *That's what everybody said on 9/10 as well. They are cunning assholes. They are not smart, but they figured out how to destroy a nation's confidence and plunge the world into extended decades of darkness with $19 worth of X-acto knives.*

What the fuck do I do? he wondered. *Pray for a miracle?*

"All right," said Swagger, "I got a last little card to play."

THE WHITE HOUSE

THE ROSE GARDEN
FREEDOM MEDAL PRESENTATION CEREMONY
1922 HOURS

How lovely it was. The flowers seemed endless, their blossoms bright even in the declining light of late summer. A kind of ambrosia filled the air, and there was just a tint of pink glow over the looming silhouette of the Executive Office Building.

The America that counted was here. The president, so charismatic that he even outshone the glowing Zarzi, his wife; the vice president, his wife; and all the others in suits and uniforms: chairmen, joint chiefs of staff; the service chairmen; the director of the Central Intelligence Agency; a dozen powerful senators, some even from the other party in the spirit of ecumenicalism; the cream of the liberal punditocracy from the great papers of the East Coast; the television heads, hair shellacked unto perfection; a variety of Washington-style women, all of whom seemed to have that tawny elegance over slender legs; and an audience consisting of dragooned staffers from the Administration, a sea of littles well primed to clamor and go wow for the TV cameras. All were gathered here to sell the world an important message: this man counts. This man we trust. This is the man who will bring us peace. This is the man we can work with. This is the man who understands. He is, well and truly, our man in Kabul.

He bowed as the president slid the ribbon necklace over his head, and he felt the weight of the huge gold disk added to his neck.

Oh the indignities to arrive at this moment: wanded, x-rayed, touched, even probed. Subjected to chemical tests, sniffed by dogs and men, touched again, touched yet again. But he had signed up for that; it was the price of the moment.

The president finished, speaking so eloquently as was his gift, of a vision of a world without IEDs and young men of any faith bleeding out in the dirt of a far-off country, and then stepped back to hand the lectern over to the Glorious Zarzi for some brief remarks.

FBI HQ

**FBI INTERROGATION SUITES
HOOVER BUILDING
PENNSYLVANIA AVENUE
WASHINGTON, DC
1923 HOURS**

They all looked at him.

"Let's hear it," said Nick.

"I want you to run a search, Google, or super FBI Google, some high-tech, high-speed data search on the following. See what links there are between our friend Dixson in there thinking he's a hero and the director of National Intelligence, that guy Ted Hollister."

"Why?"

"Dixson's clearly in on this, whatever this is. But he only knows so much and nothing more. He's told us everything and he thinks he's a hero. And he ain't heavy enough to go beyond what he's done. He knows about the contractors and the policy and that's it. I got an inkling from something Hollister said at that meeting he might know a little bit more than we think about all this."

"Swagger," said Susan, "Hollister was long gone from the Agency before Jared was even recruited."

"Please. I can't explain, ticktock, ticktock, time's wasting. Please: check it out. He said something he shouldn't have said at the meeting. Let me just see if there's a link."

Nick nodded. "Youth movement, prove your worth," he ordered.

Young people stirred and hustled. Time crept by. Up on the monitors, from a dozen angles, the U.S. Army band played "The Star-Spangled Banner" in the Rose Garden, and men and women stood with hands on hearts or at perfect salute in tribute to their country.

"Prelim," said Chandler, reentering. "Jesus Christ, turns out Dixson grew up in Braintree, Massachusetts, where Hollister lived when he was teaching at Harvard, same street, two houses apart. Dixson's father, Roger, was at Harvard and Harvard Law with Hollister in the sixties. They were both on *Law Review*. Dixson later got his master's at Johns Hopkins in Baltimore. International Law, taught by none other than his dad's old friend, classmate, and neighbor Ted Hollister. Immediately after, he joined the Agency—"

"Yes!" said Susan, in a squirt of zeal. "Yes! In those days you only got in with the recommendation of a senior Agency official or ex-official. Someone in the extended family. Jared Dixson was Ted Hollister's legacy, as we call them in the shop, protected by Hollister's rep and charisma. Dixson wasn't working for Jack Collins, not really. He was working for Ted Hollister."

"Chandler, sit down, catch a rest. Someone else under the age of thirty, call Secret Service White House right this second, see if Hollister's at the event, he should be."

"That old man's in this up to his eyeballs," said Susan. "And, ahem, allow Princess Perfection to point out to the monster Swagger, he's *not* Agency."

"Once again, you kick my ass, Okada-san."

"He's there," came the call.

"We ought to talk to him. Now, not tomorrow, not next week. *Now,*" said Bob.

"We should," said Nick.

Memphis rose, yelling at Chandler, "Get an SUV outside fast, clear us at the White House. I don't know how this is shaping up but I think I might need a sniper. Get me a goddamned sniper fast."

"Nick, they let SWAT go this morning. They're all home in Virginia resting from the gunfight in Georgetown. I could get you one from DC metro in about twenty minutes."

On all the screens, the president of the United States came to the podium.

"Hey," said Swagger, pointing at Cruz, "there's the best sniper in the world."

THE IWO JIMA MEMORIAL
ARLINGTON, VIRGINIA
1850 HOURS

The six bronze men were gigantic. They struggled with the flag, its three primary colors flapping in a wind, cross-illuminated by many beams of light that illustrated the whole piece, the ripples of muscle, the rents in the metal clothing, the hobnails in the worn combat boots, the twelve-foot rifles, all in the muted, fading green of military glory, its tarnish eroded by the ages.

"Warriors," said Professor Khalid. "You must honor their bravery."

"Infidels," said Dr. Faisal. "Brigands, crusaders, invaders, rapists, and scum."

"You haven't learned a thing, have you?" said Khalid.

"The Koran contains all the information I need to know. Other than science, the rest is delusional self-hypnosis on the part of the enemy."

"Even now, can't you control your enmity?" said Bilal.

They leaned against the van, which was in the parking lot of the Marine Corps memorial on a hill overlooking the river and the spotlit city that was Washington, DC. If anything, it was more beautiful and beguiling on this warm, comfortable, clear evening than any other. Above, pinwheels and novas blinked across cosmic nothingness, and below the city was a shimmering plain of white buildings, flags flying on many of them, the whole forming a kind of horizontal fusion of light and dark, patterns broken here and there by something of specific edge and shape, such as the spire in the center, and beyond it, the vast dome.

"Bah," said Faisal. "He talks too much. He enjoys his little epiphanies, his ironies. He is vain and prissy. He has a Western mind. He is not one of us. He thinks too much. He has no internal discipline. He has not learned the fundamental lesson, which is submission."

"You call it vanity, I call it individuality. Until we learn to value individuality, we will lag behind the West in all things and—"

"If you kill them all, there is nothing to lag behind," said Faisal.

A few other vehicles dotted the lot, and a U.S. Park Service police car had passed through a few seconds ago, noting nothing, not stopping, and it had then disappeared toward Rosslyn, a banal assortment of skyscrapers that loomed behind them. Up at the monument, a few kids scrambled around, supervised loudly by a father.

"The journey is almost over," said Bilal. "Are you prepared for what comes next? Have you accepted it?"

"Completely," said Faisal. "Never for a second did I have a doubt."

"I am without doubt too," said Khalid. "The religious subtext here means nothing to me, it's all mumbo jumbo, but I embrace the political one. My hand shall not pause, my heart shall not fail."

"That was very good ice cream," said Faisal.

"Another thing he said with which I agree. Yes, it was very good ice cream."

They had stopped at a Baskin-Robbins on the way over, three men of obvious Middle Eastern persuasion, in fresh new dishdashas with prayer caps on, waited patiently in line among the moms and dads and squealing children, some in dirty baseball uniforms, some mere babies, and each had gotten a special treat. Khalid had double strawberry in a cup; Bilal a straight sundae with walnuts, whipped cream, and a cherry; and Faisal maple praline and mint chocolate chip in a waffle cone, but with a dish beneath so that when the cone could no longer support the ice cream, the whole confection would not disintegrate in his hands.

Now, finally, they were where they should be at the time they should be there.

M emphis, Swagger, Cruz, and Okada raced through the hallway to the exit dock, where a black FBI Explorer, its blue-red lights already flashing, its engine running, waited. Memphis got behind the wheel, and Cruz went to the rear of the vehicle, opened the tailgate, removed a gun case, opened it, and pulled an H-S .308 sniper rifle from it, and a red box of Black Hills 168-grain Match ammo. He went to the driver's side and climbed in.

Memphis was saying, "I will designate target. You listen to nobody but me if it comes to that. And you do *not* fire unless I give you the green, you have that, Sergeant?"

"Yessir," said Cruz, who at the same time was reading the rifle's logbook, maintained shot by shot by its original assignee. He learned it had been fired 2,344 times, all with Federal Gold Tip 168-grain Match ammunition, for an average five-shot group from 100 yards of .56 inches. It was, of course, an H-S Precision rifle built from the design of a Remington 700 action, trued and bedded by the H-S custom shop, a Jewell trigger installed, with a Broughton barrel; its last 200-yard group, shot three weeks ago at Quantico, had been 1.06 inches, and the shooter, Special Agent Dave McElroy, had readjusted the zero to 100 yards, cleaned it, fired one fouling shot, and put it away for deployment. He had been on the perimeter of the convenience store on Wisconsin Avenue, but had not gotten a shot.

Chandler leaned in.

"Okay, you're cleared through the southeast gate. Then you can pull around past the big house to the right and take the roadway to the right straight to the Rose Garden. Secret Service has been briefed and will greet you."

"Good work," he said. "Okay, let's go."

The SUV pulled out, scooted around the block, passed several vehicles that maneuvered out of the way, hit Pennsylvania's broadness, turned right, and Nick accelerated.

The vehicle ate up the eight blocks of government architecture and hotel frontage that dominated Pennsylvania, slowing only to weave its way through the traffic at cross streets. It reached the White House southeast gate below the Treasury Department's Doric immensity. The gate to the White House, nestled in a bank of trees, loomed just ahead. A red light and too much oncoming traffic momentarily halted them just a few yards shy of the goal.

"Where's the goddamn siren?" Nick cursed.

Bob leaned forward to help him find it.

"Wait," said Susan. "Jesus, look. That's him. That's *him*."

Indeed it was. Stepping out of the pedestrian gate, a short, furtive figure paused for the same light that halted the SUV. Yes indeed, clutching his ever-present professorial briefcase, it was the director of National Intelligence, Ted Hollister. He checked his watch, looked both ways impatiently, and realized he had to wait for the shift to green like all ordinary mortals. They saw him exhale a large breath in frustration.

Nick found the siren. Blaring, he pulled ahead, as the cars before him parted awkwardly to clear a path. Nick took the left, pulled across traffic, and halted two feet from Ted Hollister.

"Mr. Hollister, sir, where are you going?"

In seconds Nick was next to him, Bob flanking the other side, and Ray close at hand. The car's blue-and-red pumped color into the scene, and around them at the juncture of 15th and Pennsylvania, traffic piled up.

"He's bugging out," said Bob.

Susan came to them.

"Mr. Hollister," said Nick, "you remember me, Nick Memphis, FBI?"

"I do. What is this about?" said the old man curtly. "I have an important appointment."

"Sir, late last night we arrested Jared Dixson and he's now confessed to assigning a contractor team to take out Whiskey Two-Two, and to authorizing a smart munition into a nonmilitary target in Qalat. There is more collateral that will have to be answered for as well. We've seen the records and clearly he is connected to you and—"

"I will be happy to discuss this with you at length in my office. Simply schedule an appointment and I will—"

"Sir, why are you leaving the White House now?" Bob said. "Ain't this your big night? Seems odd—"

"I do not intend to stand in the street and discuss matters of national security with sergeants and low-ranking agents. I warn you, gentlemen, I will take severe action against you and I have considerable influence. Now, let me go—"

"Why are you in a panic to leave now? What's happening in two minutes that you have to be far away from it?"

"I will not stand for this. I will call a policeman."

"You ain't calling no one, goddamnit," said Bob.

"I will destroy you," said Hollister. "You have no idea who you're dealing with."

But then Bob pulled Nick aside.

"This ain't getting us nowhere," he said. "Y'all take a little break. You go take a walk or something, whatever. You trusted me, I's just an old fool, said I was too tired to go with you. You're all off the hook. You leave. I guaran-fucking-tee you that in three minutes this weasel tells me everything. And I mean *everything*."

"No," said Nick. "Swagger, this is the United States. We do not—"

"Ticktock, ticktock. It's happening now. The one they said wouldn't never happen, the ticking-bomb deal. You'd risk all them lives and the morale, the humiliation, the degradation of this country because you want to feel good about yourself tomorrow morning?

That's a pretty high price for feeling good about yourself, Nick, and I have to say, it's not your ass on the line, it's theirs."

"I want this off the table," said Nick. "It is not to be discussed anymore. Instead, I want—"

"He's right," said Susan. "Ticktock, ticktock. It has to be done."

Nick shook his head. He could not believe he was having this discussion, but he was.

"Then I should be the one who—"

"No," said Bob. "Everyone here is young and has way more to contribute. Me, I'm done, there's nothing left for me. Lay it off on me, I'll go to prison, I'll be the torturer, the one everybody can hate. I'll break every one of his goddamned fingers and he'll sing before I reach number three."

Then Susan said, "Wait."

"Look, I know this guy," she said. "You're right in thinking that if this thing is going to happen, it's going to happen tonight, in a very few minutes. He is not afraid of pain or of disgrace or of failure. He is not an Islamist. He doesn't believe in seventy-two virgins. He believes in nothing, and that being the case, only one thing can frighten him and you see it in his flight. He is afraid of death. If there's death anywhere tonight, it's at the White House. Take him to the White House. What happens to them happens to him. That takes it all from him, and that and that alone frightens him."

"She's right," said Nick. "Get him in, let's get in the gates and see what we get."

They loaded the squirming old man into the front, wedged between Nick and the stoic Ray. Nick punched the siren again, pulled back, rotated the vehicle to the gate.

"Jesus Christ," he said as the gate rose, taking an agonizing three seconds. The two uniformed White House cops on duty waved the vehicle by, and it slipped into White House territory, and began to wind on the circle around Executive Drive that would deposit its travelers at the Rose Garden, in the lee of the West Wing extension. The big white mansion, with its curving Harry Truman balcony dominated by vast columns, stood out white and immaculate in the spotlights, but more to the point, through a light screen of trees to the left of the portico, nestled in the crook of the much larger building, a ceremony was clearly transpiring, and a well-illuminated crowd of people could be seen standing before a podium on which stood the distinctive figure of the president of the United States, among other men of power and prestige.

"Stop, stop," Hollister suddenly cried.

Nick halted the car.

"You have something to say?"

"Look, can we go somewhere and—"

"Yeah, the Rose Garden. That's the only place we're going."

Hollister twisted, in some kind of further existential agony, licked his lips, swallowed hard. Nick looked at him, then turned, dropped the car into gear, and began to ease forward.

"Stop," the old man said. "Oh Christ, stop."

Nick looked at his watch. It was almost 7:45.

The thing was scheduled to end at 7:45.

"Talk to us or I will drive us there in ten seconds."

Hollister swallowed again. Then he said: "They have a missile. It's a Hellfire."

Behold Hellfire.

It was a stubby thing, six feet long, seven inches wide, painted olive drab. It had tiny, out-of-scale fins, four at the nose, four more at the tail, which looked almost comical against the girth and charisma of the larger thing. In the air it looked like a flying barrel with little cartoon wings, except that it moved too fast for the eye to see, and for the first few seconds, a searing blot of flame so blinded observers it was impossible to make out further details. It was suspended on a much-modified Norwegian launch tripod, welded crudely inside the van's rear cargo area. It had a translucent nose, where the laser seeker had once been, and immediately behind it a warhead section, with the twenty pounds of a late-industrial-age witches' brew called PBXN-9 explosive. Detonating upon impact in the Rose Garden, it would surely kill everyone who was within fifty feet of its point of impact, and it would burn, mutilate, blunt-force traumatize and otherwise perforate the many others outside the immediate kill zone. It would kill all the roses.

Then came the guidance section, where so much work had been done; then the pitch gyro to keep it stable in its brief flight; the auto-pilot electronics package that made sure everything worked when it had to work and in synchronicity, and then the propulsion section, a solid-fuel rocket motor with a three-second burn, from there on controlled by the vanes of its fins, torquing this way and that on computer mandate to bite an atmosphere whistling by at 1.4 mach and guide it to its target. Time in flight from launch to strike would be about seven seconds. Nothing could stop it; no one would see it coming. It would be over almost before it began.

Professor Khalid climbed into the space in the van just under the shaft of the missile, and using a flashlight in his teeth and a sharp knife, cut through the yards of tape that had secured the one-hundred-pound weapon into stability for the long trip. Freeing it, he slid it back on the double rails that were milled into its upper torso on the launch armature until it clicked in place on the launcher housing, and when he heard it click, he knew that the plug on the missile had locked into the socket, establishing communication between the missile and its controls.

Now he had to turn the missile "on." It was really that primitive, a unit designed for simplicity, to be used under battle conditions in rough situations with time of the essence, as hordes of red T-72s were racing across the Fulda Gap and the NATO missileers would be the ones who had to stop them. This rocket happened to be Norwegian, and had once patrolled the northern NATO defensive perimeter aboard a Norwegian tank-destroyer vehicle.

Khalid went around to the front of the van—a cool breeze refreshed his moist brow as he went and now took from under the rear seat the heart of his improvisations upon the system, the original Norwegian control box, a military-strongbox with cable and a blunt, functional keyboard, ran the cable to the missile launch module, and plugged it in.

"Dr. Faisal, please run your program," he said, "and make your system checks."

Faisal came to the device, took out a small disc, found the input slot, and inserted the disc and pushed a certain number of keys. His information, concealed in Norwegian encryption that had taken him months to penetrate, flowed into the central processing unit of the missile. It held but one meaning: not to search for a specifically designated laser coding as the system had been originally designed to do, but for something much more primitive: a unique radio signal. No laser need apply; within the seeker module, behind the lenslike nose aperture, was not a laser seeker but a highly sensitive miniature FM receiver that was prelocked on to a unique frequency and would then only recognize an encoded tone. Old technology but very reliable. It would cause very tiny deviations from the path by sending signals to the servos that controlled the rocket's fins. As the signal increased with proximity, the servos continued their adjustments. They sought the strongest signal and kept making it even stronger and rode the trolley toward detonation.

Now, at the control box, facing the launch menu in glowing Norwegian, Khalid designated a trajectory: the LOAL-DIR or Lock-On After Launch-Direct mode, meaning the missile would launch blind into the stratosphere at a relatively low angle, and when it found the encoded tone on the designated frequency the CPU aboard would tweak the servos and keep adjusting the angle of attack, then plummet directly to the target on that vector.

And all it would take to—

"We are ready," he said to Faisal.

Faisal, with a police-frequency scanner purchased from Radio Shack, hunted for the signal. In the space where it should have been was nothing but static. He looked at his watch. It was 7:46:30. Not a noise anywhere on the immediate spectrum.

"Not yet," he said.

"I wonder how long we can stay here before we are discovered."

"Where is he? What is going on?"

"Agh," said Faisal. "To come this far and fail. Aghhh—Allah will not allow it."

"But will the FBI?" asked the anxious Professor Khalid.

At that point, the Park Services patrol car came slowly down the road to the parking lot.

A Hellfire missile," said Nick, incredulous. *A missile? A missile.* His mind seemed to fill with torrents of thick sludge as he struggled with the concept.

"It's Norwegian," said Hollister. "Came on the black market in Serbia, Zarzi paid for it on behalf of Al-Q. They have two scientists—an Indian rocket guidance expert and an Egyptian software genius—to decrypt it and make some basic changes. Instead of new-fangled laser it homes in on an old-fashioned FM tone at a specific frequency."

"What FM tone?"

"Zarzi's got a miniaturized FM transmitter in his wristwatch. The Russians built it for him. He pushes a button, it's good for ten seconds of broadcast, missile flying through its cone reads it, locks on, and bang. They're launching from the Iwo Jima Memorial. It will be in the air less than seven seconds. They're going to detonate it on Zarzi. It'll cut down everyone on the podium and half the audience. Now, I've told you, please, get me out of here."

Nick suddenly achieved clarity, and understood exactly what had to be done and in what order. First Zarzi. Stop him or at least lock him in place so the president could get away from him.

"Sniper, hit Zarzi, take him down hard. Do it now!" Nick snapped.

Now: clear the fucking area.

He went to his unit, hit broadcast, held the button down.

"Break-break, all units, all units, emergency, incoming missile, clear the area, clear the area, this is no drill. Incoming missile, evacuate!"

Cruz rolled from the car, saw he didn't have a shot because of a screen of trees, rotated around the iron fence until the angle came clear. He brought up the rifle, his finger ticking off the safety, and with his fine offhand skill he caught the face of Zarzi quadrasected by the crosshairs, and heard, "I lase two thirty-five, make it two and a third mil-dots above the hairs, one quarter value left windage," and felt Swagger next to him, on the laser ranger, and as the slack came out of the trigger he saw Zarzi with a hand at the watch and though he hurried, he had to hurry smoothly and even as the shot broke and the scope image leaped after leaving a nanosecond's view of shattered face, he knew he was too late.

"And so, Mr. President and my American friends," Zarzi said in his fine baritone, "I stand before you, my honor regained, and I bring you greetings from my country and the bosom of my faith," as his fingers played with the button on his watch. He smiled. He was happy. God is great. He was home. The years of debauchery, the lust for women and boys, the pleasures of alcohol and drugs, the addiction to the smoothness of silk, the softness of fine wool, the glitter of beautiful jewelry, it was all behind him.

"Incoming missile!" someone screamed. "Run, run, incoming missile!" And the crowd began to scream and disintegrate as panic filled the hearts, minds, and legs of those before him while at the same time men were tugging on the president. At that moment he touched the button on his watch, felt it click, and stepped through the gates of paradise, and then the Black Hills 168-grain Match bullet cracked into his cheekbone beneath his left eye and turned his brain to atomized jelly.

As the policeman stopped and started to get out of his car, Bilal fired an AK-47 burst into his front tire, ripping it up, the percussion of the burst driving all tourists into panicked terror and the cop back into his car.

"Hurry up," he screamed. "More will be here in seconds."

"There is nothing," screamed Dr. Faisal.

"Oh, Allah, I beseech thee," implored Khalid, "send your sinning son a signal so that he may complete a—"

The blinking red light on the scanner signified success.

"It's there," screamed Dr. Faisal. "Yes, it's—"

Khalid pushed the key.

Nothing happened.

"Oh my God!" shrieked Faisal.

His mind blanked, then came back and he remembered the launch sequence, repeated it, felt resistance in one of the keys, examined it, saw some piece of debris in the mechanism, scuffed it away, continued the sequence. Then he pushed the launch key again.

The missile's engine fired and in .0005 seconds it acquired the 800 pounds of thrust necessary for flight and it fired from the van, appearing to rip the fabric of the universe, affording a glimpse into one of hell's furnace rooms so hot no eyes could stand it, and all who saw it looked away as the rocket motor burned through its three seconds of solid fuel and in 300 yards had acquired enough velocity to arm itself, but still it accelerated, reaching 1.4 mach in another second or two.

It climbed to 800 feet and there acquired the message from Zarzi's Casio watch, for it peaked as it skidded through the air, the vanes of its fins adjusting accordingly as its CPU solved the differential calculus necessary to guide it to its destination, then it yawed, bent around the sky, and began to hammer downward.

The two old men could follow it in the dark air from the slight trail of smoke, though no eyes were fast enough to focus on the missile itself. It seemed to ride a diagonal plumb line down to earth, without deviation, hesitation, qualm, or mercy, and it disappeared behind some trees, and then a flash lit the night sky over Washington and a second later the noise of the blast reached their ears.

"Allah Akbar," said Khalid.

"You have returned to the faith, oh my brother," said Dr. Faisal. "It is a night of miracles."

A screaming came across the sky.

Two hundred thirty yards out, at the foot of the wrought-iron fence, Swagger turned on the noise just in time to see a streamlined blur incoming at a speed which has no place in time, turned again, and threw himself on Ray, driving him to the ground. In another instant the detonation cut the sky in half with a blade of light that reached the stars and simultaneously drilled a tremor through the earth and seemed to drive a nail into each eardrum. Then the blast wave struck, momentarily crushing everything erect in its mighty rush to infinity, sucking all the air from the planet. Next, an almost eerie silence, until someone began to scream.

Swagger rose.

Next to him came Ray, rising from the ground, and then Nick.

They saw the zone of destruction from 230 yards out. The missile had hit the podium and cratered a 20-foot gap in the earth, smoking now. All the windows on the walkway from the West Wing to the main residence were shattered, as were those of the West Wing, and many of the window frames were blown askew. The building's famed white flanks were seared with the ochre of extreme but brief heat. Trees everywhere were toppled or shattered and shrubbery was torn out by its roots. Flames licked out of one of the Oval Office windows, and another fire announced its presence in a line of bushes closer to the main residence.

Across the lawn, in the flickering light of the fires, the bodies lay, flattened, twisted, smashed to earth horribly. But then . . . movement. Then some more movement. One by one, then ten by ten and twenty by twenty, the frail sacks of flesh stirred and began to pick themselves up, the stronger aiding the weaker; they climbed to their feet or rolled to sit up, groggy, shaky, hair a mess, unbelieving and begrimed.

A voice crackled over the radio, "The president is unhurt, the president is unhurt," and then others, "Break-break, get emergency medical here fast, goddamnit, I have many people down," and the sirens began to sound.

"Good God," said Ray.

"Jesus H. Christ," said Nick.

"Where's Susan?" said Bob.

They walked back to the SUV as the howl of the sirens rose and the first of the emergency services vehicles roared by.

The SUV wasn't there.

Susan lay in the grass. She was so beautiful. Her hair was slightly mussed, which made her even more beautiful. The wise, serene diamond eyes were open, the face calm, the cheekbones taut under the alabaster skin.

Her throat had been cut.

PART FIVE

————

JAMESON

MARRIOTT RESIDENCE HOTEL

He awoke in a stupor. Brain foggy, memory shot, limbs in pain. Only one dream, obvious. Handsome Prince tries to save the world but forgets to save the Beautiful Princess. Part of Prince, fool of fools, played by Bob Lee Swagger. Princess played by Susan Okada, St. Louis, daughter of oncologist; Yale University; career CIA; best, brightest, most beautiful; thirty-eight years old now and forever. What was the point of saving the world if there was no Susan Okada in it?

Fuck, he thought. *If I had to do it again, I'd trade her life for all those guys in suits who think they're so important. The generals, the admirals, the president, his cabinet officers. Let the devil have them all for an eternity of punishment and take me along for good measure, torture me, it's fine, if it could spare Susan Okada's life. Fuck 'em,* he thought. *Fuck 'em all to hell forever, and me too, fuck me, just fuck me to hell.*

God, how it sucked hard and long. He wished he could sink back into dreamless nothingness. If only one of the thousands of shots taken in his direction over the years had been better aimed or untouched by wind he would not have this nearly unendurable thing festering in his brain. He just lay there for a long, long time, hoping to die, but death seemed to be off duty. Where was it when you needed it? *Come on, motherfucker, take me, not her. Okay. Me, I'm the one you want, the one you been trying to nab all these years.* But death didn't answer.

Finally, he looked around the hotel room, remembered the debriefing, the statement, the medical check, remembered that Ray and Nick were somewhere else. He wasn't sure what time it was or what time he'd gotten back, but he'd crashed hard and slept straight through after something like seventy-two on his feet. A message light blinked on the phone, and he picked it up, had twenty-six of them, dumped through them fast until Nick came on, saying, "We're going to debrief again in the director's office at one thirty today. Let me know you got this."

He tried to figure out the coffee machine, finally got it going. He looked at his watch. It was 11:17 on the first day of a rest of his life he did not want. He went to the door, opened it, and found a *Washington Post*.

He glanced at it. About three-quarters of the front page seemed to be bullshit: spin, counterspin, counter-counterspin, blame, recrimination, disavowal, analysis long term, analysis short term. What the Administration said, what the opposition said, what the English and the French said, what Al-Jazeerah said. Where the fuck were the facts? One story seemed to be the update, and he pressed through it.

Six dead, the rest contusions, sprains, a few broken bones, a few heart emergencies, and some feeling very hurt. No big guys had gone down. *Sing hallelujah. Decorate the tree. Hide the painted eggs. Get out the funny masks. Fuck all suits, uniforms, and the men who thought they deserved them. Theirs, ours, it was all the same.*

As far as the launch team at Iwo: the two dead-by-police scientists were Khalid Biswa, who worked guidance in the Indian rocket program, though he was a Muslim. Indian Secret Service suspected him of passing secrets to the Pakistanis, and he had disappeared about three years ago. The other guy was Dr. Faisal Ben-Abuljami, University of Alexandria, computer sciences, consultant for years to various bad apple groups who wanted to take their jihad into cyberspace. And the final guy, the one who survived, a real world-class Palestinian operator named Bilal Ayubi, a thousand ops, wanted all over Europe and especially by the Israelis. Evidently the sort of guy you wouldn't want to mix with on a dark night.

The phone rang.

It was Cruz.

"Hey, spotter," he said. "How's the old guy?"

"I feel like shit."

"I'm sorry about Okada, Gunny. I know she was special to you."

"You lose people. It's wrong, it's sad, it's the cruelty of the god-damn process, but it ain't ever going away. You lose people. I'll go to the funeral, I'll get over it, or at least figure out how to keep going. Anyway, hell of a shot you made."

"That was Whiskey Two-Two's shot. It's the one I was born to make. It's the one Billy Skelton died to get done. In the end, it was easy. Some old dog ranged it for me. I was just the triggerman."

"Ray, let me just say it: you're the goddamn best. Nobody ever pays the IOUs that guys like you—"

"And guys like you—"

"And Susan Okada. Whatever. Nobody pays the IOUs that guys like you and she rack up, so you end up doing it for free, for nothing. They even forget to say, hey, thanks, you saved the world, or at least a little neighborhood of it. But you and her, you saw what nobody else saw and you figured out what nobody else figured out and had the guts to move on it. Because of the two of you we're going to live in one kind of a place instead of another."

"She was the best. As for me, I just had a big charge of vitamin DNA."

"Will I see you at this meet? Ray, we ought to get to know each other, hang out. I hope you'll come and meet your sisters and step-mom. I hope—"

"Gunny, I'm calling from Lejeune. I turned myself in to shore patrol today. We'll let the corps straighten out what's to be done with me. I'll get back as soon as I know and we'll set something up."

"Can't wait," said Bob, knowing he would make it happen.

FBI HQ

DIRECTOR'S OFFICE
HOOVER BUILDING
PENNSYLVANIA AVENUE
WASHINGTON, DC
1350 HOURS

Nobody said much. They were in the suite, not the office proper, a perk that came with being heroes. They sat in beautiful leather chairs, so English clubby, around a coffee table, and the director ran the show, assisted by Walter Troy, repping the Agency, head of the damage-assessment team.

"So it's a victory but nobody's happy. It cost a lot, maybe too much. We all feel the pain of the loss. But we have to go on. That's all anyone can say."

"I don't want anything happening to Cruz," said Swagger. "Losing Okada hurt enough but that would really screw the pooch."

"I've been making arrangements, and as you might imagine, the White House is dead on board," said the director. "He should get a stripe out of this or take the damned commission they've been trying to force on him for years. We managed to get the Baltimore prosecutor's office to drop its interest in him, in exchange for the DNA samples that put Bogier in the Filipino house."

"That's good to know," said Swagger. "I'm sure the corps will treat him fairly."

"If it doesn't, I'll indict it," said Nick.

"As for you, Mr. Swagger, I'm not sure what we can pay you. Money? I doubt you'd cash the check. Peace and quiet? That's the only coinage you'd respond to. Or do you want more medals?"

"I'm fine," said Swagger. "Cruz is okay and you'll get Okada some kind of medal for her folks. Let's change the subject."

"I'm a little unclear on Arlington," said Nick. "Couldn't make much sense of it in the papers. How come the tough guy survived and the others didn't?"

"Warrior's luck. He shot it out with the Arlington police. Hit three times, too tough to die. He's in the hospital, under heavy guard, expected to recover. Won't say a word, hard to the end. The others were ordered to surrender and simply walked into the guns. The cops had no choice. They must have been good friends. They went to paradise together, holding hands."

"Anything else?" Troy asked.

Bob said, "Have you arrested Hollister yet?"

"That's the bad news. He dumped the SUV two blocks from the White House and disappeared. We figure he was going to a meet when you picked him up, and once he broke free, he disappeared. He called them, they came and got him. It had to be pro. They disappeared him well. I'm betting it was Pakistani intelligence. They're all over this."

"Motherfucker," said Bob. "Excuse my English."

"How did you know it was him? If you hadn't figured it out, we'd be sitting here with a dead national leadership cadre and a confidence crisis beyond the imagination."

"It was just something that set peculiar with me. When we all met in the Agency, he told everybody about the rifle I captured that's on display in your museum, right?"

"That's right," said Nick.

"Well, that *is* the rifle and I *was* the boy who captured it, no doubt about it. But that night, we had a big celebration at the firebase, steaks and beer, all the stuff that's bad for you. And the CIA guy running the operation calls me aside afterward and tells me I got 'talent.' The Agency, he says, is always looking for 'talent.' Did I want a job? He could get me in real high, make a lot more than I could as a marine. No, I said, I'd stay with the corps. See, I had it in my head I wanted to retire as the command sergeant major of the Marine Corps. I thought that'd make my dad proud. I didn't know I was going to lose my spotter and get my hip busted in another couple of weeks. So the guy says,

'Sure, but I'll write you up big in my reports and if you change your mind, you just tell 'em and they can look 'em up and that'll get you in.' And I said, 'Can you do me a favor? I know Marine Corps politics, and if it's out I'm connected up with you people, that could hurt me. They don't like that dual-allegiance thing in the Marine Corps. So the best thing you could do is not mention me by name at all.' He says, 'You sure, Gunny?' I says I'm sure. My name ain't in no file on that rifle. So if Ted Hollister says he heard about it in Saigon as a way of browning me up, he's lying. My file with the Agency begins six thousand quarts of bourbon later. So how's Ted know? Ted could only know from the Russians. They kept a file on that SVD case and he'd seen it. So if he's seeing Russian files on American marines, he's up to something nobody knows about. Got it?"

"What on earth motivated him?" asked Nick. "He doesn't seem like the Ames or Aldrich type."

"He left a statement on his hard drive. Crazy bullshit, I don't even know how to describe it. What do they say? 'The kind of nonsense only an intellectual could believe.' That sort of thing. And we're not going to release the news on him. It makes the Administration look too bad, and for now, they're the ones signing the checks that we all cash."

"So," said Nick, "basically this guy masterminds a plot to kill the president and the top leadership of the country by maneuvering Ibrahim Zarzi into the Rose Garden with a miniaturized FM transmitter. He uses Dixson to hire contractors to stop a marine sniper team, killing one marine and wounding another. He pursues the surviving sniper across America, kills a guy in South Carolina, kills nine Filipino immigrants in Baltimore, kills four cops in DC, kills six innocent bystanders at the White House, and . . . he gets away with it."

"It's not my decision. It's politics. But it's also reality. As I said, someone thoroughly professional got him out. As I said, maybe the Pakis. They're very good, and there are elements of their ISI that we think are jihad sympathizers."

"It's a big world out there. We'll try hard, but look how long we've been going after Osama," said the director.

"You forgot one thing," said Bob.

They looked back at Swagger. He had one of those drawn-in cowboy faces, now much cut with the wrinkles that sixty-four years of gunfights will engrave in a man's flesh.

"You forgot *me,*" he said. "My name is Bob the Nailer. I kill people."

THEODORE R. HOLLISTER

DIRECTOR OF NATIONAL INTELLIGENCE
"AN ACCOUNT OF MOTIVE"
HARD DRIVE
NATIONAL SECURITY OFFICE IBM
C:\MY FILES\ACCOUNT.1.WPD

I am no Lee Harvey Oswald, surly and bitter and luxuriating in his own self-imposed bitterness. I am no John Wilkes Booth, full of grandiloquence, theatrical self-dramatization, narcissism, and insanity. I am no Leon Czolgosz, an idiot.

I'm just a man who sees the future, understands what it must be, and humbly aspires to facilitate it as mercifully and swiftly as possible. I did what I did because the West is no longer worth defending. It has been destroyed by the people it was built to protect: its women.

The West lasted from AD 732, when Charles Martel defeated the Muslims at Tours, until 1960, where it fell without a battle. In 1960, the birth control pill became widely available. Many think of it as heaven, sexual nirvana, the route to self-expression, wish fulfillment, and liberation for millions of women. I think of it as Auschwitz in a bottle. It was and is genocide, as, using it, the women of my generation happily traded off 1,200 years of unparalleled growth, wealth, security, stability, scientific and ethical progress for a second BMW in the garage. The West ceased producing at a sustainable rate, while Islam continued to populate the world. You may look elsewhere for the demographics. This fact cannot be avoided: we Westerners currently may be analogized to upper-class Brits on the deck of the *Titanic,* April 12, 1912. My, my, why is the great ship tilting a bit? Why, dear, it's probably some minor malfunction that the handsome young men will soon fix. Meanwhile, may I have another aperitif, steward?

But not only did the pill doom the West from without by limiting population, it destroyed the culture from within by destroying the gyroscope of civilization—that is, the balance between the sexes. The sexes had existed for that glorious 1,200-year span in a kind of brilliant equipoise: men provided and protected, women nourished and nurtured. It was a sublimely efficient system, if harsh. The result was generation after generation of bold, intelligent, hardy risk takers, driven by their fathers' sense of duty but made compassionate by their mothers' mercy. They were afraid of nothing, committed to a larger thing than themselves, all united in their confident sense of destiny. The men did what they had to do, the women did what they had to do. Together, they built a thing called civilization. In all realms, from the scientific to the industrial to the aesthetic to the military to the intellectual and the medical, Western thought and culture prevailed. It was extraordinary and it seems even now absurd that we threw it away in a single generation.

After 1960, the dominos fell quickly. Once the size of a family could be controlled, it shrank; women returned to the workplace. Soon—believe me, I am not arguing that they are "dumb" or in any way "inferior"—they were making equal or even more than the males, so male authority was challenged and, metaphorically, that leveraged and ultimately destroyed the whole concept of authority. Simultaneously, with small family size, more was invested in each of 2.4 children, so that the death of one meant a shattering emotional wastage. Soldiers could no longer die in the thousands, much less the hundreds. Without defenders, we are doomed.

Thus the only question that remains for a serious man: with the West gone, what system of governance best serves the most people of the world?

If the West can no longer be defended, the East can no longer be denied. The answer to the question, "What is next?" has to be Islamic theocracy. It alone has the harshness of temperament to control the feminism that doomed the West. At its purest, Islam is simply masculinity emboldened, masculinity without moderation, hesitancy, compassion, and introspection. That force alone can save us.

You say: Islam is submission, it is barbaric in its jihad against infidels. True enough.

But once Islam has achieved hegemony and exists without challenge, all that will change. That is what truly lies ahead: Islamic hegemony over the earth, based on masculinity—self-discipline, faith, obedience, and duty. That is the system of governance that will best serve the most people and make the most people the happiest. The intellectuals and ironists will never be satisfied; wisely, Islam will execute them. They do harm far disproportionate to their numbers in any society and must be eliminated without mercy. That is the system that will finally yield the dream of paradise of economic and spiritual equality where the state has withered away and each gives from his ability and receives to his need.

The way of Islam is the only way, the predestined way, and I engineered my event to convince the West of the futility of resistance, its need to immediately abandon its adventuring in Muslim territories and to begin to study for the arrival of the Universal Caliphate.

Allah Akbar, God is great.

S wagger leaned forward. His features grew wolfish, pointed, grim, his body tense, his face a war mask; he was the hunter, the tall-grass-crawler. He was the wind, he was the brush, he was the earth. He was the sniper.

"Just a few days ago," he said, "I was beefing on security. I said we'd been penetrated. Remember that? There was a leak. No other explanation on how Bogier and his shooters kept showing up. Cruz thought I might have been the leak, somehow. Okada wouldn't even talk to me about it, it made her so mad. Memphis said they had to be using satellites. But then I shut up. So, someone ask me, why did I shut up?"

"Why'd you shut up, Mr. Swagger?" asked the director after a bit.

"I figured if it was satellites, there'd be some kind of radio gizmo in the rental car. Went down and spent an hour going over it. Not a goddamned thing. So if it wasn't in the rental car, where the hell was it?"

No answer.

"Well, I'll make it easy. You got a man and a car. And it ain't in the car."

"Okay," said Nick, "I'll be the fish. So it was on . . . the man."

"Now how could it be on the man? Hmm, so I thought hard on that one and tried to reckon as to the first time they showed up on my tail, and it was in South Carolina, in Danielstown. So I thought hard some more about South Carolina, and damned if I didn't finally recall that on the first night, some guy tries to mug me, grabs my wallet, and another guy tracks him down and takes the wallet off him and returns it. Goddamn, that wallet was out of my control for a good two minutes. Easy to slip something into it, something thin and unre-markable."

"A tag," said Nick. "They tagged you."

"Sure they did," said Troy. "An RFID. Radio frequency identifica-tion device. A miniaturized transponder. It can be laminated into, say, a credit card, complete with aerial. A satellite is always asking it where it is and it's always answering. If you can cut into that conversation, you can track . . . yes, and wasn't there a BlackBerry in their SUV?"

"There was," said Bob. "And when I looked in my wallet, there was a BankAmericard card. I hate them big banks, so I don't do no business with them. I hadn't put it in there, but like a dumb bunny, I'd carried it everywhere and they monitored me. That's how they got to the Filipino house in Pikesville and to the car wash in Balti-more."

"It's very useful technology," said Troy.

"Ain't it though?" said Bob. "So I thought: I'm gonna throw this sucker out and that'll be that. But then I thought: Hmm. It's too good a gimcrack to pitch. How can I turn it against them? How can I get it on them? And that's why I wanted the meeting. I had some arro-gant idea I'd be able to spot our man. And goddamn, if he doesn't give himself away, thinking he's all friendlied up with me. My good pal Ted Hollister. Once he blew his cover with the rifle bit, I knowed he's up to something. I picked up his briefcase. I slipped it in just before I handed it to him. Maybe he's like me. He just sticks stuff in. He never checks the whole thing or goes through it. And I'm betting if that's the case, there's a fair chance it's still with him, still in his brief-case, wherever he is. And you can track him by it."

"Where's this going?" Nick asked.

"It's going to an MQ-9 Reaper," said Bob.

W ell," said the colonel, extending his hand, "welcome back, Mr. Swagger. Now that I get who you are, I won't be such a military dickhead. Congratulations and all that bullshit. Sorry we played so dumb for you the last time."

"It ain't nothing, Colonel Nelson," said Swagger. "I'm happy to be here this time and I'm glad everything's on the up-and-up."

"We'd better get over there. She's been on him for a long time and she's getting ready to shoot. That's what you came to see, right?"

"Yes I did. Like to see this fellow closed out."

"He isn't only going to be closed out. He's going to be scattered to the four winds."

They walked to the ops center, that vast dark cave of air-conditioning and keystroke sounds and the glow of monitors, past operators hunched over their control panels and sticks, past banners that read GO GET 'EM, COWBOY, and KILL TOWELHEADS NOW, and HAVE REAPER, WILL TRAVEL, and KILLING IS OUR BUSINESS AND BUSINESS IS GOOD.

But that wasn't the only difference. The young operators wore backward baseball hats or cowboy hats, some had cups of dip parked on their panel boards, some chewed toothpicks or unlit stogies or wore one black, fingerless glove. Air Force? Never heard of it. It was more like some kind of skateboarders' meet sponsored by Mountain Dew where the events included the double slalom, the long jump and spin, and the jihad splatter pattern.

In time they found the new ace, Jameson, tucked away in a corner, her eyes glued to the screen in front of her. She wore pink Bermudas, a tank top, flip-flops, and had her blond ponytail pulled through the gap in her Cubs hat. She wore Wayfarers under the clamped headset.

Nelson whispered, "Since this is your kill, she said you could watch. Just don't move around a lot, or break her concentration."

Jameson lay off to the east about twenty miles, keeping a ridge between 107 and the Jeep Cherokee. She flew lazy circles under the crest, and every once in a while, on no set schedule, zoomed over the line, got a quick visual on the vehicle as it zigzagged along the goat track farther and farther into Pakistan's tribal regions. It was still there, as she knew it was; she checked only out of habit, for on another screen, a recon sitting much higher up watched it placidly, its electronic snooper finely attuned to the data stream the RFID sent to its satellite monitor.

Jameson's stalk was not so intense that it closed other issues out of her mind. Number one being, which color toenail polish? Nude Crushed Pearl or Pacific Dusk? They were very close, a kind of shiny translucence with undertones of cream. Hmm. Both set off the tan of her legs and she had three days off for every two on and plenty of time to work on the tan, and Randy liked her legs tan but he also liked a redder, more dramatic shade on her toes. He'd be in this weekend, and they were going to go to the steak place at the Bellagio that everybody said was so good. A convergence of days off was rare in their relationship. The Creech Operations Center was a demanding taskmaster, as was Southwest Airlines, for whom Randy was a 737 copilot, but this weekend looked like it was going to happen. Anyway, all the magazines were pushing the cream thing. She pried her eyes from the screen and peered down quickly at her ten little piggies, now rather orange, the pedi a little outgrown. She thought it was called Persimmon Sunset.

"Cowpony 3-0-3, this is Ragweed Zulu, I have a possible target deviation."

"Copy that, Ragweed," said Jameson into her throat mike, "let me get a visual confirm."

She oriented 107 in midair, took a quick glance at the ragged crest line between herself and the target, saw an upcoming gap. She eased back on the stick while giving the big bird a little more turbo, and inclined upward seven degrees. Without giving it a second or even a first thought, she toggled from the nose cam to left/lateral, and just as the lens broke free of the interfering rock mass, she brought up the magnification, waited for the self-focus, and brought the vehicle up so vividly on-screen it seemed just a few hundred feet away. Meanwhile, the compass readout above the image drifted around, quavered, and finally settled on a heading.

"Ragweed Zulu, this is Cowpony, I have a deviation, he's shifted from 123 north to about 204 west and I'm getting a slightly higher speed read, I'm putting him at close to thirty mph."

"Copy that, Cowpony."

"Ragweed, I am requesting a map indexing, can you handle, over?"

"Cowpony 3-0-3, I copy that, over, be advised to give me a minute, please, over."

Ragweed got busy with his maps while Jameson went back to the issue of feet. She always kept hers as pretty as possible. She was not one of those thin things with hardly an extra ounce anywhere, but if solidly constructed, she was still stunning, a blond, blue-eyed all-American girl, seventh in her class at the academy, the big gun on her shift, and, everybody said, every bit as good as the legendary Dombrowski.

"Cowpony 3-0-3, this is Ragweed Zulu, over."

"Go ahead, Ragweed Zulu."

"Cowpony, I have a village called Pesh el-Aware a couple of clicks ahead. We ran a 114L gig there two years ago, so it has been an active Taliban and Al-Q site but there was a collateral issue, I am advised. Do you want to shoot him now before he gets into it? We'd cut down on the collateral."

"Ragweed Zulu, I'll take that under advisement. But maybe these guys will send someone out to meet him, and we'll get a twofer. That's my play, Ragweed, over."

"Cowpony, this is Ragweed, I support that call, you stay low and off, over."

"Copy that, Ragweed."

The journey had been so long, and he was tired. He was scared too, and had a major melancholy going on, a case of buyer's regret. He tried not to think of the things he'd never sample again or the moment of horror when he'd cut the woman's throat. The weapon was X-ray proof, an intensely sharp plastic blade nestled in the lapel of his tweed sports jacket. He took no pleasure in using it. *That's not me. I had to do it.* But the look when he slashed her, and the amount of blood, so unexpected, and the ease with which it transpired, all of it, so vivid, so awful, yet also somehow *satisfying*.

On either side: nothing, as if out of a Beckett play. A denuded rural landscape of high desert, rock scut, leathery vegetation without flower or color, mud, dirt, stones, and sky. In the distance, the Hindu Kush showed its snowy magnificence but it was a sight one grew used to quickly. He thought instead about the nothingness he saw now, and how out of that nothingness, inspired by the desert's emptiness, a man had created a vision and it was, after all was said and done, the moral vision. He had committed to it. He was a moral man. He clutched his briefcase to his chest.

"Not much farther, I think," said his bodyguard from the front seat, "the village just ahead, and we are there."

Except of course there was no there there just as there was no here here.

"That is good," he said.

"You must be a very great man," said the guard, holding his rifle close. "They value you a great deal and honor you. Your comfort will be my duty. I cannot give you New York and bright lights, but I do bring you the clarity and the beauty and the serenity of the high desert."

"That is all I want," he said. "I have seen enough of those cities. I have tasted their wickedness to my content. It is now time to dedicate myself to further learning and meditation and to prepare myself to be of use in the next great development."

"Oh look," said the bodyguard. "They sent a delegation. Oh my goodness, look who it is! A very high commander! Oh, I am so impressed."

The Land Rover closed the distance with them, and came to a halt. Five fighters tumbled from it, and then a distinguished man hung with bandoliers of magazines, a smile on his bearded face.

"My friend!" he called. "My brother!"

Hollister climbed from the Jeep, felt stiffness crank through his old legs but did not want to acknowledge it at this high spiritual moment, and opened his arms to embrace his new leader.

"My brother!" he said. "God is great."

At that moment, a screaming came across the sky.

Nude Crushed Coral! It had to be! The other had too much orange in it and with the dress she planned to wear might be too matchy-matchy, because the dress had an orange tone to it that somehow, with the tan, made her teeth look very white. Randy liked that too.

"Cowpony 3-0-3, this is Ragweed, do you read?"

"Ragweed Zulu, this is Cowpony 3-0-3, I copy, over."

"Cowpony, the big bird is picking up a heat-emission signature, possibly another vehicle, maybe the greet you figured on, over."

"Ragweed, this is Cowpony, I will take a recon and advise, over."

"Go ahead, Cowpony."

She vectored 107 left, and went high, high, high, so the bird, though a Reaper was as big as a B-25 bomber on the ground, would be at twenty thousand feet nothing but a white speck, its roar lost in the tides and surges of the atmosphere. *Look at me way up high, suddenly here am I, I'm flying!* She loved this part. Breaking the surly bonds of earth. Too bad it wasn't an F-15, but a Reaper was still a good ride and it did what had to be done.

From twenty, she put the white cruciform on the small blot of illumination that signified the RFID data-stream source, brought up the magnification on her primary screen, and again watched as the tiny objects leapt to recognizability. She saw the Jeep, a new Land Rover, and a crowd of men engaged in hugging and congratulating one another. Many had weapons.

"Ragweed, this is Cowpony, I read armed targets, request permission to engage."

"Cowpony, this is Ragweed Zulu, I am acknowledging request,

confirming weapons, waiting for any comment from the Six, getting none, assuming shot clearance in place, entering it in the logbook. Go to weapons, Cowpony, and engage when ready, over."

"Ragweed, this is Cowpony, acknowledging permission."

She snapped a button and a computer icon of her weapons choices came up on the screen; given the altitude and the high value of the targets, she designated Paveway II, with the thermobaric 500-pound warhead.

"Ragweed, I have designated left inboard Paveway Two, am now arming weapon, and switching screen to secondary feed."

"Copy that, Cowpony, over."

She lifted one wing while dropping the other, circled majestically, bird of prey, soaring eagle, riding the invisible superhighways of rushing wind, held the group of men and their two cars stable under the cruciform, seemed to take an involuntary breath.

"Ragweed Zulu, I am engaging."

She pushed a button, then watched from the nose camera as the bomb took its long, last ride to earth, as internally the CPU sent minor corrections to the vehicle's vanes, tweaking this way and that as it sought its destiny under the white cruciform imposed from on high, nothing radical, just turning a good trajectory into a perfect trajectory, and the earth and its bounty of men and vehicles and justice rushed ever so fast toward her until it resolved into a complete blur. She switched the secondary readout to the long shot from 20,000 and saw the screen blank out and then return to quasiclarity. The center ruptured in a spew of radiance, an outgoing circular wave of pure energy registering as an incandescence that overwhelmed the screen.

A cheer rose in the room, and somewhere close by, a couple of operators jumped up to slap out some high fives.

"Hoochie mama," someone called.

"He didn't like that," came another.

"Welcome to hell, pilgrim."

"Dead zero," said Swagger.

ACKNOWLEDGMENTS

This book began in 1977 with the best idea I never had. The man who had it was a British thriller writer named Patrick Alexander. In that year he published a novel entitled *Death of a Thin-skinned Animal*. It crossed my desk—I was the book review editor of the *Sunday Sun, of Baltimore*—and immediately attracted my attention.

I had written two unpublishable thrillers and was about to take my last swing. I had decided, from hard experience in failure, that the next book must extend from a tight premise with a limited set of characters in a small geographical area over a specific time frame and should be about a sniper. *Death of a Thin-skinned Animal*, at least from the flap copy, offered all that. I immediately placed it on my must-never-read list. I was afraid of my larcenous tendencies.

Death of a Thin-skinned Animal reflected Britain's obsession in the seventies with the bad-boy dictator of Uganda, Idi Amin; I'm guessing it had a whisper of le Carré to it as well, as he was the colossus who bestrode the thriller-writing world in those days.

As Alexander had it, British intelligence decides a crackpot African dictator cannot be dealt with in his leftward slide, and must therefore be terminated. A British army sniper is sent on the job, but after he's in country, the politics change. Now, the dictator is a friend, and must be protected at all costs. As the sniper is beyond recall, he is coldly betrayed and disappears. Five years later the dictator arrives in London for a celebration but is preceded by a radio message, in a code five years out of date. It states that the sniper will complete his mission in London.

Great setup and I suspect it's a fine book. I still haven't read it (though now I own it). In the end, I let it go, and instead of stealing from Mr. Alexander stole from Mr. Pynchon. I managed to publish *The Master Sniper* in 1980. Sometime thereafter I realized that *The*

Master Sniper was really Pynchon's great *Gravity's Rainbow* reimagined through the prism of a more concrete, less gifted mind.

I continued, stealing left and right. *The Spanish Gambit* was *Homage to Catalonia* combined with *For Whom the Bell Tolls* and with a dash of *Brideshead Revisited* thrown in, even though I had not then and have not now read *Brideshead Revisited*. (I saw a little of the TV movie.) Most flagrantly, *The Day Before Midnight* appears to be *Dr. Strangelove,* beat by beat, scene by scene, and revelation by revelation, though told from Colonel Bat Guano's point of view. If I had noticed it then, would I have changed it? Probably not. *Dirty White Boys* was anything by Jim Thompson, although again, I had never read anything by Jim Thompson. On and on it goes: *Pale Horse Coming* was Aeschylus, Faulkner, and Charles Askins. *The 47th Samurai* was a movie, not a novel, as directed (in my head) by Hideo Gosha in 1978. For crying out loud, I stole Bob Lee Swagger from Carlos Hathcock.

Cut to 2009 when I'm looking for a plot, and what should drift before my nostrils but whiffs of *Death of a Thin-skinned Animal*. It was not the second time I considered the premise but the third, as evidently I almost wrote a book like this in 1993 instead of *Point of Impact*. But this time, I couldn't resist. It's a great premise, and I saw how it could be updated to the war in Afghanistan and the high-tech milieu that sniping and other forms of state-sanctioned killing have become, as well as provide an opportunity to crank the Swagger family history in another direction and express my contempt for the leftward drift of the American press over the past decade or so. Plus I got to write love poems to Susan Okada. I had great fun. So thank you, Mr. Alexander—he died in 2003—for being there when I needed you. I hope this plug sells a billion more of your books.

The question remains: is this theft or inspiration? Or where does the inspiration end and the theft begin? If you didn't know of the origin of *Dead Zero* and you read it and *Death of a Thin-skinned Animal,* would you see the connection? I'm not sure but I hope Mr. Alexander wouldn't be too put out at my light fingers—it's a tribute to his imagination, after all—in our mutual quest to keep readers awake all night and give them a nice vacation from their actual lives.

In more mundane matters, much thanks, once again, is due Gary Goldberg who has become my technical intelligence adviser. He's the one who understands transponders and RFIDs and Thuraya satellite phones and that sort of stuff. He also helps me send pages to New York via e-mail, a task that will remain permanently beyond my pay grade. (Alan Doelp pitched in when Gary was on vacation.)

Gary and I also went to Vegas for a look at Creech and while out there we took a course in Suppressor Theory and Practice from Long Mountain Outfitters and there met Dan Shea, president of LMO and one of the most knowledgeable guys in the world on certain subjects. Dan, editor and publisher of *Small Arms Review*, was far more helpful than the U.S. Air Force in understanding the intricacies of Hellfire ACM-114, though at Dan's suggestion, I have blurred and faked a lot of the technical stuff to keep mischief makers in the dark.

Jeremy Woody, a marine combat veteran of the war in Iraq, loaned me his official Marine Corps manuals, by which I tried to solve the organizational, communications, tactical, and equipmental mysteries of that great organization, though mistakes are mine, not his. Good friend and co-author (of *American Gunfight*) John Bainbridge turned his steady eye to proofreading for me.

On a sad note, it hurts to report that Weyman Swagger, former photo editor of *The Sun*, Bob's namesake and my original mentor in gun culture way back when dinosaurs roamed the planet, succumbed in the spring to lung cancer. He was, in the best Swagger tradition, cool, funny, and calm through the end. I hope I go out half as well.

My steady readers Lenne Miller, Jeff Weber, Jay Carr, and Gary, of course, were supremely helpful. The great aviation writer Barrett Tillman pitched in with info on military radiospeak, a poetic subdialect I happen to love. Through Gary, I met two retired FBI Special Agents, Bernie Murphy and Peter Ahearn, who talked to me about various security issues. At S & S, my new editor, Sarah Knight, was aces; at ICM, my agent Esther Newberg was her usual stalwart self throughout; and every morning as I headed upstairs into the slovenly pit where I put these things together, a thermos of hot coffee awaited me, courtesy of my wife, Jean Marbella. Without the coffee, I fear, most of these pages would have remained blank.